Copyright TXu655-937
Cover Design © 1996 Press-Tige Publishing

All rights reserved, including the right to reproduce this book or portions therein in any form whatsoever.

For information address:
    Press-Tige Publishing
    291 Main Street
    Catskill, NY 12414

First Press-Tige Edition 1996

Printed in the United States of America

ISBN 1-57532-016-9

"KALUTI"

By: Michael T. Luckett

"UTOPIA"

Headquartered in the bowels of the United Nation's building, **Utopia's** beneficence was legendary, and in spite of its innumerable international, political, and industrial adversaries, it has championed every environmental issue throughout the globe, in addition to aiding the indigent of every society. But that was on the surface. Within its inner sanctum, **Utopia** was not a proponent of goodwill as the world believed. It was something sinister. And something deadly.

THE PREMISE

A respected minister and his teenage son are murdered in a manner that baffles the authorities. Two detectives are assigned to ferret out the murderers. In the process they uncover a conspiracy that threatens America, and possibly the world. Enlisting the aid of two civilians, the four men attempt to rescue the decedent's widow and the unsuspecting inhabitants of America's largest city.

This is a story of a spiritual evil that has survived countless generations, and of its trek from the Caribbean islands to America. It is also a story of a family consumed by its demonic power, and of how they propagate their faith throughout America in the guise of Christianity. Four shall stand against them, and should they fall, the lives and souls of countless millions are forfeit.

ACKNOWLEDGEMENTS

For My Daughters, Keisha and Tiffani
With All My Love

I dedicate this work to my Heavenly Father, the true hero of **KALUTI**, and to my earthly father who has since passed on. Between them, they have taught me how to be a man. And to my mother, who was always there when my earthly father couldn't be.

To my daughters, who have been nothing but a source of pride for me.

And to Shortie. In addition to being my fiance', she is my critic and the Nellie in my life.

Finally, I would like to thank my agent and my publisher for taking a chance on me. You haven't seen nothin' yet.

And thanks to my editor for making my work appear as I envisioned it.

WINTER, NEW YORK CITY--1997

Almost faster than the eye could follow the pianist's slender fingers caressed the Steinway's glistening keys. Each touch was lighter than a feather. Each chord was flawless in its intonation. A seemingly effortless exercise for the classically trained virtuoso, as a result, a gay, quiet melody soared from the elegant grand piano.

"A nice tune," said Ricky Caldwell. "Whadaya call it?"

"Wind Song," Kevi Stone replied. His concentration broken only slightly, he stretched his thumb and baby finger outward on both hands.

A musician himself, Ricky Caldwell nodded with approval. "Sounds like your mother's wind chimes on her back porch."

"My inspiration," Stone remarked, playing the scales he selected in rapid four octave runs.

Ricky realized his associate was only experimenting, but because he was so overwhelmed by the simplicity and beauty of the composition, he adjusted his controls to get some of it on tape. By then, the tempo changed and with it, a somber, haunting melody. "Mixylodian mode." A statement.

"You have a good ear." said Kevi.

Ricky smiled. "I had a good teacher. You know, after all our years together, there's one thing I still enjoy about your music."

"Yeah? What's that?" As Stone peered through the studio window, he noticed a puzzled expression etched on his friend's face. "Rick? Wassup?"

"The elevator," Caldwell muttered distractedly, "someone's comin'."

Stone glanced at the jeweled Rolex his mother had given him more than a week ago. It was a Christmas gift. "At this hour?"

Caldwell was equally perplexed. For some time the Mammoth Record building had been closed, and since the other members of their quintet were en route to Australia, the talented engineer and bass player could only assume an intruder, possibly a fan, had somehow managed to circumvent the security force patrolling the floors below. It wouldn't have been the first time. The day their quintet, **The Pains of Love**, announced their signing with the huge conglomerate, an additional security team had been added. What good it did them. The elevator bell chimed twice before its doors slowly slid open. Then, almost majestically, a mountain of a man brandishing a gleaming solid gold shield stepped into the lobby. Ricky's eyes widened with surprise. No words had been exchanged, and yet, a clear understanding of extreme urgency was instantly communicated. "Yo', Kev!" he called out, "Someone would like a word with you." Quite abruptly, a dissonant chord echoed loudly throughout the luxurious recording studio. It was followed by a grumble Ricky knew well.

"Be out in a sec," Kevi snarled.

After he had gathered his charts scattered around the piano, Kevi sorted them neatly before placing them within a Spanish-made calf skin briefcase; a Christmas gift from his stepfather. A furtive glance told him the investigator was studying him through the large bay window. Kevi didn't mind at all.

Two could play that game.

Impeccably dressed, the policeman was wearing an elegant Royal Blue Brooks Brothers suit made of the finest silk, and he carried a smooth dark brown cashmere overcoat folded neatly over his arm. His initials were monogrammed above his shirt pocket in italicized print while solid gold links within its french cut sleeves flashed brightly in the studio's fluorescent lighting. Lastly, his lizard-skinned ankle boots bearing the mark of Stregas decorated a pair of over-sized feet.

Kevi was genuinely impressed. Everything the detective was wearing was tastefully coordinated and fit his three hundred pound, six foot two frame neatly. Although his face wasn't particularly handsome, one knew instantly this was a man you could trust. The officer's wavy brown hair was clipped military style with feather touches of grey at the temples, while a thick brown mustache, neatly trimmed, stood prominently over his wide but unusually thin lips. It was only a guess of course, but Kevi believed the well dressed detective was in his late forties, or at the very least, his early fifties.

"Wesneski...Homicide," the investigator said, extending one hand, displaying his identification with the other.

Hiding his surprise, while Kevi shook the detective's massive paw, he sensed a keen intelligence lurking behind his twinkling dark brown orbs.

"Who'd you bump off?" kidded Ricky, offering the officer a chair.

Too fatigued to be amused, particularly when his session had been interrupted, an occasion so rare it defied memory, Kevi replied, "Let's find out," before taking a seat at the mixing board.

After a pause to study the two entertainers the officer said, "A few hours ago I was assigned to investigate..."

"Who?", Ricky asked anxiously.

"Reverend Dr. Leon Braithwaite and his sixteen year old son..."

Within a heartbeat of the detective's declaration, an agonizing scream enveloped the recording studio. Much like a wounded wolf crying in the night, a piercing, lugrubious wail sent a sliver of fear traveling along the spines of Ricky Caldwell and the Manhattan investigator.

Stone's reactions were quite different. He was completely petrified. Even so, as fear's icy knife stabbed at his pounding heart, he was certain he had recognized that anguished, tortured cry. To confirm his suspicions, his eyes searched the room for the source of the ghoulish howl. Failing to find it, his fears heightened even more and reached deep into his soul. Springing to his feet, he twisted his head from side to side.

That's when he saw it.

A face. A horrible, frightening face. Floating in mid-air.

By far the ugliest thing he had ever seen, it moved towards him, slowly, purposely, halting only when their noses were inches apart.

Cringing helplessly, Kevi wasn't at all surprised a screamed hadn't escaped his lips. His throat felt quite frozen, his tongue felt like marble, and an unexpected tightening seized his rapidly beating heart. He had never been more afraid. But that was nothing. His worst fears were realized once he discovered...he was **already** screaming.

Unaware that his body was trembling, Kevi studied the grotesque image glaring back at him. Afraid to match the creature's gaze, he squeezed his eyes shut and gripped his long straight hair by the roots until each tight fist was filled with black. Finally, once he had found the courage to open his eyes, another howl, not as guttural as the first, nearly a perfect eighth in pitch slipped between his tight, quivering lips. His suspicions were confirmed. The horrible grimace glowering so sullenly was a mirrored reflection of himself.

The detective leaped to his feet. "Sir, are you all right?"

"Nellie," Stone whispered, heartsick, struggling to remain conscious.

The Lieutenant placed a meaty hand against the entertainer's forehead and instructed him to sit. Turning to Ricky Caldwell he snapped, "Quick! Get him something to drink."

Ricky bolted through the doorway to the studio cafeteria and returned a moment later with a large glass of ice water. "I-Is Nellie all right?" he asked, his voice tight with concern.

Kevi placed the glass his friend had given him against his right temple, and held it there for a moment before taking a drink. The frigid liquid soothed his parched throat almost immediately but his stomach remained wrenched in knots.

"If you like, I have something stronger," the detective said, removing a solid gold flask from the inside pocket of his suit coat. "For medicinal purposes," he added, his manner infectious, ingratiating.

After Kevi had shaken the crumbled sheets of ice into a nearby wastebasket, the police officer poured a clear liquid into his glass. Kevi took a sip. It was gin. Downing it in one gulp, the liquor shot to his stomach like a bolt of lightning, setting his insides aflame, and just when he thought he was ready to heave, at the last moment his body responded to the liquid fire burning inside his gut.

"Better?" the detective asked.

"Much..."

"What about Nellie?" Caldwell asked again.

"What about her?"

"Dammit, Lieutenant!"

Stiffening suddenly, the police officer's face flushed red in embarrassment. "Forgive me," he said in apology, taking a moment to study the taut expressions of the two men sitting before him. "The decedent's wife was visiting a neighbor at the time of the murder."

"Thank God," Kevi Stone said, trying to feel at ease, failing in spite of his efforts.

"Do you have any leads?" Ricky Caldwell inquired interestedly.

"I'm sorry...but no. It's why I'm here. I was hoping **you** could tell me what you knew of the decedent." Taking a moment, the Lieutenant allowed himself time to regain the comportment he had lost moments ago. He then extracted a note pad and solid gold pen from his coat before returning to his seat. "I'm hoping you'll know something that isn't exactly public record. Something personal, perhaps, that'll help me in my investigation."

"There's not much I can tell you," Stone said weakly. "I haven't been in contact with the Braithwates in years."

"Please call me Harvey," the investigator said, flashing an array of slightly yellowed teeth. "And if you don't mind, I'll call you Kevi." The detective offered an experienced smile. "From your reactions, I gather you've known Mrs. Braithwaite **better** than her husband."

"You could say that."

"Why do I get the feeling you didn't like him?"

"Let me put it this way, Lieu...er uh, Harvey, at one time in my life there was no one I hated more."

A curious look appeared on the investigator's beefy face. "Start from the beginning, if you don't mind. I wanna know **everything** about the decedent... his family, friends, associates, habits...everything."

"Won't be much."

The officer shrugged. "Then tell me what you can."

"Before I do...answer me a question."

"Shoot."

"How'd you connect me with the Braithwaites in the first place?"

"You were our first suspect," the detective said evenly.

"M-Me?"

"Yes. Under sedation, the widow repeated your name."

Stone's body began to twitch uncontrollably, each spasm more powerful

3

than the last.
Once again, Lt. Wesneski pulled his solid gold flask from his suit coat pocket. "You look as if you could use another snort."
"Do you mind?"
"Not at all," the detective said, emptying his flask into the handsome entertainer's glass.
"I hope you don't mind my telling you," Stone said, allowing the gin to burn another path to the pit of his stomach, "but I think you're wasting your time asking me about Leon."
"The detective released an impatience sigh. "**Anything** you can tell me will do."
"You don't understand."
Wesneski's eyes narrowed a little. "You're not making it easy."
Stone hesitated. "It's just that the things I know about Leon and his family you might find a little...**bizarre**, and will probably be of little use."
"Why don't you let **me** be the judge of that."
At first, Stone offered no reply. He was quite reticent when it came to discussing the Braithwaite's, even with those close to him, and being a public figure for so many years, he had become an intensely private individual. But that's not what bothered him. His greatest concern was that in revealing what he knew about Leon Braithwaite and his family, he would be, in fact, revealing much about himself. "Ok, Harvey," he said grudgingly, "what I'm about to tell you I think you'll find extremely difficult to accept, let alone believe. But before you start judging me, or challenging the things you hear, I must ask you to try to keep an open mind. Can you do that?"
The officer nodded.
Bong! Bong! Bong! As the luxurious grandfather clock standing in the corner chimed the hour of 3 AM, its ominous ring echoed softly throughout the immaculate lobby. Only a few minutes had elapsed since the detective entered the recording studio, but for Stone, it seemed an eternity. It was almost as if time had stood still.
Time. Now that was a topic Stone could never keep from thinking about. Since his youth he was fascinated with it, and more than time--time travel. Other than music, it remained one of his greatest passions. Having read nearly every book on the subject, fact and fiction; his favorite being "<u>The Time Machine</u>," by H. G. Wells, he would often lie on his bed day dreaming, imagining himself traveling backwards in time, reveling in all sorts of adventures with his favorite figures of mythology and history.
Like Rod Taylor in the movie version of Wells's story, to navigate through time and space Kevi Stone employed a very unique ship. Only his was fabricated by a very fertile imagination. Nevertheless, his vessel, actually a trimaran, and very much like the one he purchased a summer ago, size and model the only differences, enabled him to sail through his imaginary time stream as easily as Wells's fictional character.
His body relaxed, with every deep breath, the doors of Kevi's mind began to open. A moment later his small sailing vessel began to take shape. Once its deck was beneath his feet, he turned it into the wind and sailed headlong into the gentle breezes of the past. With each rapid beat of his heart, his life began to unfold, slowly, much like a photograph develops, in stages. Then, when there were just enough images, he flipped through them as if in a photo journal, taking note that each picture depicted a significant moment in time, an event already a part of history.
No longer an adult, Kevi felt himself traveling back, back, back in time, to a miscellany of forgotten moments, forgotten memories, and forgotten feelings and while each year passed, the fears he had hidden deep within himself reached out for him like a hand from the grave. Shuddering, Kevi realized there

were many events in his past that disturbed him, most of which had been purposely buried, deep, so deep he hadn't recalled a single image in almost thirty years. Shuddering even more, as his ghosts returned to torment him, every thought, every emotion he had experienced before, he relived all over again.

And **that** was his greatest fear.

PART ONE

VENGEANCE

**CAMERON, NEW JERSEY
1996 TO 1968**

CHAPTER ONE

Cameron, New Jersey--1966

Winter had been so brutal most of Cameron's citizenry had looked forward to spring. Shorter and warmer than most, it seemed like summer, which was only a few weeks away. Presently, the evening was hot, but not at all uncomfortable. As a matter of fact, nearly everyone in town was at one of Cameron's three beaches, and yet, on this unseasonably temperate evening, five teens from Cameron's upper east side decided against visiting their city's sandy shores. Not because they wouldn't have enjoyed it. Nothing could have been further from the truth. Quite often they indulged in the same pleasures as their teenage peers. But not today. While most of their friends were frolicking in the sun, sand, and sea, these five young men chose a small, run-down, stifling hot church as their place of recreation. Three days during the week, and twice on weekends, the young quintet would meet after school, willingly sacrificing their normal teenage pursuits for much more loftier goals.

Like most kids from their impecunious community, a common bond brought these ragged teens together. In this particular case, it was the dream of winning a very special contest. Exceedingly confident, they had every right to feel elated. Individually and collectively, each possessed the raw talent necessary to win, and because they were quite cognizant of their own strengths and weaknesses, in addition to those of their competitors, most of which attended similar schools in the communities contiguous to theirs, the thought of failure simply did not exist.

But that doesn't mean they weren't without problems.

"Daggone it, Ricky!!!", Kevi Stone admonished. "I keep tellin' you, it's A-flat." He pounded the note repeatedly on the piano. "You see? A-flat."

"Man," Ricky Caldwell replied, winking to his friends who flanked him, "I wouldn't know "a" flat if it was on your old lady's beat up De Soto." As the youth had expected, giggles began to fill the choir stand.

"Come on, you guys," Kevi said, doing his best to ignore his friend's poor attempt at humor. "Don't encourage him. The contest's Friday."

"Look man," Ricky said, hitching his thumbs around his frayed red and black suspenders, "I keep tellin' ya', I ain't no singer." With another wink he boasted, "I'm a comedian."

"Right," Timmy Witherspoon said, knocking the checkered beanie from Ricky's head, giving him a knuckle rub. "The only thing funny about you is these BB balls on this melon shaped skull of yours. Them kinks look like a million cock roaches marchin' with their fists balled up."

"Aww, you stole that line offa Redd Foxx," Ricky replied, wrestling free.

"Sure did." Timmy grabbed Ricky again. "But I'm willing to bet money, he made it up when he saw you. Conkalene cain't straighten these kinkabucks."

Seated behind the piano, Stone watched as Caldwell was wrestled to the church's tattered carpet floor. If his friends followed their usual routine, for the next few minutes they would give their wisecracking colleague knuckle noogies until their fingers were sore. Always the serious one, Stone often wondered why he tolerated his friends' childish antics. The answer was simple. He loved them, and loved being around them.

In addition to being the group's leader, lead tenor and pianist, Kevi Stone was also its composer, vocal arranger, musical director, and choreographer. Like most child prodigies, his eclectic musical abilities developed at an early age, and since developing an interest, both parents, his mother mostly, forced him to take piano lessons. Making him practice two hours everyday after school, by the time he was six, he had become a virtuoso and performed piano recitals throughout the state, including those at his church's worship services.

But the night he had heard Sam Cooke, a former gospel singer crooning "You Send Me," live on the Ed Sullivan show, his life was changed forever. Although Kevi truly enjoyed the classics, they were much too strict in form. Rhythm and Blues, however, offered him a greater freedom of expression. "This is an opportunity of a lifetime," he told his friends the day their local radio station announced the contest. "Not only is there a two hundred dollar first prize to claim, but a trip to New York City, and a guest shot on the "Hy Hope Amateur Hour."

"And," Timmy Witherspoon added, "there's a good possibility a record deal might be offered."

"Yes," Kevi Stone said, smiling like the Cheshire cat in Disney's, Alice in Wonderland, "there's that too."

Like most musicians, the young quintet had many musical influences. But none inspired them more than the Temptations. Each, a lover of the tight, doowop, bluesy, soulful harmonies of Motown's popular icon, it was only natural their group developed a similar singing style and lineup.

Ricky Caldwell--the group's **first** tenor. Of the five voices, his was the most articulate, but because of his asthma--he's had it since birth--there were moments when his soaring falsetto would crack in the upper registers--the only flaw to an otherwise perfect voice.

Timmy Witherspoon--the group's **second** tenor and its youngest member. Nicknamed "Honey Boy," Timmy reached seventy-two inches on his thirteenth birthday, and he was the spittin' image of his father; a cocoa complexioned man with wavy black hair and pearly white teeth. Unquestionably the best natural dancer among them, Witherspoon's reputation as a hoofer was preceded only by his success with the ladies, most who were his senior by four or five years. Rumored to be blessed with an extraordinary gift, Timmy Witherspoon was the only one in the group that didn't have to lie about how much sex he was getting.

Ronnie Gant--the group's **baritone**. There was no question that Ronnie was in possession of the most powerful voice in town. Born prematurely at home, he announced his arrival into the world by keeping his household and neighbors awake day and night from his incessant wailing. Just where his voluminous voice came from, no one seemed to know, especially when his skeleton-like frame looked as though a whisper would have been an agonizing effort. Nevertheless, despite his thinness, Gant's powerful voice never needed amplification. And though he often denied it, he and Caldwell could pass for brothers. First cousins, both were tall, gaunt individuals with red hair, freckles, and high yellow complexions. Red bones for sure, few ever dared calling them that. The two boys could scrap like wild cats.

Finally, rounding out the group, the quintet's **bass**, and its most uncoordinated member was Terrence "the Dancer" Jackson. Get within six feet of Terry on the dance floor--look out! You're going to get stepped on. Once, while working on their choreography, all five members of the newly formed quintet ended in a pile on their church floor. In the middle of the heap was Jackson. "Dancer" stuck ever since.

"You guys through clownin'?" chided Kevi, pointing to the clock. "We've only got a few minutes before the evening service begins."

Though no one answered, they all continued to nudge one another playfully until Ricky said, "Look man, you know I don't belong in this group...especially the way my asthma's been actin' up. What happens if my voice cracks?" Sighing heavily Ricky added, "For nothin' in this world do I wanna be the reason we don't win Friday."

"Gee whiz, man, it's too late to back out now."

"I didn't say I was backin' out," Ricky snapped, not meaning to. "I'm sayin' you guys need a first tenor who can carry his own weight. I'm not the man for the job, and y'all know it as well as me."

Because Stone understood his friend's concerns, he purposely held his tongue. For months, he and the others had tried to boost Ricky's confidence, but each time the red-headed tenor's voice would fail him he'd become so sullen he'd talk of quitting.

"I think you should find a replacement for me too," Terry Jackson muttered diffidently.

"What's up with you?" inquired Gant. "There's nothing wrong with your voice."

"It's not my voice I was referring to," Jackson said shyly. "It's the choreography. You guys have done your best to teach me the moves. Heck, you've built them around me. I **still** screw them up." Terry looked at his feet with disgust. "Knowin' me, I'll probably goof things up for all y'all."

"What're you guys afraid of," Timmy Witherspoon asked, "embarrassing yourselves...or us?" The looks he received from Jackson and Caldwell provided him the answer. "I thought so. Geez guys, it's only a contest. Nobody's gonna blame you if you make a mistake. Heck, we all want perfection, but ain't none of us perfect. Besides, we can beat the pants off the competition no matter how many mistakes we make." Witherspoon was right, and everyone knew it. "Look," he said patiently, "no one's gonna force you to do something you don't want. If your heart's not in it, you don't belong on that stage come Friday. But after six months of rehearsals, the rest of us want what may be our only shot. So, why don't we do this. If you guys are really serious about wanting out, I have in mind two cats that'd be the perfect replacements. Especially in the little time we've left to prepare. I'll check them out, and see if they're interested. If they are, then you guys are off the hook. If not, we still want you, **but** with an understanding...no **one** person **is** or will ever be responsible for the group's success or failure." Taking a deep breath he said, "Now, can you accept that?"

A nod from Ricky.

"Terry?"

"I-I guess so."

"Good," Timmy said, relieved.

"So, who do you have in mind?" Ronnie wanted to know.

Timmy Witherspoon flashed his brightest smile. "The twins."

"Yeah, yeah, yeah," Caldwell acknowledged brightly, nudging Jackson with a bony elbow. "The twins would be perfect. With them in the group, you'll have a natural first tenor on top and a natural bass on the bottom."

"Just like the Temp's," Gant confirmed.

"Yeah," Jackson added with enthusiasm, "and those boys can really step too. I've seen 'em a couple of times at their school's pep rallies. Man, can they turn it on."

One less in making it unanimous, it seemed Stone was the only one that wasn't pleased with Witherspoon's suggestion. The twins were definitely the best. That fact he would never dispute. They were also gospel singers. But that wasn't the reason he was so adamant. "I don't know," he said slowly, failing to suppress a shudder. "Don't you think they're a little weird? What I mean is, haven't you heard the rumors about 'em?"

"What rumors?" Gant asked.

"You know, about them keeping snakes as pets and stuff?"

"Snake," Witherspoon corrected, holding up a finger. "One snake. A boa constrictor."

"Whatever..."
"They don't have it anymore."
Stone raised an eyebrow. "What happened to it?"
"It got run over by a dump truck."
"That's nothin'," Jackson jumped in. "Remember ole man Farber? Everyone indicated that they did. "Well, he used to keep a hoot owl as a pet. Used to feed it field mice and everything."
Kevi remained intransigent. "But did you ever get a real close look at 'em? Except for their mother who's dang near an albino, everyone is black as coal. But all of 'em have those weird blue-grey eyes that **glow** in the dark."
"I couldn't care less what they do, or what they look like," Timmy said pointedly. "All I know is, once at a recital given right here at Second Baptist, the twins had the whole congregation under their spell. Me included. I'll never forget the day they sang "Jesus Wash Away My Troubles." The reason I remember it is because that was the **first** time I felt I was in the presence of The Almighty. As far as I'm concerned, the twins'd be **perfect**."

If you were just talking entertaining, Kevi would have agreed wholeheartedly, but when it came to them being just plain folks, that was something else. The strangest thing, though, was that in all the years he had known them, he couldn't begin to explain his antipathy towards the Braithwaite family. At this late date, he didn't wish to try. It was enough to know the four of them scared the living daylights out of him.

"So," Ricky said, deliberately pressing his best friend, "what do you say? You've got to admit, the twins are good."

Grimacing, Kevi replied, "If it's cool with everyone else, It's cool with me."

"Then why the frown? With the twins the contest is in the bag. This'll probably be the best thing that could ever happen for ya."

Kevi seriously doubted it. It didn't take long before he discovered he was right.

CHAPTER TWO

Stone just couldn't believe it. Though unfamiliar with his music, and his way of doing things, the twins managed to exceed his every expectation. As he had anticipated, their singing and harmonic sense was remarkable, but what really astonished him was their ability to dance. They moved as one. Almost as if they were sharing the same brain. No matter how complicated he made the steps, they mimicked them perfectly; the first time. Then, without discussion, always in unison, and using polysyncopated rhythms, they assimilated his ideas into something so simplistic, so perfect, so very much their own, it just blew his mind.

Much to his surprise being around the two boys hadn't made him uncomfortable at all. Not once during the long hours of rehearsal did he experience the powerful fears he normally felt in their presence. On the contrary; he found them pleasant, hard working, and easy to get along with. Everyone liked them, and in spite of his previous apprehensions, he did too.

The day of the contest--it was also the last day of school--the five teens arrived early at the Community Center to do a final tuning up of their harmonies and steps. While rehearsing in the boys lavatory--they liked the echo effect it gave--outside in the center's parking lot, a temporary stage was being erected in the warm afternoon sun. Precipitation was in the forecast, showers weren't expected until late in the evening, but just in case the weathermen were in error, as they often were, the Community Center's maintenance staff were prepared to move stage, bleachers, everything, indoors at the first sign of rain. By late afternoon, the Community Center's public address system had been set up, and once the sound check was completed, the program started promptly at five.

To best represent the twin's inimitable talents, one of the Temptation's earlier recordings, a song called "Paradise," was selected. From the moment the elder twin began singing its introduction with his thunderous basso profundo, Kevi knew he had made the right choice. Leon's voice was so powerful, so much lower than Terry's, it resonated through the on-stage monitors, traveled along the floor, and slithered upward into his body. The sensation was so exhilarating, so seductive, so incredibly hypnotic, it gave him goose bumps the size of marbles. One look at his female audience, Kevi knew that nearly all were affected by Leon Braithwaite's cold, sensuous, gritty, gravelly, graveyard voice. While he, Ron, and Timmy provided the background support for the elder twin's explosive ostinatos, Leo, whose voice is as naturally high as his brother's is low, delivered the lead with equal ability. Effortlessly, the younger twin executed a quivering legato as clear as glass while modulating from key to key, warbling the scales like a songbird singing to its mate. Born to sing, the two boys worked the stage in tandem, completely enthralling their audience.

"Ladies and gentlemen," the master of ceremonies began, "as we near the end of our program, I must say, you've been a very supportive and responsive audience." A slight pause to clear his throat. "This afternoon you've had the rare privilege in hearing the finest talent from your surrounding communities. You should be exceedingly proud of each and everyone of them. Regrettably though, there can only be one winner. That winner shall receive a two hundred dollar cash prize, a free trip to New York City, and an appearance on the "Hy Hope Amateur Hour." The judges and I have already cast our ballots, but we think it would be unfair to the contestants if we didn't allow you, **their fans,** to also take part in the voting. So, without further ado, I shall reintroduce these fine young men and women, and by your applause, you can show them just how appreciative you are."

With the introduction of each act, the audience applauded excitedly, each wave of excitement greater than the one before. But when the **Pains of Love** were introduced, it was sheer pandemonium. "Ladies and gentlemen," is as far as the MC got before a thousand screams filled the air. The sudden furor was so voluminous it caused the audio system to emit a piercing shriek through its on-stage monitors. No one seemed to notice.

Later that evening, the party to beat all parties was given in a local high school gymnasium. In addition to the music and refreshments, booths had been set up with the express purpose of taking photos of the victorious teens. Kevi couldn't remember ever being so happy. At the same time a sadness touched his heart. *"If only Poppa could've been here."*

But that was impossible.

Seven years ago, his father had been working the third shift at the foundry when word came that he had suffered a fatal heart attack. He was only thirty five. "One day son, people are gonna mention your name in the same breath as Basie, Ellington, and Gershwin," he used to say.

With those words of encouragement, Kevi would diligently apply himself to his piano lessons, hoping one day he could make his father's dream come true.

"I'm not there yet, Poppa," he said to himself, "but I got my feet in the door."

"H-honey?"

Lost in thought, Kevi turned so quickly he nearly spilled the glass of lemonade he had poured for himself all over the floor. "Mama," he regarded searchingly, "what's wrong? This is no time for tears."

"That's what I told her," Nellie Bryson affirmed, her tone gently scolding.

"I'm so happy for you," mama said, sniffing between each word, blowing her nose with a tissue Nellie had given her. As she craned her neck upwards, she kissed her son lightly on the cheek.

Kevi had to hunch over to hug his mother's full round form. Less than five feet in height and as round as she is tall, most of her friends called her Mama, or "Mrs. Butterball." In either case, Kevi knew that nearly everyone in town loved her as much as he did. "Poppa would have been so proud of you," he heard his mother say, and before he realized what was happening, his eyes began to swell.

"Don't you dare start," Nellie teased.

Almost as if operated by a switch, Kevi's tear ducts slammed themselves closed. More than a trifle embarrassed, he knew he'd be unable to cry even if he wanted to.

When his mother finally released him, she turned and hugged Nellie with gentle affection. "Be good to her, son. Girls like your Nellie come only once in a lifetime."

"Don't worry, Mama," Kevi said taking Nellie into his arms. "I will."

It never failed, but whenever they danced, Kevi would recall the day he and Nellie met. Having seen her many times--she lived in his neighborhood, and attended his church--except for the fact that they were classmates--both were in the second grade--he had never felt anything special towards her. One evening, though, as she rode her brand new bicycle down their narrow street, he watched her pass in front of the fire house. With consummate skill, she whipped her bike around a pile of scattered leaves that had fallen during a recent thunderstorm, unaware that a diminutive dalmatian--the firehouse's newest mascot--had gotten free, and was streaking towards her. Swerving at the last moment, she managed to avoid the yapping, excited pup, but in doing so, her bike slipped from beneath her and spilled her onto the slippery, leafy pavement.

Sitting on the front porch with his parents at the time, Kevi knew the instant Nellie hit the ground she was unlike any other girl he had ever known. Instead of bursting into tears or bawling like most girls, she just picked herself up and cleaned herself off as if nothing had happened. A nasty gash on one knee, and an ugly bruise on her right elbow were the extent of her injuries, but if they bothered her, she never showed it.

"Oh dear! Are you all right?" Mama called, forgetting the basket of laundry she had been folding, her huge waddling form rushing into the street.

Nellie Bryson shrugged her shoulders.

"Would you like me to bandage your hurt for you?" Mama asked, flashing her toothiest smile. "There's a bowl of chocolate ice cream in it for you."

Kevi knew that this was an offer no kid could refuse. Naturally, Nellie accepted the invitation. While he picked up her bike, the front wheel had been bent slightly, his mother helped the injured second grader across the street where his father awaited them with the first aid kit.

On the porch Mama said soothingly, "This might sting a bit."

"Sting my eye!" Kevi bellowed without shame. "That stuff burns like the dickens!"

Nellie didn't even wince.

His mouth agape, Kevi could only shake his head. Later, after her parents were notified, he was awed even more as the pretty girl from down the street seemingly inhaled his mother's homemade ice cream.

Thinking about it now, Kevi knew he had fallen in love that rainy Autumn evening, and as he recalled the expressions on his parents' faces, he knew they had fallen in love too.

"Why the smile?" Nellie asked, angling her head purposely to kiss Kevi on his ear lobe.

"How'd you know I was smiling?"

"I can tell." When Kevi didn't answer Nellie said, "Is it a secret?"

"N-No secret," Kevi said shyly. "I-I was just thinking about...how much I love you."

"May I cut in?" a nasal voice asked from behind.

Without turning, Kevi recognized the coarse, labored breathing that belonged to his best friend.

"Come on," Ricky wheezed. "Let a real man show you how to slow drag."

"Where is he, this reeeal man?" Kevi quickly retorted, realizing he hadn't seen Ricky or Terry a single time in the past few days.

The silence became thick.

"We were right about the twins weren't we?," Ricky asked pensively.

Unable to read his friend's expression Kevi mumbled, "Yeah, you were right."

Suddenly, Ricky's eyes twinkled at the corners. When he extended his hand, Kevi took it. "I'm happy for you, partner. Happy for all of you. But when you make it to the big time, you're going to need an opening act. Probably a comic. So, don't forget me."

"Deal," Kevi said, pumping Ricky's hand, "but you've got to come up with some better material than the cornball stuff you've been doin' lately."

"Cool. By the way, Terry gives his best. He wanted to make the show, but his mother went into labor just before school let out."

"That's okay. When you see him, give him and his family **my** best."

"I sure will," Ricky said before melting into the thickening crowd.

By midnight it had become so incredibly hot in the overcrowded gymnasium, the overhead lights were dimmed to reduce the heat, and the moment the rain began, the doors were opened to let in some cooler, fresher air. Still, in spite of the sporadic thunder and lightning outside, or the cacophonous activity inside, the entire gymnasium became a tranquil, cozy setting for nearly everyone.

Having made their request earlier, when "Ooo Baby Baby" began to play Nellie instinctively placed her arms around her sweetheart's neck. This was their song, and only the foolishly ignorant would attempt to cut in.

His heart soaring, Kevi's euphoria was irrevocably shattered the instant a voice as cold as death announced his presence.

"Good evening," Leon Braithwaite said thickly.

Kevi's body had stiffened so suddenly, the hair on the back of his neck stood straight up. Sick with fear, his stomach felt as if maggots were eating him from the inside out. Almost choking on the bile collecting in his throat, sweat from his brow ran down his face in icy trails. The worse feeling, though, was the way his fears spread from his constricted throat to his pain-filled gut.

Alarmed, Nellie asked, "Honey, what's wrong? You look as if you've seen a ghost."

Kevi fought to take a breath. "I-I'm all right," he lied, his heart slamming against his ribs. "I-It's the heat...I-I guess I need some air."

"Hello fellas," Nellie said, addressing the twins with her usual bubbly exuberance. "I just luuuuvd your performance today. You were soooo good."

"Thank you," the elder twin replied, his younger brother offering a nod.

If Kevi thought he felt bad before, he felt even worse when Leo slapped him on the back. It wasn't a heavy blow, a light one in fact, still, the physical contact left him weak and shaken. It was as though part of his life force had been stolen from him.

"What's up, Stone?" the younger twin asked.

"N-nothing m-m-much," Kevi rasped, his words catching in his throat, as if filled with saw dust.

"Do you mind if Nellie and I dance?" Leon asked politely.

Kevi wanted to scream, "Nooooo!!!" but his tongue felt wooden in his mouth. After he had taken the hanky Nellie had removed from her purse, he stumbled towards the open gymnasium door and stepped out into the drizzling rain. Miraculously refreshed somehow, he watched his sweetheart wave to him as she was being held in Leon's arms. Another bolt of fear shocked his innards, making him feel even sicker than before.

Unaware of her presence until she had touched him, Nellie pulled Kevi inside, wiped the rain from his face, and placed the back of her hand on his forehead. "I'm not sick," he told her.

"I don't know, honey. For a second back there, I thought you were gonna pass out." Nellie paused to make sure. "You seem all right now."

"I'm fine," Kevi grunted, the pain in his stomach, although still a presence was subsiding slowly.

"The twins are wonderful, aren't they?"

"They give me the creeps," Kevi said abruptly, his tone as cold as ice.

Shocked, Nellie Bryson's walnut colored eyes stared uncomprehendingly. "How could you say such a thing?" she asked, her eyebrows perched high.

"Haven't you ever found them the least bit...strange?"

"Strange? No. And I've known them most of my life." Concerned, Nellie pressed. "Honey, what's the matter? This isn't like you."

"I don't know", Kevi muttered discontentedly, hating the fact he had allowed his fears to get the better of him. "Every time they look at me, it gives me the willies. It's like they can see into my soul." A brief pause. "Aww honey, I can't explain it."

"Shhh," Nellie said, kissing him on the forehead. "I'm sure it's nothing more than your imagination."

"Kevi seriously doubted it. Something had happened to him tonight. Something beyond explanation. The pain was unendurable and the fear. The last time he recalled such terror, he was ten years old. Worse this time, it struck deep into his psyche, reached into his soul, and deposited an acrid, cretaceous taste in his mouth. It was a feeling he didn't relish at all.

About 1 AM, the party started to break up and like so many others, Kevi and Nellie decided to leave before another shower started. The second they stepped outside their high school gymnasium, they paused to breathe in the sweet night air. Rain. How they loved it. Therapeutic for both, one of their greatest joys was strolling together down the middle of a street after a spring or summer shower.

For Kevi, snuggling on Nellie's front porch was a perfect end to an almost perfect day. Except for a few bad moments, most of which he had been able to push to the back of his mind, it had been absolutely wonderful. His only wish was that it could go on forever. A little after three, he finally said goodnight and while he walked the five blocks to his home, the memory of his sweetheart's warm lips and intoxicating fragrance filled every corner of his mind. Completely exhausted, he laid across his bed without undressing, falling asleep almost immediately.

His last thoughts before closing his eyes were of Nellie.

CHAPTER THREE

A tremendous weight was pressing heavily against Kevi's chest. How it had gotten there, or how long it had been there he had no way of knowing. Every attempt to remove it met with failure. It was as though his limbs were made of marble. To compound his futility, he was unable to determine what it was that set upon him. The blackness surrounding him was total, but moved as if a living thing.

"Nellie will be mine!"

There was only one voice that could chill Kevi so completely. One voice so devoid of emotion and yet so powerful its gritty timbre could create excruciating pain. *"Leon! But how?"* Kevi's mind flashed backwards. After leaving Nellie's last night, he had gone straight home. That was all he could remember. Everything else about yesterday was erased from his mind, as if it had never existed. *"This can't be happening! This has got to be some kind of horrible nightmare!"*

Dream or not, Kevi's lungs felt as if they were ready to burst. Even worse, blood from his tongue bubbled through his locked, trembling lips and trickled from the corners of his mouth down into his ears. *"Aarrrggghhh!!!"*

Pain. In all the universe, how could there be such pain?

Suddenly, light. Blessed light. And finally, release. Sweet release from whatever it was that pressed heavily against him. Was he truly awakening from this horrid nightmare? He certainly hoped so. He couldn't take much more. Off in the distance, movement.

Something approached.

Whatever it was, it was huge. Baffled by the horrifying, hissing sounds that were undoubtedly getting closer, Kevi began to tremble. His first thought was that an old steam train had engaged its brakes, or that possibly a huge balloon had been punctured, in which case minute amounts of its precious gas was being released through a tiny aperture. Fearfully, he peered into the inky blackness, seeing nothing at all. Suddenly, there was a flicker of light. From all appearances, a duo of vehicles raced towards him, their headlights growing more intense the closer they came. In another moment, they would be upon him. Then, while he was trying to decide which way to run, the blazing orbs leaped from the ground and headed for the blackened sky.

Following its smooth, unerring arc, Kevi looked upward. What he saw made his blood run cold. High above him stood a gigantic two-headed snake, its eyes a fiery bluish-grey hue. Moving faster than light, each of the beast's slimy elongated tongues whipped around his neck and tightened its grip. Kevi screamed. Not so much from the pain of contact, but from the repulsiveness of its touch and the stench that filled his nostrils. Taloned appendages, more ethereal than corporeal, clasped his feet. Twin tails working independently, one tightening around his chest, the other encircling his midriff, squeezed in tandem, increasing the pressure with each second. As his skin burned from the snake's scaly touch, the acid-like bile he felt in his throat shot upward into his nasal passages scorching the tender insides of his nostrils.

"There issss no esssscape," the reptile hissed. "We shall destroy you. And those you love."

Kevi's thoughts turned to his mother and then Nellie. His fear was replaced with rage. "The hell you will," he cried defiantly, his vomit spewing from his mouth in a gushing stream, striking the serpent's hideous, scaly faces.

As its hissing grew intensely louder, Kevi sensed somehow that his regurgitations had caused the reptile pain. Relentlessly, his vomit continued to flow, showering, devouring, scalding the monster, until there was nothing left but the sound of its faint screams, and the noxious odor of its rapidly decomposing flesh. Then, the light began to dim. After a time, the blackness consumed everything, leaving nothing but a still emptiness in the ether.

The next morning Kevi's agonies resumed. In addition to a bleeding mouth, every muscle in his body ached intensely. His senses reeling at the stench of his own sweat and bile, the second he recalled his macabre nightmare, he raced to the bathroom to retch up the remainder of his guts.

After he had cleaned his room and had settled himself in the scalding hot waters of his tub, the phone in the hallway started to ring.

"I got it honey..."

"Ok, Mama!" he yelled.

When Kevi was through bathing, he discovered the clothes he had taken out were already pressed and lying on his bed. "Mama," he mumbled with a smile, "sometimes you treat me like a baby", adding, "but I wouldn't have it any other way." Dressed finally, Kevi bounded down the steps in search of his mother. But each time he had called out to her, his only response was an empty echo. Heading for the kitchen, he knew that if she had gone out, a note would be tacked on the refrigerator door, but this time it was next to the lunch she had prepared for him.

The note read, "Honey, my sisters and I are gonna spend the day together. Hope you don't mind. If you need me, call me at Crestview 7-4112. That's your Auntie Bonita's number. I'll be home some time around eight."

"While you were in the tub, Ricky called. He'll meet you at the "Y" about one o'clock. I saw Nellie in the market this morning. She wants you to call her this afternoon."

"I fixed a couple of sandwiches and made some iced tea for your lunch. If you get hungry around dinner time, there's some leftover meat loaf and green beans in the fridge. There's also some potato salad your Auntie Bonita brought over this morning."

"See you some time tonight. Be good. Don't forget to call Nellie. Love, Mama."

By 12:45, Kevi caught the Park Street bus that would take him uptown to the YMCA. A short ride, give or take a few minutes, he'd probably arrive the same time as Ricky. While he looked out the window, the nightmarish events of last evening pushed its way into his thoughts, but disappeared the instant the vehicle had stopped. Suddenly, he felt safe and secure, as if he had come home. Nothing could've been closer to the truth. In a way, the "Y" **was** his home. Through the variety of athletics the club offered, he was able to fill the void his father's passing had left inside him.

Still a painful memory, Kevi had never felt more heartsick, or totally lost then when his father died. No matter how many images of him were stored in his memory, the one of his father lying cold in the casket, he remembered most. It was the last time he had seen him.

New emotions were born each day. Among them, bitterness, betrayal, desertion. Even hatred. Being seven years old didn't help at all.

For days, Kevi refused to go near any of his friends, which included Ricky and Nellie. Since there was nothing they could do to bring his father back, or change the way he was feeling, he avoided them. And whenever they'd visit him, he would treat them horribly, mostly because he believed no one could understand what he was feeling. He was wrong. His mother could. She had lost her father to cancer when she was just about his age. "Mama?" he asked, crying uncontrollably since discovering his mother's loss.

"Yes, dear?"

"Were you mad at your Poppa when he died?"

"Yes, darling, I was the youngest, his favorite...and was deeply hurt by his passing. Like you, I couldn't make any sense of it. But I was fortunate. I had three older sisters who loved him too. Without their help, I don't know what I'd have done." Embracing her son in her warm, fleshy arms, she stroked him gently. "Always remember, honey, as long as you have someone who loves you, you're never alone. Don't ever shut out those who care for you. Nellie and Ricky are your friends. They need you in their lives as much as you need them in yours. Don't ever forget that. Do you understand?"

"Yes, Mama," he said, wiping his tears away. He hadn't shed a tear since.

A few weeks later, Kevi became a member of the "Y" and was enrolled on its boxing team. He also joined the Boy's Club, and participated in football, baseball, basketball, and track. In short, athletics provided an additional focus to his young life. With school, music, and his burning hunger for physical competition, he had very little time to feel sorry for himself. More importantly, contact sports taught him how to deal with the smoldering anger burning deep inside him.

As time went on, everyone but Kevi's mother was in awe of his athletic prowess. "Takes after his father," she would say, "who was an exceptional athlete in his day." But by the time her son reached his teens, he had exceeded her expectations. Especially in boxing. Kevi had found his niche. Since stepping into the ring he had never been put down. After seventy-six amateur bouts, he was undefeated.

In nearly every neighborhood within the tiny community of Cameron, being able to defend one's self is an absolute necessity. Youth gangs of every ethnicity were on almost every street corner, and there were many turfs you purposely avoided unless you were prepared to fight. To hone their street-fighting skills, most of Cameron's teenage hoodlums boxed at the "YMCA". Impressed by his pugilistic abilities, the gang members often observed Kevi from ringside. At a respectful distance, of course. On the streets, it was the same. Kevi Stone was one of a few teens in Cameron that could go anywhere he pleased.

Whenever Kevi stepped into the "Y's" crowded gymnasium it set his blood afire. Other than sitting behind a piano, or being entangled in Nellie's arms, this was the one place in which he truly felt alive. As if by osmosis, he absorbed the nuances of his surroundings, particularly the smell of the sweat soaked leather, and the grunting sounds of bodies being pushed to the limit in their eclectic pursuits. These were like a heady nectar; invigorating, stimulating, intoxicating.

Standing at ringside, he watched Ricky spar with a kid from one of the uptown street gangs. The boy didn't stand a chance.

With great skill, young Caldwell easily picked his opponent's defenses apart. Somewhere in the middle of the first round, the kid conceded defeat and hastily retreated from the ring.

Another win under his belt, Ricky Caldwell practiced his Ali shuffle, threw several combinations, and concluded his routine with a victory walk around the ring. And while coach Edwards, a former heavy weight contender of the early fifties assisted Kevi with his gloves and head gear, Ricky mimicked his hero. "Get in here, you little whippersnapper," he challenged. "I'm going to beat you like you stole something." Adding:

"Now, I'll say this only once,
"It won't be repeated,
"But if you mess with me,
"You will be defeated."

The coach's guffaw rocked his heavy body, shaking his once muscular torso like a huge vat of gelatin.

Kevi, however, had heard Ricky's lame limerick before, and wasn't at all amused. "Ha, ha, ha", he sneered playfully. "When I get into that ring, I'm gonna introduce you to one of your closest friends."

Ricky snorted. "Yeah? Who's that?"

Exhibiting a lightning quick flurry Kevi said, "The canvas."

"Man, you'd rather go into a lion's den with meat-packed drawers on than mess with me."

"Oh yeah? Well, you'd rather tongue kiss an alligator than mess with **me.**"

Caldwell's expression turned thoughtful. "Gee, Stone," he said, his smile replaced by a frown, "you're stinkin' gross, you know that?"

For more than an hour, the two teens boxed each other before moving on to the weight room. Although Ricky was a natural all around athlete, he couldn't begin to compete with his best friend. No one could. Kevi was just that good. Nevertheless, for the past three years, every Saturday afternoon the two boys would get together at either the YMCA or the Boy's Club and have a great time.

With much reluctance, Kevi managed to tell Ricky what had happened, or what he believed had happened last night at the party, but decided to say nothing about his dream because he feared his friend might think him crazy.

"What're ya gonna do now?" Caldwell asked, grunting heavily as he pushed the barbell upward a final rep. Taking the weights with an ease contradictory to his slender frame, Stone placed it securely within the hooks as his buddy reached for the towel at the end of the bench.

Caldwell wiped his face. "If the twins got you so spooked, how ya gonna do the show?"

"Beats me. But I can tell you one thing. The next time I see 'em, I'm gonna know if it's my imagination or not. I hope it is...cause if it isn't, I'm gonna make 'em wish they were never born."

"Sounds like you've gotta plan."

"Oh, I gotta plan all right," Stone imparted. "I'm going to tear their freakin' heads offa their freakin' necks."

"Stunned at first, Caldwell's features turned pleasantly mischievous."Works for me..."

CHAPTER FOUR

Sundays, Kevi Stone and Nellie Bryson usually attended Second Baptist's worship services. The only exceptions were when they were invited to another church, which was the case with this particular Sabbath. Both were guests of the Good Shepherd Church of Cameron, the Honorable Calvin V. Braithwaite, pastor and teacher, presiding.

Ordinarily, a team of wild horses wouldn't have been able to drag Kevi into the twin's church. But Nellie could. "I know you're only doing this for me," she acknowledged. "You won't be sorry. I promise."

Kevi wasn't convinced. As soon as he entered the old tabernacle, an uncomfortable feeling seeped deep into his bones. There was no mistake. An undercurrent of tension filled the air, and from every indication it seemed only he was capable of sensing it.

Barely noon, the temperatures outside were rapidly approaching the mid-nineties. Inside, the temperatures were significantly higher. Even with the large, dusty, metal fans spinning full tilt in every corner, the heat was sweltering. The doors and windows were opened wide, and offered an occasional breeze, but not nearly enough to keep the church's patrons from fanning themselves profusely.

The music, however, was gospel singing at its best. For the better part of an hour, the jubilant, sweating congregation were entertained by three of west-side Cameron's finest choirs. First, a dozen three to five year old dressed in white, appropriately called the "Angels Without Wings," performed an exciting accapella arrangement of "Jesus Loves Me," and in spite of their frequent wanderings from key to key, Kevi found the tiny preschoolers a pleasant diversion.

The junior and senior choirs followed. Led by Leo and Leon, respectively, with each selection, Kevi became more and more astonished by the impressive vocal tapestries that only the twins could weave. Surprisingly, though, for the first time since entering the church, he was beginning to relax.

"Let us prepare for the altar prayer," a deacon announced.

Like a herd of stampeding buffalo, the church members responded, and rushed eagerly towards the altar in search of a place to kneel and pray. In just a few seconds, every inch of space had been usurped by the elder, more frenetic holy rollers that were already seated up front.

Time passed. So slowly in fact, the oaken bench that Kevi had been sitting on seemed like an ancient instrument of torture. No matter what he tried he was unable to find any comfort. To add to his miseries, two humongous women, one on his left, the other on Nellie's right, sandwiched them together so tightly, he imagined himself his sweetheart's Siamese twin.

Noticing his discomfort, Nellie touched his hand lightly and smiled.

"I can't believe her butt doesn't hurt too."

Kevi shifted his weight to one side, but the pain persisted. For some time his rump had been asleep, and any attempt to wiggle, squirm, or readjust his delicate bottom resulted in agony. And if a numb tail bone wasn't bad enough, Miss Gargantua on his left emitted an odor so foul, he was certain she could be used as the nation's newest secret weapon. It would be simple. Just stand her upwind of the enemy, blow a huge fan on her, in three seconds flat--capitulation. *"Somebody get this fat, funky, collard green eating heifer offa me before she kills me..."*

As if in answer to his silent prayer, the deacon bellowed in a powerful baritone, "Will everyone please rise."

Kevi waited patiently for the two leviathans to get to their feet. It took much effort to lift that tonnage. Miss Bovine on Nellie's right was the first to stand. Miss Buffalo was next. It seemed minutes, but the moment both ladies reached their feet, he let out an audible sigh, at which point he received a sharp elbow to his rib cage. Caught off guard, Kevi attempted his best "please forgive me, but I'm being tortured" look, but Nellie wasn't buying it. Next, he tried a look of sorrow with a hint of anguish added, but she wasn't buying that either. Finally, he gave up. There was just no fooling her. At least not today.

While everyone else was standing, Kevi was the only one that remained seated. Still trying to get the circulation flowing into his lower extremities, for Nellie's sake, he acted as if he were a paraplegic. But the instant Miss Big Booty's sweating, ample derriere' was planted inches from his face, he sprung to his feet as if shot from a cannon.

Elbowing him again, Nellie whispered between muffled snickers, "That's what you get for faking."

"It's a miracle, ma'am, but I'se been cured."

Snickering again, Nellie pushed Kevi away as he leaned against her.

"Are you feeling all right, young man?", Miss Biggest Butt in the world inquired, her concern genuine. "You don't look so good."

"I'm fine, ma'am," Kevi replied, a little ashamed by his demeaning, dehumanizing thoughts. "My legs are a little stiff, that's all. Thank you for asking."

Miss Buffalo Butt beamed a toothless smile and offered her sweaty, fleshy paw. Taking it, although much to his dismay, Kevi was unable to believe that his hand, which was considerable for a fifteen year old, had completely disappeared in a mound of fat, sweating flesh. When he took Nellie's hand, he smiled. It was soft and warm. Nothing at all like Miss Meaty Paws. Then, with genuine amazement he studied the girl he loved so much. She had endured the same hardships as he, but showed no indication of discomfort.

How could she do it?

Simple. Nellie was just being Nellie. It was her nature to smile in the face of adversity, while his was to scowl at every opportunity, good or bad.

While the minister prepared to deliver his sermon, the congregation began to fidget with nervous anticipation. Everyone it seemed, but Kevi. A sudden, unshakable feeling of dread had come over him, forcing him to shiver in spite of the church's rising temperatures. A single thought echoed in the back of his mind. The devil himself was preparing to speak.

"Our text for todaaayy!" the minister began," comes from the book of Revelations." In a few short moments, he delivered his voluminous diatribe with all the fire and brimstone he could muster.

Throughout the sermon, Kevi studied the minister's fiery blue-grey eyes, and understood, in part, why his congregation seemed to hang onto his every word. There was definitely something hypnotic about those blazing orbs, and though the stately backwoods preacher wasn't the most eloquent speaker he had ever heard, his presence was certainly one of the most powerful.

The entire sermon was such an eery thing, minutes passed before Kevi realized something was wrong. With a subtlety that completely surprised him, everyone sitting in the pews had become bewitched by the minister's fiery oratory and blazing eyes. Including Nellie. Other than the minister's dynamic discourse, not a single word had been uttered.

Kevi was stupefied and quite honestly, afraid. At first he thought the congregation had been subjected to some sort of mass hypnosis, but it was much more than that. As the preacher droned on in his soporific, husky baritone, Nellie's breathing became increasingly shallow, so shallow Kevi could barely detect the rise and fall of her chest. The moment he touched her, he snatched his hand back as if he had grabbed a red hot poker. It was just the opposite. Nellie's hand was colder than ice. It was like touching the dead. *"Oh honey, what's happened to you?"*

More importantly, what could he about it?

Purposely, Kevi brushed against the fat lady sitting at his left. In spite of the sweat oozing through her light-colored cotton garments, she reminded him of a glacier; huge, cold, rigid. Sitting as he was, amongst the comatose immobile members of the congregation, helpless in aiding them, for the first time in his life he felt completely alone. Even the infants that had wailed as if there were no tomorrow prior to the minister's sermon failed to offer him hope. The dozen or so tots were as stiff and as silent as their unfortunate parents.

With each minute that passed, the church soared to inferno-like conditions. Still, no one moved, not even to fan themselves. Which gave the flies and mosquitos a rare opportunity. Like two allied military formations, they flew at warp speed striking without protest from their rigid sweat-soaked targets.

"Aaaaaoooooo!!!"

Kevi stiffened in his seat. Except for the minister's voice, or the sound of his own frantic breathing, the unexpected wail forced itself upon the awful silence. His every sense alert, even without looking towards the altar, he knew the unexpected utterance had come from someone in the minister's family.

He was only part right. Caught up in the passion and delivery of their leader's sermon, each of them moved to a smooth undulating rhythm. Whenever the minister would build his oratory to a fever pitch, their moaning and swaying would increase proportionately, and each time he diminished in religious fervor, their moaning and swaying would then also diminish.

"Aaaarrrrrgggghhh!" The pain was so unexpected it had taken Kevi completely by surprise. Believing at first, the Braithwaite's were somehow responsible, he was quite relieved to discover a brightly colored yellow jacket was the source of his misery. Certain that it must have wandered through an open window, why, of all its prospective targets had it singled him out for its attack?

Kevi's eyes swept the room. Except for the twins and their parents, no one had heard his scream. The minister's wife, who had been sitting behind her husband stood up and stepped towards the altar. The twins, who were sitting on the choir bench also rose and flanked their parents. As if guided by radar, their blazing eyes searched the pews to find the root of the disturbance. His resolve hardened, Kevi ignored their hateful glares and swallowed his fears. And then a wonderful thing happened. A sudden stirring at his side took him completely by surprise. Feeling a joy beyond description, he touched his sweetheart's hands.

Kevi's joys were instantly magnified.

Nellie's deathly chill had gone.

With his sweetheart free of the Braithwaite's spell, or whatever it was, Kevi was confident that the others would also be roused from their trances; and they were, two and three at a time, until everyone had shaken the hellish thing that possessed their bodies. As each of them became cognizant of their actions once more, a variety of expressions were displayed on their faces; fear and bewilderment the most prominent.

Kevi then wondered if any of his fellow congregants would remember what had happened. It didn't matter. For as long as he drew breath, he would never forget the day a spiritual evil had been loosed in his presence. Thankfully, no, blessedly, its power paled in comparison to that of the

Almighty.

It seemed strange somehow, but growing up in the church as he did, Kevi had never considered himself a religious person. Even now. And yet, at this very moment, he felt a great comfort in believing somewhere in the universe there existed a power of good capable of defeating evil wherever it reared its ugly head.

Feeling one with the heavens, an unbelievable warmth seeped into his bones, completely replacing the dread he first felt entering the Braithwaite church. Overwhelmed by this strange sensation, his every pore seemed charged with an incredible energy.

This too, he would remember.

*****

While Nellie greeted her friends gathering outside the small tabernacle, Kevi stretched his weary limbs across an old wooden bench beneath the only shade tree in the churchyard. Grateful to be out in the fresh air again, he breathed in the sweet fragrance of the honeysuckle blossoms, filling his lungs to capacity, realizing that it was only a matter of time before the Braithwaite confronted him.

He didn't have long to wait.

"You should try to pay more attention young man," the twin's father said acidly.

"I **was** paying attention," Kevi replied, undaunted. "I must apologize, though, for my outburst, he added, displaying his right hand which was begin to swell. "A bee stung me." A brief smile touched his face. "Seems the only one I disturbed was you and your family. Strange, don't you think?"

"Strange?" the twin's father asked, flustered a little. "What's strange about it?"

Kevi shrugged absently but retained his smile.

"Have my sons told you about an idea we have for your upcoming television debut?"

The minister's question was so abrupt, Kevi's mind whirled in confusion. "N-No they haven't," he said hesitantly. "What exactly are we talking about?"

"I was thinking about the enormous opportunity you have to reach out and help those who are less fortunate than yourself." Putting his hands together, the minister formed a steeple with his fingers and repeatedly rubbed his chin. "I'm hoping you can be persuaded to sing a gospel number written by my sons instead of the secular music you've already chosen," he said after collecting his thoughts. "Before you begin voicing your objections, let's discuss it for a moment. Think of the good you could do. Think of all the young men and women you could help find grace and salvation. My dear boy, in just one song, you could reach more Christians in three minutes than I have in my thirty years of ministering. You, your young friends, and my sons could become a blessing to so many ."

"*Or a curse!*" Kevi wasn't fooled for a moment. After witnessing the incredible power the minister and his family wielded only moments ago, he was certain with the media behind them, their influence could be expanded, effecting thousands, maybe even millions, and that horrified him. Suppressing a shudder he said, "I'm sorry, sir, but I can't do that. The **Pains of Love** are a rhythm and blues group...**not** a gospel group."

"I thought you of all people would have a more Christian attitude," the minister said icily. "Especially, since your mother..."

"Leave my mother out of this," Kevi said vociferously, more angry at himself because he'd lost his temper. He always prided himself on remaining cool, regardless of the circumstances. It was one of the many things he learned in the ring. "She's not a member of my group, and even if she was, she would expect me to do what I think best for everyone. Now, if your sons are having second thoughts, and no longer wish to be with us on the terms they agreed upon, I assure you they can be replaced."

"Since you choose to be stubborn as well as selfish," the preacher said coldly, "maybe my sons should talk with the other members of your quintet. Maybe then you can be made to appreciate things from a different perspective."

Kevi became furious. But this time he kept his temper in check. "You can talk to Timmy and Ronnie until you're blue in the face," he said coolly, "but I don't think you could change their minds in a zillion years."

The Reverend glanced quickly to his right.

His defenses ready, Kevi acted as though he hadn't seen what had passed between father and son.

"Look, man," Leon said, his thick voice deceptively warm, "I'm sure there's no need for concern. Everything will work out to everyone's satisfaction."

While Leon created the diversion, Leo attempted to slap Kevi on the back, but before the younger twin's hand could make contact, it was caught in mid-air. Leo blinked in surprise. So did everyone else.

"I'm gonna say this only once...I don't like it when people put their hands on me." Kevi yanked Leo forward until their noses touched. "Especially by you. So, let me give you some reeeaal friendly advice...don't." Sneering acidly, Leo attempted to free himself, but Kevi's grip was like iron. "You wouldn't want to get hurt now, would you?"

"Are you threatening my son?", the twin's mother roared, moving towards him, restrained an instant later by her eldest boy.

Kevi Stone smiled. "No ma'am, I'm giving him a warning is all..."

"Young man, I dislike your violent attitude," the Reverend hissed savagely, attempting to release his son.

One squeeze from Kevi's powerful limbs and Leo winced in agony.

Getting the message, the minister retreated quickly and reclaimed his place between his wife and Leon.

"Sir, with all due respect," Kevi said derisively, releasing the whimpering twin, "the only time I'm violent is when I'm **attacked**, or in the ring. So there is no misunderstanding, let me make myself perfectly clear. In the ring, my violence is tempered with mercy because boxing is a sport I quite honestly love. But as far as violence goes outside the ring, if I, or any of my loved ones are threatened, believe me, I'm quite capable of exceeding your wildest imaginings."

"You sound just like your father," the minister said indignantly, "and like him, your arrogance knows no limits."

Kevi blew up. His father was the world to him, and no one would be allowed to demean his good name. Not while he lived. Choosing his words carefully he said, "Sir, many times throughout the years, I've heard ministers like yourself promising "peace in the valley." I give you fair warning, you push **me** too far, you're gonna find **Hell** in that valley."

That afternoon while Kevi was having dinner with Nellie and her folks, Timmy Witherspoon called. "Hey buddy...didn't mean to interrupt your eats."

"That's ok, man...what's up?"

"Dunno," Timmy replied strangely. "I just got off the phone with the twins, and believe it or not, they tried to convince me we should sing a gospel number instead of the tune you wrote."

"How do you feel about it?" Kevi asked, holding his breath, preparing for the worst.

"Are you kidding? All I dream about is being in a group like the Temps, and maybe one day sharin' a stage with 'em. There's no way that'll happen singin' gospel. Besides, soul music is where my heart is. I'd be unhappy doin' anything else."

"Didya tell them that?"

"Sure I did, but it didn't do no good. They got ticked at me for some reason and hung up. No explanation. No goodbye. Nothin'. What'd I say that was so wrong?"

"Nothin', Timmy. Don't sweat it. I wouldn't be at all surprised if they called Ronnie next."

"They already did. What's up, Kev? Why the change of heart? It's not like they didn't know what they were getting into...cause they did. I laid everything out for them the day I approached them, and you know what? Both were excited about it...**really** excited. The three of us must have talked for hours about how **baaad** we were gonna be. I wonder what could've changed their minds?"

"Beats me," said Kevi, his mind filled with doubt. "I can tellya one thing though, after church today, I had a discussion with the boys and their parents, and they were quite displeased when I rejected their offer." A short pause. "What does Ron think? How does he feel about the twin's idea?"

"Come on, man, you know Ron."

Kevi breathed in a sigh of relief and said, "Yeah, I guess I do. Well, maybe it's for the best. I've already informed the twins they can be replaced. For right now, being in the group is entirely up to them. But you know me, I've never been a patient person and I don't jump through hoops for anyone."

"Me neither," echoed Timmy. "I'm almost sorry I suggested them. Rehearsal's tomorrow at one, right?"

"Yep. If the twins show, they show. If they don't, they don't. Either way, I'm not gonna lose a second's sleep over'em."

"Well, I'll catch you tomorrow then. Say hello to Nellie for me. Later gator..."

"Later, T..."

*****

"Do you think they're gonna show?" Ronnie asked Kevi.

"To tell the truth, I really don't care."

After yesterday's experience at church, Kevi had plenty of time to think about the twins and their family, and he wasn't at all surprised at the decision he made. Leo and Leon would remain in the group up to and including the New York trip; a week on the outside. Afterwards, whether his group managed to secure a record deal or not, the twins would have to go, and though he'd never admit it, the unusual confrontation in the churchyard disturbed him more than he thought it would. His instincts told him a similar encounter was inevitable. This being the case, he decided to remove those obstacles that might represent a danger to his friends. Scarcely able to believe he hadn't thought of things in those terms before, he was glad he did. The Braithwaites might have everyone else fooled, the whole town possibly, but given sufficient provocation, Kevi believed they could and would resort to violence. For himself, he wasn't concerned. He was quite capable of taking care of himself. But Timmy and Ron, now that was something else. Which only made his case against the Braithwaites stronger. The twins had to go. They were expendable. His friends weren't. Besides that, there was Nellie to consider. She was in danger as well, and much too susceptible to the Braithwaite's unholy power, which made protecting her a problem in itself.

"What time is it?" Timmy asked.

"1:15," Ronnie answered impatiently. "How much longer are we going to wait? Maybe we should call and see if they're on their way."

"Nah!" Kevi said scowling. "If they ain't here in the next fifteen minutes, the only call I'm gonna make is to Ricky and Terry. They've already greed to rejoin us if the twins don't work out."

Nudging Kevi with an elbow Ronnie's powerful baritone boomed, "Guess you don't get your wish...'cause here they come."

Meeting the twins halfway down the church steps, Kevi gave them each an icy stare. Clearly, a message passed between them. But just in case they didn't get it he said, "I would like to clarify a few points. If either of you have a problem with the direction in which this group is going, you better say so now. There is only **one** leader in this group." Kevi thumbed his chest. "And that's **me**. If you have any goals other than those explained to you prior to your joining us, you don't belong in our organization. It's as simple as that. Have I made myself clear?"

No reply.

"Any questions?"

Again, no reply After a few moments, the twin's nodded.

"Good," Kevi said triumphantly, "then let's get to work."

CHAPTER FIVE

While the young quintet anxiously awaited their turn to perform, the raw energy they exuded occupied every molecule of space within their closet-sized dressing room, and though there was little activity inside the cramped quarters, the air had become so saturated with electrically charged particles, physical contact with another was purposely avoided.

Within the tiny room, Kevi's mother was the only one unaffected. Somehow she seemed immune to the spine tingling shocks the teens discharged to one another. Much like a busy little bee, she buzzed about the diminutive dressing room, making small talk, easing the tension, giving encouragement wherever it was needed. "Don't worry," she told them. "Y'all do just fine."

"Ten minutes before curtain time," someone yelled. "Wardrobe. I need someone from wardrobe."

"Keep your pants on," a man answered. "What's the problem?"

"Mr. Hope wants a change in clothing for the next act," the director said.

"Why? They look fine to me."

"Haven't seen their test, have you?" The man from wardrobe shook his head. "I suggest you check it out," the director ordered, motioning to the monitor.

The man from wardrobe took a brief glimpse at the black and white screen. He jumped back a moment later. "Geeeez," he said, shaking himself, his face turning crimson, then pale. "Those twins have got some spooooky eyes."

"See what I mean? If we don't do something quick, we're gonna scare the pants offa everyone in our viewing audience and that's not all..."

Because of the bluish-grey hue of the twin's eyes--they appeared glassy white, and blazed with fiery intensity when viewed over the studio monitor--and because the "Hy Hope Amateur Hour" was a family-oriented variety program, it was the host's concern the twin's unusual occulars might frighten some of its younger viewers. The only available recourse was to have them cover them. Understandably so, the twins were diametrically opposed to this suggestion, even after viewing their screen test. Unfortunately, they had no choice.

"Why don't we all wear shades?" Ron Gant suggested amicably.

"Yeah," Timmy Witherspoon added. "At least that way we can keep our look of uniformity."

Which is exactly what everyone did, once the wardrobe department managed to find the "Stevie Wonder-like" glasses Ronnie had suggested. But in solving one problem, another resulted. Their costumes. Presently, everyone was dressed in shiny black satin outfits. By itself, that wasn't a problem at all; the uniforms were quite stunning, but five black kids, dressed in black, wearing dark shades, made them look less like a singing group, and more like members of a militant organization. And with the attention certain civil rights leaders were getting, in addition to the recent rioting in the news, **black** wasn't especially beautiful, but more or less, a necessary evil to the show's sponsors.

Fortunately, the young quintet brought along additional clothing and once they changed their attire, in egg shell white this time, their dark glasses contrasted with their immaculate dress but was an agreeable improvement over their previous costume.

*****

"Camera one, pan right please. Camera two, zoom in on Mr. Hope.

Closer...closer...hold it. Your cue in twenty seconds, sir."

While he waited for the curtain to rise, Kevi took a moment to study his colleagues. He noticed a nervousness in everyone but Timmy. Since coming to New York, Witherspoon's beaming smile hadn't left his ebony face a single moment. Unquestionably the merriest member of the group, and possibly the most jovial person he knew, Timmy amused himself by displaying his dazzling footwork to a few of the show's female crew members.

Every second he waited, Kevi's stomach twisted into knots. Even after taking the antacid tablets his mother had given him, his stomach imitated a roller coaster ride at Coney Island. Nothing seemed to rid him of that thick, chalky taste on the tip of his tongue. Knowing the reason he felt so badly didn't help either. In fact, it only added to his misery. It was his song they were about to sing. This was the reason for his anxiety. Though everyone knew it cold, his greatest fear was that it wasn't nearly **good** enough for a national audience.

"Ok, laddies," the director said with just a hint of his Irish brogue noticeable. "Remember your marks, and to always face camera three, the one with the red light...you got that?"

Nods from everyone.

"What if we bomb?" Kevi muttered, horrified by his own thoughts.

A second later, the director turned to cue the nervous quintet, the host, and finally the cameras. "Alright everybody...quiet!" he yelled, getting set in his chair. "Your cue sir, in ten seconds ...9...8...7...6...5..." Holding up his hand, he counted the remaining numbers silently on his fingers. When he reached...1, he pointed purposefully to the show's host.

"And now, ladies and gentlemen," Mr. Hope began in a brittle, nasal, tenor voice that almost made him sound like Woody Woodpecker, "Tonight, I have a very special treat for you. From Cameron, New Jersey, singing an original composition, I give you...**The Pains of Love**."

In unison, two members of Hope's crew, one on each side of the stage, but outside the angle of the cameras held signs in front of the studio audience instructing them to applaud.

A moment before the curtain had risen, Kevi managed to catch his mother winking at him from the wings. As if by magic, the sight of her warm, cherubic smile erased all of his fears. By the time the first three bars were played, he was completely relaxed and had become one with his music.

Moving nimbly in front of their microphones, each of Kevi's colleagues were perfectly in sync with the other. While the young girls swooned in their seats, the boys' piercing whistles punctuated the air. So elated by the audience's immediate acceptance of his music, and his group, Kevi responded instinctively by throwing his microphone high above him, and though he had never done it before, he spun around, dropped to the floor into a split, only instead of catching the mike in front of him, he caught it behind his back. With that move alone, scores of teenagers leaped to their feet screaming their approval. But before he could rise, Timmy Witherspoon whirled suddenly from his group's formation and somersaulted into a split right next to him.

Kevi's heart pounded in his chest. Timmy's unexpected move had caught him completely off guard. Taking a moment, he glanced furtively towards Ron and the twins. From all appearances they acted as if nothing had happened. Then, looking directly at Timmy, ready to admonish him with an icy glare, Kevi saw something too marvelous to believe--Witherspoon's big, fat, beautiful smile. Somehow Kevi knew everything was going to be all right.

Slowly, Timmy started to rise but without the use of his hands. As his long legs seemed to stretch into infinity, inch by inch he began his slow scissor-like ascent. Once erect, he gyrated to the music while placing his baby finger at the point of his colleague's shirt collar.

Understanding, Kevi Stone duplicated his young friend's movements by also rising slowly, his hands at his waist. A seemingly foolish act on stage, from the audience's perspective, he knew that it would appear that Timmy was lifting him from the floor to a standing position with only a finger. Finally, when both were standing side by side, Witherspoon executed a pirouette that even Nureyev would have envied and stepped back into the group's formation without missing a beat.

The studio had become a madhouse by then. The entire audience was on their feet cheering, clapping, shouting, standing in chairs, and dancing in the aisles.

"Be Still My Heart," ladies and gentlemen," the host said over the rising clamor. "The **Pains of Love**...a rare performance by a huge talent."

Unable to wait for the curtains to close, Kevi rushed towards Timmy and lifted him from the floor. "Way to go "T," he said exuberantly, giving his young friend a powerful hug, "because of you the **Pain** are on their way."

Later, after many congratulatory remarks from Mr. Hope and his staff, the exuberant teens were introduced to Jonathan Sparks, president and producer of Sepia Records, who routinely attended the show's live performances. From the beginning, he expressed considerable interest in "Be Still My Heart" and other songs Kevi had written, and to everyone's amazement he offered the young quintet a standard recording contract. All were elated by the producer's unexpected proposal, but none more than Stone. This is what he had hoped for. This was the greatest day in his life.

To be signed with Sepia Records would be the pinnacle to any young entertainer's dreams. The small Harlem based company, jointly owned by Jonathan Spark's younger sister, a DJ for WSOL AM, and an older brother, a host for a show called "Dance Party," had considerable success with their stable of teen acts. As a matter of fact, the trades often proclaimed the Sepia family of companies as the country's newest Mecca for young Rhythm and Blues artists, and were often referred to as the "Motown of the East."

While Johnny, as he preferred to be called, discussed his successes, failures, and insights of the music business, Kevi's admiration for the Harlem record mogul grew with every moment. His keen instincts told him that Sparks was a man that could be trusted. A look from his mother confirmed his opinion. Surprised at first, Kevi recognized something else in his mother's features. Some thing he hadn't seen since his father was alive. Regarding her with interest, he realized his mother had more than a liking for this quiet, humble stranger.

"When are you leaving for home?" Sparks asked.

"We're catching the Greyhound that leaves the Port Authority at 7:00 P.M."

"You've almost six hours then. Do you plan on doing any shopping or site seeing, if you don't mind my asking?"

"I don't mind, and yes, we thought we'd see as much of the city as time allows."

"Then please, let me offer you my services, and allow me to act as your guide. I know all the best places to shop, and you can see," Johnny grabbed his stomach,"from my build that I know the best places to eat."

"He ain't lying," Kevi said to himself, noting that although Johnny was only a few inches taller than his mother, his corpulence exceeded hers by at least a foot around.

"I like to eat too," Mama said sweetly, displaying her full figure, also without shame. "It would be our pleasure to have you as our guide...but only on one condition."

"Name it."

"I expect you to call me Anita."

Johnny Spark's flashed a gleaming set of teeth.

Kevi had always believed that Timmy had the brightest smile in the world, but after a quick look at Johnny's brilliant pearly whites, he decided he wouldn't want to bet his life on the difference.

"Anita, you have no idea how happy you've made me."

As would be expected, Johnny showed his guests the main points of interest in New York city; the Bronx Zoo, the Empire State building, Time's Square, Broadway, and finally Harlem, where they toured Sepia Records. Afterwards, they met his sister and brother for dinner at a place on Lenox Avenue called "Geechie's," where the best soul food in the world was served.

"What would you recommend?" Anita asked.

"I think you'll find all of the specials delightful," Johnny replied taking a menu from the center of the large rectangular table, "especially if you're as famished as I am."

"It's been quite a day. I can certainly eat something."

"Personally, I recommend the number eight...the Creole Special. It's more than enough food, and I'm certain you'll be amazed at the variety of side dishes you get, each designed to tease and tantalize the taste buds."

"You make it all sound so wonderful."

"No offense, Anita, but the first time I ate here, I wanted to go home and slap my mom." Johnny had made a quick motion in the air. "I wanted to tell her, get out of the kitchen, mom. You can't even cook."

"That's nothing," Ricky Caldwell interposed, his eyes twinkling with amusement. "Mrs. Stone's so good she can cook the fart out of beans."

If it would have been humanly possible for her chocolate features to blush, Kevi's mother would have been red as a beet. The best she could do, however, while everyone else including Johnny were overcome by laughter, was to slap Ricky on top of his head with her menu. She missed both times.

"I was only paying you a compliment, Ricky told her, an innocent look upon his face.

"Good one," Kevi said, giving his red-headed friend some skin. "Good one."

*****

Promptly at 7 PM, the huge Greyhound pulled out of the Port Authority terminal and headed for the tunnel that would spill them onto the Jersey Turnpike. With the traffic in New York City, and all the stops on and off the toll road, it would take at least four hours to get back to Cameron. Wearily, Kevi, his mother, and the others seated themselves in the rear of the bus, each readying themselves for their arduous journey home.

Too exhausted even for small talk, everyone but Kevi had fallen asleep before they had reached the West Newark boundary. Sleep was the last thing on his mind. For hours he stared out the window, and replayed every nuance of the day's events over and over in his head. Somewhere around ten, though, his eyes began to get heavy, and in just a few seconds he fell into a deep, black void.

The first indication that he was actually dreaming was the sensation of a million insects with hot tiny feet crawling all over his body. In contrast, something cold wrapped around his neck, entangling him, strangling him, cutting off his breath.

"No! Not again!" A familiar force had tried to push its way into Kevi's mind. Fortunately though, before the ominous invader could obtain its control, he managed to sever its hold by forcing himself awake. Realizing his narrow escape, He exploded. This was more than just another nightmare. This was an attempt on his life. *"And to think I was concerned about treating those bastards unfairly..."*

As his rage amplified, Kevi initiated the breathing exercises coach Edwards had taught him long ago. Taking several deep breaths, he tried envisioning something idyllic. The song, "Quiet Village," a composition from Les Baxter's "Sounds of Adventure" LP was the first thing to come to mind. Slowly, as the sweet strains of the violins filled his brain, his emotions were vented, and in less than a minute his hot blooded rage had turned into a controlled smoldering anger.

Ever since that day at the twin's church, Kevi hadn't relaxed his guard for an instant. Here, however, during a moment of weakness, in a place where he felt completely safe, that mistake nearly cost him his life, and though it might be inconceivable to others, he was convinced the twins were trying to destroy him. They would try again, if he let them. After he had shaken the cobwebs from his brain, Kevi took a moment to study his mother who was resting quietly in the seat next to him. Looking across the aisle, his eyes fell upon Timmy, who was snoring like a bull into Ronnie's ear. One, or both were sure to have a stiff neck upon awakening. Behind him and his mother, the twins were seated in the last two seats on the bus, directly across from the lavatory.

Cautiously, Kevi crawled over his mother's legs. He didn't dare wake her. What he had to do he could never do if she was awake. Standing in the aisle, he glanced quickly at the other passengers seated towards the front of the coach. Everyone appeared to be resting quietly. Even though the cabin was dimly lit, from the mirror hanging above the cockpit, he could see the driver's brow furrowed with concentration as he snaked the bus down the serpentine highway. Turning then towards the twins, who appeared to be sleeping, he leaned over and listened.

"Your soul is ours...," they intoned in unison, followed by some words that were quite unintelligible, yet vaguely familiar.

If Kevi had thought he was imagining things before, it was the twin's whispered uttering that convinced him everything he had experienced in the past weeks was not only horribly real, but done with malicious intent. Consumed by rage, he seized the two boys by their throats, and nearly crushed their fragile larynxes with his prodigious might. Shaking them violently, he quickly realized the temptation to end their lives was almost too strong to resist.

Incapable of uttering a sound, the twins squirmed in their seats as Kevi's powerful grip tightened. Tears flowed from Leo's eyes, while his brother's tongue protruded obscenely from his mouth.

Leaning closer, Kevi glared menacingly. "Let me make a suggestion," he said in a savage whisper. "I think it would be in your best interest to leave the group. This issue is neither arguable or open to debate." After a momentary pause to reconcile the fact that if pushed too far he could commit murder, extermination might be a better word, he said, "I give you fair warning, if you **don't** do as I say, I promise you before the sun sets tomorrow, I'll kill the lot of you, and that includes that vermin you call your parents."

This was no bluff and the twins knew it.

Quite effortlessly, Kevi lifted the two boys upwards and banged their heads together roughly before depositing them back into their seats. The bus driver looked up for a moment, but because his vision was impaired by the darkness, he returned his attention to his driving. None of the other passengers had been disturbed.

A minute passed, then two. In that time, Kevi could feel the twin's hatred of him grow like a living thing, emanating from them with incredible force. A few more minutes passed. By then the twin's hatred for him had dissipated into nothingness. It was replaced by fear.

"You'll pay for this," Leon croaked in agony, his powerful voice, no more than a husky whisper. "If it's the last thing I do, I'll make you pay."

"Don't make me say it again...but if you or your slimy brother mess with me just once more, it'll be the **last** thing you'll ever do."

"We've done nothing to be treated this way," Leo ranted harshly.

Kevi's mouth twisted into an ugly gash. "Don't think me a fool," he scolded, "and spare me the denials. I'll kill every last one of you if you force me to, and there's **nothing** you can do to stop me."

For a long moment, Kevi regarded the twins until their presence had become so repugnant he couldn't look at them anymore. His mother awakened just as he was trying to regain his seat.

"Everything all right, dear?"

"Everything's fine, Mama," he said softly, taking her hand. "Go back to sleep."

*****

Skipping breakfast, the next morning Kevi went to the Farrow Hill library in downtown Cameron, spending most of his time reading everything he could find on the occult, voodoo, and paranormal experiences. A few weeks ago, if someone had tried to convince him such things existed, he would have laughed in their face. Satanism, demonism, vampirism, possessions, hauntings, paranormal activities which included all forms of ESP, pyrokinesis, telekinesis, telepathy, psychometry, astral projection, and teleportation were just a few of the topics he researched. As his mind hungrily devoured each word, he realized how little he knew of the world outside of Cameron, New Jersey.

Cults. That particular subject caught his eye. Certain that Cameron hadn't any, Kevi was enlightened, entertained, even horrified to discover there were people in the world that worshiped everything from snakes, cats, bats, owls, and insects such as spiders, locusts, and even the praying mantis.

After more than an hour of relentless research, he had found nothing remotely resembling his experiences, until he picked up a book called "*Island Folklore, Myths, and Legends*," by Dr. Hector W. Vasquez. It was then he recalled what Reverend Thompson had told him years ago, and what was common knowledge to almost everyone in Cameron--the twin's father, while an infant, had emigrated from tribal Jamaica.

As Kevi's fingers explored the pages, mysteriously guided by some unseen, inexplicable force, a fresh chill embraced him when they rested beneath a single word.

Kaluti.

He was certain he had never heard the term before and yet it seemed familiar. **Kaluti**. Loosely translated, it was defined as "the possessors of gifts." In present day, these gifts were referred to as paranormal abilities, and could take many forms. In addition to telekinesis, pyrokinesis etc., it was believed the ancient tribe could cause sickness or kill simply by touch alone. Reading further, Kevi learned the **Kaluti** often practiced possession through dreams and incantations and though this ancient civilization was reported to have many different powers, the aforementioned abilities, surprisingly enough, paralleled those he had experienced with the twins.

According to Dr. Vasquez, though some believed in the ancient, heathen race, there was, in fact, no supportable evidence the **Kaluti** or their paranormal abilities ever existed. Still, as Kevi's research continued, he discovered other anthropologists boldly refuted Dr. Vasquez's theories. They agreed the unusual size of the cerebellum and medulla oblongata from various cadavers and skeletal remains discovered throughout the Caribbean could possibly support the existence of the **Kaluti**, as well as the high probability of them possessing natural psychic ability. It was also their contention the **Kaluti's** innate powers could be increased substantially simply by invoking the demons they worshiped, in which case, snakes were used as their medium. Unlike the snake worshipers of ancient Egypt that believed in man-to-snake transformations, or the snake worshipers in tribal Africa who believe mankind evolved from land bound reptiles, the **Kaluti** imprecated many snake gods.

One in particular. **Daagon**.
Not much else was mentioned about the heathenous deity.

Reading on, Kevi learned the **Kaluti** were the most misunderstood of all the pagan beliefs. Not entirely Jamaican, Cuban, Haitian, or Bermudian, the **Kaluti** language in addition to their respective tenets were quite independent of each of its island races. Light years from Christianity, or any religion that accepted the prophets of the King James Old Testament, it was quite unfathomable how this singular belief could proliferate from such biologically and evolutionary diverse cultures.

Before placing the dozen or so books back on their shelves, Kevi realized he had discovered nothing he could use as a defense from the Braithwaite's demonic abilities. "Maybe there is none..."

No. He didn't dare believe that.

On his way out of the library, Kevi's eyes rested on an album prepared by the Cameron Chamber of Commerce. In summation, the thick tome included the history of his community, its historical buildings, a list of its pioneers in politics, business, and its most influential leaders. His curiosity aroused, he peered inside and discovered Cameron's first black pastor was the twin's grandfather, Reverend Calvin C. Braithwaite. The twin's father, Calvin V. Braithwaite became the church's pastor in 1940 when the elder Braithwaite passed away. The shocker was the middle name beneath the picture of the Good Shepherd's first minister.

Calluti.
Coincidence? Doubtful.

CHAPTER SIX

"Would anyone like more pie and ice cream?"
"No ma'am," answered Ricky.
"None for me," said Kevi.
"What about you, Miss Bryson?"
"I'll have some more pie, please," Nellie said, holding out her plate.
"Here you are, hon," Mama replied. "I gave you just a smidgin' more ice cream. I know how much you love chocolate..."
"Especially when it's homemade," Nellie grinned, scooping a spoonful into her mouth. "Thanyouverymush."
"You're quite welcome," Mama intoned. As much as she loved to watch Nellie eat, she often wondered where the girl put it all. She had already consumed more than a pint of ice cream, and three heaping slices of pie. More than Ricky and Kevi together. Noticing that her watch had stopped, she tapped the crystal a couple of times, frowned, placed the watch against her ear, frowned again before removing it from her meaty wrist and placing it in her apron pocket. "What time is it?"
"7:20," Mrs. Stone," Caldwell said, muffling a snicker. "In another ten minutes we're gonna see if your son is as ugly on TV as he is in person."
"Ricky," Nellie scolded.
"Pay him no mind, honey," Mama said dryly. "Come Halloween, Mr. Caldwell and I are gonna be partners in my new cookie business."
"Cookie business?" Ricky asked curiously, one eyebrow arched slightly higher than the other.
"Uh huh. I'm gonna sell monster cookies...so I'm gonna need you to stick your face in the dough."
Nellie laughed so hard she nearly choked on her ice cream. Kevi, also in stitches, held his ribs as if they were ready to burst. Ricky's features remained expressionless. But after a few moments his face lit up with amusement."Hmmm", he said thinking aloud, "I'm gonna have to remember that one. Good one, Mrs. Stone...good one."
Once Kevi had learned when his group's debut would be aired, he invited Ricky, Terry, Ron, and Nellie to watch it with him and his mother. Only Ricky and Nellie were able to attend. Terry and Ron planned to watch the program with Timmy Witherspoon and his folks, and play basketball afterwards.
"Did you hear what happened to the twins last night?" asked Ricky.
"Isn't it a shame?" Nellie said. "Both of them are in the hospital."
"What happened to 'em?" Kevi inquired, uninterestedly.
"Leo was found unconscious lying on the street. Beat up. I think he has a broken jaw and a concussion."
Kevi's ears prickled with curiosity. "What do you mean...found?"
"According to the police, Leo and his brother were lying in the streets along with three other kids. But get this...they were dressed in hoods and jackets worn only by the Red Dragons."
Kevi's heart skipped a beat at the mention of the west side street gang. Without realizing it, he began to chew his bottom lip. Where did this happen?", he asked, his heart beating excitedly.
"On Grady and Calley," Ricky replied. "The police found their bodies laid out all over the streets."

33

"I still can't believe it," Nellie said shaking her head. "They've always been such nice boys."

"That may be, but the condition they're in suggests some kind of rumble took place." A slight pause followed by a snicker. "They certainly didn't get those injuries at a church social."

"Ricky Caldwell," Nellie responded, her tone acidulous, "how can you be so unfeeling?"

Embarrassed, Ricky said nothing in reply. A spiritless shrug was the best he could offer.

"Is Leon ok?" Kevi asked, his heart still fluttering.

"He has a severely broken nose, broken knee cap, and two broken ribs," answered Nellie. "His doctors believes he was beaten with either a baseball bat, or maybe a pipe."

The doctors were wrong. Kevi knew better than anyone. He also knew he couldn't tell a soul what had happened. The moment he did, he'd be faced with a dozen questions he had no ready answers for. Besides, a confession at this point would only upset his friends and loved ones needlessly. His only option was to remain silent, at least until he learned what the twins or their parents would say concerning the incident.

Briefly, a smile touched Kevi's face. As much he wanted to chortle openly, he denied himself the pleasure. Realizing the events of last evening would doubtlessly cause considerable interest to the nosy citizenry of Cameron, and because of their proclivity for gossip, he was confident the Braithwaite's illusionary cloak of respectability would be finally penetrated. Knowing his community's busy bodies as well as he did, he was certain the twins and their parents were about to subjected to the intense scrutiny of their neighbors. Amused, Kevi reflected on the circumstances that precipitated the twin's misfortunes.

With choir rehearsal over, he had stopped by "Shortie's" Pharmacy on Seneca to pick up his mother's prescription. Upon exiting the neighborhood drug store, a crack of thunder signaled the beginning of the shower that would soon follow. With the scent of rain already in the air, and the clouds growing blacker by the second, to save time and himself a needless wetting, he decided to take a short cut through Finney's Park. Once through the park, which really wasn't a park at all, but actually a playground for the inner city kids, he turned onto Grady Street, and noticed three boys standing on the corner ahead of him. Even thirty or forty feet away, it wasn't difficult to recognize the colorful red and black leather jackets of the Dragons. What they were doing on the east side of town was anybody's guess. The Dragons usually didn't venture far from their turf unless they were "gang walking," which could only mean trouble.

As for who they were, he had no way of knowing. Two had their backs facing him, and the third's face was blocked by the others. As he approached the intersection, one of the kids with his back facing him tossed a cigarette into the sewer, pulled a black and red hood from his back pocket, and tugged it over his head.

The others did the same.

Kevi knew then, they were waiting for him.

Unconcerned, he approached them, amused, and actually looked forward to a struggle others would fear. Although it had been years since he had been in a street fight, considering his skills, Kevi believed he could defeat the leather clad bluejeaned trio easily. Taking a hefty breath of the sweet night air, he held it in his lungs a few moments before letting it out slowly. Completely relaxed, his adrenalin flowed through his body so rapidly it gave him a heightened sense of awareness and charged his sinews with the power he would need. The three gang members turned quickly, spread apart, and with a move that indicated practice, they surrounded him. Two in front, the other at his rear, and to his

right.
　　Retreat was impossible.
　　"Where do you think you're going punk?" the tall one said, removing a pair of brass knuckles from his back pocket.
　　The voice sounded familiar, but Kevi couldn't be certain he had recognized it. The red and black cowl muffled the hoodlum's voice as well as disguised his features. Even his eyes were hidden. "That's my business chump."
　　"Oh, tough guy, huh? Well, we'll just have to..."
　　With impossible speed, Kevi hit the boy with a bone crushing overhand left, dropping him as if a ton of bricks had fallen upon him. A split second later, he followed through with the same motion and elbowed the delinquent behind him in the throat. He had heard the boy's painful gasp but didn't let it distract him. The other rowdy facing him had just launched a pretty fair right hook. Ducking beneath it, Kevi slammed the boy flush on the jaw with his left, spun around, and hit the kid who was still clutching his throat with an uppercut that sent him flying. He landed about five feet away. Out cold. Kevi smiled at his handiwork. *"Three down in as many seconds. Not bad. Not bad at all."*
　　Thinking no more of the incident, or what provoked the attack, Kevi continued home, heading south on Grady. But when he turned onto Calley, he discovered two more Dragons were waiting for him. *"What in the world is going on? "*
　　The bigger of the two was swinging a chain high above his head. The other held a knotted piece of wood the size and thickness of a baseball bat in both hands.
　　Deliberately, Kevi moved towards the chain swinger, forcing him to make the first move. Faster and faster, the chain swished above both their heads. Calculating its length, and its striking distance, Kevi realized the only the way the hoodlum could strike effectively was to use his weapon like a whip. That was his opponent's weakness.
　　Dodging the chain easily, Kevi delivered a blow to the thug's flabby stomach. Lifting him to the tips of his toes, the boy doubled up in pain, stumbled for a moment, then dropped face first into the concrete, his weapon tangled around his neck. Only seconds had passed since the chain swinger had fallen, but somehow in that time his club wielding crony had disappeared. Expecting an ambush, Kevi walked towards the corner avoiding any area his hidden adversary could use to spring from before moving to the middle of the narrow street. With the street lights broken, and the gloom of the impending storm blackening the night, this was the smartest move he could make. If the Dragon member still wanted to rumble, he'd have to come out of hiding.
　　A flash of lightning illuminated the night. In that infinitesimal moment, Kevi saw where the youth was hiding. Casually, he walked from the middle of the street back to the pavement, leaned against the telephone pole, and crossed his legs. "Hey stupid," he shouted, "even Stevie Wonder could see your dumb butt behind that truck. Let's get this over with so I can get on home?"
　　No reply.
　　"Hey moron...did you hear me? Or are you deaf?"
　　Still no answer.
　　Kevi started to get annoyed. "Look chump, don't make me drag your sorry tail outta there," he said, attempting to sound as menacing as possible.
　　Finally, the obstreperous youth with the club came from behind the pickup truck and started towards the street. Tiring of the whole scenario, Kevi eagerly headed for his opponent who held the club in both hands like a batter stepping up to home plate. His hands at his side, Kevi purposely leaned forward, offering his head as a target, inviting the kid to strike.
　　Taking the bait, the kid swung as hard as he could. But his opponent was

no longer there. He had completely disappeared. But that was impossible. He couldn't have missed. The kid felt a tapping on his shoulder and turned quickly.

"Strike one," Kevi drawled, mimicking Mr. Jensen, his high school's baseball coach and umpire, "batter swings high and on the outside."

Grunting in frustration, the youth swung once more, but this time in a clubbing downward motion. Nimbly, Kevi side-stepped his adversary's second effort, moved to his left, and out of range. "Strike two, fuuulllll cooount to the baaatter," he sneered, his southern drawl becoming more pronounced. "Last chance chump. Only three swings in this game."

The hooded youth growled angrily, feinting several times trying to trick Kevi into making a mistake, never realizing that he was telegraphing his every move.

A drop of rain smacked both combatants on the forehead. A moment later, the pitter patter sounds of rain filled the two warriors' ears.

Kevi looked up into the dark clouding sky for a moment, holding both hands out innocently. "We haven't much time fella," he said smiling. "We wouldn't want this game to be called on account of rain...would we?"

Because Kevi's easy cockiness had angered him, the hooded youth closed quickly, swinging his club with all his might, believing it impossible for his foe to evade the blow. Kevi didn't even try. Catching the knotted limb in his bare hand, he wrestled it from the youth with incredible ease. The delinquent stood like a statue, rigid, unmoving. But when Kevi snapped the knotted piece of would like a match stick, and tossed it at his feet, the hooded youth felt an overpowering desire to flee.

Deliberately goading him Kevi said, "Whatcha gonna do now...sissy?"

Cursing, the Dragon took a desperate swing.

Blocking it with one hand, Kevi riddled his opponent's body with powerful blows from feet to head. Then, with a quickness too impossible to measure, he changed positions, and repeated his attack, striking one blow each in the ankle, calf, knee, and thigh, followed by blows to the kidney and rib cage. The leather clad youth was already toppling to the right when Kevi caught him with a final left to the nose. Like a tree cut down by lightning, the street tough fell to the ground the same moment the sprinkle had turned into a torrential downpour.

Drenched, Kevi Stone looked around for other Dragons to slay. For some reason that particular thought amused him. Seeing there was no one else to challenge him, he raced for home, giving little thought to those who suffered defeat at his hands.

"Is it on yet?"

"Yes, Mrs. Stone," Ricky answered, fidgeting excitedly. "It just started."

*****

In the days to come, the **Pains of Love** became the "talk of the town." Each of Kevi's friends and relatives expressed how pleased they were with his group's first television performance, although what was really in the back of their minds was how the twins were doing, were they still in the group, and did he know of their association with the Dragons. Always, Kevi remained politely evasive.

Six record companies on the eastern seaboard had seen the Cameron quintet's debut on the amateur hour, and all were interested in signing the young teens. But after careful consideration, the group's lawyer had satisfied each of the boys' parents that Johnny Sparks's proposal was the best over all. Exactly one week later, the **Pains of Love** became the latest acquisition of the Sepia family of companies.

That same evening, Nellie asked Kevi if he could meet her at the Holy Hope hospital where her mother worked part-time as an RN in the emergency room. The only hospital in town, it was where the twins were convalescing. As soon as Kevi stepped into the lobby, Nellie handed him a basket of fruit, and a card, signed in the group's name of course, that wished the twin's a speedy recovery. In spite of their unexplained misfortunes, Nellie believed it would be a nice gesture to wish them well. Kevi didn't exactly share her views, and very much wanted to tell her so. Instead, he did as she asked.

Between the hours of six and eight P. M., only the immediate family were allowed visitors. To gain access to the twin's room, Kevi had to sneak past the reception area in the hospital lobby and up three flights of stairs. Luckily, there was just enough activity in the hospital that no one paid him the slightest attention. Once he was outside the twin's room, he listened for sounds of visitors within. The last thing he needed was to run into the boys' parents. If that happened, all hell would break loose, irrevocably destroying the hospital's current state of peace and tranquility.

The room was as silent as a tomb, and like a wraith Kevi slipped inside. Even with the shades drawn slightly, he had no difficulty seeing Leo resting quietly in the bed on his right, and Leon asleep in the other. With the exception of the openings for his eyes, nose, and mouth, the younger twin's bandages completely covered his head. Leon, however, had a metal brace taped to his nose, and most of his upper body was wrapped and in traction.

Even standing in the shadows as he was, the moment Leo opened his eyes, Kevi knew he had been recognized. Placing the basket of fruit on the table, he moved between the two beds. Slowly, the twin's hand crawled towards the nurse's call button lying at his side.

Kevi smiled.

Leo's hand stopped, as if struck by a sudden paralysis, and though the switch was less than an inch away, he made no further attempts to grab it.

"The card and fruit is Nellie's idea," Stone said with another smile, picking up the nurse's call button and handing it to Leo. "She's also responsible for me being here this evening." A slight pause. "However, I must admit I was thinking about visiting you some time in the near future...once I discovered it was you and your brother that attacked me."

Leo's eyes tensed.

Stone continued. "I warned you. You and your brother are lying here because you ignored my advice." Another pause. "Both of you can consider yourself fortunate. Believe me, if I had known the two of you were with that gang, you wouldn't be in the hospital today...you'd be in the morgue." Leaning closer, his glare hardened. "My patience with your family has reached its limit, Leo. The next time we cross paths..." A pause. "Do we understand one another?"

Leo's body was shaking so violently, it was impossible to distinguish a nod from his other motions. As Kevi opened the door, he regarded his enemy one last time, taking note that a single tear had seeped out of the corner of the twin's eye, crawled down his face, and was instantly absorbed by his bandages.

Closing the door behind him, Kevi strolled down the hospital hallway, his sharp ears picking up the strangest sounds he had ever heard. More animal than human, he could only compare them to the whimperings of a cringing, cowardly, beaten dog.

CHAPTER SEVEN

Johnny Sparks wasted no time getting his latest discovery back to the "big apple." Instead of sending a subordinate from his staff as he did with his other clients, he went himself to pick them up, meeting them the moment their bus arrived. As he explained the day's agenda, his five young proteges were given the scariest ride in their lives en route to the studio. "Time is money," he told them, aiming his automobile through the rush hour traffic.

The young quintet nodded in unison, feeling an excitement they had never known. Not because of their mentor's Indy-style driving. Or for even being in New York again. Nor was it because the original group was back together. It was Johnny. His every word seemed to supercharge their emotions.

As his big, black Buick Coupe sped its way from Manhattan to Harlem, he continued to enumerate from his agenda. "There's a full orchestra," he said, "complete with combo, an arranger, some of the city's best wardrobe experts, painters of various styles--including serious portraits and caricatures, and several freelance photographers awaiting your arrival."

The selection and fitting of costumes, two different photo shoots--one casual, the other formal--meetings with vocal coaches and choreographers started out the teen's busy day. The recording session followed, and amazingly, in just a few hours, the group's first single had been rehearsed, orchestrated, recorded, and mastered.

Kevi was astonished. He had expected things to move fast in the music industry, but not that fast, and though he certainly didn't wish to tell Johnny his business, the project meant so much to him, he felt it necessary to express his concerns.

"You never want to **overproduce** a song," was all Johnny would say at the time.

At first, Kevi didn't understand. But once he listened to his songs on the master tape, and heard how beautiful they had become, he knew Johnny was right. The gospel-like doowop harmonies were even tighter than he had hoped, and the funky bass lines doubling with the bass drum were syncopated, polyrhythmic, and just as he envisioned. But what thrilled him most was how the orchestral arrangements captured the very essence of what he hoped to convey lyrically and melodically. "I take back everything I said."

"No need to apologize," Johnny returned, his meaty hands clasping the young entertainer's shoulder. "You have every right to be concerned. These are **your** songs but I guess now you can see what I mean."

Within a week, more than 2,000 demos were pressed and distributed to every major radio station from Boston to Richmond, and as far west as Cleveland, Ohio. Naturally, WSOL in New York City, was the first station to play the group's debut single. It was an immediate success. In the second week, the **Pains of Love** appeared live on "Dance Party," in which they not only sang "Be Still My Heart," but also its flip side, "No Other Love". In short, both songs had taken the city by storm.

Just shy of a month, "Be Still My Heart" reached the #3 spot on the Billboard charts. Following closely in its wake, "No Other Love" reached #9, and was expected to mimic their debut single's success. By August, the quintet embarked on a bunch of grueling one-nighters all over the eastern seaboard, singing to capacity crowds wherever they went.

Summer was almost over when their tour ended, and of all their performances, the young quintet gave their best when they returned home. A **free** concert was their gift to the community that bore them. It was held at the Community center. Where it all began.

*****

In two short years, the **Pains of Love** became an unprecedented success story. Routinely, they led the industry in "number one" chartings and sales in both R & B and Pop categories. Without a doubt, Kevi Stone's songwriting skills coupled with his colleagues exciting delivery of his material, and the inspired arrangements from Johnny Spark's talented staff made Sepia Records and the **Pains of Love** one of the most successful collaborations in the music business. These were the best of times for everyone, and just when Kevi began thinking things couldn't get any better, a week before his graduation his mother and Johnny announced their intended nuptials. As it turned out, theirs were the shortest engagement in history. Or at least, in Cameron's. They were married three days later.

Looking out into the pews Reverend Thompson smiled. His gold crown flashed brilliantly as a stray sunbeam bounced off his gleaming tooth. "Dearly beloved, we are gathered here today..."

"She looks so beautiful," Nellie said, wiping the tears from her eyes.

"Soon it will be our turn," Kevi hoped, giving his sweetheart's hand a gentle squeeze. Though wedding plans were often discussed, the young couple understood the importance of pursuing their respective careers. In the fall, Nellie would attend the Nursing Academy in Cameron, and Kevi would continue to perform and record in addition to attending Julliard. Both abhorred a lengthy separation, but accepted it willingly.

Although Timmy had two years of school remaining, his parents were allowing him to move to New York with the rest of his friends, but only as long as he continued his education. With this in mind, Johnny leased a spacious apartment overlooking Central Park, with room for everyone including Tracy Hartwell, who besides being a blood relative also managed the young teens. Tracy was also a qualified tutor, Witherspoon's education was assured. Barely in his mid-twenties, Hartwell looked more like one of the teens than the group's guardian. A New Yorker by birth, blessed with an even temper, and considerably experienced with big city life, he was perfectly suited for watching over the young entertainers.

Just the thought of living in New York City filled the young quintet with an energy that was so forceful it could be felt by anyone in their presence. It would not last. Ricky Caldwell was the reason. The day after Labor Day, he would have to report for induction at Ft. Bragg. With the Vietnam conflict very much in the news, nothing could have been more upsetting to his family and friends.

"Things like this happen," Johnny Sparks said distressingly. "But it's not the end of the world. While we will certainly **pray** for Mr. Caldwell's safe return, we must get together and regroup." A lengthy pause. "I think I've got a solution that'll satisfy everyone."

Johnny went on to explain that while Ricky was doing his hitch in the Army, the band would take a two year hiatus to pursue some of the business-like areas in the industry they were all very much apart of. He also suggested a revision of Caldwell's contract, the terms and conditions, such that, in case of the unlikelihood their colleague failed to rejoin the group, for whatever reason, one-fifth of all monies the group earned in his absence, for as long as they remained together, would be awarded to his family.

Ricky tried not to show it, but he was completely overwhelmed by the kind-heartedness and generosity of his friends and mentor. "That's all I'm gonna get?"

Puzzled, Johnny said, "You don't think the offer is fair?"

Ricky snorted. "Nope. If I'm gonna go and fight for a bunch of sissified panty waists like you guys...I want more money."

With deceptive speed, Johnny pounced and knuckle-rubbed Ricky's beady red hair. Barely a second later had passed before the others had joined in.

"You may now kiss the bride," Reverend Thompson said.

As the newlyweds sealed their union, everyone within the crowded church stood up applauding, shouting their joys. There wasn't a dry eye in the house.

After the reception, Kevi and Nellie were entering Tittle's Ice Cream Parlor when they bumped into the twins. It had been two years since Kevi had seen them, the last time, in the hospital. As he watched them approach, his keen eyes picked up Leon's limp, an injury he acquired as a result of their street brawl.

And though Leo didn't exhibit any noticeable scars or disabilities, Kevi could see that his hatred for him hadn't diminished at all. If anything, it flourished. Unafraid, Kevi was quite prepared to take on the two boys at any time, to the death if necessary.

But one look into the younger twin's shining eyes changed everything. Leo was absolutely terrified. Leon was a different story altogether. His eyes and demeanor didn't express any of his brother's emotions or fears, and yet, there was a quiet calm about him Kevi failed to understand. Not a shred of malevolence or that all too familiar scent of evil surrounded the elder twin, even though Leo reeked of it.

"Hi fellas," Nellie said gingerly.

"Hello," boomed Leon, nodding to Kevi. As usual, Leo said nothing. "I understand congratulations are in order."

"It was a beautiful wedding," Nellie imparted.

"I'm sure she'll be very happy," Leon said kindly.

"Thank you," Kevi said, his face contemplative.

"Did you record that gospel album yet?" Nellie asked.

"No," Leon said in reply, "we haven't. It's in the works though. We go into the studio this month."

"Good. I'll be looking forward to hearing it."

"Best of luck to you," said Kevi.

Then, almost timidly Leon said, "Nellie would you mind if I have a private chat with Stone? It'll only take a minute."

"Certainly not," she purred, "as long as your brother doesn't mind buying me an ice cream soda."

Quite nervously, almost fearfully, Leo muttered, "I-I don't mind."

"Deal," Nellie said, taking the younger twin by the arm.

Once she and Leo were through the revolving door Leon said, "You still hate us, don't you?"

"I've **never** hated you Leon...although I think you and your family have given me more than enough reason to."

Leon shuffled nervously, looked towards the ground, and deliberately avoided Kevi's eyes. "You just don't know how lucky you are," he said in a deprecating tone.

Kevi lifted an eyebrow. "Lucky?"

"That you weren't born in a family like mine."

"What is it you want, Leon?" Kevi asked callously. "I'm sure you don't wish to discuss the differences in our family tree."

"You're right. Wouldn't do no good no way. You can't help where you come from, **or** who your parents are." A brief pause. "The truth is, I've been wanting to thank you."

Kevi lifted another eyebrow. "Thank me? For what?"

"For showing my family compassion when you could have easily done otherwise. This may surprise you, I'm a little surprised myself, but I'm exceedingly grateful for what you've done. I know you don't believe me. And why should you? But you see, when I was laid up in the hospital, for the first time in my life I became aware of my own mortality, and though the lesson I learned was quite painful," he said, not realizing he was rubbing his knee, "for me it was necessary. It changed my way of thinking entirely. Because of you, I've found something to live for."

Kevi shook his head. Nothing the twin had said made any sense at all. Even so, he recognized an opportunity to find out some of the things that had been bugging him over the years. "A moment ago you asked me if I hated you. I think it's only fair that I put a similar question to you. What is it that I've done to you and your family that merits such ill feelings between us?"

"You haven't done anything," Leon reported. "I myself don't understand why mother and father resent you. I asked them once...that first time, when my brother and I were ordered to attack you. They told me it wasn't important enough for me to know."

"Do you always obey your folks without question?" Kevi asked, his tone accusatory.

Leon Braithwaite's eyes flashed hurt and anger all at once. "They are my parents," he replied, "and you can't imagine the severity of punishment for disobedience."

"Then what's the point to all this?"

"To warn you of the danger that still exists."

"Danger?"

"Not from me, please believe me. From my brother, and my parents. They've never forgiven you for turning them down, or for the beating you gave us. They've vowed to see you dead."

"I didn't start any of this," Kevi pointed out, growing angrier by the moment.

"They don't care who started it...only who finishes it."

"I-I don't understand."

"Neither do I."

Leon was telling the truth. Kevi could see it in his eyes, but knowing it did him little good. He was as much in the dark as ever.

The sound of Nellie's bubbly giggle and Leo's pure falsetto laughter made both boys turn simultaneously. Nellie was shoveling a large scoop of chocolate ice cream into her mouth, while Leo toyed with a cherry on his banana split.

"What I do know is," Leon continued in whispers, leading Kevi away by the elbow, "my parents fear you as much as they hate you. But that won't stop them. Something else. Somehow your family is linked to the **Kaluti**. Are you familiar with the word?"

Desperately, Kevi attempted to control the beating of his heart. "No," he lied, "what's it mean?"

When Leon noticed his twin had taken a more than curious interest in his conversation he said, "This is not the time or place to go into it, but if I were you I'd learn everything I can about them. I could be wrong, but it may be the key to both of **our** problems. And Stone, whatever you do, don't ever turn your back on my family. If you do...you'll live to regret it."

"There's something you're not telling me," Kevi said suddenly, his eyes fierce.

"Wha-what, do you mean?" Leon stammered, caught off guard.

Kevi pressed, "You're hiding something. I can feel it. What is it?"

Leon shook all over. "Nellie," he said trembling, "I'm in love with her...have been ever since she started visiting us in the hospital." A pause. "In all this time, I haven't had the courage to tell her, **not** because I feared what you might do," he said with a gentle laugh. "I guess love makes you brave. But because it would be disastrous for her, **and** for myself if anyone in my family discovered

I had such feelings."

Kevi continued to press. "That's not all of it."

"You're right," Leon ventured slowly, his voice sounding like gravel churning in an empty cement mixer. "You have the right to know..."

"Know what?" Kevi prodded, his impatience nearing its limits.

"Nellie's in danger too."

"What?"

"Quiet," Leon whispered, turning towards his brother and Nellie, forcing a smile.

His palms bathed in sweat, several trails of the salty fluid proceeded to run from Kevi's forehead down each side of his face. While his blood boiled, he clenched both fists so tightly his fingernails cut gashes into his sweating palms. Opening them finally, each hand had four bloody half moon indentations pressed in them. At best, the pain was a momentary distraction, but it at least kept him from slipping over the edge where seething rage turns into cold blooded madness. Desperately, he tried to subdue his anger. But regarding Leo with Nellie continued to fuel the rage growing inside him. Then it happened. He had lost control. The primeval berserker madness that is in every human being consumed him. His mind was blank of all thoughts but one, and that was to extinguish the lives of those who would wish injury to his beloved. With blood in his eyes and murder in his heart, Kevi made his move.

"Stop," Leon commanded softly. "Stop it I say, and listen...listen...listen."

Incredibly, Leon's deep, husky, whispered tones reached into the darkest corners of Kevi's mind, tugged at his emotions, and literally pulled him back from the brink of madness. And though his mind had told him that his powerful hands were already around Leo's naked throat, in reality he hadn't moved an inch. Somehow, Leon's uncanny vocal abilities had vanquished all traces of hostility within him. As he continued to listen to the elder twin's soothing deep hypnotic tones, his emotions became even more quiet.

With real concern Leon asked, "Are you all right?"

"Yes." Kevi raised both hands to his temples and rubbed them lightly. "I almost lost it for a moment."

"I know. Look man, I'm gonna tell you like it is. To destroy you, my family will stop at nothing. If they can use the girl we both love as a lever, believe me they won't hesitate. Putting it simply, Nellie's safety is in our hands, and ours alone. Now, I'm willing, if you are, to lay aside our differences and devote our energies towards her protection." A pause. "Will you help me?"

Still massaging his temples, Kevi nodded.

"Then I give you my hand, and with it a promise...as long as breath resides in my body, Nellie will not be harmed."

That evening, after Kevi had more time to think about it, he realized that life was indeed a funny thing. If nothing else, it was certainly full of awe and mystery. Because of Nellie, the impossible had happened. He had taken Leon's hand, and his word. In doing so, he believed that under the most incredible circumstances he had found an ally.

More than that. He had found a friend.

CHAPTER EIGHT

Because Johnny had shared so many wonderful moments with his young friends, he was quite disheartened to see them filled with such hopelessness and despair. Ricky was leaving them, which meant severing a relationship that had spanned many years. And though young Caldwell seemed to accept his fate, the possibility that he might end up in Viet Nam had a demoralizing effect on everyone.

Since the very beginning, Johnny recognized the comradeship between the young quintet as something very special. **A family of friends** they called themselves. It was the only way to describe their affiliation. But regarding them as they were now nearly broke his heart. Something had to be done, or else everything they had all worked for would go whirling down the proverbial drain. But what?

Then, like the mythological Phoenix rising from its ashes, the answer came in the form of an invitation requesting his proteges to participate in an overseas "Rhythm and Blues Extravaganza." This, Sparks knew with a certainty would be the transfusion that everyone needed, and he was right. The moment he shared his news with his five young friends, he witnessed a miracle. It was as though each of them had been granted a new lease on life. Caldwell more than anyone. He would be going with them. The BBC's show in England would be his farewell performance.

In addition to the **Pains of Love**, the other acts that planned to attend the one of a kind extravaganza included the Drifters, the Dells, Little Anthony and the Imperials, the Ojays, Motown's Smokey and the Miracles, the Four Tops, and the group's favorite performers--the Temptations. But once the widely publicized concert began, what started out to be a live four hour televised performance for many of the acts, turned into a three week tour of the bistros, clubs, and concert halls throughout France, Switzerland, and Germany; amazingly, to audiences in some countries that couldn't speak a word of English.

For Kevi, it was an incredible dream come true. The day he had set foot on English soil he cried, "Pinch me somebody...but not too hard. I don't want to wake up just yet."

Unfortunately, the talented teen was in for a rude awakening. Soon his dreams would become a waking nightmare. Beginning the day they were to return to the states, his horror was manifested in the form of a wire that simply said, "Call home." At first, he didn't think much about it. Johnny was with his mother, and Nellie was okay. He had just talked to both of them. But the instant his call had been put through, the very fabric of his life was ripped to threads.

"Honey, I hate telling you this," his mother sobbed over the phone,"but Nellie was just married to Reverend Braithwaite's boy, Leon."

"Nooo," Kevi cried out in protest, his heart exploding in his chest, the phone slipping from his fingers. Emotionally eviscerated, he prayed for death before slipping into an agonizing oblivion.

*****

During the entire flight to the states, Kevi purposely remained aloof and hadn't uttered a single word since leaving London. At his request, no one met him at the airport. The last thing he needed was a public teary-eyed reunion. Arriving home, his mother and Johnny were sitting in the kitchen drinking iced tea when he and Ricky entered through the back door.

"Honey, I would suffer anything than see you hurt," Mama said, moving her considerable bulk from her seat. "You've loved Nellie all your life, and now she's married to another. It isn't fair," she moaned tearfully, "it just isn't fair."

"What happened, Mama?," Kevi asked, his eyes swelling.

By then, Nellie had walked into the room.

When Kevi turned to look at her, he nearly went into shock. This wasn't the beauty he had left behind. The dark circles beneath her eyes had turned one of the loveliest persons he had ever known into a ghostly, ghastly, harridan. His heart pounding in his throat, he gaped in horror at the unhealthy pallor of the girl he loved more than life. With outstretched arms she ran towards him. Scooping her up, he kissed her hard upon the mouth.

"Oh dearest, I'm so sorry," she cried softly, her sobs racking her body.

"Hello, Stone," a deep voice boomed unexpectedly.

Gritting his teeth, Kevi watched Nellie's husband stroll into his mother's kitchen. As if he belonged there. *"You filthy maggot! Today you die."* Grabbing him by the throat, Kevi lifted Leon from the floor.

"No honey...don't," his mother screamed fearfully.

"You don't understand," Nellie shouted from the floor where Kevi had unwittingly shoved her.

But Kevi was too far gone. Even Ricky and Johnny were unable to stop him. In agony, Leon's eyes bulged from its sockets and his tongue dangled from his mouth. Smiling grimly, Kevi waited for the light of life to fade from his enemy's blue-grey eyes. *"Look into my face you cur,"* his mind screamed, *"and see what death looks like."*

As if reading his thoughts, Braithwaite's empty gaze leveled upon him. It was in that moment Kevi realized his foe wasn't putting up a struggle. *"You fool...don't you realize this is your last moment on earth?"* Shaking him like a rag doll, he looked searchingly into Leon's eyes. *"He wants to die. All right then you bastard, you'll get your wish. One squeeze and it'll be all over."* But his fingers would not obey. Time and again he tried, but his fingers just wouldn't close. Cursing his foul weakness, and Leon's good fortune, Kevi realized he could have taken the twin's life quite easily if he had shown the slightest sign of fear. Killing him then would have been a joy. *"Fear me, damn you! Come on...give me one sign and I'll crush the life from you forever."* But Leon's eyes remained vacant, as though he had accepted the inevitability of his fate. Once more Kevi tried to make his fingers complete the task his mind and heart begged for.

An instant later, Leon fell to the floor. While Ricky and Johnny helped him into a chair, Mama rushed to Nellie's side.

"Give me one good reason why I shouldn't kill you," Kevi said.

"I almost wish you had," Leon croaked.

Kevi digested the twin's words for a moment. "There's still time," he replied savagely."There's still time."

"You don't understand," Nellie said, weeping. "None of this is Leon's fault. What he did...what we did, we had to do...to save Mama and Johnny."

Kevi became incensed. "What in hell is that supposed to mean?"

"Nellie's right," Mama replied, taking the brightly colored handkerchief her husband had just offered her. "If it wasn't for Leon, when you returned home you would have found Nellie, her folks, Johnny and myself...all of us, dead."

"I warned you," Leon squawked, rubbing his throat gently. "I told you my family'd never rest until they've destroyed you."

"I trusted you," Kevi growled, his rage augmenting. "The devil take me for a fool, but I trusted you. Under the guise of friendship you betrayed that trust."

Calmly, Leon removed some ice from a glass on the kitchen table and wrapped the cubes in a small hand towel hanging from the refrigerator door.

"No," he said weakly, "I didn't". Placing his makeshift ice pack against his throat he added, "I promised you I'd do anything to protect Nellie. I meant what I said."

"Sit down, honey," Mama suggested. "Give Leon a moment to explain."

While Kevi waited, a dozen different scenarios flashed through his brain. It was a waste of time. In a million years he would never have guessed the horrifying events that had taken place in his absence.

Returning home from an errand he had been running for his parents, Leon had overheard his family discussing a plan to use the Dragons and a few other gangs his brother controlled to break into Kevi's home, kill his parents, and set their home afire as they made their escape. Once the Sparks were eliminated, Nellie Bryson and her family were to be next. To confuse the authorities and to hide their crime, other families in different parts of town would die in a similar manner, making it appear as though several street gangs had gone on a rampage of death and destruction. Each of these senseless deaths had but one purpose.

Destroy Kevi Stone.

It was then that Leon intervened. "I don't think that's being very smart," he said with casual indifference. "If any harm comes to Nellie or Kevi's family we'll be inviting the one thing we don't want."

"Which is?" his father prompted.

"Stone coming after us," Leon answered. "And don't think for a second he won't. With all that's happened between us, he'll know we're responsible. You know him. He won't need no proof. His suspicions will be enough. Besides, he's much too dangerous for us to deal with physically."

"You sound like you're scared of him," Leo sneered.

Leon turned to his twin and glared with contempt. "You're the one that's scared," he declared, unfazed. "You know it, and I know it. If you recall, he took on five of us without working up a sweat. Remember?"

Leo rubbed his chin thoughtfully. He remembered all right. It filled his mind with a hate that intensified every day. Though surgery had repaired his broken jaw, the emotional scars would remain forever.

"Personally" Leon said, "I want to continue breathing. And I certainly don't wish to see any of us killed by that maniac." A pause. "I suggest we try something else."

"You have a plan?" his mother inquired interestedly.

"I do. Nellie." As soon as Leon spoke his beloved's name, he wished he could have had his tongue cut out, but it was already too late. Too late for a number of people if his plan failed.

Leo was puzzled. "Nellie? Now, where does that get us? You said it yourself, if she's hurt, Stone's gonna hot foot it over here like a bloody angel of death and wreak holy hell on us."

"I wasn't thinking of hurting her," Leon said, managing a smile. "I was thinking of possessing her."

As his mother and father's eyes glowed with interest, Leon could see the seed he had planted was already growing in their minds. With a little guile, accompanied by a bit of luck, he hoped to convince his family that he could make Nellie his slave. If they bought it, then all he'd have to do is persuade Nellie to go along with the idea, at least for a little while. That was the only hole. If Nellie didn't believe him, or refused to take part in his scheme, many innocent people would die. And she would be one of the first.

"You think you can do it?" Leo asked skeptically.

"I'm certain of it. We did it once in church. Since that time in the hospital, Nellie and I have become extremely close." A lie. "And don't you see, this way we can punish Kevi every single day of his life."

"He's still gonna suspect us," his mother stated.

"Sure he will. But there's a lot less risk to us than by do something so blatantly stupid like attacking his family. I assure you, if Stone believes he has lost Nellie to me as a rival, that will become a clear beginning to his inevitable destruction."

"That's cool, bro," Leo said evilly, "but you'd better not fail. Cause if you do..."

The elder twin went cold inside. His plan had to work. If it didn't, nothing would stop the untold bloodshed that would be unleashed upon their unwitting community.

"At the time," Leon explained, "it was the only thing I could think of. The first chance I got, I called your mother and Mr. Sparks. I told them everything. They, in turn, called Nellie."

"Mama, you believed him?"

"We had no reason not to."

"We know it's hard for you to accept right now," Johnny offered, "but Leon has been telling the truth."

His anger mounting Kevi asked, "How would you know?"

Johnny folded his hands and rested them on the table. "I grew up in Bedford Stuyvesant son, the worst ghetto in New York City, and I've lived in and around gang activity my entire youth. It didn't take much to discover several of Cameron's gangs were keeping company, all with a history of being the fiercest rivals. But just on the slim chance Leon might have been mistaken, I called a friend of mine on the force, and he confirmed my suspicions."

Unconvinced, Kevi shook his head. "That doesn't explain why they're married."

"The wedding was **my** idea," Nellie announced.

Kevi could have been knocked over with a feather. Those were the last words he had expected to hear. His eyes leveled on Leon, and burned intensely.

"I know what you're thinking, honey," Nellie said, touching his hand gently, "but Leon's powers had nothing to do with my decision."

Kevi's tone was sharp. "You have no idea what you're talking about."

"She wouldn't," Mama said abruptly, "but I would."

Kevi stared at his mother, his mouth agape. Under normal circumstances, he knew of no one capable of deceiving her. Intuitive by nature, his mother could see through people as easily as a pane of glass. But the twins and their family were a different breed of cat entirely. Their unusual brood possessed powers outside the realm of human understanding, and reached deep into the supernatural.

"Son," she began tentatively, "your father was a direct descendant from an ancient tribe in Haiti called the **Kaluti**, just as Leon and his family are descendant from the **Kaluti** of Jamaica, and though you are in fact Leon's tribal cousin...you are also his sworn enemy."

Shock first, astonishment next, an uncontrolled fear stabbed at Kevi's aching heart.

"It's true, son. It's one of the first things your Poppa told me when we met. He thought being **Kaluti** was a curse, and he tried everything in his power to keep me from marrying him. But I wouldn't listen. Your father was my first love, and from the day I laid eyes on him, I knew I couldn't live without him. You may find this hard to believe, but Poppa was afraid. Not of any man, that I can assure you, but of his heritage, and what he perceived as evil. It's why you were born so late. Poppa was convinced that if we had no children, the curse in his line would die with him. In the beginning, I don't know if I believed him or not. I only knew I loved him, and wanted his child." A brief smile. "And since your father never could deny me anything, we were married."

"Before you were born," Mama continued, "Poppa taught me everything he knew of his ancestors. As his parents showed him, he showed me all the different ways to recognize demonic possession, and how to defend my unborn child from his natural enemies." Gripping her son's other hand tightly she said, "It's been quite some time since I've used those skills...I thought I had forgotten them, but your father was a good teacher. Now that I know what to look for, I know your sweetheart is not being influenced by another."

"Tell him the rest," Nellie urged.

"Tell me what?, Kevi asked.

"When you were about two years old, your father provided you with the psychic tools necessary to defend yourself from your enemies. Without realizing it, these abilities have enabled you to repel every attack Leon's family has attempted thus far..."

"Why haven't you ever told me any of this before?" Kevi interrupted, his voice pained and pleading.

"Poppa," his mother continued, "made me promise never to reveal your heritage until you reached adulthood. Today, I break that promise. And gladly. Because even though the blood of the **Kaluti** flows strong in your veins, you are my child, and there's no way I can believe you've been cursed. Poppa was wrong, honey. If he could see you now, he'd know that being a **Kaluti** is something very special, something to be proud of...as long as the gifts you've been blessed with are used for good."

"Gifts? What gifts?"

"Honey, haven't you ever wondered why you've never been sick, why you're so much stronger than other boys, or why when injured you heal so quickly?"

Kevi shrugged his shoulders. It had never crossed his mind before. He always believed a rigid regimen of athletics for the past decade was responsible for his physical conditioning.

"And your name...haven't you ever thought it the least bit uncommon? Kevi is not an Anglo-Saxon name. In **Kaluti**, however, it has two meanings, "indomitable spirit" and "invincible one.""

"That would describe you perfectly," Ricky commented.

"Son, how much can you remember about Poppa?"

"I don't know, Mama. I guess I remember how much I loved him, how he towered over everyone, and that he died so young."

"You remember what is important to you," she said gently, "and that's as it should be. You're right though, your father was big. And strong. Believe me son, your father was possibly the strongest man in the world. But few knew of his enormous strength. He purposely hid his abilities from everyone except those in his immediate family. He was right in doing so. Poppa knew that many would fear him simply because he was different."

"In many ways honey, you're just like your him. You're kind, considerate, and in addition to being incredibly strong, you have the sharpest reflexes and senses I've ever seen. You also have the ability to become so focussed your body will instantly obey your mental commands. But dear, this is only the beginning. Once you reach manhood, you'll find these are just a **few** of your many gifts."

It was all true. Kevi realized that now. Every trial, every hurdle, mental or physical, almost everything came easy to him. He had always thought it was due to the way he disciplined his life. Still, even if he believed everything his mother had told him, a nagging thought continued to haunt him. "If Poppa was so strong, Mama," he said hesitantly, "how come he died of a heart attack...and so young?"

Mama's eyes darted in Leon's direction. Her voice turned cold. Her glare became daggers, steely and dangerous, so much that the twin shifted uncomfortably in his chair, completely stunned by the quiet malevolence she projected towards him. "I can't prove it son," she said grievously, "but I believe Poppa died of **unnatural** causes. Although the autopsy stated cause of death was due to a weak heart, there's no way anyone could make me believe it."

Kevi watched his mother as she watched the twin. "Do you think his death was caused by the **Kaluti**?"

Mama's eyes softened a little. "I don't know honey." she said sadly. "I admit it's what I've always suspected. But I've never found the proof." A pause. "A few weeks before your father passed away, he made me promise to tell you that should anything out of the ordinary happen to him, when you were old enough I was to charge you with the responsibility of seeking out and destroying those responsible for his death. I gave him my word, even though many were the times I prayed this day would never come." Her head hung low for a moment. When she looked up, her mood had changed. "It's just as well, I always hated secrets. I've never known one that could be kept. The time has come son for you to accept your heritage as well as the charge your father has given you. Not just for me or for him, but for yourself."

If there was even the remotest possibility his father had been taken from him before his time, and if the **Kaluti** were indeed responsible, Kevi knew he would do as his mother asked.

"Darling, I know this is hard for you to accept," Nellie said shaking, taking Kevi's hand. "It's hard for me too. All my life I've known only the love we've shared. And until just a few weeks ago, we were living in a world I'd give anything to be able to go back to. But my dearest, dearest love, please believe me when I tell you marrying Leon was the only way I could think of preventing a terrible tragedy. Even as we speak, to assure the safety of our loved ones, friends, and neighbors, Leon and I must convince his parents that I am bound to him body and soul."

"What about the police?" Kevi asked frustratingly. "Why didn't you go to the police?"

"We thought of that," Nellie replied, sniffling. "We planned to request protection for both our families. But what about all the others that might be endangered? Would they be safe? Besides, without concrete proof," she sobbed, "do you think the authorities would believe us?"

When Nellie began to weep, Kevi's heart broke into a thousand pieces. Taking her into his arms, he realized that all of their hopes and dreams, everything they had lived for had come to a bitter end. There was nothing left for them. Nothing at all. A lifetime of living, loving, and happiness was forever lost.

"Can you ever forgive me?" she asked, her body convulsing.

What could he say? His own hurt ran deep. Not only did he feel defeated by life, he was left without purpose. A single day ago, he had a thousand reasons for living, and was completely comfortable with who and what he was. Now, he didn't know anything anymore. What was he to do? Where would he go? And what was life without Nellie? "I don't know," he said gravely, feeling his sweetheart's body shake in huge tremors. "I just don't know."

Those few words were like a knife in Nellie's heart. And though Kevi desperately tried to imagine her suffering, he discovered he could only see his own. Holding her in his arms, possibly for the last time, he wondered if he'd ever love again. He doubted it. First, he'd have to find a way to purge the hate occupying his heart, realizing that if he didn't, it would surely destroy him.

PART TWO

DECEPTION, TREACHERY, AND DEATH

CHAPTER NINE

It was a nervous thing the detective did, his twirling his slender pen through his meaty fingers; right hand first, left following, his right again. A subconscious habit, in times of mental distress Lt. Wesneski would often display an extraordinary ambidextrous ability that would disappear the instant his normal thought processes resumed. And so, taking a moment to write in his note pad, his flashing quill ceased its whirling suddenly, becoming steady and sure. For nearly five minutes the portly investigator wrote in frantic haste, almost as if he was trying to take down every word that had been spoken in the last hour. Placing the pad on the end table next to him, he reached inside his jacket pocket, selected a cigarette from his gold cigarette case, and lit it. While he exhaled the smoke from his lungs, he looked up for the first time. Angry, his wrinkled brow and flaring nostrils twitched nervously, his steely brown eyes glaring at the two men facing him.

"Look, Mr. Stone," he said disapprovingly, smoke spewing from his lips, his eyes narrowing into slits. "I didn't come here to waste your time. I had hoped you'd at least offer me the same courtesy. Now, before you say another word, I'd like to say that I drew this case quite against my wishes, and because of it, my first night out in months has been ruined." He paused to take a drag from his cigarette. "I'm tired, frustrated, and for the moment, extremely irritated, so what I don't need, particularly at this late hour, is a fanciful tale about voodoo, witches, and goblins."

"To be honest, I hadn't planned on telling you as much as I did," Kevi admitted, becoming quiet for a moment. "I guess I needed to get some things off my chest. But in spite of what you might think, or believe, everything I've told you is true."

The detective's eyes turned cold. "If you expect me to tell my superiors this cock-and-bull story of yours, you're nuttier than I think you are. They'd have me in Bellevue so fast it would make my head spin. And that would only be the beginning."

"You said you'd keep an open mind," Kevi said patiently.

"An open mind," Harvey retorted, his jowls reddening, his veins pulsing noticeably at the temples.

"I understand your reluctance to believe such a story. Really, I do. If I were in your shoes, I'd probably feel the same." A short pause. "Suppose I give you proof. Would that help?"

Harvey's brow furrowed in to several broken lines. "It would."

"I must tell you...the proof I'm referring to is not necessarily the kind you're probably accustomed to."

"As long as it corroborates your story," Harvey stated quite cynically, "that'll be enough."

Nudging him first, Ricky Caldwell whispered into his colleague's ear. Smiling, Kevi took note that Harvey wasn't at all amused with his and Ricky's behavior. Nor was he surprised. Most cops rarely possessed a decent sense of humor; probably due to the seriousness of their profession.

The investigator eyed them both thinly. "Look, you two," he advised, his mein souring, "I don't have any time for games."

"No games," Ricky said wryly.

Though Kevi's movements seemed casual at first, they were, in fact, deceptively swift, so swift that within the space of the next heartbeat he stood directly in front of the detective's huge leather chair. And before the Manhattan police officer could complete the gasp that had started in his belly, Kevi had stooped to the floor and with one hand, lifted the chair and its occupant easily over his head.

"Wha-What the?" sputtered the startled investigator, his cigarette landing squarely between Caldwell's feet, nearly six feet away.

Guffawing uproariously, Ricky extinguished the burning cigarette in a nearby receptacle.

"Stop squirming. I'm not going to drop you." Turning slowly, Kevi took a moment to observe Harvey's reddened face and awestruck expression in the wall-length mirror. "Relax...and watch."

Once Kevi was certain he had gained Harvey's undivided attention, he bent into a sideways incline position, and while holding the chair aloft in his right hand, he effortlessly executed a half dozen one handed pushups in as many seconds. Up...down...up...down, the detective went, his artificially tanned hands showing white around the knuckles, his eyes as big as silver dollars. Reaching ten, Kevi tossed the chair two feet into the air, and in one quick motion, he changed positions and resumed his exercise.

A throaty gasp forced itself from Harvey Wesneski's lips.

Smiling, Kevi wished he could see the detective's facial expressions. After he had executed a total of twenty pushups he rose to a standing position, faced the mirror once more, and held the chair containing the flustered policeman outward to his left for nearly thirty seconds. Slowly, he passed the huge leather chair from one hand to the other, holding it outward to the right for another thirty seconds, before placing it gently upon the floor.

Despite the coolness of the studio lobby, Lt. Harvey Wesneski was sweating quite heavily. His expensive suit with its elegant french cut shirt had soaked clean through and stuck to his body.

"I think Harvey needs a drink," Kevi commented.

"So get him one," Ricky replied, finding delight in the policeman's discomfort.

"Quit clownin', this is serious."

"What am I today...the water boy?"

"Rick, please," Kevi said, giving his friend an impatient stare.

"Yessuh, massa boss man," Caldwell quipped, rolling his eyes, snapping to attention, giving his friend a Gestapo-like salute. Returning seconds later, he handed an ice cold glass to the sweating, shaken police officer. "For medicinal purposes," he said, his gaze and laughter both sardonic.

"Harvey," Stone began, "you weigh in the neighborhood of three hundred pounds, am I right?"

Wesneski nodded shakily, drained his glass in huge gulps, and placed the empty container on the coffee table in front of him.

"And would you agree the chair you're sitting in weighs somewhere around a hundred fifty pounds?"

Nodding once more, Wesneski patted the leather seat as if it had become his best friend.

"That's approximately four hundred fifty pounds. I weigh one-eighty. Now, I'm willing to bet that no bodybuilder, professional weightlifter, or anyone else you might know can do what I've just done."

"I'm inclined to agree," Wesneski squealed, his voice sounding very much like a canary in the clutches of a hungry tom cat. Clumsily, he lit another cigarette.

"The **Kaluti** exist Harvey," Kevi Stone proclaimed. "One stands before you."

The detective's eyes widened. "I don't know what to say," he muttered, utterly confused. A pause. "What you've shown me is not exactly what I'd consider evidence, still, I must admit, it certainly substantiates parts of your story. The problem is, I wouldn't begin to know how to make my superiors believe the rest of it."

"That's not important, Harvey...just as long as **you** believe."

Wesneski mulled it over for a moment. "Are there anymore like you?"

"You mean as strong?" A nod from the detective. "Honestly, I don't know. In the first place, the **Kaluti's** powers vary from person to person...and these days, we tend to keep our abilities secret, even amongst ourselves. Believe me, it's best. If the unsuspecting populace ever discovered our existence, they would either try to exploit us...or destroy us."

"Now that," Lt. Wesneski said emphatically, "I can believe."

"Well," Stone asked, "have I helped at all?"

"I haven't the faintest idea," Wesneski said stubbing out his half-smoken cigarette, aware of the concern on Stone and Caldwell's faces. "And even though we have yet to determine just how the minister and his son were murdered, I'm certain there's nothing supernatural about it."

"Pardon me, but how would you know?"

Thinking it over for a moment, Harvey realized he hadn't an answer. "I guess I wouldn't", he admitted. Then, with a distinct lack of enthusiasm he added, "Mr. Stone, I'll be perfectly honest, I haven't a clue to what really happened, that's why I'm here. Should I need your help, may I call on you again?"

"Certainly." Kevi gave the detective a fax and cellular phone number where he could always be reached. "Thank you both," Harvey said, shaking Kevi's hand first, then Ricky's. "Thank you very much."

"Before you go," Kevi said tentatively, his voice acquiescent, "I'd like to know if it would be possible for me to visit Nellie."

"I'm sure something can be arranged," Harvey assured him. "Right now she's under police protection, as well as a doctor's care. I'll let you know something soon, okay?" And then he was gone.

As the elevator doors closed, Kevi wondered how'd he react to seeing Nellie again. There really was only one way to find out. It had been many years since they had seen each other, and he decided that if she needed him, neither Heaven or Hell would keep him away.

*****

As soon as Harvey Wesneski left the Mammoth Records building, he drove straight to his Staten Island home. Actually it was more than that. It was an estate if anything else. Costing in the millions, he hated it with a passion. The house itself was more than 32,000 square feet and was entirely too much for just two people. Even a staff of twenty live-in servants, most who he never saw more than a couple of times a month couldn't rid himself of the terrible loneliness he felt each time he entered the immense dwelling.

Then there was his wife; one of New York's busiest and most public socialites. Most of the time she'd be off gallivanting from one place to another, and would never be there. Whenever she returned, though, it was never alone. The house then would become so packed with her rich bitch friends he felt positively suffocated. You would think they could leave at a reasonable hour. Not!

Very often his wife's raucous crowd would party through the night till noon the following day. Those were the times Harvey dreaded most. Luckily, this was not one of those mornings. His debutante' wife was presently out of the country doing charity work for some impoverished ethnic group of suspect origins. And though she had no way of knowing it, her husband was extremely grateful.

*****

A few minutes before the sun had come up, Harvey Wesneski turned his vehicle towards Floral Park. Within the last eight hours this was his second trip to the affluent community in which the decedents once lived. And very much to his own surprise, the image of the murder scene continued to haunt him. After sixteen years on the force, he believed he had seen everything. He couldn't have been more wrong.

Although he had never met him before, Wesneski considered himself quite fortunate to have his Floral Park counterpart assisting him in this particular investigation. For once, no bureaucratic red tape existed between their respective police forces. "Isn't that always the way?" he muttered aloud. "For one cop to show another professional courtesy, somebody important has to die."

He had just passed through the toll gate when his car phone began to ring. It was his office informing him that Mrs. Braithwaite had been discharged from the Darian Hospital Psychiatric/Crisis Center about four AM. She was staying with a neighbor. Under police protection, of course. Smiling, Harvey remembered seeing the recent widow many times on television, and besides being a stunning beauty, it was his opinion she was one of those most remarkable ladies in the world today.

As he pulled onto the Braithwaite's premises, the early morning sun offered him a better view of the lavish Tudor style home. By Long Island standards it would never be considered a mansion. Still, it was one of the finest homes in the state. After he had parked his car behind a string of police vehicles in the Braithwaite's elliptical driveway, he lumbered up the snow-covered walkway. Nearing the entrance, he flashed his badge and ID to the two uniformed officers guarding the front door.

"Mornin', Lieutenant," a patrolman said respectfully.

While offering both men a nod, Harvey noticed a tall, lanky officer wearing a dark blue coat sauntering towards him. The man looked familiar, but he couldn't be sure he knew him.

"Lt. Wesneski, it's good to see you again," the officer said pleasantly.

Harvey wrinkled his brow. "We've met before?"

A sly smile. "Yes, sir. I was one of your students when you taught at the academy. Hennessey's the name, sir. You may remember me, because I beat you in the small arms contest a few years ago."

Beaming, Wesneski recalled his only defeat in his lengthy career. "Yes, I remember you," he said, shaking the officer's hand vigorously. "You were the best shot I've ever seen with pistols. But if I remember right, you couldn't hit the broad side of a barn with a rifle."

"Yes sir, that's me," Hennessey replied, smiling, "I've improved considerably since then."

"I'm sure you have," Wesneski told him. "I'm sure you have."

Escorted by his former pupil, Harvey took an opportunity to admire the beauty and grandeur of the elegantly decorated home, noting particularly, that while the furnishings were quite expensive, they accurately reflected the tranquil and peaceful characteristics of its occupants. Heading up the marble staircase towards the murder scene he encountered several police officers along the way. All were busy hustling about doing the jobs they were trained for in a quick and professional manner.

Recalling his first visit, the closer Harvey came to the master bedroom, a familiar ache swelled in the pit of his stomach. Even though the bodies had been removed hours ago and sent to the morgue for their post-mortem, the room was still a mess. The silken drapes and sheets, the thick white Persian carpeting, the walls, almost every piece of furniture was coated with blood. Feeling a little light headed, a new experience for him, Harvey was glad he skipped his usual breakfast of cream-filled danishes and coffee.

No unusual fingerprints had been discovered. Those lifted, belonged to the two decedents, the widow, and a couple of their servants. The strangest evidence, though, were the burn marks on the floor. Four patterns in all, one in the bathroom, the rest in the bedroom. As he studied the bathroom tile and porcelain toilet for a moment, he tried to imagine the heat that could turn those materials into so much melted slag. In the bedroom, his eyes rested on the silver plated vanity table sitting in the corner. It was warped and misshapen. Next, he studied the double king-sized water bed sitting in the middle of the spacious room. All of its water had been evaporated, and there was no evidence of its thick polyethylene mattress. It was as if it had been dissolved into nothingness. At the base of the bed in the burned and bloody carpet were two impressions of the bodies. The blackened silhouettes gave the appearance that Leon and his son died in each other's arms.

When Harvey turned, he discovered a lean-looking man standing next to Hennesey had been glaring at him.

"You Wesneski?" the officer asked authoritatively.

"Yeah," Harvey countered, offering an amiable smile, "you Conklin?"

One look into the detective's swirling blue eyes and Harvey knew that his Floral Park counterpart was cut from the same cloth as himself.

Conklin nodded. "I know you haven't had time to find out much from your end", he said despairingly, "but any information you think we can use will be appreciated. The Braithwaites were...are close personal friends of mine, and I'll bargain with the devil himself to find those responsible for this tragedy."

In the police business, first-impressions are often everything. Harvey's were no exception. His instincts had already told him that he and Conklin would work well together. Not only did the brash younger officer exhibit the keen intelligent eyes of a trained professional investigator, but he projected the courage and conviction to stand by his actions.

"Let me bring you up to speed," the Floral Park detective said purposefully. "We're still unable to determine how the murder occurred. The bedroom door was locked from the inside. The lock is a dead bolt type, the key was still in it, which makes you wonder...how in hell did the murderer, or murderers get out?"

Wesneski looked towards the window. It was the only possible exit.

"Not that way," Conklin stated. "The windows are iced shut and the snow outside hasn't been disturbed... with the exception of the occasional bird."

Unconvinced, Wesneski looked out the window anyway. "Well, I certainly don't believe they beamed themselves outta here like on Star Trek."

"Me neither," Conklin assented, missing Harvey's intentional witticism. "If indeed, some kind of incendiary device was planted without the decedent's knowledge, prior to their entry, a device working on some kind of timer, where is it now? We've looked everywhere for it."

"Have you been able to determine what kind of device it was?"

"Not yet. The natural assumption would be a flame thrower of some type, but we ruled that out once we were unable to discover any trace of gaseous or flammable fuels present. If it was a chemical fire, we've been unable to ascertain the types of chemicals used. Whatever caused this damage doesn't fit any profile we can think of."

"Why not?"

"The problem is the heat. Everything that came in contact with the fire was burned horribly. You've seen the bodies. Both of the decedent's teeth and jewelry suffered unbelievable damage. Even the marrow in their bones were an ash. Our experts believe it would take in excess of five thousand degrees Fahrenheit to cause this damage. Now what could create such incredible temperatures and not set the rest of the room on fire?"

"I dunno, but once we find the device or method used, we'll be able to find the murderer as well."

*****

Someone had to interview the widow, and since Conklin was busy at the murder scene, Wesneski was elected. Presently, she was convalescing in one of the most ostentatious homes in the Crenshaw Circle section of Floral Park, reportedly the largest in Long Island, owned by Congressman Clayton Harper--a political heavyweight and his wife Lillian, a former Senator of some distinction.

"Allow me to extend you my condolences," Harvey said humbly.

"Thank you, Lieutenant," Nellie replied, with just a hint of a smile. "Would you care for some tea?"

"No ma'am," he replied politely.

In spite of her recent hardships the widow was one of the loveliest women Harvey was privileged to meet. The pictures in her home could never do her justice. The sheer radiance of her smile made his heart pound with excitement. Inwardly, he smiled. Though she had suffered much in recent hours, the bright light in her eyes and the tiny crow's feet around them indicated she was a person who enjoyed laughing. Suddenly he wanted to hear the laughter he had only heard during television interviews, a laughter that was honey sweet, seductive and melodious, a laughter that reminded him of a muted trombone solo by the highly articulate jazz trombonist, J. J. Johnson.

"There's no need for you to stand, Lieutenant," she said softly. "Please sit here...next to me."

Harvey removed his outer garments and sat in the chair a few feet from her bedside. "I don't want to appear cold and unfeeling," he began, "but these questions must be asked. I hope you realize that."

"I understand," Nellie said uneasily.

After he had given her a moment Harvey asked, "When was the last time you saw your husband and son?"

"Last night...about 8:00 PM, during the telethon at Radio City Music Hall." Noting her distress, Harvey allowed the widow a few moments more to compose herself. "After the telethon, did you speak with your husband and son at anytime?"

"No," she said. "Both of them knew I'd be getting home late. The Harper's and I routinely discuss "Utopia's, Issues and Answers" program the same time every month."

"What time did you get home?"

"A little after midnight, I guess. I'm not sure. All the servants were gone for the day, that I know. They usually leave around eleven."

"I see. You entered your home and..."

"As soon as I walked into our living room, I knew something was wrong. I thought I smelled smoke...coming from upstairs." Shivering, Nellie paused a moment. "I ran up the steps as fast as I could and nearly fainted when I noticed the pool of blood coming from under our bedroom door." She shivered again. "I tried getting in, but the door was locked. I didn't know what to think. We haven't locked our bedroom in the ten years we lived there. I must've banged and kicked the door for some time before even thinking of Lex. But when I looked in his room, he wasn't there. I was so terrified I completely forgot he was staying with friends. I guess that's when I realized I had my keys still in my hand. But I couldn't find the one to our bedroom door. I know now, I never had it. It was where it has always been. Stuck in the dead bolt." A lengthy pause. "After that I can't tell you much of anything. I must have collapsed, because the next thing I remember is waking up in the hospital."

As Nellie sniffed softly, a tiny tear emerged from the corner of an eye.

Harvey moved the box of facial tissues from the dresser at his left and placed them at her side.

"Thank you very much," she said, blowing her nose lightly. "You're very kind."

"Not at all," Harvey said gently. With genuine praise he added, "You know, Mrs. Braithwaite, you're a very remarkable woman. Before blacking out you were able to notify the Harper's and the police. I wish I could say I would be as capable under similar circumstances."

Nellie tensed a little. "I'm sorry, Lieutenant," she said, leaning forward to adjust her pillow, a confused expression on her face, "but I didn't make any phone calls." The bed she was lying in was one of those motorized reclining types, and she manipulated the controls until it raised her up at an angle of forty-five degrees.

"Perhaps you don't remember ma'am. Under the circumstances I can understand why, but Senator Harper and his wife came to your aid only minutes after your call. The police arrived seconds after your neighbors."

Nellie shook her head firmly. "I assure you, Lieutenant, I called no one." Briefly, she closed her eyes. When she opened them again she said, "I remember now. The stench of the fire choked me even from outside our bedroom door. When I saw the blood, I panicked, and I knew I had to get help fast. But when I turned to run, I tripped over something. No, I broke a heel, fell down the stairs, and blacked out before hitting the bottom." Displaying the bruises on her arms and head Nellie stated as-a-matter-of-factly, "Believe me, Lieutenant, after that fall, I was in no shape to do anything."

Envisioning the marble spiral staircase in her home, and remembering the broken heel that was found at the top of the stairs Harvey couldn't help but think, *"It's a miracle she didn't break her lovely neck. But she had to make those calls...the 911 operator has her voice on tape."*

"And I'm willing to bet," Nellie said, "you'll find no calls were made from my home after 11:00 P.M."

Making a mental note to check into it Harvey stated, "Your husband was a very popular man in many circles, Mrs. Braithwaite. Would you know of enemies he might have had?"

Nellie froze. Even a blind man could have sensed the change in her mood. She was angry. No. It was hate. Her walnut colored eyes were filled with it. "It's an occupational hazard being a minister **and** a politician, Lieutenant. A man such as my husband had many enemies."

"You suspect someone, though," the detective stated, his tone curt, but not intimidating.

"No, Lieutenant," Nellie answered in a defeated voice.

"Please, ma'am," Harvey said imploringly, sensing her lie. "I can see it in your eyes. If you have any suspicions at all, you must tell me. It's the only way I can help you."

Nellie's reply was quite bitter."I'm sorry, Lieutenant, there's nothing in this world I want more than to see the murderers of my husband and son captured. And not so they can rot behind bars either. I want them dead, Lieutenant. Can you understand that? For destroying my family, my life, I...want...them...dead." Nellie shook herself before continuing. In a small voice she said, "I'd like to help, really I would. But if I told you who I believe is responsible, you'll only think I'm mad, or possibly that I'm on the verge of a breakdown." Nellie blew lightly into another tissue. "And maybe I am, Lieutenant. Maybe I am."

"I don't believe that for a second," Harvey assured her. "I'm a pretty good judge of character. You have to be in my profession. In spite of what's happened, I believe you are the most rational, clearest thinking person I've ever met." The detective sighed. "Please, let me help you. Tell me what you know...or at least what you **think** you know."

Nellie said nothing for awhile. The minutes ticked away slowly as she laid in her bed staring towards the ceiling. Desperately wanting to help her, the hurt in the widow's eyes caused an ache in Harvey's gut.

"Will you pour me a cup of tea please?" she asked.

"Certainly," Harvey replied, reaching for the steaming pot on the stand next to her bed. As he began to pour, he was delighted when Nellie rewarded him with a glimpse of her perfect white teeth.

"Lieutenant, after I was told how my husband and son were found, I must have died a thousand deaths. I knew then, those responsible would probably go unpunished." Nellie paused to sip her tea. "And that there was only one person in the world capable of helping me destroy them. Unfortunately, he's hated me for almost thirty years."

It was an educated guess at best, but Harvey was certain the bereaved widow was referring to Kevi Stone.

"Now," she said, placing her cup on the tray, "I'm not so sure even he'd be able."

"Ma'am, you have the resources of two of the finest police forces in the country in addition to the federal services working for you. I assure you if we can't help you...no one can."

"Perhaps you're right," Nellie replied thoughtfully, "but I seriously doubt you'll believe me anyway. It's so incredibly insane, I have trouble believing it myself."

Harvey hid his surprise. Just a few hours ago, Kevi Stone had made a similar statement. Something told him what the widow was about to reveal he had already heard before.

CHAPTER TEN

Cameron, New Jersey--1968

"I always knew it would be like this," Nellie purred, running her fingers across Kevi's naked flesh. Snuggling closer, she held him tightly and sighed. "You know, I was beginning to think you'd never make love to me. I've always wanted you to. But you'd never make a pass. How come?"

"Dunno," Kevi said with an embarrassed shrug. "Guess I was scared."

Nellie began to giggle. "You? Scared?"

"Does it surprise you that something can frighten me?"

"Yes. I've seen you get into the ring with some awful brutes, and I'd swear you weren't the least bit afraid."

"I wasn't. But when it comes to girls, and you in particular, I'm not as sure of myself as when I'm fighting."

Thinking it over for a moment, Nellie recalled their first kiss. At the time both were ten years old. Although she was quite willing, Kevi relented only when she twisted his arm. "You know, Mr. Stone, I do believe you're just a shy little boy hiding inside a grown man's body."

Kevi whacked Nellie on the behind.

"Owww, that hurt!" she cried happily, pulling herself upward, placing her arms around his neck, hugging him with all her might. While she lay atop him, his strong, gentle fingers ran up and down her back causing a shiver of excitement with each stroke. *"I must be the luckiest girl in the world. I have the lover every woman dreams about--tender, caring, patient. Oh God, five wonderful climaxes in the first hour. He'll probably kill me with his lovemaking once we're married."* Nellie released a thoughtful sigh. *"But what a way to go..."*

"Honey, your folks'll be home soon," Kevi said softly. "We'd better get back to the prom party before someone misses us."

That's when Nellie began to sob.

"What's the matter? A moment ago, everything was wonderful."

"It still is darling...that's what's wrong. For the first time in my life I feel like a woman...your woman."

As Kevi held Nellie's face in his hands, he kissed her lightly on the lips. "You'll always be my woman, honey. Always."

Nellie buried her face in her lover's neck and kissed him behind the ear.

"I know it's late," she began enticingly, "but will you make love to me just once more?"

With an eager smile, Kevi kissed her waiting mouth. When their tongues met, Nellie knew by his breathing that he was ready for her once more. Shifting slightly, she positioned her body directly on top of him and sucked him deep inside. The next few minutes were filled with intensely heated passion as his muscular body drove into hers like a powerful unrelenting piston, filling her insides with his warmth. Hungrily, eagerly, gratefully she accepted everything he had to offer. Once more he brought her to ecstasy. And once more she succumbed to it, before falling headlong into a dark pleasurable abyss.

*****

"Final boarding call for flight number 1322, non-stop to London. All passengers should be boarding now."

"Gotta go, honey," Kevi said, giving his sweetheart a hug. "Can't miss my flight. After he picked up his garment bag and hung it from his shoulder, he grabbed Nellie by the buttocks and said quite unabashedly, "Love you, love you, love you."

"Oh, honey, I'm going to miss you," she sniffed, as if he would be going away forever. Three days, that's all it would be. Three days. Almost a lifetime.

"Shhhh," Kevi whispered, squeezing his sweetheart's buttocks again, "be back before you know it. Love me?"

"Terribly," Nellie replied, near tears.

"Good," Kevi said, giving his mother a loving embrace. "You two have a safe trip back, ok? I don't want anything to happen to my two best girls."

Thirty two steps. Nellie had counted them. It had taken Kevi exactly thirty two steps before he disappeared into the plane. It was silly of course, her watching him the way she did. But she wanted to remember everything about him. His voice. His kiss. His touch. How they had made love all through the night. Suddenly, a strange feeling rocked her insides. Something was wrong. By the time she discovered what it was, the plane was pulling away.

Kevi had left without saying goodbye.

"Come on dear," Mama said, handing Nellie the car keys. "It's getting late. You drive the first hour or so. It'll take your mind off things."

*****

As soon as Kevi was settled, he called home. Just by the sheer exuberance in his voice Nellie could tell he was deliriously happy, and so was she. Even when she learned his group's stay had been extended a few weeks more. In the beginning, she thought she'd miss him more than she could bear, but after the first few days, she never got the chance. Kevi consistently filled her lonely hours with post cards, letters, and souvenirs from all the places he visited. Something arrived nearly every fourth day. Three times a week he would call to share his experiences. It was almost like being there herself. And each time before he'd hang up, he would say, "love you, love you, love you," like he did the day he left. It was those few words that made her miss him less each time.

While Kevi was away, Nellie and his mother met often, usually at the cafe down the street. Excellent therapy for both, it helped chase the blues away. Late one evening, though, in the middle of the week, Kevi's mother had asked Nellie to drop by her home.

It was a meeting both would regret later.

"Sit down, dear," Mama said hesitantly. "What Johnny and I have to say won't be easy for you to accept, or understand."

"W-What's the matter?" Nellie asked anxiously. "Has something happened to Kevi?"

"No, dear," Mama said, pouring herself a cup of coffee, "Kevi's fine. He'll be home in a few days."

Nellie should have felt relieved, but she didn't. "Then what's wrong?" Mama and Johnny explained. *"Why would the Braithwaites want to harm me? We've been friends for longer than I can remember."*

The rest of the day Nellie had become nothing less than a bundle of tangled nerves. The slightest sound frightened her. And whenever her parents expressed their concerns, her only explanation was that she missed Kevi terribly. Which wasn't too far from the truth. Nellie was glad they understood. It would have been a terrible ordeal trying to explain the real reason behind her fears.

Wanting to feel closer to her lover, she visited his home the following day. Much to her surprise, Leon was there. Easily, the first thing she noticed was his fear. That wasn't all. She also discovered that he was in love with her. Often, while they sat across from each other, she would catch him staring. To hide his embarrassment, he'd go to great lengths to avoid further eye contact.

That night, around ten, Nellie got out of bed and sat out on the front porch swing for awhile to try to sort things out. *"If Kevi was here...he'd know what to do."* But he wasn't, and Nellie felt completely helpless without him. Someone had to find a solution to their problems, otherwise innocent lives might be lost. And for what? God only knew. After racking her brain for several hours, she finally gave up and went back to sleep.

An absolute wreck by morning, Nellie crawled out of her bed and headed for the bathroom. On her way through the narrow hall, she looked in on her mother; her father had left for work hours ago. Precisely at eight AM, she called Leon Braithwaite and asked him to meet her, and within the hour, she trudged the few blocks to her church, hoping the short walk would refresh her somehow, as well as provide a solution to her predicament.

The elder twin was sitting on the hood of his father's sky blue Cadillac when she turned the corner. With head hung low and shoulders slumped forward he shuffled towards her. As soon as he looked up, Nellie noticed the puffy bags beneath his eyes. Leon hadn't slept well either. Nellie felt defeated. She had spent most of the night agonizing over her troubles, and she hadn't a single suggestion to make regarding her dilemma. Neither did Leon, it seemed. If he did he was keeping it to himself. Neither dared to speak, and for long minutes, Nellie stared at the elder twin as if he was a complete stranger. Suddenly, she recalled the vicious rumors she had often heard about his family, rumors she had always defended, rumors she had refused to believe. *"How could I have been so wrong?"*

Nellie gave Leon another long, hard look. His head still low, only when she had touched him did their eyes meet. In that instant, she knew what had to be done. "I know you love me," she blurted. Leon turned quickly, but before he could walk away, she grabbed him by the forearm. "It's true, isn't it?"

"Y-Yes."

"Why haven't you told me before?"

"You weren't supposed to know. N-no one's supposed to know."

"I see," Nellie said, but she didn't really. Changing the subject she said, "Look Leon, we haven't much time. Somehow we must prevent a very serious wrong from happening. Do you understand?"

"More than you know," he said morosely.

"I know **you** personally aren't responsible," Nellie started. But then she became incensed. "Dammit, I can't begin to understand why your family hates me so. I thought we were friends. What have they got against Kevi anyway?" Leon offered no reply. "Whatever their reasons," she said furiously, "I will **not** stand by and watch my loved ones destroyed. I won't, I won't...I can't."

"Nellie, I promise you, if my folks ever comes near you or your family, by all I hold holy, I swear I'll kill them. I'll kill them all."

Nellie had never been more stunned. Even though Leon's hatred was directed towards someone else, it terrified her to no end.

The elder twin opened his car door, got in, and turned the ignition. "I don't know what we're gonna do, Nellie, but your family will be safe. That's a promise."

"Don't go," she said gently, noticing his tears.

Ensconced behind the wheel, Leon hid his head within his arms. "Go home, Nellie," he said, "please."

Nellie tried to get him to turn but he resisted. "Leon, look at me." "Please, Nellie. I don't want you to see me like this."

There probably isn't a girl in the town of Cameron more compassionate than Nellie Bryson, and under normal circumstances she might've done as Leon had asked. But these were far from normal circumstances. Her actions were the proof of it. "Damn you, Leon," she blazed hotly, shaking him as hard as she could. "This is no time for crying. You look at me this second or I'm gonna slap the living hell out of you. Do you hear me?"

Leon turned slowly, the whites of his eyes already reddening. "I'm sorry," he said, swallowing down each word. "I guess I'm not a very strong person."

"Nonsense," Nellie said, kissing him lightly on the forehead.

Flinching suddenly, Leon's eyes widened with surprise.

"Move over," Nellie commanded, "there's something I want to tell you." Once she noticed the early morning worshipers gathering outside on her church's front steps she added, "And roll up your window. What I have to say to you is private." Then she said, "I think we should get married..."

Startled, Leon backed himself against the passenger side door. "Are you crazy?" he asked, his pale eyes nearly popping out of his head.

"I'm serious."

Tiny globules of sweat appeared on Leon's forehead. "No, Nellie, no. There's got be some other way..."

"Think about it," she interrupted. "It's the **one** way we can get out of this mess. Perhaps the only way."

"But what about Stone?" the twin asked sheepishly.

"Kevi is the reason why I'm willing to do this, you fool. Kevi, his family, mine...everyone."

"Oh Nellie, this isn't right. There's got to be some other way."

"Short of killing your entire family, there isn't. And believe me," she said contritely, "that idea has crossed my mind several times in the past twenty four hours."

Leon believed her. It was written all over her face. And who could blame her? If he were her, wouldn't he have felt the same?

"Stone'll kill me, you know that, don't you?"

"No he won't," Nellie promised. "He'll hate you, yes. And maybe even me. But once he realizes this was the only way to save his folks, that'll make the difference."

"For all our sakes, I hope you're right," Leon said thoughtfully. "Stone has quite a capacity for violence if he's pushed to it. Believe me, I know."

"No one knows my man better than me," Nellie said assuredly, praying all the time she was right. If she was wrong, Leon and his family would pay, dearly, possibly with their lives. There would be no one on earth that could prevent it. "One last thing Leon, I love Kevi with all my heart. I've always loved him, and will always. And its because of my love for him, I'll do whatever's necessary to assure that no harm comes to him and his family. But I want to make one thing perfectly clear. If there's ever a chance we can get out of this mess, I intend to have this marriage annulled and go back to him...if he'll have me. I will not go back as damaged goods. In no way, I repeat, in no way will this marriage ever be consummated. It will be a marriage of convenience and appearances only. Now, feeling as you do, can you accept this?"

"Yes Nellie, I can," Leon said determinedly, almost as if he had gained a new resolve. "And I promise you, as long as there is breath in my body, no harm shall come to you or your loved ones...that includes Kevi."

Nellie believed him.

And believed in him. Later that day the two of them crossed the Maryland border and were married at a Justice of the Peace.

CHAPTER ELEVEN

Hurt, heartsick, feeling quite despondent, Kevi slipped out of Cameron like a thief in the night. And even though he had taken Nellie's aching heart with him, she couldn't find it within herself to blame him. More than anyone, she understood his pain. It was a reflection of her own. Still, what had hurt her most is that he had left without saying goodbye. For the second time.

"Give him time," Mama soothed, after telling her that her son had gone. "He still loves you, and soon...very soon, he'll forgive you."

Mama was wrong, and Nellie knew it. On Kevi's sixteenth birthday, she had given him a gold pocket watch with their picture inside. He kept it with him always. But a few days after his unexpected move to New York she received the watch in the mail along with everything else she had given him. Only then did she realize how much she had hurt him. After all they had meant to each other, Kevi wanted nothing to do with her. Ever again.

Four long months went by before Nellie discovered she was pregnant with her lover's child. A product of their love, instead of being elated, she wanted to crawl into a hole and die. Several times she had begged her husband to help her get an abortion but Leon was considerably adamant. Besides being an extremely dangerous procedure, especially for someone so far into term, and against the law in most states, he wanted nothing to do with the taking of an innocent life. "Why," she asked, failing to understand his objections, "would you want to burden yourself with the responsibility of raising a child that isn't yours?"

"Because," he told her, "I owe you and Kevi more than I can ever repay."

Nellie didn't understand, and Leon would say nothing more on the subject. But as time went on, her husband proved he fully intended to live up to his part of the bargain. Studying Theology at the Community College during the day, in the evenings he labored at the foundry, and on weekends he worked afternoons part time at the supermarket. And in spite of his busy schedule, he took care of Nellie better than she had thought possible

A month later, the newlyweds moved from Nellie's home into a nice apartment in Cornwall, a little town a half hour outside of Cameron. Objections from both sides of the family were many, especially with Nellie being in such a delicate period of her pregnancy. Leon had his reasons. Each time his parents visited his in-law's home, his wife had suffered. That could not be allowed. Although his folks vehemently disapproved at first, they no longer pressed the issue once they realized their son refused to budge. Leon knew that as long as they believed the child was his, they would do anything he asked. Which was the other reason for moving away. Once his parents discovered the baby wasn't his, he had no way of knowing how they would react.

Then, tragedy struck. At the beginning of Nellie's sixth month, she miscarried. When her baby died inside her, everything she clung to in those unendurable months, died with it. Sinking to the lowest depths of despair imaginable, she would have died if not for Leon, having spent more than five months in the hospital, needing both physical and psychological therapy. Nellie was never alone. Every step of the way her dutiful husband was at her side nurturing her, comforting her, providing her with the emotional support she so desperately needed.

The day she was released, Nellie was quite surprised to learn that she wasn't the only one that had suffered. Not once in those long, hard months was it ever mentioned, but Leon was crushed by the loss of their child. Even though it wasn't really his, he genuinely cherished the tiny life that had been growing inside her.

"I would have like to have raised him as my own," he sobbed, "it would have been a small payment for the suffering my family and I have caused his father."

Nellie was stunned. Never had she known such compassion. Nor could she believe that she could have been so heartless. Not once since their wedding day had she considered her husband's feelings. It was time to change all that. Somehow, someway, someday, she was determined to find a way to repay her husband for his kindness, his unswerving devotion, and his incomparable generosity.

*****

Within the next eleven years, the young couple became extremely busy, and both realized moving to Floral Park, Long Island was the best thing that could ever happened to them. By itself, the affluent community opened doors neither knew existed. Leon had become successful in real estate back in Cornwall, but his business flourished even more once he moved to Long Island. In less than two years he was appointed his own ministry, and was soon regarded as one of New York State's most respected statesmen. Almost over night his popularity soared, his influence approaching that of Jesse Jackson's, and as his wife who actively supported him, Nellie acquired her own measure of notoriety.

Exceedingly happy, in a million lifetimes, Nellie would have never believed she could have ever fallen in love again. She had loved Kevi for so long, and so completely, she didn't think it possible. Nevertheless, to her great surprise she had not only fallen in love, she had learned to love her husband with the deepest commitment and the greatest of passion. *"What a waste. How does the saying go? If I only knew then what I know now..."*

Looking back, Nellie remembered. She hadn't talked to Kevi a single time since his leaving Cameron. Each time he called her, he refused to speak to her, and all of her letters were returned unopened. Tiring of torturing herself, she finally gave up.

Years rolled by and just when she thought she had gotten him out of her system, she discovered she was in error. It happened one night while she and her husband watching the Grammy's at a friend's home. Throughout the years, Nellie always made a point to catch Kevi or his group's performances whenever they aired. It was like taking a step back in time to more pleasant days, so seeing him was nothing new. But the moment the camera panned through the audience in search of its many celebrities, her heart sunk to the pit of her stomach once she discovered the only man she had ever loved was in the arms of another woman. This was a new experience entirely. Kevi and the gorgeous starlet looked so happy, Nellie's mind became consumed with hate.

"How could he do this to me?" she asked herself, her hate growing. Her lover had found happiness while she continued to suffer in a suffocating endless purgatory.

Intuitive by nature, Leon sensed the sudden change in his wife's mood. When he asked her what was bothering her, she told him.

"Don't be ridiculous," he grated, his laughter tinged with contempt. "You don't hate him. You're just jealous." Nellie was wounded, mostly because Leon was right. "You're acting like a spoiled child," he added. "Don't you think it's about time you grew up?" And that really hurt.

For a long time after that Nellie felt totally lost. At first, she refused to believe Leon's analysis of her feelings, even though in her heart she knew he was right. But once she learned to accept the cold and bitter truth of her existence, her brooding ended, and with Leon's help and infinite patience, she was able to get on with the business of living again. With her husband at her side she found purpose, and helped him in every avenue of his church, business, and political career. But what pleased her most was that he always sought her advice before seeking others. Each day of their lives together, he made her feel exceedingly proud, and much more than that, he had made her feel needed and though she might not have remembered the actual moment she began to love him, there was one moment in their lives she would never forget.

That was the night they first made love.

"Honey?"

Leon was lying in bed reading the evening edition of the Times and drinking his favorite tea. Whenever he had the chance, this is what he enjoyed most, especially at the end of a busy day.

"What's the matter?" Nellie asked curiously. "You have the strangest look on your face."

"You never called me **honey** before. Its always been either Lee...or Leon."

Nellie smiled. "It's about time, don't you think? After all, you **are** my husband."

Sitting up straight, Leon reached for his tea on the night stand. "Ok Nellie," he said, "what's on your mind?"

Leaning forward, Nellie ran her fingers through the soft curly hairs on her husband's chest. Stiffening at her touch, Leon snatched her hand away. "Ow, you're hurting," she squealed.

"Sorry..."

"What did you do that for?" she asked, rubbing her wrist.

Leon was firm. "I wanna know what's bugging you."

As Nellie got up on her knees, she removed her house coat. The nightie she was wearing underneath wasn't very sexy, but with her large, firm breasts, she could still provide her husband with a perfect view of her ample cleavage. Pursing her lips sexily, in her deepest sultriest voice she said, "I want you to make love to me."

Leon's expression soured.

Missing it entirely, Nellie moved closer and tried to stick her tongue into her husband's ear.

"Stop it!" he barked, pushing her aside. "I'm in no mood for games."

"Is that what you think I'm doing? Playing games?"

"As a matter of fact...yes."

"I'm not," Nellie said truthfully.

"Get away," Leon said disdainfully, shoving her forcibly.

Nellie winced. She knew that Leon desired her. She had always known it. And even though he was never concupiscent, she believed if given the opportunity, he would take her. What had happened? The one thing she had never expected was a refusal. Frightened, her mind became clouded with doubt. If her feelings could change after all this time, wasn't it possible his could change as well? Maybe he didn't love her anymore. *"Wouldn't that be the cruelest of all ironies, if after all this time, I find myself loving someone who no longer loves me?"* "Don't you love me?" she asked worriedly.

Leon sighed, his eyes softening a little. "Of course I do. I'll love you until the day I die, but that doesn't mean I'm going to fool around with you."

"I don't understand," Nellie said, shaking her head.

"Remember our wedding day? You told me then our marriage was never to be consummated. Those were the rules **you** laid down. I agreed to them. At the time, I had nothing to offer you but my word. And you know better than anyone what my word means...then and now. We made a bargain Nellie, and I intend to live up to my end, even if you don't want to live up to yours."

"That's silly, honey. Things were different back then, and a lot has changed in the last seven years. Why shouldn't my being in love with you be one of them? I admit I never thought it possible, but I love you. I really do. And for the first time in a long, long time, I want us to be a family...a real family, honey, and not the roles we play for your folks and the public. I want to have your children...as many as we can produce, and if you give me a chance, I want to show you how grateful I am for all the sacrifices you've made for me, my friends, and my family." A long silence followed. "Don't you have anything to say?"

"No."

"No? What do you mean, no?"

Leon's tone was both caustic and dismissive. "I've nothing to say."

Nellie didn't know what to think. Her husband's attitude was most puzzling, and for some reason she believed he wasn't being completely honest. It's true she hadn't been the perfect wife, hardly a wife at all. In truth, she was nothing more than a stranger in his bed. There was no love, no compassion, no touching, no nothing. But given the opportunity, she planned to change all that.

While Leon continued to read his paper, Nellie carefully regarded the man she had been married to for nearly a decade. The way he ignored her was quite disturbing. He had never done that before. Even when they weren't getting along, he was always underfoot. It was something she had gotten used to. Even more distressing, she discovered that there was a harder, crueler edge to her husband's personality. Quite frankly, she didn't know how to deal with it. But once she noticed the smug, contemptuous smirk on his face, particularly the one he used against those who opposed him in his many political forums, she began to understand. The bastard was laughing at her. And after she had bared her soul to him. Outraged, she knocked the cup from Leon's hand, spilling tea all over him. While he sputtered in surprise, she jumped on top of him, straddled his waist, and snatched him by the lapels of his pajamas. "Listen here you sanctimonious cold-hearted son of a bitch," she fumed, yanking him forward until their noses were inches apart, "I'm in love with you. Get that through that thick skull of yours. Believe me, if I didn't mean it, I wouldn't say it. I'm telling you right now, if you don't treat me with the same respect I give you, if you don't start being as honest with me as I am with you, and if you don't make love to me **this** instant, I'm gonna beat the living crap out of you." Nellie shoved Leon's head roughly into their bed's head board. "So...what's it gonna be?"

Rubbing his head tenderly, Leon's face displayed a variety of emotions. First, there was shock, and then a look of confusion. Next, a boyish grin appeared, which was quickly followed by an uncontrollable fit of laughter. In the next instant he surprised Nellie completely by tossing her from him as if she were a paper doll. Then, quite athletically he leaped from their bed and began to run around the room like a crazed person.

"What's so damned funny?"

Leon couldn't have answered even if he wanted to. Falling to his knees, he held his stomach, rolled onto his back, and kicked his legs as if he were riding an invisible bicycle.

"I want an answer," Nellie said sternly, hating the idea that she was being laughed at. "What's so damn funny?"

His laughter spent, Leon got up from the floor and sat on the bed, wheezing in huge gasps. "Remember," he said, "the day we were married...how upset I was I was reduced to tears?"

"Yes. So?"

"Don't you remember? You threatened me."

"Get to the point," Nellie demanded, her eyes like twin daggers.

"Don't you see? Twice since I've known you, each time when you just had to have your way, you've threatened me with bodily harm. Now isn't that like the black calling the kettle pot? You talk about all the changes we've been through, when you yourself haven't changed a bit."

Nellie was as confused as ever. She hadn't a clue to what Leon was babbling about. She needed to think, and time. Time to get her head together. She didn't get either. Leon had seized a pillow from their bed and whacked her in the face so hard she went flying off the bed where she landed unceremoniously on the floor. Lying there for a moment, Nellie was positively stunned by her husband's startling act of violence. He had never struck her before. And for some reason, her being sprawled about on the floor, her legs and arms akimbo, was much more humorous than whatever he was laughing at in the first place.

Nellie went beyond being outraged. She went ballistic. Though, on the inside she was a raging volcano on the verge of eruption, on the outside, she was calmer than a desert breeze. Slowly, casually, almost nonchalantly she got up from the floor, sat on the bed, and waited. Tired of her husband's frantic antics, principally because they were at her expense, she awaited her opportunity. When it came, she grabbed a pillow of her own and smacked Leon in the face with all the strength she could muster. *"Payback time, you bastard."*

In striking her husband, Nellie thought it would have at least made him stop laughing. It did. For about two seconds. Enough time for him to arm himself with another pillow. Then, with a devilish grin, he proceeded to beat her over the head with brutal regularity.

Nellie being Nellie, could never allow any man to treat her in such a cavalier fashion, so she resisted with everything she had. And before long the two of them were involved in a pillow fight that would have made history. Like two naughty children the couple whacked each other until their entire bedroom was covered with feathers and their hands held nothing except empty pillow cases.

Later that evening, lying in front of the fire place in their bedroom, Nellie snuggled in the comfort of her husband's arms for the very first time. "Honey, I do love you," she said sweetly, kissing him on the neck. "I really do."

"I'm glad, dearest," Leon replied, kissing her hungrily on the lips, "because I love you more than you'll ever know."

Fourteen months later, their son Lexington was born.

CHAPTER TWELVE

Nellie beamed happily as she watched her husband hold his son for the very first time. His chest thrust forward, strutting about like a peacock, Leon was the epitome of a proud father. And though their son was barely an hour old, even she was surprised when she had intimated to him that she wanted another child.

"I'm ready whenever you are," he replied happily, kissing his infant son.

As contented as they were, in the weeks to come much of their joy would flee as if on wings of flight, leaving the new parents listless, disheartened, and fearful. Every bit of joy they had known in years past would become overshadowed with an aura of hate and evil.

Only one thing could mar such happiness. Leon's family.

All because of their new born son.

Anyone could see that Lex resembled his father. A point of fact: Their son was an exact carbon copy of Leon when he was a baby. This was the problem. In the last eight generations of the Braithwaite family, siblings born with blue-grey eyes almost always indicated an important trait--the inbred gifts of the **Kaluti**. It was because of these circumstances Lex's grandparents intended to take him to the islands of their birth in hopes to discover if he possessed the gifts they had desperately hoped for.

Agony for both, Nellie could see the hopelessness of their situation etched plainly on her husband's face. She also knew that even though Leon wanted to voice his objections, he didn't dare. In addition to putting Lex and herself in danger, those their deception had protected throughout the years would also be put at risk. And no one knew better than Leon just how unforgiving and vindictive his parents could be.

Upon their return, both Nellie and Leon were completely taken aback by the elderly couple's uncharacteristically pleasant demeanor. The very first thing they did was congratulate their son for bringing another member of the **Kaluti** into the fold. His mother went on to explain that although Lex was only a few weeks old, the "Kotha"--an old, island witch doctor--assured them their grandson's gifts would manifest before his second birthday.

"If his blood hadn't been tainted," Leo Braithwaite said, indicating Nellie, "he would probably exhibit his gifts even sooner."

Angered by his brother's nasty remark, Leon struggled to remain cool.

"Knock it off," the aged minister said sharply, turning then to his eldest sibling. "Your brother has done a fine job." As an after thought he added, "Better than you've done lately. Where's the son **you've** been promising all these years?"

Cold with hate, Leo glared menacingly at his twin.

"Your brother has not only brought **new blood** into our family," the popular minister continued, "he's established himself as one of the foremost political figures and evangelists of our day. Already his following exceeds that of my own ministry."

"That's no small feat," his wife acknowledged, "particularly when its getting harder and harder to find subjects that can be manipulated so easily. It's not like in the old days, when a revival meeting and a few well-chosen invocations could net us three, four, or five hundred new followers a night."

"And even with the media behind us," the minister posed, "our influence has waned much. I suspect it's because our audiences are much more intelligent than in times past, therefore, making it harder for us to get inside their minds."

"I agree," his wife said, giving her eldest son a rare embrace. "And with so many cultists that keep springing up out of nowhere..."

"Children compared to us," Leo interrupted.

"Nevertheless, the 80's and 90's cultists as well as many legitimate evangelical orders have given us much competition. Still, the weak shall always find their way to us, and that's good enough. While we gather the weak, Leon shall gather up the strong."

"*God, how I hate them.*" As soon as that thought entered Nellie's mind, she knew her loathing was nothing compared to her husband's. She also knew that because of her in-laws's considerable influence, Leon was convinced that if his family's malignant presence should continued, they would inevitably contaminate and destroy all of mankind. And though he thought of it often, the only thing that kept him from actually destroying them, besides the convictions of his Christian faith, was the fear that if he failed, she and Lex would be the ones that would suffer.

After his family had gone, with Lex safely in Nellie's arms again Leon said, "One of these days I'm gonna kill that brother of mine."

"Honey!"

"I'm sorry, dear," Leon said, failing to hide his anger, "but I'd give anything if we could live a normal life...instead one of so many lies and deceptions."

"Darling, it's those lies and deceptions that have kept my family and friends alive these many years. Don't ever forget that. Besides, as long as you're honest with yourself, your son and I, your congregation, and your business constituents, I think we can consider ourselves fortunate."

Nellie knew her husband would never be satisfied, no matter how she rationalized it. It was true that his ministry exceeded that of his father's, and there was little doubt that it would continue to flourish as it had done from the beginning, but in spite of the image he conveyed to his family, Leon took his Christian faith seriously. And he despised hypocrisy, particularly his own.

Leaning over her shoulder, Leon kissed Nellie on the neck."What would I ever do without you?" he asked affectionately.

"I don't know, darling, and I really don't want to find out."

Leon smiled at his infant son with pride. "Lex'll be all right honey...you'll see. No harm shall come to either of you. I promise."

"I believe you, darling," Nellie said, "but what will we do if our son possesses the gifts your parents are hoping for?"

"I wouldn't worry about it. You can't tell outwardly, but Lex is as much your son as he is mine, and it's quite possible none of the traits of the **Kaluti** will **ever** surface."

"You sound so sure," Nellie said, feeling hopeful.

"I am," Leon affirmed. "My family once believed that I had the special gene in my DNA that all true **Kaluti** are born with. I didn't. The paranormal abilities I possess weren't inherited...they were acquired by my family's teachings. My brother was different. Before his second birthday, there was little doubt that he'd been born with the gene that would prove him **one of the chosen**."

"One of the what?"

"Defti Garugatu...**one of the chosen.** It's the one thing I've never told you. Our race believes that **two** shall be born into this world...to bring about a new order, if you will. Father and son. They shall have great power. Through them, all the power from beyond will be at their fingertips, and with **Daagon**, they shall be one. Ever since we were kids, my brother has believed that. He still does. I guess my parents do too. But just in case they're in error, they look to our son so the prophecy can be fulfilled." A brief pause. "In either case, for mankind's sake I pray they're wrong."

"Why?"

Leon's voice turned graveyard cold. "Because instead of being a Messiah, the **chosen one** will be a harbinger of doom."

Nellie didn't like the sound of that. "Our son," she said with some hesitation, "if by some chance he **does** possess this extra gene, would you know it?"

"Before anyone else."

"What will you do once you find out?"

"You mean..."

" If he's **one of the chosen**," she completed.

The look in Leon's blue-grey eyes chilled Nellie to the bone. "He will be born of evil, honey," he said in a dry, emotionless voice. "He will not be the son whom we love. He'll be an abomination spawned in Hades. In that instance, I will destroy him...before he's able to destroy us. Should he survive long enough to have a son, they will eventually destroy the world."

"No!" Nellie cried fearfully, "not our son."

Leon held his wife as she cried in his arms. There was nothing either of them could do that would change a thing. They could only wait and pray. Somehow be prepared for the uncertain days that lay ahead.

*****

Time went by so quickly Nellie found it extremely hard to believe that her son was already in the seventh grade. What a great kid; intelligent, handsome like his father, and nearly as tall. Observing the two of them together always filled her with pride. The years had been good to them. As Leon had predicted, their son escaped the horrible curse of being born with the gene that would have signed his death warrant. Although incredibly disappointing to his parents, he and Nellie were deliriously happy. That didn't mean there was no longer any danger.

Far from it.

As long as there was a chance that Leon's family could penetrate the deception they perpetuated for so many years, no one could be truly safe. To prevent such a thing, Leon began teaching his son about his heritage almost from the cradle. An eager student, before his fifth birthday, Lex had a firm grasp of the role he must play and proved himself equal to the challenge.

Since their son's birth, each year for two weeks during the summer, Leon's parents made their annual pilgrimages to Haiti, Jamaica, and Bermuda, taking their grandson with them. During those times, Nellie was always terrified, thinking the worst would happen. Leon was unconcerned. His son's lessons were complete. Even the formidable talents of the "Kotha" wouldn't be able to circumvent the things his son had been taught.

Vigilant, and extremely perceptive like his father, Lex learned to sense the presence of **everyone** within his **Kaluti** family, particularly those emanations that always accompanied his grandparents and uncle. Because of his father's intensive training, he could recognize their psychic signatures from a block away and having done so, he could react appropriately. But there was one spring afternoon the incredibly perceptive thirteen year old allowed his defenses to slip. It was a day he and his parents would always remember.

Lex had just returned from a school field trip when he entered his home screaming. In response, his startled parents rushed to his side, discovering that after things had settled down a bit, their son was smitten by the lovely wide-eye beauty he had been dragging behind him.

"Mom, dad, I want you to meet Carter Ann Benton," he said nearly out of breath, "my girlfriend."

Alerted by the expressions on his parents' faces, Lex trembled the moment his grandmother and uncle entered their living room. With each step they drew near, he sensed the rancidness that always seemed to accompany them, and for a brief moment he wondered how he could've missed their horrible, putrefying stench. Only until he turned towards his sweetheart did he realize the seriousness of his error.

For the first time in her memory, Nellie saw her son's eyes burn with anger. But only for an instant. Regaining his composure quickly, Lex assumed his role in what he like to call the Game.

One look into Carter Ann's lovely brown eyes, and then her son's, Nellie could see the feelings they shared were real. Remembering her first love, she knew she could never allow her son or his young lady friend to be hurt by the abrasive tongues of her in-laws. Her mind was made up. She was tired of living in fear anyway. In spite of the obvious dangers, she pushed aside the dread she felt and welcomed Lex's young lady into their home. "How nice to meet you, dear," she said warmly, taking her son's sweetheart into her arms.

"I'm Lex's father," Leon said, winking to his son. "Don't I get a hug too?" Lex's smile shined like a beacon. "Miss Benton, I would like you to meet my mother, Sister Nora Braithwaite, and my twin, Leo Braithwaite, a very eminent gospel singer."

"I'm happy to meet you both," Carter Ann said politely.

"We're happy to meet you too, dear," Leon replied quickly. "Are you staying for dinner?"

"I haven't asked her yet, dad. Er uh, w-would you?" Lex asked hesitantly, his eyes hopeful.

"I'll have to check with my parents first," Carter Ann said, "but I'm sure it'll be all right."

"Good! We will be six for dinner," Nellie announced.

"I know you'd like a little privacy," Leon said with another wink, "and since your young lady needs to call home, why don't you make yourselves comfortable in the den until dinner's ready?"

"Come on, Annie," Lex said, grinning from ear to ear, taking his girlfriend by the hand.

"I can see you've become **lax** in teaching Lex our ways," Leon's mother scolded, watching her grandson close the den's thick sliding doors behind him. "And I think it's quite possible your influence over your wife is not as complete as you would like us to believe." The Braitwaite's matriarch then turned to her youngest sibling. "Wouldn't you agree?"

"I would indeed," Leo replied hatefully.

"Do you really believe," Leon asked calmly, "that after all my teachings, some I might add that were extremely difficult receiving, I would be foolish enough to betray my family, my birthright?"

Leo's evil glare wavered slightly when looking into his brother's cool steady eyes. "I must admit, it is a little inconceivable," he said, shaking his head, "but how else would you explain your wife and son's behavior?"

"Easily," Leon returned. Facing Nellie he said, "Leave us woman. This does not concern you."

The day they were married Leon had impressed upon Nellie the importance of obeying him without question. No matter how awful a thing he asked of her, or how ridiculous it might appear, it was absolutely imperative that she comply. It was the only way he could convince his family of his power over her. And though it was very much against her nature, Nellie agreed. In the beginning, it took much practice, but after a time, on cue she could become Leon's unthinking drone, totally obedient and subservient to his will. Hating it at first, later, Nellie didn't mind at all. To safeguard the lives of her family, it was a role she could play competently and willingly.

Their deception had never failed them, but it was hardly an infallible device. To further protect his wife and son from his family's formidable powers, Leon used his considerable skills to create a psychic defense around them. In his absence, it would protect Nellie and Lex from almost every form of psychic attack his family could devise, and though his mother and father hated Nellie intensely, Leon had no real fears they would harm her, not as long as she remained useful in perpetuating the continued growth of the **Kaluti**. But there was one within his family that would always be a danger.

Leo.

Several times throughout the years, he had tried to bend Nellie to his will. Every attempt failed. Leon's psychic defenses would not be breached.

While Nellie acted as if she were preparing dinner, she listened intently to the conversation being held in the other room.

"In the first place little brother," Leon replied coolly, "never doubt my control over my wife. It is total and absolute. Who should know better than you? Several times you've tried to possess her. Quite unsuccessfully, I might add. And isn't it your boast that your abilities are so much greater than mine? Another thing, I've found it necessary to allow my wife and son certain liberties that don't necessarily follow our tradition. If I am to maintain this facade as a man of the people, and increase my influence in the political and religious arenas, I must be the paragon of virtue they expect. So must my family. Both of them must be able to interact with my constituents and their families as competently and efficiently as I." A pause. "I repeat, my control is complete. Nellie appears as I desire her to appear...as an outspoken, free thinking wife of an outspoken, free thinking minister. With Nellie's help, I have used subtlety and guile instead of our exacting, exhausting, manipulative abilities to achieve our desires." Leon paused once more to allow his family time to digest what he had been saying. "Until the **Kaluti** nation is strong enough to make our presence known throughout the world, this is the path we must take. Last of all, Lex will do as I wish, always...because before all things, he is my son."

The silence within the living room sent chills into Nellie's bones. Her husband had made his best pitch. She could only pray it was convincing enough to satisfy his family. If he failed, a terrifying hell would be unleashed in their home. Envisioning such a prospect, Nellie began to tremble all over again.

"Mother?" Leon asked, "do you still share the same doubts as my brother?"

"No son," she replied, "I do not."

Nellie nearly choked with delight. If her mother-in-law could be swayed, Leo would have no choice but to defer to her judgement.

"I'm certain you'd never betray our family," Leo said, a little less cocky than before, "and you certainly know the ways of moving in political circles far better than I, but I'm not completely convinced of your control over Nellie. She's always been a strong-willed, clever girl, and though it appears that only you can possess her...well, let's just say, I have my doubts."

"Then, brother dear, what you need is proof even you will not question."

Leo arched both eyebrows. "What do you have in mind?"

"What would you suggest?"

Leo thought it over. "Whatever this proof might be, it must meet with mother's approval as well as mine. Do you agree?"

"Absolutely."

The seconds that followed filled Nellie with more dread than she could imagine. Her mind worked feverishly as she tried to determine what her husband could possibly ask of her that would satisfy Leo and his mother so completely.

"Let me make a suggestion," Leon said boldly. "I shall command my wife to escort you to our bedroom, where she will undress before you and submit to whatever physical desires your mind is capable of conceiving. She will do this not only willingly, but without shame, **and** with wanton passion. If that doesn't

satisfy you, nothing will ."
Nellie almost fainted where she stood. *"Noooo! Not that. Anything but that..."* Shuddering at the idea of having Leo's filthy hands upon her, a sickening, revolting fear crept into her heart. An even more horrifying thought, she couldn't believe her husband could suggest something so vile, so despicable, so perverse.

"You would allow this?" Leo asked, disbelief in his eyes.

"I would," Leon said firmly, "if you think it proof enough?"

"Yes," his brother said, rubbing his hands together quickly, "I believe it would. Mother? What do you think?"

Once she had given her approval, Leon's deep booming voice echoed from the living room, reverberated throughout the dining room, until it finally reached into Nellie's shivering spine. Cold from fear, goose bumps spread quickly all over her body, leaving her skin feeling rough and clammy. Even so, she crushed her fears, gathered her wits, and prayed that her husband knew what he was doing.

"Harlot!" he said contemptuously, "you will go with my brother to our bedroom, and fulfill his sexual desires. You will obey his every wish. Do you understand?"

Nellie said nothing. Even if she wanted to, her tongue wouldn't allow her to speak. Her mouth felt as if she had swallowed sand. Finding the strength somehow, she marched up the spiral staircase to their bedroom without giving her husband a single glance.

"You're not coming?" Leo asked, surprised.

"Surely you can handle this on your own. Besides, it's not often I get to see mother, and we have much to discuss."

"If that's the way you want it" Leo snickered. "If you hear a few screams, it won't be me."

Unsure of what Leon was planning, Nellie entered her bedroom filled with fear and trepidation. While she waited for Leo, her heart beat heavily in her chest. Listening intently, when there was no sign of her husband, her fears began to grow. Did he really intend to let his brother have his way with her?

No! That was something she refused to accept.

Leo wasn't a heavy man. Still, the sound of his approaching footfalls echoed loudly in Nellie's ears. Only moments away, she managed to clear her head before he reached the top of the stairs. Since she was wearing nothing beneath her housecoat, she let it fall to the floor. The temperature throughout their home was at least seventy degrees, but Nellie felt deathly cold.

She felt even colder when Leo stepped into her bedroom.

Even with her back facing him, Nellie could feel Leo's lust-filled eyes ogling her naked body. As she laid down on the bed, her husband's instructions echoed loudly in her ears. She must be "wanton and shameless." And she had been. Many times before. But only with Leon. Now, against her will, she must do so again, and with one who hated the very air she breathed. Writhing sexily, her long slender legs spread lewdly apart, she stared into Leo's blazing eyes. Never had she seen such unbridled lust. For long moments, his wandering eyes covered every inch of her nakedness, taking in every detail. Nellie did the same. As Leo removed his clothes, she compared his well-muscled body with that of her husband's. It was amazing. There were no visible differences anywhere. *"How could two people so similar in appearance be so different in everything else?"*

Once naked, Leo's avidity and chilling, lascivious smile made Nellie retch inside. To boost her courage and to disguise her trembling, she cooed lustily, in spite of the fact that her stomach was on the verge of spilling the chicken fajitas she had for lunch all over their king-sized waterbed. Stealing a desperate look over her brother-in-law's broad shoulders, she prayed for her husband to appear.

Her hopes were crushed. Leon was nowhere in sight. *"How could you do this to me? How could you say you love me and allow this animal to have his way with me?"* Nellie then decided that should Leo penetrate her, she would force herself to imagine it was her husband. But even that thought revolted her. At the moment, she hated Leon more than anyone in the world. It was he that had suggested and condoned her rape.*"You swine. You dirty, filthy swine. I'll kill you for this. I'll kill you..."*

As Nellie's fears turned to rage, she was just about to resist her brother-in-law with all her might when something caught her eye. *Now what in hell does he have to be nervous about?"*

As Leo climbed onto the bed, his eyes remained fixed on Nellie's naked breasts. He wanted to touch them in the worst way, but each time he tried, his hands would begin to tremble. Purposely, Nellie pushed her arms together, forcing her breasts to balloon up. Once again, when Leo tried to touch them, he yanked his hands away as if they had been singed.

Since the birth of her son, Nellie had worked hard to maintain her school-girlish figure. To stay in shape, she played tennis and racquetball religiously, and spent many hours on various courts throughout the country. Her efforts were not in vain. Her breasts were larger and firmer then when she was a teen, her legs were shapely, supple, and athletic, and her waist, waspish.

Licking his lips with anticipation, Leo managed to conquer his nervousness and grabbed Nellie's breasts firmly in both his hands.

Cooing openly, Nellie shrieked inside at his touch, and crushed the need to puke.

"For a tainted bitch," Leo said panting heavily, "you're quite lovely. I see now why my brother enjoys having you around."

Though Leo's comportment carried a resounding ring of confidence, Nellie managed to penetrate his veneer of steely resolve. The first thing she noticed was that his body shook frequently, and that he sweated as if he had endured some great exertion, and though she couldn't begin to understand what was happening inside her brother-in-law's perverted mind, Nellie realized things weren't going the way he had planned. Releasing her breasts finally, Leo climbed between her legs, and prepared to mount her. As his hungry eyes burned with lust, Nellie knew the moment he entered her, she would kill herself at the earliest opportunity.

Inches away from penetration, Leo growled like a hungry beast.

Visualizing his hot organ pounding inside her, ripping her guts out, feeling the pain before it happened, Nellie's reverie crumbled when Leo suddenly pulled away.

And then she understood.

He was afraid.

That had to be it. Nothing else made sense. After all his arrogant posturing, after all the bluster and pontificating he'd done since she'd known him, Leo was afraid of her. Oh, he still hated her, all right, nothing could ever alter that fact.

Taking a desperate gamble, Nellie opened her legs wider, reached down and grabbed Leo's hot, erect organ in her hands. Yelping in surprise, he leaped from the bed as if his genitals had come in contact with a searing flame.

Puzzled and relieved in the same moment, Nellie lowered her legs and looked at her brother-in-law with longing. "I want you," she said in a husky voice, groping for his diminishing member. "I want you **now**."

Leo's eyes shot a bolt of hate towards Nellie even as his pulsating, throbbing organ shriveled into limp, lifeless flesh. Dressing quickly he blazed, "I don't intend to soil my loins with the likes of you...you filthy bitch." And hurriedly fled the room.

Nellie grabbed the comforter on which she had been lying upon, covered her nakedness, and began to cry. She had escaped a fate worse than death, and yet, gratitude was not in her heart. The only emotion she felt was hate. Hate for Leon. Hate for his cursed family.

Some time later, after his mother and brother had gone, Leon entered the bedroom where his wife lay weeping. Nellie was so preoccupied with replaying her degrading experience over and over in her head, she was totally unaware of his presence. *"What can our lives be like now?"* Her concerns were well warranted. Should Leon touch her ever again, would she remember the experience with his evil twin? Could she ever forget that he was responsible?

When a drop of water fell upon her shoulder, her first reaction was to look towards the ceiling.

Nothing.

Tensing suddenly, she turned. In that instant, her hatred consumed her once more. But as soon as she noticed her husband's tears trickling through his fingers, she realized how wrong she had been. Pulling Leon onto the bed, Nellie drew his head to her naked breasts.

"Oh honey, I'm so sorry," he sobbed plaintively, "it was the only way...the only way."

Gently, tenderly, lovingly, Nellie held Leon in her arms, and kissed him repeatedly. Tears ran down both their faces. "Shhh," she comforted, realizing her husband had suffered too, perhaps more than she. In that moment, all the hate and anger she felt throughout her ordeal vanished completely. Before either of them knew what was happening, both were coupled hungrily in the throes of passionate lovemaking. Suddenly, all the horrible memories of the day vanished with every touch, every kiss, and with each groan of pleasure. Draining each other completely, the couple laid in each others arms blissfully, happily, contentedly.

Later that evening, after an enjoyable dinner with Lex and Annie, the happy couple excused themselves before making their way back to their love nest. Sharing a hot bubble bath they drank champagne until both were giddy, and made love all through the night.

About two AM, Nellie and Leon discussed their dreadful experience for the first and final time.

"What made your brother act like that?" Nellie asked uncertainly. "I thought he wanted me."

"He still does," Leon affirmed. "Leo's one true weakness is his appetite for beautiful, big breasted women...**you** in particular. I knew if he had an opportunity to screw you, he'd take it. I also knew his hatred and disgust for you was much stronger than his lust for that luscious body of yours."

"I don't understand."

"Leo's fears are real, honey. In his mind, he believes he will fall prey to your fleshly pleasures as believes I have." Leon kissed his wife on the throat. "Don't you see? It's inconceivable for my brother, or anyone else in my family to believe that I'm in **love** with **you**, and not your body."

Thinking of how close she had come to being raped, Nellie asked, "But what if you were wrong, honey? What if you were wrong?"

Leon's mood darkened. His voice turned cruel. "Then neither he or my mother would have left this house alive."

*****

The clock on the vanity table blinked to 03:36. Nellie had been asleep for almost an hour when she heard the tapping on their bedroom door.

"M-Mom?"

The moment the door opened, Nellie could see her son's pajama clad silhouette slip into the room. Before closing the door, he switched off the light in the hallway. "What is it, honey?" she whispered. "Is something wrong?"

Slowly, quietly, Lex tip-toed around to his mother's side of the bed, stumbled over something on the floor before sitting at her side. Even in the almost total darkness, Nellie could see her son's bright blue-grey eyes illuminating his ebony features. When she touched his face, she discovered he'd been crying. "Oh honey, what's troubling you?" she asked quietly, hugging him closely. Lex sniffed a couple of times and put his head on her chest. "Tell me darling, but let's not wake your father. He's had a lot on his mind lately."

Click! The bedroom was suddenly filled with light. Nellie and Lex were both blinded by the unexpected brightness. Sitting up in bed Leon said, "You should both know by now what a light sleeper I am." Once he had placed a pillow comfortably behind his back, Leon leaned against the head board. "What's bothering you, son?"

"I guess I blew it today," Lex said tearfully," bringing Annie home I mean. What's gonna happen now?"

"Nothing," Leon said, running his fingers through his son's curly hair. "Everything's fine. In fact, things couldn't have worked out more perfectly."

"Really, dad?" Lex asked, his eyes wide with surprise.

"Absolutely. So there's no need to lose any sleep over it. Ok?"

"Ok," Lex said happily, rubbing the tears from his eyes. "You know dad, I don't know how Grandmother and Uncle Leo were able to slip past my defenses. Usually I can sense their presence a couple blocks away." Shaking his head he said, "Today, I don't know what happened."

"Don't you think Carter Ann might have had something to do with it?" his father asked.

A puzzled expression appeared on Lex's face. Scratching his head he said, "Annie? What would Annie have to do with anything?"

"Oh honey, your father and I could see how you looked at each other," Nellie said. "It's obvious you care for her. From the moment you burst through the door, Annie was of paramount importance, wouldn't you agree?"

Lex thought it over for awhile and smiled. "Yeah, I guess so."

"You like her a lot don't you, son?" Leon asked.

"Yeah dad, I do. Annie's so much like mom, I guess that's why I'm stuck on her."

No compliment in the world could have meant as much to Nellie than the tribute her son had just paid her. and she couldn't have felt more proud.

"I guess that makes the two men folk in this household the luckiest guys in the world."

"Dig that, dad," Lex agreed, giving his father the high five. "Well, I won't keep you up any longer." Leaning forward, he kissed his mother on the cheek, then ran around the other side of the bed to hug his father. "Good night, Mom, Good night, Dad. Love you both."

"Goodnight, son," Leon said.

"Goodnight, son," Nellie said, leaning over to kiss her husband on the lips.

"What was that for?" he asked.

"Do I need a reason?"

"Of course not. But you have one," he said. "I can always tell."

"Darling, sometimes I believe you know me better than I know myself."

"I do," Leon replied, clicking out the night light.

They were in the darkness only a second when Nellie heard her husband's pajamas hitting the floor. A moment later, she was lying naked in his arms. Once more they were locked in a passionate embrace that lasted until the sun came up.

CHAPTER THIRTEEN

Floral Park, Long Island--1997

Nellie felt as if she had been floating on a huge, billowy cloud. Which was strange when she thought about it. Instead of it being a wonderful experience as she often imagined it would, it was most unsettling. Especially when she realized she had no sensation of touch, or even an awareness of things of substance around her. The strangest part of the whole thing was that all of her senses, with the exception of her hearing, seemed to have ceased functioning. What in the world was she listening to? Music? No. A fog horn? Possibly. Whatever it was, its warm hollow sound seemed to call to her from a distance.

"Mrs. Braithwaite, are you all right?" Harvey Wesneski asked, his heavy hands shaking her gently.

Nellie shook her head slowly. "I-I'm sorry, what did you say?"

"I asked if you were all right," the detective repeated, his concerns, real. "You seemed to blank out for a second."

Nellie placed her tea cup on the tray, pushed it aside, and tried to smile. What was she to do? There was no way she could reveal her suspicions without also disclosing her most shameful experience. It was certainly possible the detective could help her, but at what cost to herself. Even if the murderers were caught and punished, would it bring back her husband and son, or any of the happiness they had shared? *"God in Heaven, why couldn't you have taken me also? Without my family I'm nothing. Nothing at all."*

"Pardon me, ma'am, but you were about to tell me of your suspicions."

"I'm sorry, Lieutenant," Nellie said disconsolately, amazed that so much of her life had flashed before her eyes, "but I've changed my mind. I realize now that any information I give you would only be libelous slander."

"Maybe. Maybe not. I need to know what you're talking about first."

Nellie's voice lowered a notch. "I wish I could help, Lieutenant, but I can't. I apologize for wasting your time."

"I beg you to reconsider, ma'am," Wesneski implored. "Any information is better than none." A pause. "If it's fear of reprisals that concerns you, I assure you my inquiries will be discreet. No one will ever know."

"Please, Lieutenant, I want nothing more than to point you in the right direction", Nellie said ruefully, "but you see, if I tell you who these individuals are, I must also tell you why I suspect them. I can't do that. In doing so, I'd have to divulge something so horrible, so personal...well, it's not the kind of thing I can talk about. With anyone."

"I'll have to respect your wishes then," Harvey said disappointedly. "It makes my job that much harder, you understand. But should you change your mind", he added, taking a gold-embossed card from the tiny case that held his shield, placing it next to the pot of tea, "please give me a call. You can reach me any hour, day or night. And ma'am, anything you tell me will remain in the strictest confidence."

"Thank you, Lieutenant...at least for understanding."

"Good day to you, ma'am," Harvey said before exiting the room.

Even before her door had closed, Nellie felt cold, alone, and singularly defeated. And though she was confident the police would do their level best to find the murderers of her family, she knew their meager resources would prove inadequate. *"Leon, my husband, and Lex, my darling son, I guess I will be joining you soon. It's just as well. I want no more of this life, if you're not in it with me."*

*****

More than two hundred passengers were on Flight 52 to Chicago, but only two sat in silence the entire trip. And though both had just come from Atlanta, their general appearance would have assured even the most casual observer they were not Georgia-bred. Moving purposefully from the crowded 727, speaking for the first time in several hours, in whispers they discussed their itinerary for the next few days. St. Louis, Denver, and Los Angeles were on their list of cities to see. And yet, they were not tourists. Still, within the last 48 hours, prior to Atlanta, the two men had visited New York City, Boston, and Philadelphia.

Fareless, the cabby pulled his battered yellow vehicle into the first available position at the O'Hare cab stand and studied the two men. The moment they stepped into the wintry Chicago air attired in what he liked to call their Miami Vice business rags, his eyes saw dollar signs. At first, he thought they might be drug dealers. But then, he thought that of most of the affluent looking black men coming from Florida. The cabby honked his horn. "Where to gents?", he asked through the half opened passenger window, chewing on a smelly cigar.

Eyeing the cabby thinly, the shorter of the two men entered the rear of the vehicle first.

"Sears Tower," the taller of the two instructed, his head nearly touching the roof of the cab.

"That'll be twenty bucks," the cabby said, striking a wooden match against the dashboard, relighting his cigar, "a piece."

Because the two men were out-of-towners, the cabby boosted his fare, but was ready to haggle on the off chance his patrons knew they were being extorted.

"Get us there before one," the taller of the two men said with a thick island accent," and your fare is doubled."

Through his rear view mirror, the cabby looked at the man who had spoken, and then, the other. Bahamian was his first guess. Cuban, his second. They were neither. "But that's..."

"We know where it is," the tall man interrupted.

The cabby's eyes smiled into his mirror. With the noon traffic it would be next to impossible to get to the Sears Tower by one o'clock. But if anyone could do it, he could.

In hardly any time at all, the cabby reached the busy expressway and headed for the city. Demonstrating an innate ability maneuvering through the heavy traffic, he darted from lane to lane, instinctively avoiding the slowest. "Youse guys work for Xerox?" he inquired interestedly, peering into his rear view mirror..

The tall man nodded.

"Thought I'd recognized the logo on those cases. Where you coming from? Miami? Didn't notice no overcoats."

The tall man nodded again.

"Been there once," the cabby recalled. "Spent two weeks on the beach about two winters ago. Best vakay I ever had."

Though he was unsuccessful in eliciting additional vocal responses from his patrons, the cabby continued his discourse. Because he considered himself a conversationalist, as long as he received a nod, a smile, or maybe a hand gesture to let him know that he was communicating effectively, he was never offended by his patron's silence. In either case, during the frenetic drive into the city, his topics ranged from sports, politics, crime in the city, and always his favorite subject, big butt women. His wife being a big butt woman made him more knowledgeable than most when discussing their temperament, attitudes, and general disposition.

Five minutes before one, the cabby pulled his battered taxi in front of the Sears Tower building. "Been nice talking to you," he said chewing his cigar, taking the four crisp twenty dollar bills that had been promised.

The taller of the two offered a diminutive smile. The other nodded. The cabby served up a quick salute before whipping his car back into the heavy traffic.

A black man of incredible girth dressed in a security officer's uniform approached the bogus Xerox men the moment they entered the Sears Tower's immaculate lobby. Once they had shown their credentials, which were of course impeccable, the two men were escorted to a service elevator reserved just for them.

They reached the roof in less than a minute. Despite their summer dress, the two men seemed comfortable in the freezing clime. Both worked quickly. They had another plane to catch in just a few hours.

The electrical apparatus they had taken from their cases was quickly assembled and placed at the base of the tower's huge antenna. Its purpose was known only to them. Once they were certain the device was secure, it was switched on.

Beep! Beep! Beep!

Satisfied that the device operated properly, the two men left the roof and rejoined their contact who had been waiting inside. Given a pocket-sized contrivance to monitor the device remotely, the security guard was delegated with the task of seeing that it remained undisturbed. Noting the time, a brief smile touched both men's faces. It had taken less than thirty minutes to complete their mission.

Arranged earlier by their bogus contact, another cab awaited the two men as they exited the Sears Tower lobby. And while they sped on their way back towards the O'Hare Airport, the two men discussed their itinerary.

St. Louis was their destination.

CHAPTER FOURTEEN

Conklin hated shaving. Especially with the new cordless razor his kids had given him as a Christmas present. Each time he used it, the blades would bite into his chin, leaving tiny circular marks where the stubble had been. "I'll give it a try for a couple of weeks," he had said that early Christmas morning, assuring his three girls he was still quite pleased with the gift. "If at the end of that time my face doesn't look like hamburger, I'll keep it. If not..." Smiling to himself, Conklin knew his kids had understood. They were just like their mother. Each of them thought he was the handsomest man on earth and they all wanted him to stay that way.

When Conklin's office door swung open, he didn't have to turn to know who had entered the room. Harvey Wesneski's expensive cologne was unmistakable. Pausing a moment, he studied his Manhattan counterpart's reflection in the mirror before returning to his shaving. "I know that look," he said with a smile.

"What do you mean?" Harvey growled.

"You didn't learn anything from Nellie, did you?"

Harvey raised an eyebrow. "How'd you know?"

"I know that look."

Harvey snorted. "She was about to tell me something, I'm sure of it...but at the last second she changed her mind."

Conklin switched off his razor and placed it in his top desk drawer. "Don't sweat it my grumbling, gravel-voice friend," he said, rubbing his face, his lips twisted into a smirk. "If I know Nellie, we'll being hearing from her soon enough."

"If you say so," Wesneski said doubtfully. "I did learn one thing though."

"Yeah? What's that?"

The Manhattan police Lieutenant removed some charts from the manila folder he was holding and tossed them onto Conklin's desk. "Tell me what you make of this." While his Floral Park colleague looked through the documents, Wesneski fished a cigarette from his gold cigarette case. "I know that look," he said with a boyish grin, smoke blowing from his nostrils in identical streams.

Conklin looked up quickly. His eyes had narrowed into thin slits of blue. "Where'd you get this?"

"Your lab. You've got a guy down there with coke bottle glasses and hair as long as Crystal Gale's that claims to be a wizard with voice print analysis."

"That would be Jacobson," Conklin affirmed, looking at the charts once more, "and he's right, he **is** a wizard. If these charts are correct, and I have no doubt that they are, you realize what this implies?"

"Uh huh,", Harvey Wesneski said, flicking his cigarette ashes into a receptacle on Conklin's much-too-tidy desk. "Someone other than Mrs. Braithwaite is responsible for alerting the Harpers and your 911 E.U. The phone records show the last call from Braithwaite Manor was made by one of the servants, some time around noon."

For the moment neither detective cared to discuss what they were thinking. Both were reasonably befuddled.

A knock on Conklin's door broke the silence.

A buxom policewoman entered. "Here's the lab report you've been waiting for, sir," she said, placing it on her superior's desk.

"Thank you, Sergeant." A quick smile passed between them. As the officer turned to go, Conklin instructed her to leave the door open.

Picking up the report, Wesneski studied its contents while Conklin reached for his phone and hastily punched in four numbers. "Doctor Thomas, please." A short pause. "Doc, could you come to my office? Thank you."

Shortly, the sound of heels tapping on a cold marble floor could be heard. When they stopped, Wesneski turned, and was noticeably stunned by the statuesque figure that had entered the room.

"Dr. Thomas," Conklin said pleasantly,"I'd like you to meet Lt. Harvey Wesneski from Manhattan South. Harvey...Dr. Thomas."

"A pleasure, Dr. Thomas," Harvey said, extending his hand warmly.

"Don't be so formal," she said sweetly. "Please call me Mike."

Harvey wrinkled his forehead. "Mike?"

"I was named after my father...before I was born. He expected a son, but got me instead."

Taking a moment to admire Mike's vivacious figure, Harvey grinned unabashedly. "In either case, I'd say he wasn't the least bit disappointed."

"What a nice thing to say," she murmured appreciatively.

"Knock it off you two," Conklin said abruptly. "This is a police station, not a lonely hearts club."

Harvey arched an eyebrow. "Hey, I was just being friendly."

"Sure you were," Conklin said, teasing, not really blaming his colleague for being attracted to the young criminologist. Dr. Thomas was quite beautiful. A knockout would be more accurate. Her long blond hair shimmered in the light, and her light grey eyes flashed almost as brightly as her perfectly straight teeth. Even with the long white lab coat she was wearing, it was obvious she had a remarkable figure. "The Doc is on loan to us from the FBI. Because of Leon's political connections in Washington, the bureau has offered to take a supportive role in our investigation." Refilling his coffee cup Conklin said, "Doc, since you compiled most of the data within this report, why don't you explain your findings?"

"Gladly," she replied, putting on a pair of horn-rimmed glasses. Anyone else would have looked nerdish in the granny style eye wear, but in the young criminologist's case, they only served to accentuate her lovely features. "First, let's discuss the blood present at the scene. It corresponds with both of the decedent's blood types, "A" positive, and covers almost every square inch of the bedroom. Next, it was first assumed there had been some kind of explosion. There wasn't."

"I don't get you," Harvey said, forcing himself to recall all the blood he had seen.

"Even the smallest explosive device would have damaged the floor, ceiling, or walls. There was no such damage, and no traceable fragments of shrapnel. Besides that, the decedents' internals should have been splattered all over the room. They weren't. A second incongruity is the heat. No conventional explosive we know of can create temperatures so excessive that it can evaporate all the water in the waterbed and not set everything else on fire. And where did all the blood come from. Shouldn't it have evaporated too? Third, the bodies were charred beyond recognition, but remained completely intact. Conclusion: no explosion."

When Dr. Thomas walked around Conklin's desk to get herself a cup of coffee, Harvey couldn't help but admire the way the shapely criminologist moved across the floor. She had a wiggle that could put Cindy Crawford and Naomi Campbell's to shame. Her every movement oozed sex. Only after Conklin had cleared his throat did Harvey realize he'd been leering at her like some old lecher with a rain coat.

"Then there's the scorch marks," Mike continued. "Although we've been unable to determine the device that caused them, we're reasonably certain it wasn't a flamethrower. Based on the available evidence, we can only conclude the deaths were caused by some type of chemical device capable of generating intense heat...which would later consume itself once spent."

"That's ridiculous," Conklin flared. "Nothing like that exists."

"It does now," Mike assured. "Upon examining the bodies, the burns, and every inch of the bedroom, we've discovered sub-microbic traces of sulfur."

"Sulfur? Where in hell did the sulfur come from?"

"The device perhaps. Wherever it came from, it escapes a complete analysis. As far as we can tell, this particular type of sulfur hasn't existed in several thousand years. As a matter of fact, several hundred years ago, it wasn't called sulfur at all. It was called brimstone..."

"Wait a cotton picking second," Harvey interrupted. "Are we talking about brimstone, as in **fire** and brimstone?"

Mike nodded.

"Get out of Dodge..."

"I, too, find it hard to believe. But the truth is, after analyzing and testing the substance in most of its component parts, it is indeed the enriched brimstone of old. Once ignited, it will burn intensely until it is completely consumed. All it needs to start the exothermic reaction is an ambient temperature of sixty degrees or more."

"But that would mean almost anything could set it off," Conklin concluded skeptically.

"That's correct. Almost anything wet or dry can act as a catalyst."

"Fascinating," Wesneski said, running his fingers through his thick wavy hair. "Are you sure you haven't made a mistake?"

"No mistake," Dr. Thomas said assuredly. "Unfortunately, we haven't enough of this substance to do anymore testing, but in every analysis conducted by our labs here and in D.C., the results were the same. This unusual substance resembles oxygen chemically but is less active and more acidic, and suggests properties toxic in nature, as if it were a sulfur dioxide. And in addition to the sulfonyl compounds we've found, there are a variety of **organic** constituents we haven't been able to identify, at least not yet. We believe it is these agents that cause the self-destruct mechanism to perform so efficiently. A pungent odor is present during the exothermic reaction, but disappears completely after the heat and/or fire is consumed. How this sulfonyl compound can generate such intense heat is still a mystery. My guess would be the unidentified organics."

A still silence filled the room.

"You know, Doc," Harvey Wesneski said appreciatively, "you're a remarkable young lady."

Thomas smiled." I am?"

"Yes. When it comes to chemistry and stuff, I must admit to being somewhat dimwitted. What's amazing is...you've been able to make me understand just how this thing works."

The FBI criminologist smiled what the detective would later call a bee-yoo-tee-fool smile and said, "I just assisted in the lab analysis, Harvey. And only because of a peculiar piece of evidence turned up by forensics was I asked to coordinate with the Floral Park police in their investigation." Another smile. "It was Bob's idea," she continued. "It seems he'd heard of my somewhat peculiar, yet very particular expertise."

Curious, Wesneski furrowed his forehead. "Which is?"

"Mike's specialty is the study of ritual killings," Conklin said helpfully. "You know, the methodology, philosophy, ideology, and psychology of etc. etc. etc."

Puzzled, Harvey asked, "What does ritual killings have to do with this case?"

Mike handed the Manhattan detective a photo of a painting of the decedent's family. It was a typical pose. He remembered seeing it the first time he entered the crime scene. "What's so special about this?"

"Look closely," she said. "You'll see blood has stained the portrait above and through the painter's signature." Mike handed Harvey another photo. "This is the same corner of the portrait, only blown up. Notice the blood stain?"

"Looks like some kind of writing."

"A very ancient form of writing...considered nonexistent in our times, and indicative of the native tribes of Haiti, Jamaica, and possibly the Bahamas. Right now, I'm not certain which. It may be a mixture of each, but I've no doubt this particular form of writing dates at least two thousand years."

"Whew!" Wesneski exclaimed. "This gets more confusing by the minute."

"You said it," Conklin agreed.

Recalling what Stone had told him about the **Kaluti**, Wesneski suddenly realized he might have been a bit judgmental in declaring the entertainer's unusual discourse as fiction. After he had studied the blowup a little more closely he asked, "Have you been able to decipher it?"

"Yes. The word is **kotaii**. What it means exactly escapes me, but I'm working on it. I do have some knowledge of ancient island languages, but not enough to give an accurate translation. I'm convinced, though, it refers to some form of tribal assassination." A pause. "When my learned colleague from the Smithsonian completes his research, we'll know for sure."

"Forgive me, doctor, if I think you're a little crazy," Conklin said moodily, "but the Braithwaites have nothing in common with ancient island tribes."

"You're wrong," Harvey Wesneski announced, and briefed Bob Conklin and Dr. Thomas on what he had learned from Kevi Stone. Before he had concluded his report, the Floral Park detective was looking at him as if he were measuring him for a very large straight jacket. The young FBI agent, however, at least seemed entertained by his story.

"If what Stone has told you is true, maybe he knows what **kotaii** means," Mike suggested.

"There's only one way to find out," Harvey replied, offering an endearing smile. "Let's ask him."

CHAPTER FIFTEEN

Kevi had just finished packing and was waiting for Ricky's arrival when his phone began to ring. Because a few of his female fans had recently gotten his private number, and because he hadn't had time to implement a change, he decided not to answer it. It didn't really matter. With the phone's next ring, it was set for two, his answering machine would click on automatically. No message would be heard on either end. Only a beep. If the caller didn't begin his message within the next five seconds, the machine would immediately disconnect, and set up for the next call.

"Mr. Stone," a gritty voice began, "Lt. Wesneski. Please call me at your earliest..."

Picking up the phone quickly, Kevi reset the machine. If Harvey was calling there might be news about Nellie. "Stone..."

"Kevi?"

"Yeah Harvey, what's up?"

"Hold on a sec, Kevi. I wanna put you on the speaker." After a few annoying squawks Harvey said, "Can you hear me all right?"

Kevi abhorred conference calls. He always felt like he was talking to someone in a cave. "I hear you fine," he replied frustratingly.

"Kevi, with me is Lt. Conklin of the Floral Park police, and Dr. Thomas from the FBI crime labs. We've uncovered some unusual evidence in the last few hours, and it's our hope you might help us understand it."

"I'll do whatever I can."

"I was hoping you'd say that." Harvey paused for a moment. "What can you tell us about the word **kotaii**?"

Kevi's mind was instantly thrown into a maelstrom. More accurately, the very fabric of his sanity unraveled a thread at a time once he realized a horrible truth that few knew.

"Hello?" from Harvey.

Although a reply had formed in Kevi's mind, the words remained locked in his throat.

"Stone, are you there?"

"Who told you of **kotaii**?" Kevi Stone asked finally.

"It was written in blood on one of the paintings within the Braithwaite home," Harvey replied. "You know what it means?"

"It's a number," Stone said fearfully.

"A number?" Wesneski repeated, his disappointment evident. He had hoped for something more. What exactly, he didn't know.

"Yes. It is a promise of death from the **Kaluti**. It means **three** shall die." Stone choked on his next few words. "Nellie's in danger Harvey...the worst kind."

"I think we should get together as soon as possible," Wesneski said quite frankly.

"There's nothing I'd like better, considering the danger that Nellie faces. Unfortunately, the earliest I can meet with you will be some time next week."

The detective erupted. "Next week?"

"Yes," Stone said disappointedly, "my band and I are hosting an international AIDS benefit in Sidney, Australia. You might have read about it in the Times."

"Yeah, now that you mention it, I do remember hearing about it. But can't you postpone it or something?"

"I wish I could, but not only am I contractually bound to this engagement, the President of the United States, who will also be there, has personally requested my presence. I believe he intends on giving my band a citation, or something."

"I see" was all Harvey could say.

Kevi could sense the detective's frustration. He wasn't alone. But there was nothing else he could do. "Harvey, I don't know what measures you've taken in Nellie's behalf, but I'd double them, triple them if you have to. The **Kaluti** won't rest until she meets the same fate as her husband and son...in the same manner."

"We'll do that, don't worry. You just hurry back. Something tells me we're gonna need your help."

A knock on Kevi's front door made him turn. An instant later, Ricky Caldwell and his wife, Lia entered, both displaying similar hurried expressions on their faces, each encumbered with a considerable assortment of luggage. "Harvey, I gotta go," Kevi said quickly.

"Wait a second," the detective said, "there's something else we need to know."

After Harvey Wesneski explained what both labs had ascertained he asked the entertainer if he knew of any device capable of creating similar conditions in the Braithwaite home. Indicating that he didn't Stone said, "If you wish to reach me, fax me, or call me on my cellular phone."

"Have a safe trip then," Wesneski told him, "and hurry back."

*****

"We've just received our clearance to take off," the pilot announced over the plane's speaker system.

As Kevi prepared himself for departure, he discovered he was unable to get comfortable in the luxurious aircraft. Any other time he would have enjoyed traveling in his band's customized Lear jet. This was not one of those times. Comfort, at least for the moment, was the farthest thing from his mind. The news he received from Harvey couldn't have been worse. After all these years, the **Kaluti** were back to torment him once more.

Suddenly, Kevi realized why he had disclosed those things about the Braithwaites that night in his studio. Some inner sixth sense he hadn't known he possessed, or some dormant precognitive ability must have awakened him to the dangers that lay ahead, and not just for him. For someone he'd forgotten he'd even cared about.

Almost certainly, the deaths of Leon Braithwaite and his son, and the warning promising Nellie's death could mean only one thing. A grievous error had been made by someone in Braithwiate family, and it was quite possible the entire brood was marked for death.

Kevi could care less about the evil minister, his wife, and Leo. Or even the boy. If Lexington was anything like his father, he deserved to die. Nellie, however, was quite innocent, and had been forced into the Braithwaite's evil family long ago. There was no reason she should be made to suffer, and she wouldn't if he had anything to do with it. "Damn their black hides," he growled aloud. The **Kaluti** were an unforgiving people and wasn't he just like them? No. One of them, yes. **Not** like them. But just as vindictive if provoked, and just as cruel. Looking through the small port hole window at his right, Kevi Stone carefully studied his reflection. Surprisingly, his grim features reflecting back at him served a purpose. "So be it," he muttered to himself, "the war begins anew."

Across the gulf of time, the race that had spawned him was challenging him once more, promising death. Unafraid, one thought lingered in his mind. Anyone even remotely responsible for hurting Nellie would die. Even if it took the rest of his life to find them.

*****

As suggested, Conklin assigned a dozen additional men to the Harper home. **No one** could get in or out without his verbal authorization and in addition to the Swat team, a canine corps patrolled the grounds. To many of his peers, Conklin's measures might have seemed like overkill, but considering whose home his troops had seized, and the importance of the occupants within, he decided he'd rather be safe than sorry. As long as Nellie remained within the Harper's home, the Congressman and his wife would be provided with an armed police escort wherever they went. If there was even the slightest possibility the decedent's killers would try to use them to get to the widow, Conklin wanted it covered.

While Dr. Thomas awaited Stone's return, she called upon her various resources and those of her colleagues in search of all data referring to the **Kaluti**. Wesneski and Conklin decided to take a more direct approach. They visited the decedent's immediate family.

"I hate sounding like a detective from an old "NYPD" rerun," Harvey began, "and I'm sure you've already been asked this more than once, but just for the record, can you think of any enemies your son might have had?"

The retired evangelist's eyes twinkled at the corners. "Enemies, Lieutenant? Imagine if you will, that you are an outspoken minister and politician, a successful businessman, a champion of civil, political, and human rights issues, you wield more power, more influence than most government officials, **and** the fact that you've attained such status in spite of being a black man from the ghetto...don't you think **you'd** have enemies?"

"I see your point," the detective replied, "but I was hoping you could be a little more specific."

The elderly minister looked towards his wife and son. They both shook their heads. "I'm sorry, Lieutenant, but it would be impossible to think of any **one** individual. My son's enemies were many, and from many walks of life."

Harvey had expected such an answer. He had heard a similar reply from the minister's daughter-in-law. "Then, if you don't mind, sir, I would like to ask your son a question?"

"What is it, Lieutenant?"

Harvey stared fixedly into Leo's empty blue-grey eyes. "I know that there has been enmity between you and your brother, and that it's existed since you were children. Some of your feuds have become public record, I might add," he said, studying the twin's impassive features, "but that's not important."

"Really? What is?"

"How you did it?"

Puzzled, the twin asked, "How I did what?"

"Murder your brother," Harvey stated as-a-matter-of-factly.

While Harvey ignored the choking sound that had just come from his right, his intense brown eyes studied the reactions of the three individuals facing him.

The minister's face went slack for an instant, while his wife's expression remained unchanged.

Leo's poker face, however, formed a grin. "Me?" he replied without missing a beat. "Kill my brother? Tell me, Lieutenant, how did you ever arrive at such an amusing, obtuse conclusion?"

"Please forgive my colleague for his over-zealousness and insensitive methods," Conklin sputtered quickly, wiping his forehead nervously, realizing only then he hadn't a handkerchief. "I assure you that Lt. Wesneski's intentions were not to offend anyone, and that he was only making an awkward attempt in finding the truth."

"Lt. Conklin's absolutely right," Harvey said humbly. "I am sorry. But in search of truth there are moments when I **must** employ crude methods. Again, I apologize, and I beg your forgiveness for my insensitivity as well as my appalling bad manners."

When Leo's mother spoke her tone was icy. "What did you expect to gain from such infantile trickery?"

"Well, ma'am," Wesneski said slowly, "by your reactions, I hoped to discover if there was motive enough for your son to murder his brother."

"What about my husband and myself, Lieutenant? If you suspect our son, why not us? Aren't we equally suspicious?"

"I hadn't ruled you out either," Wesneski said evenly.

"That's enough," Conklin vociferated, his blue eyes aflame. "We're conducting an investigation, **not** an inquisition. It's not our job to make accusations that have no basis of fact." Rising from his chair, Bob took Harvey by the arm and forcibly led him from the living room. After a few harsh words between them, Harvey stormed out the front door. "My apologies to each of you," Conklin replied sincerely, his brow covered with sweat. "Please understand, Lt. Wesneski's only interest is discovering those responsible for your son's, and grandson's murder. You see, in his experience the most unlikely suspects often turn out to be the most probable ones. If you've been offended in any way, I do apologize."

"That's little consolation for his accusatory behavior," the minister's wife said coldly.

"You're right, ma'am, but please try to see it from Wesneski's viewpoint. When there are **no** suspects, everyone becomes suspect, which must include the unlikely ones. And if you think about it, he's exactly the kind of cop you'd want on your side. Oh, he's cold and callous, but he's also objective and diligent and his persistence is without equal. Harvey'll bend over backwards to get the job done. To him, murder is the most heinous and cowardly of all crimes, and he takes it very personal when **any** citizen is deprived of his right to live." Conklin paused a moment before sitting down. "Now, if you don't mind I have a few more questions, then I promise to leave you alone."

"All right, Lieutenant," the minister's wife said tightly, "proceed."

Conklin swallowed hard before saying, "We've uncovered some unusual evidence that leads us to believe your son may have been a victim of a ritual slaying."

"It is no less than what we've already suspected," the elderly minister replied, getting to his feet and moving behind his wife's chair. As he placed a gentle hand upon his wife's shoulder he added, "The way our son met his death can only mean that our progenitor's past have finally caught up with us."

"Then it's true?" Conklin asked. "About the **Kaluti,** I mean. They exist?"

The minister raised an eyebrow. "I assure you they exist, young man. They are a formidable force to be reckoned with. If you knew of them as we do..."

"Forgive me, sir," Conklin said scoffingly, "but even if I believe in the existence of this tribe, or cult, or whatever they are, I've a problem in believing in the voodoo tales associated with them."

The minister's face displayed a vague smile. "Spoken like a professional policeman," he said. "One day soon, Lieutenant, I think you're going to learn there are things in Heaven, Hell, and earth that you are incapable of understanding, and quite helpless in dealing with. I believe in the abilities of the **Kaluti** because I have no choice. My father used to frighten me with the tales, as you say, of my ancestors when I was a child. Later, I discovered they weren't tales at all. They were, in fact, the reason my grandparents came to this country. It was their hope they might escape the bonds of their pagan heritage, and for many years our fears were at rest. Until, that is, when my son became obsessed with our progeny. In the past twenty years, he has made several trips to the Caribbean islands, always against our wishes. What he did there we don't know, but with each trip, he returned a different person."

"Different?" Conklin asked. "In what way?"

"Just different," the minister replied without elaborating.

Conklin had dealt with religious fanatics before, and some were demon worshipers or Satanists that believed they possessed supernatural powers. That he could handle. His only fears were of how far the cultists would go in the name of their perverse gods. "What then can you tell me of these **Kaluti**?" he asked. "I'd appreciate any help you can give me. We believe your daughter-in-law is in serious danger."

"Nellie isn't the only one in danger," Leo said abruptly.

"Pardon me?"

"Anyone who stands in their way, anyone who attempts to prevent them from carrying out their vendetta, and **anyone** who interferes in their affairs will also be eliminated."

"That's crazy," Conklin exclaimed.

"Exactly," the minister's wife confirmed. "I assure you the **Kaluti** will stop at nothing. My family is endangered the moment they discover we've aided you. And **you**, Lieutenant, your fat, fatuous friend outside, and your families are also subject to their vengeance."

"I think you'd better explain," Conklin said grimly.

*****

"Well, what do you think?" Wesneski asked.

"About what?"

"The Addams family back there."

"What's wrong with them?"

"They're ooky and they're creepy..."

Conklin chuckled. "Isn't that supposed to be the other way around?"

"Whatever..."

Conklin chuckled again. "I admit they're a little eccentric..."

"Eccentric my big, fat behind," Wesneski snarled. "They give me the piles, **and** they're damned evasive."

"What did you expect with your belligerent line of questioning? As far as I'm concerned they reacted appropriately. And next time, give me some idea when you want to play 'good cop, bad cop'."

"I wasn't playing."

Conklin said nothing at first. When he did, he replied in an even tone, "I would have expected more professionalism from one with your record."

"You saying I was unprofessional?"

"Not only unprofessional, but tactless and offensive. Didn't you ever here of diplomacy?"

"Okay, okay, okay, I came on a little strong. But it rubs me the wrong way when people try to hide things. First the widow...now them."

"Well, if you've had a little more patience, you would've found out everything you wanted to know."

It had taken Conklin only a few moments to summarize everything he had learned from the minister and his wife, and though he had tried to hide it, Wesneski was visibly shaken by the seriousness in which his colleague spoke. A gut feeling told him the immediate future held things that didn't bode well for either of them. When the two officers returned to the Floral Park precinct to discuss the security arrangements for the Braithwaite funeral, Dr. Thomas was waiting for them in Conklin's office. After she showed them the information she compiled in their absence, Conklin shook his head several times in disbelief. Wesneski, on the other hand, was able to accept the data much easier. Most of it included the things Kevi Stone had told him earlier. Reading through the report a second time, Wesneski discovered that he was trembling. Conklin and

Dr. Thomas were similarly affected. For some reason, each of them had been overcome by an inexorable, strangely disquieting net of fear.

CHAPTER SIXTEEN

The citizens of New York City were outraged when they discovered the Braithwaite funeral wasn't going to be a public ceremony. Only a few close friends, business associates, political figures, and members of the press were invited. They were even more outraged, if that's possible, once they learned the ceremony would take place in New Jersey, instead of the state their renowned bureaucrat had served with distinction and honor. In reality, the announcement to the media was just a ploy; its purpose: to prevent the general public and the groupies that often haunt celebrity funerals from turning a tearful, solemn occasion for one of the city's beloved statesmen into a media circus. Unbeknownst to the general public, two services would take place, at the same time. One in Jersey. One in New York, both with the tearful presence of the bereaved family. Only, at one of the ceremonies the participants would be genuine.

Prior to his departure from New York City, Stone had instructed his attorneys to keep him apprised of all noteworthy events surrounding his former sweetheart and her family. He also instructed a private investigator, one that often worked with his attorneys, to ferret out any information concerning the forthcoming funeral. Should the P. I. be successful, he would forward his data to the contracted attorney(s), who would then forward theirs along via E-mail.

From Sidney, Stone used his personal computer to retrieve his messages from his desktop back in the states. It was easy. As long as the password was known and an active phone line was available, the Compaq sub-notebook's internal modem was capable of tapping into any network in the world. Because of the overseas exchange, it took a few extra minutes for his computer to make the call, but once the link was established, he cursored down the main menu to "E-mail", and struck the Enter key. The messages were listed in the order of their occurrence. Interested in only one, he highlighted the fifth message, and struck F2 to read.

Two days later, he was on a commercial plane heading for home.

*****

As soon as the "fasten seat belt" light went out, the cabin attendants prepared a light lunch for their passengers. Not particularly hungry, Kevi decided he'd rather have a Manhattan cocktail.

"Would you like anything else, Mr. Stone?" a honey sweet voice chimed.

The flight attendant was a breath taking brunette with light blue eyes peppered with flecks of jade and her smile was bright as the sun. What impressed Kevi most was her bubbly personality. It was genuine, not practiced. A native of Sidney, the lovely attendant had a deep, rich tan that would make George Hamilton envious. Giving her voluptuous figure careful consideration, Kevi also knew that should the attendant decide to delight the male voyeurs of the world by posing for Playboy, their sales would not only shoot through the roof, it would cause the reigning Playmate of the Year so much consternation, she would probably throw herself off the nearest and highest precipice. "I'll have another of the same," he replied with a smile.

While the attendant prepared his cocktail, Kevi's thoughts turned to his friends he had left behind in Sidney. As much as he wished to remain, the Braithwaite funeral was Thursday morning, and he wanted, no, he needed to be there even more. Because his band had concluded their contractual obligations earlier than expected, the remainder of their stay was more or less a holiday for them and their families. That's what bothered him. Johnny and Mama were there, and he hated leaving them. Months ago, the three of them had made plans to get in some deep sea fishing. Marlin. But that would have to wait for another time.

Her smile, demure, the lovely attendant handed Kevi his drink. "Thank you," he said, taking a sip, his tongue tingling at the taste. "Perfect."

"If there's anything else you need, don't hesitate to ask."

"I'll do that."

This was the last leg of Kevi's trip from Sidney to New York. In another two hours, he'd be home. Once he finished his drink, he settled back and closed his eyes. When he opened them again, his plane was docking at the Kennedy International Airport. Once he cleared customs, he rented a brand new Mercedes coupe for his drive to Long Island. With the early morning traffic, it would take more than an hour to reach the Floral Park Cemetery.

Upon arrival, Kevi surveyed the grounds, particularly the area where the ceremony would be held, but more importantly, for places of concealment.

By 09:30, the grounds keepers pulled up in an old, seventy-ish, olive green, worn out van. Arriving a few minutes after them, the police positioned at least a dozen officers at various places upon the grounds, Others gathered beneath the large canvas tent that would serve as a shelter for the guests, set up the padded wooden folding chairs, and ignited the huge industrial heaters that were placed in each corner. Stone doubted the heaters would do much good in the frigid morning air. The winds were already howling like a banshee and forcing the temperatures well below zero. A brief meeting ensued, followed by the policemen dispersing. Some to control ingress to the cemetery, the rest, to patrol the grounds.

Stone had been watching from a large snow-covered oak thirty or forty feet away from the massive tent. Confident he could observe the proceedings without being discovered, for his own reasons he wanted to be closer. To accomplish this, he would need a disguise. It was the three grounds keepers that gave him the idea. Of the trio, one African-American, the other two Hispanic, each wore a light, brownish green insulated snow suit, a woolen toboggan of the same color over their heads, and black rubber boots. Some fifty feet away stood the maintenance shack where their tools and foul weather gear were stored. Within it, Kevi hoped to find what he needed.

Silently, he dropped from the tree into the ankle deep snow, his ivory white three-piece suit blending in with the terrain. Using the larger head stones and monuments for cover, he sneaked to the east end of the cemetery towards the maintenance shack. Once inside, the cold fled from his body in an instant, and though he had spent the better part of two hours in the brutal temperatures without an overcoat, he was genuinely surprised by the sudden chill. As a rule, Kevi was immune to cold weather, and as for an overcoat he almost never wore one. His recent trip to the tropics was responsible. In either case, it would take little time for him to become re-acclimated to the harsh New York winters. After he had shaken the snow from his feet, he began to look for the foul weather gear the grounds keepers were wearing. None were in sight. Three lockers were open. Two others had padlocks upon them. Hopefully, what he needed would be in one of them. If not, he'd have to settle for playing Tarzan again, and hopefully regain the perch he had recently vacated.

Starting with the locker to his left, Kevi took its padlock in his hand and gave the cool metal a gentle squeeze. Snap! The lock crumbled like a month old cookie between powerful fingers. He peered inside.

Bingo!

Everything he needed was there. As quickly as he was able, Kevi stepped into the insulated coveralls, tucked his expensive garments neatly inside, and zipped it up. Sitting on the bench, he hastily donned the black, rubber snap-up boots, and pulled them over his shoes. From the top of the locker he removed a thick woolen ski mask, pulled it over his head, and tucked his long black hair inside. The cracked mirror hanging above the smelly, rust-stained sink caught his eye. His disguise was complete. None of his features were distinguishable. The only problem he could foresee would be if some astute individual discovered an additional man was on the grounds. If such a thing should happen, he was prepared to pretend he was a new worker called in at the last minute to help out. It might work. It might not. It was a risk he was willing to take.

Donning a pair of thick work gloves, Kevi grabbed a shovel and returned to the elements. Luckily, everyone around him was so busy with their assignments, no one paid him the slightest attention. Moving away from the others, while the three grounds keepers maintained the temporary shelter, he cleared an area near the dark green tarp that laid across the huge gaping hole that would serve as the eternal resting place for the decedents.

In less than an hour, the guests began to arrive. With each minute that had passed, limos of every type rolled onto the snowy cemetery grounds.

Judging from what Kevi had overheard while working next to the large canvas tent, Nellie and her in-laws were en route.

As the arctic-like gale continued to increase, most of the guests huddled themselves in small groups around the heaters. Uncomfortable for everyone, it was the photographers that grumbled the most. The morning air was so frigid, their efforts to defog their camera lenses became increasingly frustrating, and as the wind grew even more intense their muttering became even more voluminous.

Suddenly, an angel white double-stretch limo rolled into view, its duplicate trailing a car length behind it. In unison, the driver and patrolman from the first vehicle exited and opened each of the passenger doors.

His mouth suddenly dry, an ache in his chest, Kevi Stone's heart skipped a beat the instant a pair of long shapely legs stepped from the shining limousine. First one leg, then, the other. There was no mistaking that body. It belonged to Nellie Bryson-Braithwaite. Smiling excitedly, in a single glance Kevi's keen eyes took in every detail of the breathtaking beauty he had once loved. Still a vision, she was wearing a thin black veil that hung from her charcoal mink hat, and a long black mink coat which fell an inch or so above her knees. Suspended from her shoulders was an elegant Louis Vuitton bag, compact enough for the barest essentials, make-up and things of that nature, while minuscule star shaped sequins decorated her high heeled ankle boots and stockings, both of which sparkled like jewels in the early morning light.

The other passengers exiting Nellie's elongated vehicle Kevi recalled seeing on television--Congressman Harper, and his wife, a former Senator.

A sudden gust of wind blew Nellie Braithwaite's veil upward. Kevi Stone had only a glimpse, but he could plainly see the pain and anguish in her walnut-colored eyes. Deftly, she reached for her veil and pulled it down upon her face before being escorted to the small assemblage waiting below.

Kevi's heart pounded as his childhood sweetheart approached. Fidgeting, he could feel his sweat trickling down the small of his back, his sweat glands going into maximum overdrive as she drew closer.

Then, as if stricken with a sudden seizure, Nellie stopped. Noting the surprise in her eyes, Kevi, at first, thought he had been discovered, but discounted it immediately. Just in case, he became a statue. Even his eyes didn't move. A slight yelp slipped through Nellie's lips. Those nearest her were so startled by her sudden outburst they searched for the cause. The widow yelped again, and pointed, her entire body shaking uncontrollably. Realizing that his disguise had been penetrated, Kevi removed his mask. That same instant, Nellie fainted.

In making a desperate attempt to catch her, Kevi was completely unaware that he had inadvertently knocked the Congressman and his wife to the ground and because of Mrs. Harper's fearful cry and the hateful invectives from Nellie's in-laws as they emerged from their limo, he was besieged by policemen from every direction.

Even with Nellie in his arms, Kevi moved like a whirlwind. The four officers closest to him were knocked senseless the moment they came within reach. Six more assembled to attack. Striking with lightning rapidity and sledge hammer force, he evaded their every blow while delivering one of his own. In just a few seconds nearly a dozen bodies littered the ground.

His every sense alert, out of the corner of an eye, Kevi noticed an officer going for his revolver, but before the weapon could clear its holster a shot rang out. Although the report was muffled somewhat by the scores of frightened screams, the second shot, shockingly louder than the first, was the catalyst that had transformed a group of fearful mourners into a panic-stricken mob.

With weapon drawn, Harvey Wesneski was the first to reached his side. "I thought you were in Australia," he said tightly, his brown eyes aflame.

Before Kevi could reply, Nellie's father-in-law poked a jeweled forefinger forcefully into the Manhattan police officer's chest. "I want Stone arrested immediately," he said acidly. "He is not welcome here."

"This is your fault, Conklin," the minister's wife shrieked. "You incompetent bastard. You were supposed to prevent this from happening. Remove this man from these premises at once."

While the minister and his wife berated the two police officers with their caustic tongues, Kevi attempted to awaken his childhood sweetheart. Shaking her didn't help. Nor did slapping her lightly. Kneeling, he filled his hand with snow and placed the icy crystals lightly against her cheek. A frightened look appeared in Nellie's eyes almost immediately, but disappeared the instant she saw his smiling face. "Hello," Kevi said softly, his voice melodious, comforting. "It's been a long time."

Tearfully, Nellie reached around his neck and sobbed into his shoulder. "Oh honey," she cried, "thank you. Thank you for coming."

With the exception of Conklin, the majority of the guests were interested in the violent oboloquy from the decedent's parents. Even the ever-vigilant Wesneski failed to notice the scene that was developing. "Nellie, dear," the Floral Park police officer said purposely loud, "you should have told us Mr. Stone was invited to this ceremony."

All heads twisted suddenly in the widow's direction. Kevi had just put her down, but she continued to hold onto him firmly. Observing the bodies littering the snowy earth, the frightened faces of her guests, and the harsh stares of the policemen assigned to protect her, it didn't take long for Nellie to realize what had happened. "I-I'm sorry, Bob," she said shakily. "I meant to tell you a few days ago."

Conklin knew that she was lying. It's what he hoped she do. No one would dare dispute her word. And for the moment, he and Wesneski were off the hook. But this put Nellie's in-laws in an unenviable position. They also knew she was lying, and glared at her intensely. It did them little good.

With Kevi Stone at her side, Nellie Braithwaite would not be intimidated.

As soon as the photographers realized the danger was over, they developed a professional interest in the proceedings, and flashed their bulbs incessantly. This not only angered the police, but the bereaved family as well. As a result, their cameras were confiscated and the film within them exposed. Outraged, the photographers threatened to sue, at which point, each of them received a warning. If they failed to behave accordingly, they would be physically escorted from the premises, detained until the services were over, with a promise that one of their competitors would sit in their place. That quieted them in a hurry.

Once the injured policemen had been attended to, and some semblance of order was attained, the ceremony began. As expected, the Braithwaite's patriarch delivered the eulogy without a single trace of the anger he exhibited moments before. In seconds, the gifted preacher had the entire assemblage in tears with his impassioned, solemn, somber oration.

*****

Sitting alone with Nellie, Kevi asked her how she'd been able to recognize him so easily.

"Your eyes," she told him with a confident smile. "I recognize everyone by their eyes. Yours, I could never forget."

Kevi wasn't at all surprised. He had a similar gift. As soon as the Harper's approached, he politely excused himself, removed the foul weather gear he borrowed, and headed for the other side of the tent where Conklin, Wesneski, and another officer appeared to be in conference.

"You know," Conklin said, "after seeing Stone take out nearly a dozen of my best men, I'm almost ready to believe in this **Kaluti** business."

"I know what you mean," Wesneski agreed. "Some of the best bouts I've ever seen were with fighters like Ali, Foreman, Leonard, Duran, Benitez, Hearns, Chavez, Hagler, and Tyson. None of them possesses Stone's abilities. Hell, he's better'n all of em, and he's got to be at least forty years old."

"Forty seven," Kevi said helpfully. When the three officers turned, Harvey exhibited an amiable grin. His was the only friendly face. Conklin and the other detective scowled deliberately. "My apologies, gentlemen. If I'd known my presence would cause this much trouble, I wouldn't have come."

"No problem," Harvey replied, meaning it.

Conklin exploded. "No problem? Are you nuts? Ten of my men are in need of hospitalization because of Stone's unwelcome intrusion."

"Unwelcome?" Kevi flashed and innocent smile, and handed Conklin a small white envelope. "Intrusion? I don't think so."

"What's this?"

"My invitation."

Conklin's eyes thinned to a razor's edge. "Don't get flippant, you bastard. You're in enough trouble."

Kevi's smile widened. "See for yourself."

Angrily, Conklin tore open the envelope and read from the four by five card. Before handing it to Harvey, Conklin's face gave the color purple a couple of new shades.

"She was telling the truth," Harvey Wesneski said, surprised.

Kevi Stone nodded. The invitation was indeed genuine. No post mark was on the stamped envelope because Nellie had not made up her mind to mail it. For days she had kept it in her purse, and had given it to him just a few minutes ago.

"I still have a good mind to run you in for disturbing the peace," Conklin said coldly, "and assaulting my officers."

"Give me a break," Stone retorted, not meaning to sound insulting.

"That did it," Conklin said, reaching behind his back. "I've had enough of your crap." And in a blink of an eye, his cuffs were securely on the entertainer's wrists.

Realizing his mistake, Stone didn't bother to resist. He had caused enough trouble and didn't wish to cause anymore. But trouble of a different kind was already heading in their direction. Conklin hadn't noticed it yet.

Wesneski did. "Uh, Bob," he whispered in Conklin's ear, "if I were you, I'd let him go."

Conklin blew his stack. "Are you crazy? Because of your Mr. Stone here, I have to explain how my men were injured, possibly answer several complaints I'm certain that will be lodged against the department, not to mention the bad press we're sure to receive." A snort. "The **last** thing I'm gonna do is let him go."

Wesneski sighed. He knew exactly how Conklin felt. In his shoes, he'd probably feel the same. Forcing his colleague to turn around, Wesneski pointed towards Nellie who was heading their way. "Well then, Bobby, old buddy, I guess I'm going to get to see what happens when an immovable object such as yourself, meets an irresistible force...meaning **her**."

Conklin swallowed hard.

Nellie didn't notice the handcuffs at first, but when she did she said, "Bob dear, why is my guest being treated like a common criminal?"

Conklin opened the top button of his shirt and loosened his tie. Even in the cold morning air, he was beginning to sweat. "I beg your pardon, ma'am, but Mr. Stone has managed to disrupt this ceremony as well as injure several of my men in the performance of their duties. He will be detained and brought up on charges."

When Nellie smiled, her perfect white teeth gleamed brighter than the snow. "Don't be silly," she said pleasantly. "Release Kevi at once."

"Can't do that, ma'am."

Nellie's smile turned colder than an arctic wind and when she spoke, her tone was just as icy. "Listen, Lieutenant," she said with the emphasis on the Loo, "we've been friends for a number of years, and I'd hate to see that friendship end over something as silly as this. But if you don't release Mr. Stone this instant, all the influence of the press," she turned and pointed in their direction, "and all the influence my husband's constituency can muster will be brought to bear on you and your precious department, and that will only be the beginning. Once my attorneys get through with you, a job as a dog catcher will be a step up from where you'll be. Do I make myself clear?"

Conklin hoped no one would notice but his bottom lip quivered slightly.

"And Bob," Harvey added, unable to resist a prod, "the Braithwaites are personal friends of your boss, the chief of police. And this being an election year, I don't think he'd appreciate it if they discontinued their support. That's not all. Mr. Stone's wealth is in excess of a hundred million dollars, and his political friends include the Mayor, the Governor, and more recently, the President of the United States. Finally, his attorneys make the Braithwaite's look like Romper Room graduates. No offense ma'am."

Nellie giggled. "None taken."

Conklin was not only a good cop, he was a smart one too. He knew when the cards were stacked against him. "My apologies ma'am," he said, capitulating. "And my apologies to you, sir," he said to Stone.

A warm smile returned to Nellie's face.

"No apologies are necessary, Lieutenant," Kevi said sincerely.

"Come, Mr. Stone," Nellie said, reaching for his arm. "You and I have much to talk about."

"Lieutenant," Stone said, holding his hands outward, "I believe you'll be wanting these back." Tugging lightly, he snapped the center link as easily as if he had broken a single strand of thread. Then, with a slight twist of his wrist, he tore the cold metal bound around his right arm in two. After he had done the same with the other cuff, he tossed the torn pieces of metal into the Floral Park detective's shaking hands.

"Sheesh!," Conklin sputtered, astonished.

"You can say that again." Harvey said.

Conklin obliged.

*****

The snow had begun to bluster a little, the temperatures hadn't improved at all, and most of the guests were preparing to leave until a black and gold Jeep Cherokee skidded to the side of the road. A moment later, a tall ebony figure emerged from the glistening snow-covered four wheeler.

Leo.

The reporters and photographers were the first to reach him. All of them asked the same questions. Where had he been? What could have been so important to keep him from his brother's funeral? Ignoring them completely, the handsome twin headed straight for his parents.

Stone was genuinely surprised he hadn't noticed Leo's absence before. With all that had happened, it completely slipped his mind. Judging by the mob close on the twin's heels, he was not alone. His curiosity aroused, Steve took Nellie by the hand and started towards the growing gathering.

The widow resisted. Seeing her husband's twin was not what she needed right now. It would only remind her of the man and boy she had just buried. Realizing that fact, and wanting to kick himself, Kevi gave her a reassuring smile as her brother-in-law approached.

"My deepest sympathies," Leo said, kissing Nellie lightly on the cheek.

Nellie shuddered, almost violently. It might have been the brisk wind that had suddenly come up that caused her to react in such a fashion, but Kevi doubted it.

Leo extended his hand. "Good to see you, Stone," he said politely, his countertenor voice both melodic and pleasant. "It's been many years."

"Sixteen, to be exact," Kevi recalled."The last time we ran into each other was at the Soul Train awards in Hollywood."

"I believe you're right," the twin reflected.

"Was your trip successful?," his mother asked.

"Trip?," Conklin said.

"It's the reason I'm late," Leo explained.

"You picked a helluva time to take a trip," Wesneski said, venom in his voice, his glare, wintry.

"It was necessary. I've just returned from the Caribbean with two people who are probably more knowledgeable about the **Kaluti** than anyone else in the world. With their help, we might discover those responsible for my brother's and nephew's death. Otherwise," Leo paused to return Harvey's frigid glare, "nothing else would have kept me from being here."

"I'd like very much to meet your friends," Conklin said, regarding his portly, Manhattan colleague. Something was bugging him. Whatever it was, it had to do with the twin.

"That was my intention, Lieutenant," Leo stated, taking a business card from his wallet, handing it to the Floral Park police officer. "Would tomorrow noon be convenient?"

"It would," Conklin replied, sticking the card into his coat pocket.

"Uh, would you mind if I tagged along?," Kevi asked.

"W-Why should I mind?," Leo replied hesitantly, pulling his collar up around his neck as if to ward off the chilling wind.

Kevi knew that it wasn't the cold that bothered Leo because he had already sensed the fear he was trying to hide. At first he didn't understand why the twin was afraid, but then it struck him.

Unable to ignore Stone's penetrating glare, a bead of sweat appeared at Braithwaite's temple. With a quick and casual move from a gloved hand, he wiped it away.

"I'm tired of being alone," Nellie announced suddenly. "Kevi, honey, if you don't mind, you can be my escort."

"That's not a good idea," Harvey said pointedly. "Until we get things sorted out, I think you should remain under cover. Under police protection."

"I agree," Conklin acknowledged.

"I'm going," Nellie argued, taking her former beau brazenly by the arm, her tone leaving no room for further debate.

"Will you also be in attendance?," the minister's wife asked Harvey, her smile vague, mysterious, even taunting.

"Ma'am," the portly detective replied with a wry smile, "I wouldn't miss it for the world.

CHAPTER SEVENTEEN

"The view is breathtaking," Mike Thomas said with genuine fascination. "Simply breathtaking."

"That it is," Bob Conklin agreed. "Looks like something out of "Lifestyles," doesn't it?"

"Bet it costs a pretty penny," the criminologist posed.

"In the millions," the detective assured her.

While Harvey Wesneski remained in their vehicle smoking a cigarette, Conklin and Thomas took a moment to admire Leo Braithwaite's elegant home. Standing alone in the quiet valley of Cherrywood, in spring and summer the beautiful mansion would be surrounded by a growth of greenery consisting of oak and the more predominant cherry trees. Presently, a blanket of snow covered the rolling hills and glistened as far as the eye could see.

An imaginative architect; either a little crazy, or possibly ahead of his time, was the designer of the odd, but beautiful habitat. Right angles were nonexistent in the energy efficient home, and there was as much glass as wood and brick. Even the driveway was unusual. Viewed from the top of Leo Lane, where Conklin and Thomas were standing, it appeared as if some gigantic feminine hand had written a beautiful looping "L" in the earth.

When Leo answered his door, he was dressed in a colorful smoking jacket, fire engine red silk pajamas with slippers to match, a burnt orange scarf about his neck, and a sash the same color tied around his waist. Mike was impressed. Everything she had heard about the twin from Bob and Harvey were in startling contrast to the man that stood before her. Ruggedly handsome, the famed gospel singer was the epitome of graciousness and charm.

While Harvey and Conklin waited in their host's tea room, Leo took Mike on a tour of his beautiful home. "Would you like to see my bedroom?".

"I'd be delighted," Mike purred, not at all surprised by her host's flirtatious behavior. From the moment she walked through his front door, she could feel his eyes undressing her. Thomas didn't mind. Truth to tell, she was quite flattered by her host's attentions, particularly since he was considered one of the most eligible bachelors in the country.

As soon as they returned, Conklin scowled at Dr. Thomas's school girl silliness and resented Leo for being so damned charming. Harvey's expressions for the moment seemed contemplative.

"While we're waiting for the others, would anyone care for some refreshment?," Leo asked politely.

Mike sniffed the air. "I'll have some of that wonderful tea you're brewing," she said pleasantly.

"It'll be my pleasure," the twin replied with a slight bow.

Conklin grimaced. "Nothing for me."

"What about you, Lt. Wesneski?" Then, as an afterthought Leo asked, "Would you mind terribly if I call you Harvey?"

His true feelings effectively concealed behind his warm, almost humble expression, Harvey wanted to say, "Hell No!" In his friendliest tone, he somehow managed, "You may. Mind if I smoke?"

"Not at all." Leo handed the detective an ashtray from the mantel over the unlit fireplace. "Often enough, I find myself having a taste for tobacco. As a matter of fact, I have some excellent French cigarettes you might like."

"No, thank you," Harvey said politely. "I've tried imported cigarettes before. Never could get used to them."

When the doorbell rang, an angelic theme filled the room.

"Isn't that Steal Away?," the beautiful criminologist asked. "If I'm not mistaken...a Norman Luboff rendition?"

"Very good, Michael," Leo said, impressed. The theme was more than thirty years old--at least six or seven years older than Dr. Thomas. "It appears my friends have arrived."

A minute or so later, Harvey's eyes nearly popped from his head when Leo's guests were ushered into the elegant living room. Both men were so dark, their eyes and teeth seemed to float on the air. The bigger of the two was so incredibly emaciated he looked two hundred years old if he was a day.

Dressed in a cream colored suit that was in startling contrast to his ebony skin, his Medusa-like dreadlocks were blacker than coal and looked as if they would spring to life at any moment. The whites of his eyes were a blazing blood red and his pupils were completely dilated. And yet, despite his startling appearance, Dr. Elizondo Pothiz, was considered one of the foremost parapsychologists in the world, in addition to being a noted archaeologist, paleontologist, and eminent authority of island cultures and religions.

The moment Harvey clasped the aged professor's hand, he imagined himself in the grip of a man recently risen from the grave, and one glimpse into the Jamaican's cadaverous eyes sent a chill racing up his spine.

The other man, an inch or so shorter than six and a half feet, was called "Mourla." No last name. It seemed a title of sorts. "Mourla" was considerably younger than Dr. Pothiz, that's if you can call a man in his eighties considerably younger. He was dressed in an elegant dark blue double breasted pin striped suit. His smooth features and athletic figure gave him the impression of a man that knew his way around women. By any standard, or in any culture the octogenarian would almost assuredly be considered a handsome man.

While Leo prepared some tea and Espresso Cappuccino for his guests, his parents had called and expressed their apologies. The funeral had been too much for them to bear, and both were too distressed to meet with anyone, but both felt confident their son could handle things in their absence.

The Harpers also called. Nellie and Kevi would be arriving soon.

Born inquisitive, and recognizing an opportunity of a lifetime, Mike was unable to wait for the other guests. "Dr. Pothiz, I once thought my knowledge was extensive concerning tribal religions, cults, and customs. I was wrong. The **Kaluti** are an interesting subject of which I...of which we know little about. Would you care to enlighten us?"

"Certainly, uh, uh Miss..."

"Thomas," she said helpfully.

"Yes, Miss Thomas," the scholar said, pursing his lips. "I don't believe anyone living today really knows their true origin. With the exception of their bible, record keeping was not a practice of the primitive tribe. Because of their warring natures, the Haitian, Jamaican, and Cuban factions have nearly succeeded in annihilating one another. Even today, they remain the fiercest of enemies. The only difference is their number." Dr. Pothiz paused to sip his Espresso. "I must admit, though, it is most surprising to find they've migrated beyond their homeland. Surprising indeed."

"Pardon me for interrupting Dr. Pothiz, but what Conklin and I would like to know is if the widow is in danger or not, and if so, how do we **find** the murderous bastards before they manage to kill her."

"Patience, Lt. Wesneski," the doctor said, placing a gnarled, vascular hand into a jacket pocket, "patience." Slowly, he removed an old, worn, dark brown leather tobacco pouch that was rolled tightly and held closed with a thick rubber band. The instant it was opened the bitter sweet smell of marijuana filled the room. Taking a pack of rolling papers from another pocket, he tore off a single sheet. With just one hand, he nimbly rolled a long torpedo shaped joint, lit it, and inhaled the smoke deep into his lungs.

"I hope you know," Conklin announced, "what you're smoking is illegal in this country."

Dr. Pothiz offered a confident smile. "I have glaucoma. Are you planning to challenge my legal right to possess this drug?"

Conklin shrugged.

The doctor took another long toke, held the smoke in his lungs for about thirty to forty seconds, exhaled it, and handed the joint to "Mourla."

"Does your colleague have glaucoma too?" Harvey Wesneski wanted to know.

"No," Pothiz replied with deliberate frankness. "He just likes to get high."

Mike giggled.

Giggling also, Leo went to the central air controls in the middle of the room and turned on the fans. An efficient system, in less than a minute the thick, pungent odor disappeared through hidden vents.

"You have every right to be concerned," Dr. Pothiz continued. "The evidence found in the Braithwaite home is unquestionably a death threat, and the widow is most definitely in danger. As for finding those responsible," he said placing the roach on the tray beside him, "you must look for what the **Kaluti** refer to as **koth fura**."

"A what?," Mike asked.

"Not a "what" Miss Thomas. A who. Today we would call a **koth fura** a person with pyrokinetic abilities. Do you understand the implications?"

"I do, but I find it difficult to believe," she said, her eyes popping.

"Well, don't keep the rest of us in the dark," Conklin said testily. "I don't know what either of ' em is."

"It's the ability to cause fires or extreme heat," Mike explained, "but the incendiary device is the mind."

Conklin's mouth hung open. "Are you trying to say the person were looking for is someone who can cause a fire just by thinking about it?"

"That's precisely what she's saying," the elderly scholar related.

"That's preposterous," Wesneski exclaimed. "People simply cannot do the things you describe."

"Mourla!!!"

Everyone jumped at once. Seemingly on its own, the unlit fireplace erupted into a fury of flames, producing unbelievable heat. From nothingness the flames appeared, and burned each of the freshly cut logs into cinders in the space of a few heartbeats.

Pothiz offered a slight smile. "You were saying?" Not a single word was uttered. All eyes remained locked on the fireplace. "Though 'Mourla's' pyrokinetic abilities are considerable", Pothiz continued, "they pale in comparison to the individual you seek."

Harvey Wesneski's flesh began to crawl. Feeling another chill at his spine, to calm himself, he lit a second cigarette and puffed on it furiously.

"What in hell is that smell?," Conklin mused, his nose wrinkling.

"Brimstone," Mike answered knowingly, removing a plastic pouch and some smears to wipe the blackened ashes. "It's not even hot anymore. Amazing," she said, "simply amazing." Once she had taken several different samples, she placed them carefully within a plastic pouch and tucked them carefully in her bag.

"What in hell are we up against?," Conklin asked, fighting to control his twitching body.

"A killer, or killers who exhibit various paranormal abilities. And fanatics. The worst kind. Fear is not a part of their vocabulary. The **Kaluti** will embrace death itself to serve their demon god. They are unbelievably cunning, and ruthless beyond imagination. That gentlemen...and miss, is what you're up against."

"Sheesh," Conklin muttered.

"Knock it off, Bob," Wesneski said angrily. "This is no time for jokes."

"Who's joking?"

CHAPTER EIGHTEEN

Hours before Kevi had gone to pick up Nellie from the Harper mansion, he was informed by one of Conklin's men that other arrangements had been made. He would **not** be escorting Nellie. Neither surprised or bothered by the change in plans, his only concern was that she remained safe.

A road block was the first obstacle he encountered approaching Crenshaw Circle. After he had properly identified himself, he learned only the citizenry living within the Harper's block were allowed access to the adjoining streets. If you didn't have a legitimate reason for being in the area, you didn't get in. That's all there was to it. Luckily, Conklin had verbally authorized him inside the perimeter. Without such authorization he would have been politely turned away.

Pulling into the Harper's driveway, Kevi counted at least thirty armed policemen moving about the premises. Some with attack dogs. Impressed by the police's ostentatious display of armaments, he believed the huge mansion was nearly as impregnable as Fort Knox. As long as Nellie and the Harpers remained inside, their safety was assured.

The designated transport vehicle essentially became Kevi's rental car. Conklin and Wesneski decided earlier against using a police vehicle because it would draw attention they wanted to avoid. The two escorts assigned to drive Kevi and Nellie were dressed in nondescript clothing and wore nothing that could associate them with being police officers. The only exception would be the automatic weapons they hid beneath their heavy winter clothing.

The trip to Cherrywood went without incident until one of the police officers announced, "I think we've picked up a tail." After his associate looked into his mirror, the sound of metal against metal clicking in the front seat echoed loudly in the car's interior. "Let's not get hasty," the driver stated grimly. "We don't want to take out innocent civilians."

Kevi whispered into Nellie's ear. At the first sign of trouble she would get down on the floor and should it become necessary to leave the vehicle in a hurry, it would be with him carrying her.

"Whoever it is, they're playing it safe," the driver said, "keeping out of range."

"Doesn't matter," the other officer intoned. "We've sufficient firepower to withstand any attack, at least until reinforcements arrive."

"I don't know if you can see' em," Kevi said, "but their car has stopped at the top of the hill."

"I see 'em," the driver noted.

Kevi's Mercedes had just reached the "L" shaped driveway when something told him to take another look back. What he saw made him think he had taken leave of his senses. "Get outta the car," he screamed, his powerful shoulder knocking the door completely off its hinges. With Nellie in his arms, he leaped into the foot deep snow at the roadside. Before he could take another breath, a meteor about the size of a medicine ball struck the rear end of the car he and Nellie had just exited. Exploding on impact, the vehicle was completely obliterated.

Neither of Conklin's men had time to get clear.

Out in the open as they were, Kevi assessed their vulnerability. They had to get inside. He only hoped Leo's home would provide them adequate shelter.

A single glance filled him with doubt.

Nellie's screams filled the air. Another meteor was on its way. A second later, Leo's huge front window was disintegrated completely and his living room became a torrent of flames. Nellie screamed again. A meteor, much larger than the others was hurtling towards them. Just missing them, the blazing object whooshed into a grove of snow-covered cherry trees incinerating them as if they were dry kindling.

While Kevi raced towards the house with Nellie in his arms, a door had opened. In it stood Harvey. His face was filled with shock and fear. "Get back," Kevi screeched. Whether Harvey heard him or not, the startled detective complied. Feeling the intense heat at his back, Kevi knew that he had less than a second to act. The difference between safety or a horrifying death was thirty-five feet. Gripping Nellie tightly, he marshaled his great strength and leaped the entire distance through Leo's paneless front window.

An explosion occurred. The fireball meant for Kevi and Nellie disintegrated Leo's massive Colonial front door completely.

Inside the burning structure, Braithwaite, Conklin, and Thomas were clutching the walls in fear, all afraid to move. Howling in agony, Wesneski rushed towards the horrified trio, his coat sleeve aflame. Shedding the expensive garment, he joined the others in a tight corner.

Before Stone's feet had touched the living room floor, his sharp eyes peered through the smoke and flames and picked out Wesneski's stout form racing into a shallow cul-de-sac. Others were with him. Dodging the flames, leaping over the burning furniture, he carried Nellie in their direction.

Baaarrrooommmm!!!

Another explosion rocked the house.

In the seconds that followed, a series of fireballs blasted through two walls perpendicular to the other before landing in Leo's pool, turning a foot of snow and ice into a growing cloud of vapor.

A woman screamed.

As Kevi turned, two elderly gentlemen he assumed were Leo's guests had just stepped from around a corner. "Get down," he shrieked. Once more his warning had come too late. Another ball of death hurtled through the open window, burned the two men to a crisp, and knocked out a portion of the wall before settling in Leo's backyard. "It's not safe here," he choked, a horrible stench burning his lungs. Through the gaping holes the fireballs created, Kevi's alert eyes noticed a concrete work shed forty yards or so away running parallel to a half frozen pond. This would have to suffice as their refuge. "Everyone outside," he commanded. "Get to the rear of that shed. If need be, immerse yourself in the pond." Nobody moved. "Dammit, Harvey," he shouted, striking the detective across the face just hard enough to get his attention, "move your ass!"

Pushing Conklin ahead of him, Wesneski and Leo ran like death was on their heels. As a matter of fact, it was.

Shifting Nellie beneath one arm and the screaming blond under the other, Kevi jumped through the gaping hole with the both of them, and just in time. A trio of fireballs had just come through what was left of Leo's roof.

Baaarrrooommmm!!!

That was the death knell to Leo's home. The entire structure had been destroyed.

"Watch the women," Kevi ordered, racing up the hill.

"Where in hell do you think you're going?," Harvey shouted.

Consumed with rage, Kevi moved like a cheetah around the burning debris, and headed up the winding lane towards the two men standing on the rise. Meandering his way out of the path of several bowling ball-sized meteors, he poured on more speed. Frantically, the two men above him piled into their car. Wheels spun, kicking snow and dirt in every direction. But the car wouldn't move. With a grim smile, Kevi promised two deaths for the four innocent dead that burned with Leo's home.

Fifty feet to go.

The car's passenger side door opened suddenly. Moving quickly, a heavy set black man jumped out, ran to the rear of the vehicle, and began to push. Fishtailing from left to right, the wheels spun in the snow before finally grabbing concrete. A moment later, the vehicle was tearing away at breakneck speed, dragging the fat man who had been able hang onto its bumper.

"Noooooo!!!," Kevi screamed, leaping into the air, missing the portly black man by inches.

Scarcely touching the ground, he was on his feet again racing after the speeding vehicle. Grabbing a smooth football-sized rock lying on the roadside, in one swift motion he through it with all the strength his powerful limbs could muster. Like a guided missile the rock careened towards the car, destroying its rear window, striking its driver in the neck and shoulder. The car swerved suddenly, several times, in fact, before ramming headlong into a telephone pole.

The man that had been dragged had never known fear before. Not until today. Today he had looked death squarely in the eye. The one who had dove for him would have killed him with his bare hands if he had gotten the chance. What speed. What strength. He had never seen the like.

But the heavy set man was strong too. Not nearly as strong as the one that pursued him, but strong enough to dig his fingers into the fiberglass bumper and to hold on, even when the car had crashed. Ignoring his innumerable aches and pains, he looked upward, realizing he had been whipped under his automobile. As he peered between his feet, he saw the fiery eyes of the demon that continued to give chase. Squeezing his considerable bulk from beneath the automobile, the portly man tore open the door and got behind the wheel. If his master willed it, he would die this day. His brother, also, who was already near death. Judging by the blood that was seeping through his comrade's clothing, the rock that was thrown must have broken his shoulder, and quite possibly, his neck. Through his mirror, the heavy set black man continued to watch his pursuer racing towards him. Suddenly, he realized that fear was an excellent motivator. Because of fear, he willed the car to start, got it in gear, and had it on the road an instant before death could reach him.

Kevi Stone bellowed out his rage as the vehicle sped off. As if in answer to his cry, a half dozen fire engines, policemen, and ambulances raced past him, lights flashing and sirens blaring. To the astonishment of the fireman riding the rear of the hook and ladder, an extra passenger rode with him towards the conflagration below.

There were no serious injuries among the survivors. Just a few bumps, scrapes, and minor burns. Dr. Thomas suffered the worst. Shock mostly, brought on by fright. Seconds after her collapse she was rushed to the hospital. She would be ok.

"I'm sorry about your two men," Stone had told Conklin. "My warning came too late. I barely managed to get Nellie and myself clear."

Conklin remained silent. He had said nothing since the death of his two officers. For long moments he stared sullenly into space as if the world around him had ceased to exist.

"He doesn't blame you," Wesneski said. "Bob was particularly close to the two men he had assigned to drive you. Both were married to his two sisters."

"Where's Leo?," Nellie wondered. No one could remember seeing the twin since everyone had fled towards the shed. "Coward," she hissed.

"He's got some serious explaining to do," Conklin said coldly, his dull eyes indicating sorrow and rage.

"That he does," said Stone.

"Don't worry," Wesneski replied grimly, "we'll find him. And when we do..."

PART THREE

BIRTH OF A CONSPIRACY

CHAPTER NINETEEN

While Leo watched from the woods his eyes bulged wide with horror. He had never seen such destruction. What had taken more than a year to build was destroyed in minutes. A full score of firemen tried desperately to save the elegant dwelling he had hastily vacated, but they were pitted against forces beyond their experience; the same forces that filled his heart with terror.

It might have seemed a cowardly act, running like he did, but the truth of the matter was that he had hoped to lead his enemies away from the others. Even so, no matter how fast or how far he ran, it was impossible to outrace his fears. The dread he felt was so inescapable it hovered over every moment of his flight, and because he was left with no other choice, his eyes wary for even the unlikliest of dangers, he continued to run, doggedly, guardedly, fearfully.

Suddenly, though, he had nowhere else to go. Weary from wandering aimlessly, his grueling trek had ended fifteen hours later in front of a Manhattan precinct.

"Now, why would I come here?," he asked himself.

A fair question. What would prompt any man to travel so far, on foot no less, through back alleys and dark streets, risking death from exposure? Leo could only assume that in a state of panic and distress his subconscious mind had taken him to the one place where he knew he'd be safe.

The moment he entered the precinct building, half frozen, bruised, bleeding through burned and tattered clothing, he took one look at the coffee vending machine just inside the door, searched for a coin--none were in the pajamas he was still wearing--turned to beg assistance from an officer exiting the building, and collapsed in the middle of the yellowing tile floor before uttering a single word. Barely cognizant of those huddled around him, he told a fantastic tale to the desk Sergeant who felt compelled to lock him up, at least until such time he received both medical and psychiatric care.

Despite Leo's disheveled appearance the Sergeant recognized him as the brother of the minister recently murdered, and after he had been deposited in an empty cell, a call was placed to the Long Island precinct for confirmation of his story. What the desk Sergeant learned chilled his blood. Realizing then that his frightened guest wasn't as loony as he first thought, the veteran police officer moved the twin to the most inaccessible cell in the station, at which point he placed a guard at his door and put the entire precinct on station alert. Absolutely no one would be allowed near the prisoner. Until his superiors arrived, Leo would remain in the protective custody of the Manhattan police.

Every time Leo Braithwaite closed his eyes, his nightmare would pick up where it had left off. Dr. Pothiz, "Mourla," and the two policemen were dead. That fact was unavoidable. In his dreams, however, they rose again and again from their burning ashes only to die once more. He could actually smell their flesh as it was being burned from their bodies. An even more horrifying sensation was that he actually felt scalded by the intense heat that had turned their bloody, internal organs into a steamy mush, and he reeled from the sickening scent of their deaths. He could even see them standing as they were hours ago, each being consumed by the hell-spawned conflagration, each pointing their fingers in accusation. They had good reason. The four men might be alive today if they hadn't gotten involved in his family's problems.

Lying upon his back, his arms covering his head, Leo rocked himself restlessly. No matter what he tried, respite continued to elude him. Biting back the pain, a powerful ache pounded his brain. His arduous trek from Long Island to Manhattan had taken its toll. Every muscle, organ, and nerve ending in his body throbbed with agony.

But there are worse things than pain. Guilt is one of them. Much more absolute than any physical experience, Leo's guilt fed upon his soul like a starving cancer, eating his life away little by little.

Desperately, he tried to flood his mind with images of better times. But none would come. Finally, he gave up. If he couldn't expunge his guilt, he'd have to learn to live with it. It didn't matter in either case. He felt certain his death was inevitable, and that his fearful flight had done nothing but postpone it.

Even if his mind hadn't been in such total chaos, Leo doubted seriously he could rest in his damp, gloomy prison. How could anyone get comfortable on the soiled, smelly mattress he found himself lying upon, or get used to the horrid stink saturating the air?

Leo had just closed his eyes when something scurried across his face. Sitting up quickly, his senses alert, his shuddering beyond his control, he sought out his prison's unwelcome intruder. With the lighting as bleak as it was, he didn't spot it right away.

Suddenly, a three and one half inch insect darted across the cold cell floor, instinctively dodging this way and that. Leaping to his feet, Leo stomped at it several times before finally stepping upon its back. It was the largest water bug he had ever seen. Twisting his heel into the floor's crumbling concrete, a crunching noise echoed loudly throughout his cell. Sick to his stomach, an involuntary shiver rocked him the moment he realized the brownish-black insect wasn't dead. Disgustedly, he watched with unwavering interest as the huge waterbug crawled across the floor through the bars of his prison. Inch by inch it dragged itself, leaving a trail of its shiny guts in its wake.

At once, the guard in the hall noticed the crippled insect crawling towards the foul smelling water in the half-filled floor drain the moment it had reached his feet. Not at all repulsed, instead of stepping on the creature and giving it a merciful death, a spurt of hot, steamy tobacco juice spewed from his lips, covering the insect completely.

A wave of nausea rocked the twin as he watched the final death throes of the horrible insect swirling around and around in the clogged and smelly drain, amidst a graveyard of its brethren.

Beep! Beep! Beep! Beep!

His heartbeat pounding in his chest, Leo jumped in surprise as his watch's alarm signaled four AM in the empty silence. After he had removed the gaudy jewel from his wrist, he inspected it for damage. Even though the opaque crystal and solid gold band had been scorched by the fire, the time piece continued to function.

Four AM. For more than a decade, it had been his practice to rise at this hour, stretch aerobically for twenty minutes or more, run at least five miles, shower and shave, and breakfast on a bagel with either Philadelphia Cream Cheese or Musselman's Apple Butter as a topping. But that was a lifetime ago.

As Leo prepared his regimen, the sound of footsteps moving in haste reached his ears. Before the guard in the hall snapped to attention, his automatic rifle at the ready, he knew the echoing footfalls belonged to three determined individuals.

They had found him at last.

*****

"This is the one place I never expected to see you," Conklin said fiercely.

"For those who seek my death, it's the last place they will look," Leo replied calmly.

"You've got a lot of explaining to do," Wesneski growled, eyeing the twin closely.

"You're right, I do," Leo said halfheartedly, "As you can see, I'm completely at your disposal."

Stone said nothing. For the moment, he thought it best to observe.

Once the guard had unlocked Leo's cell door, the four men were escorted to a vacant interrogation room on the top floor of the precinct. Two armed guards remained outside the room the entire time.

"You led us here deliberately," Conklin accused. "Why?"

Picking up a pencil from the table, Leo fumbled with it for awhile before putting it down. "For the best of all reasons," he said candidly. "I feared for my life. In coming here I have secured myself a safe haven, and an environment more conducive to discussing our future plans."

"What plans are those?," Stone inquired interestedly.

"If you don't mind, before I get inundated with a bunch of pointless questions, I'd like to ask one or two myself. The first being...would anyone care to tell me what they know about Utopia?"

After Wesneski and Conklin had exchanged puzzled looks with one another, the Floral Park police officer said, "Utopia is an advocate of almost every environmental issue of concern today, i.e. the green house effect, the rapidly dissipating ozone layer, the protection of the earth's rain forests, its endangered species, and possibly a hundred other worldly issues. They've also been instrumental in providing food and shelter for the homeless all over the world, and their operations parallel and work in conjunction with the Green peace and the World Life organizations, but exceed them both in reputation as well as the scope of their operations."

"Succinct and eloquently put, Lieutenant Conklin, but that's not the answer I was looking for," Leo said. "Allow me to pose it a little differently. Has anyone heard anything **unusual** about Utopia recently?"

"There was a fire," Wesneski answered, "in Utopia's main headquarters. At the United Nation's building."

Conklin snapped his fingers loudly. "I remember now. It happened earlier this week. Arson was suspected."

"Oh, it **was** arson all right," the twin confirmed. "I should know. I'm the one responsible."

"You what?," Wesneski exclaimed, nearly leaping from his seat.

"I'm responsible for setting the fire in Utopia's headquarters," Leo reiterated.

"But why?," Conklin asked uncomprehendingly. "I've watched you and your brother nurture Utopia as if it were a suckling child. Why would you do such a thing?"

Leo picked up the pencil and tapped it repeatedly on the table before setting it down. "Because it has become possessed by evil, gentlemen," he said, forcing the lump from his throat, "the coldest, blackhearted, merciless evil that man can imagine."

"Why don't you get real?," Harvey said with disdain.

The twin's eyes turned wintry. "What is your problem?," he said angrily, leaping to his feet. "Since I've met you, I've endured your foul humor and your insinuating remarks. I've had about enough of it."

Wesneski had tried to rise but he was unable to move.

"Before things get out of hand," Kevi said, pressing firmly on Harvey's shoulders, his eyes sending a clear message for Leo to take his seat, "I suggest the two of you put your attitudes aside for the moment, and try to concentrate on the business at hand."

His anger cooled, Leo did as he was instructed. Harvey, on the other hand, had become even more incensed. Immobilized so easily by Kevi, his brown eyes burned intensely. The thick vein in his forehead pulsed noticeably. Leo was no longer the focus of his rage, which is exactly what Kevi wanted. Once Harvey realized this, he relented, and offered a reluctant smile. "You were saying," he said, as if nothing had happened.

"I was saying, my brainchild had been corrupted by an evil beyond imagination, and that the Utopia the world has known doesn't exist anymore. In the beginning, the organization I principally created was meant to be an instrument of hope for our world. Its fundamental aim was to solve the plight of the downtrodden, the sick, the homeless, in addition to preserving our planet's environment. In the past few months, though, possibly the past few years, it has gained a hidden agenda. On the surface, and to the world at large Utopia retains its saintly image as mankind's best hope for survival. But on the inside, it has become an organization bent on nothing less than its domination. It might surprise each of you, the person behind this hidden agenda, this new order if you will, was none other than my brother."

Wesneski and Conklin stared at one another. Looks of surprise were etched plainly on both their faces. Stone's features, however, remained apathetic.

"I see doubt in your eyes," Leo said in a tired voice. "It doesn't matter, because I have the proof."

"Okay, okay, okay," Harvey said impatiently, "for the sake of argument, say you're right. Who killed your brother? I can't prove it yet, but my instincts say it was you, and more than anyone else, you have the strongest motive."

"Motive yes," Leo admitted, "opportunity, no. I wasn't even in the city when my brother met his death, and that's something I can prove."

"You're gonna have to..."

"We've asked you before," Conklin interrupted, "can you think of anyone that would want your brother dead?"

"Only those that tried to kill each of us a few hours ago." A brief pause. "They're going to try again, you know, and not just for me. But for each of you. Your families too."

None had doubted Leo's words. Nor did this information spark any need for immediate concern. Kevi's folks and Harvey's wife were presently out of the country, and they would remain there until their safety was assured. Since the tragic deaths of Dr. Pothiz, "Mourla" and his two men, Conklin had taken the advice Leo's parents had given him. Somewhere in upstate New York his family was being watched over. Counting himself, only a handful of people knew their whereabouts.

"From what your parents told me," the Floral Park police officer recalled, "I gathered Leon was embracing the **Kaluti** faith. Why would they want to kill him?"

"Because," Leo ventured slowly, "my brother did the one thing that is unforgivable in our race."

"What's that?"

"He betrayed them." A brief pause. "Leon's biggest problem throughout his life was his megalomania. It stemmed from his childhood and continued to flourish as an adult, even to the point where he thought himself above our tribal elders. His plan was to overthrow the bonds of our pagan ritualistic religion and to reshape it into an image of his own...which inevitably sealed his fate, as well as those of his wife and son."

"I can't believe any of this crap," Conklin ranted unexpectedly, getting up from the table and shoving his chair aside. When he leaned over the table he put a stiff forefinger into Leo's chest. "You've done nothing but paint a picture of your brother as a mad, self-serving fanatic instead of the fine, upstanding humanitarian I've known personally for more than fifteen years. I refuse to listen anymore garbage maligning one of the most respected figures since Dr. King. Dammit Leo, I won't even hear it from you. I don't care if you **are** his brother."

"That's your prerogative, Lieutenant," the twin said dryly. "But tell me, if you can...who would know Leon better than those in his family?"

Reluctantly, Conklin reached for his chair and sat down in silence.

"So far all you've managed to do is explain something was wrong inside Utopia," Harvey declared, his voice harsh. "You haven't given us one shred of proof to substantiate your story."

Leo's features hardened. "I'm getting to it," he said firmly. "The explanation will have to suffice for the moment. The proof I'll show you later." Moving from the wooden table, he stood in front of the two-way mirror against the east wall and studied his face for a moment. "The day before my brother was killed we were to have lunch at "21's". While I was waiting for him in his office, his phone started to ring. As I've done often, I answered it, and was, in fact, writing down the message when a member of his staff came in. Because he assumed I was Leon, the man handed me one of our special courier envelopes. I didn't think anything of it at the time, but after I had hung up the phone, I noticed its return address. It was from Jamaica. I have to tell ya, I couldn't have been more alarmed. When I looked at the package more closely, the post mark and return address particularly, I could see that it came from our Caribbean branch."

"Forgive me," Conklin said, noticeably perplexed, "but I don't get the significance."

"Utopia has branches all over the world, Bob, but none in the Caribbean, and definitely none in Jamaica. Several years ago, there was talk of starting an office in the tropics in St. John, or St. Thomas, but we decided it wouldn't be economically advantageous so the whole idea was forgotten. At least, I had thought so. Imagine my surprise to discover differently. If there was an office in Jamaica, my brother not only had to know about it, he had to be responsible for putting it there. After I had made a few discreet calls I discovered no such address had ever existed. But that didn't alter the fact where the envelope had come from, or the fact that Utopia had something to do with it. I didn't know what was going on, but I intended to find out."

"So you opened it," Harvey concluded, uncrossing his cramped legs.

"Yes," Leo acknowledged tentatively. "I can honestly say, I almost wish I hadn't. Because of my curiosity, a frightening chain of events would follow, causing not only my brother's death, but the innocent deaths of others."

"What was in it?," Kevi asked curtly.

Leo's eyes widened a little. "A time table," he said trembling. "And yet, it's more than that. The contents of the envelope detailed a conspiracy in its last stages of implementation. In just two days, something so frightening, so shocking, is going to happen, it will irrevocably change our way of life forever. Two days, gentlemen. That's all the time we have. Two days to find a way to keep our country from being overthrown by an incredible power."

Leo paused briefly to look into the eyes of the trio facing him. "I don't blame you for not believing me," he said sadly. "At first, I didn't believe it myself. But after I read the documents over and over again, I realized the conspiracy was frighteningly real. Which brought me to my next problem. What was I to do, and who could I tell that would believe me? Who would ever believe that Utopia would be behind something so absolutely preposterous?" Another pause. "Your expressions are answer enough. Your conclusions: the same as mine. No one would believe it. As much as I wanted to confront my brother about it, I knew I couldn't. He'd only deny it. And with the stakes involved, I wasn't certain what he might do. So, I did the only thing I could. I committed arson, with the hopes that I could destroy some of the equipment crucial to the success of my brother's plan."

Leo released an uneasy sigh. "I know how all this sounds. You think I'm mad. Well, if I am, then so will you be...once you see what I've discovered."

"Where is it," Harvey asked skeptically, "this proof I mean?"

"Where it has always been," Leo declared boldly. "Utopia headquarters." Leo indicated the clock on the wall. "We haven't much time. If we don't stop my brother's followers now, come Monday morning a new order will be ensconced. If that happens, gentlemen, I fear it will be the beginning of the end."

CHAPTER TWENTY

"I saw you fight once at the Garden," Harvey said, turning his police car into the thick traffic on the Avenue of the America's. "I think it was the Golden Glove competitions, or something. Can't remember exactly."

"Golden Gloves," Kevi confirmed. "It's the only time I fought at the Garden, and the last time I put on the leathers."

"How come? You won the competition effortlessly, as I recall, and I remember reading a dozen promoters were interested in handling you at the time."

"True. But I had other reasons for not turning pro."

"Your musical career?"

"Not exactly."

The Manhattan Lieutenant raised an eyebrow. "Well, you've certainly got me curious."

"Remember the kid I fought?"

"Yeah. He was a cocky lad from my neck of the woods, Spanotti, Spagnotti, or something like that."

"Spagnoli," Kevi corrected, surprised that Harvey remembered him.

"That's right. Vincent Spagnoli. I even knew his family."

"Really? Well, it was because of Vincent Spagnoli I decided to hang up my gloves." The smoke from Harvey's last cigarette still lingered in the air, so Kevi rolled down his window a little. Turning in his seat, he faced Conklin and the twin who were sitting in the back. "Is this too much air on ya?"

Leo, who was sitting directly behind Harvey dressed in a borrowed police uniform two sizes too big, bundled up with a thick heavy coat secured from the Manhattan precinct's lost and found locker, shrugged absently.

Conklin, seemingly in another world, continued to stare out into space.

While Kevi cracked his window a little more, Harvey adjusted his rear view mirror to study the pair sitting behind him. "What about Vince?," he asked.

"If you recall, I knocked Spagnoli out early in the second round," Kevi picked up. "But it wasn't until the fight was over did I learn how badly he was hurt." A pause. "A few days later, Vince succumbed to the effects of our fight by blacking out and falling off a subway ramp. He was electrocuted."

Although Harvey didn't reply, his eyes reflected surprise.

"During his funeral, I overheard someone saying Vinces's last fight had given him continuous fainting spells which increased in frequency, and that it was his doctor's opinion the blows he received to the head were instrumental in ending his young life. I knew then that I'd never fight again."

"It wasn't your fault," Harvey reasoned.

"You're wrong," Kevi replied.

"You don't understand what I'm saying," the detective returned. "It wasn't **just** your fault, or **all** your fault, I should say. Like I told you, I remember that kid from way back. Vincey and his brothers were always in trouble with the law. I should know. I ran them in enough times. They were a large part of the crime element on my beat, having been involved in numerous robberies, extortion, and a couple gang wars. I can't count the times he and his brothers were put in the hospital from bricks, bats, bottles, and pipes up side the head. Almost every bone in their bodies was broken at one time or another."

"I can even remember when Vince started boxing for the Police Athletic League in Bushwick. Most of the times he had to box the same kids he tangled with on the streets, which meant if he won fairly inside the ring, he'd have to fight again once he stepped out of it. So you see, ever since Vince left the cradle he was in one fight after another. No Kevi, the blows that caused Spagnoli's death were cumulative and received over a period of years of fighting on the streets, and not his brief stint in the ring."

"That's what I kept telling myself, but it didn't make any difference. I met Vince only once, and liked him immediately. Even though he was grossly outmatched, he was a good sport and the gutsiest fighter I ever fought. I respected him. In spite of all the things I had heard about him, I knew in my soul he really wasn't a bad kid. He had too much heart and sense of fair play in the ring to be as rotten as people made him out to be. So, on the day Vince was laid to rest, I did the same with my gloves and my career, and I promised myself I'd never again contribute in the taking of another life."

"That's interesting," Harvey said thoughtfully. "A few hours ago, I'm almost certain I was going to see a perfect example of an eye for an eye."

Kevi didn't admit it, but he would have agreed. He most definitely had murder in his heart. The madness had come upon him so suddenly he was unable to resist it. The catalyst was the four innocent men that burned to death at Leo's home. Just the thought of them dying so needlessly, so horribly, filled him with a seething rage. "I no longer possess the naivete' or the compassion of my youth," he said, his voice cold, remote. "The stormy years of my life have made me so unforgiving, so unfeeling at times, I'm often frightened of what I might do should someone be foolish enough to anger me."

"Believe me," Harvey said, reaching for his cigarette case, "I know exactly how you feel."

"Do you? I wonder."

"I do," Harvey added vaguely, lighting another cigarette. "Remind me to tell you about it sometime."

*****

A few blocks from the United Nations building, the foursome found themselves caught in a traffic jam caused by a fender bender in front of the Hyatt Regency Hotel. But once Wesneski attached the flashing police light to the roof of his car and turned on his siren, a pathway was cleared.

Minutes later, the security guards admitted the four men into the UN building with little formality. Leading the way, Leo guided his guests towards the elevators that would take them to Utopia. Upon reaching the lowest level, they followed him to the large glass doors that was the main entrance to Utopia's headquarters. Though his keys and key card had been destroyed with his other belongings, the twin could still gain access by punching a series of digits into the nine digit card reader. Having done so, the doors to Utopia swung open automatically.

"Is Utopia the only business on this floor?", Wesneski inquired, realizing he knew little of the building's layout, in spite of the fact he was a native New Yorker.

"Business, yes," Leo said, pointing across the wide corridor, "but this level also houses the communications and satellite center, and the security force that patrols the entire building."

Kevi Stone was absolutely amazed by the damage. The fire had no mercy. A few months ago, he had read an article about Utopia's headquarters in an issue of Ebony magazine, but looking at them now, the once plush offices that had won accolades for being an exemplary work environment no longer existed.

"Most of the lights were destroyed by the fire," Leo stated, "so watch your step." A pause. "Before the fire, this was the Utopia most of the world was familiar with. Let me show you a Utopia that no one would believe."

Leo pointed at the thermostat on the wall. Standing to one side, he twisted the dial several times to the left and right, as if some invisible safe was behind it. After he had turned the dial to the left once more, a faint click could be heard. With the palm of his hand he pushed in its face plate, offered a grim smile, and moved aside. A gentle hum emanated throughout the room followed by the entire wall moving outward. In roughly ten to fifteen seconds the wall stopped moving at roughly a forty-five degree angle. A bright light beamed into the semi-darkness the four men were standing in.

"Gentlemen, **this** is Utopia..."

Inside the brightly lit room was a command center of sorts. Nearly twice the size of the outer office, it was filled with an array of elegant office furniture in addition to some very sophisticated electronic equipment.

Leo reached inside a large, beige filing cabinet that was standing in a corner and extracted several green and white binders from within its drawers, each bearing large italicized gold letters that read, Utopia, Project Alpha. "**This** is why my brother and nephew were killed," he stated, tossing the binders on the desk closest to him, "and why the **Kaluti** must be stopped."

Wesneski handed a folder to Conklin. Puzzled, both men perused its contents avidly. With each second that passed, their expressions changed from confusion, to astonishment, and finally to fear.

Studying the detectives' faces for a moment, Kevi wondered what could have caused such a myriad of emotions. That would have to wait. For the moment, his interests were elsewhere, particularly, the equipment that filled the room. None of it would ever work again. It looked as if it had met with an ax, or at least something as equally destructive. In spite of its damage, though, Kevi managed to ascertain its purpose. "This is what you were trying to destroy." A statement.

"Partly", Leo answered vaguely.

"What is it?" from Harvey.

"A very unique transmitting device," Kevi noted. "With these instruments, I'd say one could possibly jam, if not control every means of communication in our country; television, radio...everything."

"Not only that," Leo confirmed, "it can do it without detection."

"That's absurd," Bob Conklin interposed. "I have more than my share of advanced electronics experience in the Navy's nuclear program, on subs and on aircraft carriers, and I can assure you no such device exists. If it did, the military would have it."

"In the field of electronics, I am also considered an expert", Kevi Stone argued, his eyes studying the unusual contrivance, "particularly communications devices, so you'll forgive me if I should disagree."

Conklin moved next to Stone and bumped him deliberately. When he was unable to budge him, he gave the entertainer an intensely cold look. Ignoring him, Stone pointed to the wrecked equipment. As Conklin studied the console in front of him, his expressions changed several times. He had, in fact, become so shaken he was unaware the folder he was holding had been taken from his trembling hands. "H-How?" he muttered in astonishment. "How can this be?"

"With Utopia, all things are possible," Leo Braithwaite said grimly.

"This is amazing," Harvey Wesneski said, briefly scanning each page of the thick binder.

"It's more than amazing," the twin offered. "It's diabolical. With this neurotransmitter my brother planned to bounce a wave of alpha energy off an orbiting satellite, jam all of our country's communication signals, and with the alpha-adrenergic waves that are closely associated with our brain waves, he could project very subtle, yet completely undetectable subliminal messages over whatever communicative medium he desired. In essence, he would control the unsuspecting mind of everyone in this country."

"But where would he transmit from?," queried Harvey. "Wouldn't he need an extremely powerful antenna...or something?"

"Not especially, but if he wanted one..." Leo pointed upward.

"The roof?"

"The United Nation's building has one of the most powerful communication systems in the country. Because of that fact alone, I believe my brother intended to initiate his takeover from this very spot. Think of the irony and the colossal joke on the powers-that-be if he could to tap into the United Nation's communication system and subvert it to his purposes...here of all places. Imagine what a coup that would be for him. Just on the off chance there was a possibility of someone tracing the slight electromagnetic field and alpha energy emanating from here, do you think for one moment they'd ever suspect Utopia? And what are the chances they'd ever discover this anteroom?"

"What a mad plan," Wesneski breathed, "but would it work?"

"Oh, it would work all right."

"Fascinating. Mind control on an apocalyptic scale..."

"Wait a second," Stone interrupted. "Regardless what subliminal commands your brother managed to transmit, there's no way it would effect everyone."

"It wouldn't have to," Braithwaite agreed. "Think about it for a minute. If enough of the key people in our country are affected, meaning those the populace listens to each and every day, those who influence popular opinion, what would happen?"

"I see what you're getting at. If you control our leaders and the people who control the media, along with its various sources of communication, television, telephones, computer networks, such as the internet, satellites, and so on, you in effect control the world."

"Their ultimate goal," Leo imparted, his arms spread suggestively. "First America, and then..."

"Unbelievable," Kevi said, certain that this was the plan Leo's family had hatched nearly thirty years ago. In its infant stage then...now, after more than a quarter century, it had reached full maturity.

"It was a good thing you destroyed this equipment," Harvey stated.

"A wasted effort," Leo said with an angry scowl. "I'm almost certain my brother has redundant systems as backup in the event something happened to him."

Harvey scratched his head. "I don't follow."

"Leon's followers can still transmit whatever messages he made. And if you take a look at the manifest on the last page of that binder I gave you, I think you'll see at least three items are missing from this room."

Conklin snatched the folder from Stone's hands and checked the equipment against the list. Briefly, he delineated the particular uses of each of the items. "Destroying this equipment was indeed a waste of time," he assented. "The **missing** equipment is the key to the success of the **Kaluti's** plan. As long as it is in their possession, they can operate from anywhere in the city."

"If only I had discovered this room a day sooner," Leo said regrettably, "then we wouldn't be faced with this horrible dilemma. But I was too late...much too late."

"I thought I knew him," Conklin said to no one in particular, "but I was fooled, completely. The worst of it is, there isn't a man in this world I admired or respected more, and it hurts to know how much I considered him a friend."

"My brother has never had a friend in his life, Lieutenant, and to return one's friendship is something he's never learned to do."

"That doesn't help much," Conklin said somberly.

"Neither does being hard on yourself," Leo said sympathetically. "Listen Bob, my brother was closer to me than anyone in this world. But he had me fooled too. He had us all fooled."

"Tell me," Conklin said pleadingly, "I need to know. How could all of this have happened?"

"We haven't time. Every second we waste, my brother's followers get closer to accomplishing their goals."

"Dammit, I want to know," Conklin said fiercely, his eyes containing blue fire. "No one's moving from this spot until I get some answers."

When Harvey cleared his voice, Leo understood what was expected of him. "You won't believe me," he said acquiescently, staring into Conklin's flaming blue eyes, sitting atop one of the desks, "but then again you might. You've seen enough in the past few hours to realize what my brother's followers are capable of." Nervously, Leo popped his fingers on each hand, one at a time. When he was finished, he popped them all over again. "My parents have told you very little actually, not all of it the truth, and only what they felt you needed to know." Leo sighed. "You must understand, my family...we are not in the habit of confiding in outsiders, nor are we used to betrayal. But four innocent men have died, and millions more will follow if we fail." Leo sighed again. "What I'm about to tell you my parents would never admit even under pain of death, and this will be the first time one of our sect has ever disclosed such information to an outsider."

"Get to it," Conklin said impatiently.

The twin shrugged his shoulders before briefly relating his tale.

CHAPTER TWENTY ONE

Cameron, New Jersey --1963

Thirteen years ago, on Friday the thirteenth, in a hospital on Cameron's west side, the Braithwaite twins were born. Arriving first, Leon A. Braithwaite, a healthy baby boy of considerable size would have killed his mother if she had been a weaker woman. Even so, complications arose. Natural child birth for the second sibling was virtually impossible, and so, a decision was made. In order to save both mother and child, a caesarean was necessary. As it turned out, exactly thirteen minutes after his elder brother's arrival, Leo A. Braithwaite was cut from his mother's belly.

If the twins were a superstitious lot they might have appreciated the incredible twist of fate that bound them together. But these things were of little consequence to the Braithwaite siblings, and though today was their thirteenth birthday, it was after all just another day.

In most cultures, birthdays are usually a day to honor both young and old. In a **Kaluti** family things are quite different. Birthdays have no special significance at all. **Power** alone in its multifarious forms is the only achievement worth noting. Traditionally, once a **Kaluti** child enters their teens they are expected to accept the responsibilities of an adult, and to emulate their parents in every way. This was Leo's problem. Instead of having a birthday party with happy, young teens, dancing, laughing, and playing games he had only heard about, or viewed from afar, it was his misfortune to find himself locked in a battle of wills with the one person that truly despised him.

To say that Leon was cruel would have been an understatement. For most of his life, Leo had been tormented by his brother in one fashion or another. Today wasn't any different. And though they were physically equal, today's particular torture session took place in a different arena. The mind.

"You're a pathetic little weakling," Leon said spitefully.

"Just because I'm not as strong as you doesn't mean I'm a weakling," Leo grunted, pain coursing through his body.

"Really now?" Leon's face displayed a range of condemnatory expressions.

Leo scowled as best he could, but it was just a facade.

"Shall we begin anew?," his brother asked, his eyes containing a feral, strangely bestial glint.

Though he had expected the pain, Leo still screamed out in agony. Incredibly, his forearms had swelled to twice their size.

His brother chortled. "Now you look like Popeye." Pointing, Leon said, "Look!"

To Leo's complete horror, his deep, black skin had become as transparent as glass and his veins had become finger thick. But that was only a precursor to the real horror. Instead of blood being pumped through his arteries, there were snakes--hundreds, thousands, maybe even millions of them, swimming, racing, leaping about like spawning salmon. Leo knew then that he was being punished. His brother's ascension into manhood was not to be shared with anyone, least of all, a weakling child that barely made it into the world, and because it was with his parents blessing, he also knew that his punishment would continue until every manner of torture was extracted from his brother's evil brain.

There was only one way to react. Desperately.

Summoning every iota of his strength, Leo created the most terrifying image he could think of and shot it into his brother's vitals.

Caught off guard, Leon was unable to raise his mental shields in time, and while his body listed from left to right, pain became etched upon his face. "A valiant effort," he said, trying to control his twitching, "but you'll never be as powerful as I."

Leo understood that fact better than anyone. His brother was **one of the chosen**, foretold in the legends as the one called Defti Garugatu--the **Exalted One**.

"I heard screams," a husky baritone boomed suddenly. "Have you been instructing your brother as I ordered?"

"Yes, father," Leon answered obediently, shaking off the residual effects of his younger brother's powerful assault. "Leo's telepathic abilities are growing quickly," he said with a snort, "but will never equal mine."

"True," his mother replied, "but between you, we hope to create a force so formidable every **Kaluti**, irregardless of their ethnicity, will bow down and serve our manifold delights. Once we've united all the Carribean factions into one nation, the weakling outsiders throughout the world will fall before us as wheat does to a scythe."

"Come, Nora," the elderly minister ordered, "we shall allow them to continue."

"I Have to admit, you're improving," Leon said as soon as his parents closed the door, "particularly with your mind melding technique. But what can you do when an attack comes from another source...from outside the mind and body...at the core of your spirit?"

"Try me," Leo challenged, failing to hide his fear.

Leon reached beneath the bottom bunk bed and pulled out a thick black leather bound book belonging to their mother.

Leo was shocked. No one, not even their father had ever looked inside their mother's book of spells. It was forbidden for any male **Kaluti** to look into the **Kolakuu Kotorna**. "Are you crazy?," he sputtered. "Mother and father will flay you alive if they ever find out you've been messin' with that book."

"Who's gonna tell em'? You?"

"Of course not. You know I'd never do that."

"Shut up, then. The **Kolakuu Kotorna**," Leon sighed reverently, handling the ancient book with tender care, flipping through its torn and tattered pages. "In here lies the power to rule the world...if one has the strength and courage to use it, and believe me brother, I have both. Come, let me show you what I've learned."

Leon pointed to a passage in the middle of a brown-stained crumbling page. To read it, Leo had to lean over his brother's shoulder. That's when their faces touched. At first, he thought Leon was going to whisper an incantation into his ear, but once he felt the sharp sting of his brother's bite upon his left ear lobe, he realized he was in for something else. "Let me show you what true power is," he heard his twin sibling say before tumbling backward into an abyss so black he feared he might never see the light again.

Then came the pain. And it was exquisite.

"SSSSSSSSSSSssss!!! Who is it that calls on **Daagon?**"

Leo went stiff with terror. Towering above him was the incredible form of the two-headed snake that was his race's deity.

Daagon! Even his very name evoked fear.

Although the **Kaluti** had many gods, **Daagon** was their most powerful, and their most feared. To call on his unholy name meant to be eternally in his debt. To fail him meant to die horribly.

"SSSSSSSSSSSssss!!!"

As Leo leaned backwards, he tried to get some sense of the size of the leviathan standing over him. Even though most of the demon's body was coiled beneath him, **Daagon** reached at least fifty feet in height. A monstrous head bent suddenly to give him a curious look. A single blast from the demon's powerful nostrils sent him tumbling. While on his stomach, Leo looked upward. "Who calls on **Daagon**?," were the last words he heard before slipping into a void he truly believed was the prelude to death.

*****

"Wake up, damn you," Leon snarled, slapping his brother for the third time. "Wake up."

Catching the next blow just inches from his face, Leo opened his eyes slowly. Half expecting to see the face of **Daagon** standing over him, an even worse evil regarded him with interest.

Leon.

More than anything, Leo wanted to eradicate that contemptuous smirk from his brother's face. Forever. Unfortunately, his frightful experience with **Daagon** had sapped much of his strength.

"Looks as though you went and crapped yourself," Leon said laughing, pointing to his twin's crotch with one hand, holding his nose with the other.

Leo's mind was suddenly filled with hate. "You dirty son of a bitch," he croaked weakly, "I'm gonna getcha for that. You here me?"

With cool and steady eyes, Leon beamed a chilling smile at his younger brother. Rising slowly, he spat on him and walked from the room roaring with laughter.

Helpless, Leo could do nothing. Except wipe his brother's spittle from his face while lying in his own fetid waste.

*****

The day Leo Braithwaite met Olivia Leander, he knew that his life would never be the same. To his genuine amazement, the lovely New Englander stirred emotions inside him he had never felt before, or even thought possible. Unlike most boys his age, the younger twin knew what it meant to be sexually aroused by a beautiful girl. He and his brother were quite promiscuous. This wasn't like that at all. The feelings he had for Olivia had nothing to do with lust, and went beyond his basic animal desires.

"Love is for fools," his brother had often said with profound amusement.

Always, Leo had agreed. Until the day he met Olivia Leander. Every time he saw her, his emotions grew more and more strange. Though there were times he found himself delirious beyond belief, there were other moments when he was nearly crushed by his own depression. It seemed there was no other explanation. He was in love, and yes, he thought himself a fool. Still, once Leo accepted his unusual circumstance, a bigger problem arose. As much as he wanted, he had no one in which he could discuss these strange new feelings. He didn't dare tell his parents. The fact that they wouldn't understand didn't bother him half as much as what would happen to Olivia and her family should they find out. And yet, he needed to tell someone. Only because there was no one else, he foolishly divulged his innermost feelings with the one person he truly hated.

"So you think you're in love," his brother said scornfully. Leo nodded sheepishly. Leon's chiding laughter was no surprise. "You can't love, you idiot. Our people are incapable of such feelings."

"How come?"

Leon shrugged. "It's just the way it is. Look, have you ever seen mother and father kiss, hold hands, or do any of the things the outsiders do?" Leo shook his head slowly. "There you go," his brother said, as if that was an answer to everything. "If anyone would know about love in the **Kaluti** nation, don't you think it would be mother and father? Another thing, I've read the

Kolakuu Kotorna from cover to cover, and I've yet to see the word **love** mentioned even once."

"But that's just a book of spells and charms and stuff."

"Wrong, brother," Leon protested. "If you've taken the time to read mother's book as I have, you'd find it's more a bible than anything else."

"A bible?" Surprised, Leo found it difficult to believe that his parents would acknowledge a Christian symbol.

"Yes, dear brother...a bible that contains not only the spells and charms you've referred to, but a history of our people, our beliefs, and our traditions." Leon put his arm around his twin's shoulder in a genuine act of affection. "Traditional Anglo-saxon Americanized courtships or customs are not for us brother," he declared. "We are **Kaluti**. We take our mates by force of will. If necessary, by force of arms."

Leo felt crushed. He wanted Olivia Leander to **care** for him, **not** be compelled to obey him. He wanted her to come to him of her own free will, if there was such a thing, and to stand along side him as an equal, not as a subservient, submissive wench he would only use to satisfy his carnal desires. And though he tried to make his brother understand his new feelings, his efforts were in vain.

"You pitiful fool," Leon said disparagingly. "Has this girl given you any indication she's interested in you?"

"N-no," Leo said hesitantly. "I've asked her out several times, and though she's been nice enough, she's always declined."

"Hmmmm. Tomorrow at school, why don't you point her out to me?"

"Why? What do you have in mind?"

"Nothing. I just want to see the girl that could get your head so messed up, that's all."

During the first lunch period the following day, nearly every boy in the cafeteria had gathered around Olivia Leander's table. She was the new girl in town and every boy in school wanted to meet her, if for no other reason, to confirm that she was as beautiful as everyone said she was. Standing among them was Leo. As he elbowed his way through the mob of love-struck teens, he soon realized he would never get within arm's length of the statuesque beauty. A boy of average height, he was unable to see over the heads of the taller teens in front of him. In fact, he considered himself quite fortunate to even get a glimpse of her.

Dressed simply in a light blue cotton dress, pulled tight in the waist and flowing just below her knees, Leo sensed that every girl standing amongst the mob of boys would have killed to have Olivia Leander's figure. Seven times in as many minutes she had crossed and uncrossed her long shapely legs, neither wantonly or teasingly. It didn't matter. A series of muffled gasps from her male admirers could be heard whenever the event occurred. And each time the sun would touch her thickly braided ponytail, its rays were instantly reflected as if it had landed upon an elegant rope of black silk. She was tall for a girl, nearly seventy inches. Not particularly fond of girls that tall, Leo discovered he would gladly make an exception concerning Olivia Leander. Everything about her excited him. Her warm caramel skin, her dancing hazel eyes, her slightly crooked smile; each of these things stirred his blood so much, it caused his heart to thud loudly inside his chest. And her laughter - there was only one way to describe it -- cool, gentle, peaceful; much like a bubbling mountain brook on a quiet summer's eve.

A moment before his home room had been discharged for the day, Leo finally summoned his courage and asked Olivia if he and his brother could walk her home. Expecting a polite refusal, she surprised him by saying yes.

"How do you like our little town?," Leon asked.

"It's a lot different from Providence," Olivia said, "but there's a lot to like here, especially since everyone's been so nice."

"I think you'll find a lot of interesting people living here."

"I'm sure," Olivia said with a smile.

"Do you have a boyfriend yet? I've noticed that in just a short time you've become extremely popular."

Shocked by Leon's directness, Leo was about to admonish him when Olivia replied, "He's still in Providence, but'll be arriving this weekend for a visit."

"Really? Th..."

"Pardon?"

"Oh nothing, I was just thinking that Providence is such a long way to carry on a serious relationship."

"It is. But Geoffrey...that's his name, has already finished high school, and he's taken a job at the foundry here in Cameron. As a matter of fact, he starts week after next. Because he has family here, we can continue to see each other until I graduate." With a bright smile she announced, "We plan to be married right after."

Leo's heart crumbled into pieces. "It sounds like you're very much in love," he managed with a weak smile.

"Yes," Olivia purred softly. "I am."

A few blocks from Olivia's home, Leon suggested taking a short-cut across the railroad tracks and then through Simpson's field. In that moment, a series of signals rocked Leo's brain. Having experienced them before, he knew that danger lay ahead. This time, for someone other than himself.

Smiling innocently, the moment Olivia stepped into the dense waist high grasses Leon placed both of his hands firmly upon her breasts.

Stunned, shocked, even horrified, Olivia's mouth opened to scream, but nothing came out.

"No!," Leo shouted snatching his brother's hand away, pain cutting into his heart as fear appeared on his beloved's face..

"You stupid fool," Leon hissed, struggling. "You want her. Well, here she is. Take her."

"No!," Leo shouted again. "Not this way. Not like the others. Run Olivia! Run!"

Paralyzed with fear, only when the twins had almost knocked her to the ground did Olivia obey.

"Stop!," Leon ordered.

A single command and Leo could feel his brother's power pushing its way into his mind. Girding himself, with great effort he raised his shields and blocked Leon's assault. Olivia Leander wasn't nearly as fortunate. Spellbound as she was, she had stopped dead in her tracks. "Run Olivia!," the younger twin shouted, trying to aid her. Unfortunately, his psionic abilities were already being pushed to the limit. "For God's sake," he pleaded to his older brother. "Let her go. I don't want her anymore."

"Too damn bad," Leon growled, "I want her. And I'm gonna have her."

"Don't be too sure about that," Leo said savagely, finding new strength from some hidden inner reservoir.

As their struggle brought them both to their knees, neither gained the slightest advantage over the other. Leo however, had unfortunately misjudged his brother's superior mental powers.

"Strip!," Leon commanded.

"No, no, no," Leo begged, "don't do it Olivia, don't do it. For God's sake, run!"

"For **Daagon's** sake," Leon corrected. "Look!"

Completely unaware of their presence, Olivia Leander turned and began to unbutton her dress. In just a few seconds, her long slender neck and ample cleavage were naked in the warm afternoon sunlight.

Desperately, Leo dug in and increased his strength. But once Olivia's full erect caramel-colored breasts spilled free, he found himself crumbling helplessly beneath his brother's formidable power. In one quick motion the lovely New Englander stepped out of her white cotton panties. She was the loveliest thing Leo had ever seen. A caramel statue standing stark naked in a field of green.

Taking the advantage, Leon broke free of his younger brother's grip and with animal-like brutality he knocked him to the ground. Unable to move, Leo laid in the tall green grasses staring wistfully at Olivia's perfect body. A feeling of desire touched his heart. Deserting him immediately, it was replaced by a feeling of shame. Shame for having failed the only girl he had ever loved.

"She's a luscious bitch, isn't she?," Leon said hungrily, his eyes cold and unforgiving. "This is the **Kaluti** way brother. Don't ever forget that."

Too weak to move, Leo watched Leon undress. Naked in seconds, he commanded the lovely New Englander to lie on her back with legs spread wide. "Ahhh, we have a virgin, little brother," he panted, "an untouched flower."

As Leon achieved penetration, blood spilled from Olivia's womb, staining the grasses between her wide spread legs.

"Get offa her you slimy son of a bitch," Leo yelled, his blood boiling.

Totally consumed by his lust, Leon never heard him.

Forcing himself to his feet, Leo grabbed his brother by the neck, and cuffed him behind the ear. And he continued to pound him until the skin on both hands were raw with bruises. Then, like a thing of filth, he tossed his brother's unconscious body aside, shuddering in disgust as his evil seed spurt into the grass and dirt where he lay.

Now that his brother was incapacitated, Leo reached inside Olivia's mind and instructed her to get dressed. Although she obeyed, she was quite oblivious to everything that had happened to her. Soon, though, she would feel the pain of her violation. There was no power on earth that could prevent that. Gently, patiently, and with great care, Leo removed the entire day from her memory. For the remainder of her lifetime she would at least be spared the horror and humiliation of his brother's violent act.

Once Olivia had gone home, Leo stood over his brother's unconscious form. Glaring with hate, he kicked him several times in his side.

"Where is she?," the elder twin asked, rubbing his ribs.

Leo told him.

"That was an excellent piece of ass you missed little brother," Leon sneered, fondling himself.

Whatever self control Leo might have had before, he lost in that moment. Consumed by hate and a seething rage, he kicked Leon in the testicles as hard as he could, and once again in the rib cage. The force of the second blow was so powerful it turned his brother onto his side. Now that his back was facing him, Leo kicked him a third time, deliberately aiming the hard pointed toe of his boot for the crack of his brother's naked behind.

Leon howled as if he were a wild beast dying alone.

Looking at his brother, Leo recalled all of the innocent girls he and Leon had raped to slake their animal thirsts. Disgusted, he spit on his brother's bleeding rectum. **Kaluti** or not, he vowed never to dehumanize another human being in such a vile depraved manner.

Later, as he stood at the edge of Simpson's field, he could still hear his elder brother's roaring screams riding the warm gentle winds. Music to his ears, it reminded him of a somber tuba solo off in the distance. Even when he couldn't hear Leon's bellowing anymore, those mellifluous, sonorous tones echoed in his ears throughout the day.

CHAPTER TWENTY TWO

Brazen, arrogant, and exceeding in conceit, Leon openly defied all authority figures. Even his parents were unable to control his insatiable lust for power, or prevent his inevitable madness. In the final analysis, there was no need in pointing fingers. It was quite obvious they were to blame. Hadn't their youngest son warned them a thousand times? Indeed he had. And did they heed? They did not. "Jealousy does not become you," was their scornful reply. Leo could only shake his head with disappointment. His parents were in for a rude awakening, and it was not long in coming.

Throughout much of the gospel music industry, the twin's debut gospel recording was considered an undeniable success. Naturally, a recital was expected and because the Labor Day weekend was approaching, a concert was scheduled to take place in the new Union Hall in the sleepy little town of nearby Neptune. Since most churches celebrate their Holy Communion on this particular Sabbath, the twin's father and mother decided Communion services and concert should become a single ceremony. An incredible opportunity for the Braithwaite family, the minister and his wife were certain they could strengthen their influence over their flock already embracing their beliefs, and with the growing popularity of their sons' music, it was quite possible they could gather several new sheep along the way.

While it was the minister's practice to never show his emotions, with the exception of the religious ire he spouted during his services, for the first time in nearly a decade he let himself go. More than once during the service he felt compelled to share his feelings. For those that knew him, this was a most uncommon act. Even more uncommon, the minister expressed openly his love and pride in his family; particularly his twin boys.

As the program's end drew near, those assembled in the crowded hall waited anxiously for the twin's performance of their first release. Penned by Leon, "Come Unto Me" was one of the most inspirational songs Leo had the privilege of leading. More than any other, it highlighted his clear, flexible, counter tenor voice. After each verse, of which there were four, the scales would modulate a minor second interval, and with each change in key, the younger twin's pure falsetto would enthrall his eagerly enthusiastic audience. Leo had never been more moved. Unfortunately, those feelings were short-lived. They ended the moment his brother stepped to the mike a final time.

"Come unto to me and rest," Leon commanded, his eyes glistening as if he were high on dope. "Kofu cadin natu moro matu."

Before Leo was even aware of what his brother was doing, he was screaming at the top of his lungs.

Leon just smiled.

In a heartbeat, Leo assessed the situation. Horrified by his brother's bold stratagem, everything became crystal clear. For those that embraced their Christian faith, and truly believed in it, the speaking of tongues accompanied by a roaring wind has always symbolized the physical manifestation or presence of the Holy Spirit. This knowledge was crucial to Leon's mad scheme. Because the language in which he had spoken was unknown throughout most of the world, and because he planned to utilize the dark forces he had just called upon, Leo was certain his twin could duplicate the biblical experience.

Shaking like a junkie, Leon pointed towards the rear of the hall where a pair of heavy double doors had been left open. "Behold!," he said, raising his arms high. "The Holy Spirit is among us."

Out of nothingness, a heavy wind whipped through the crowded auditorium. Suddenly, three of the four heavy double doors slammed shut. Heads whipped around. Eyes widened in surprise. The winds intensified, and chilled the room. All eyes returned to the stage. Like a restless panther, Leon paced its hard wood floor. Stepping in front of the mike, he uttered another unintelligible phrase. Within the next heartbeat, the winds died as if they had never existed, and in its place, a fearful silence enveloped the once temperate auditory. A huge smirk upon his face, Leon studied the crowded assemblage. To each of the impoverished, hopeful, pitifully ignorant spectators, all would believe he had been anointed by a heavenly power.

From out of the wings, the minister and his wife rushed onto the stage. Quite purposefully, both struck their son a brutal blow across the face. But Leon would not be denied. Brushing his parents aside, he beckoned his subjects, "Come unto me, my children."

"No!," his father screamed coarsely. "Think of what you're doing."

"I know **exactly** what I'm doing," the elder twin declared, once again calling upon his dark power. "I'm going to show you, mother, everyone what it means to be Defti Garugatu."

Those that tried to resist Leon's demonic-enhanced powers were overcome just as easily as those that embraced it. In the seconds that followed, horrifying screams erupted, as though a great torment was being shared by all. None suffered more than the children. Left to their own devices, most of the infants were knocked aside, dropped, even trampled by their parents who had abandoned them.

Moving as one body, a mob of zombies pushed forward, each member ignoring the person in front, rear, or on either side. Leon Braithwaite became the only focus in their tormented lives. Those that had managed to touch his outstretched hands were shocked senseless, stunned by the dark force moving inside him. Those that had the misfortune of falling to the floor were trampled by the others still trying to reach him.

Helplessly, Leo and his parents watched in silence, powerless to do anything for the scores of tormented miscreants moving towards the stage.

"We are all of one mind, one heart, and one soul," Leon told his eager subjects. "Join me now, and we shall beckon the mighty one to hear our prayers."

Believing they would be standing in the presence of their Christian god, screams of joy echoed throughout the hall. They were wrong. Horribly wrong. Soon their minds would become filled with the image of **Daagon**, the dark horror. **Daagon**, the merciless. **Daagon**, the cruel.

"I can feel his presence, my children. But in order to join with him, we must bring him into this plane of existence." As hundreds of faces displayed their hopes and anticipation, Leo's heart wept for his brother's wretched subjects. Once they met **Daagon**, their lives would be forever lost.

"Join ye all in union my children," the elder twin commanded, "and share your life's seed with that of another, giving new life, as new life has been given you."

Selecting a coal-black, big breasted beauty from the front row, the elder twin yanked her onto the stage. Like a bitch in heat, the teen jumped into his arms. Their tongues met. Ripping the girl's dress with one hand, Leon snatched her bra and panties off with the other. Eagerly, the teen laid on her back spread-eagle, tearing at his belt until it opened. His pants at his knees, his erect organ swung free. Quickly, Leon filled the teen's young, squirming, hungry body with his own.

As if on cue, everyone tore at each other's clothing, and fell upon the floor in various forms of copulation. The more athletic tried their sexual congress standing against the wall, or in their chairs. Naked bodies were piled atop naked bodies. No one seemed to mind. Completely engrossed in their varied sexual pursuits, every type of incest and perversion was exhibited; brother with sister, mother with son, and father with daughter. Age and gender was unimportant.

Leo couldn't take anymore. This madness had to stop. But how? If his parents were powerless, what then could he do? Maybe nothing. Still, he had to try. As he struggled against the invisible restraints that held him, he was completely surprised when he was suddenly free. Gathering his strength quickly, he leaped through the air, only to be swatted away as if he were no more than a pesky fly. In agony, he rolled over onto his stomach, blood in his eyes from where his brother had struck him.

Bound once more an incredible power, Leo was forced to watch his twin pump like a man possessed into an elderly woman. Like someone one-fifth her age, she kissed, licked, and stroked his panting sweating body with youthful exuberance and enthusiasm.

For nearly an hour Leo watched his brother's orgiastic horror with increasing disgust. Equally helpless, his parents shared his fate, and hadn't moved an inch since the madness had begun. Leo wanted to feel sorry for them but he realized he couldn't. There were others much more deserving of pity.

Naked, sweaty, and stinking of sex, when Leon finally climbed to his feet, his features displayed a look of grim satisfaction. "You have served our god well," he said with pride, reaching for his tattered clothing piled in crumpled heap inches from the edge of the stage. "Many of you have seen his face each time you climaxed. Good. Very good. From this day forward you **will** serve him. And **me**...for it is I who shall be the conduit that shall lead you to he who is our everything. Now tell me, my children, **who** do we serve?"

"**Daagon! Daagon! Daagon!**"

Leon beamed. "Get to your feet then," he ordered. "Dress yourselves, and go. And always remember who you serve. Now and forevermore, **Daagon** is your lord." Turning then to his father he proclaimed, "Am I not Defti Garugatu--**The Exalted One**?"

"Truly," the minister admitted, in awe of his son's power. "You are also sorely lacking in humility."

"Humility is for lesser beings," Leon said contemptuously.

"Do you think yourself so powerful, you cannot be taught to obey," his mother asked perniciously. Leon's smirk was his reply. "You're wrong, son," his mother said, taking her husband's hand, "terribly wrong." In whispers they began to chant in unison, "Fatero, matero, delik caao, nadu toni delik caato!"

Briefly, Leon's laughter roared, but ceased the moment a power beyond his comprehension reached out and snatched him from his feet. Up, up, up, he went into the empty air, flailing helplessly, dancing like a puppet on invisible strings. In desperation, he tried a counter spell. When that didn't work, he tried another. When that also failed, he reasoned the power controlling him wasn't an incantation at all. It was his parents doing; their own power made to appear as a spell. And because he believed that only he was capable of such a feat, fear clutched at his rapidly beating heart. "Put me down," he ordered, looking to his subjects for aid. But they were oblivious to the scene transpiring on the stage.

"Let the lesson begin," his mother announced sternly.

"Aaaarrrggghh!!!"

As Leon writhed in agony, his clothing began to burn, surprisingly, with no flames. In a few seconds, though, a pile of ashes smoldered below him.

"Aaaaaaaahhhhh!!!"

Real or imagined, invisible flames licked at Leon's naked body and filled his nostrils with the smoky flavor of his own flesh. Sickened by the bittersweet odor, he retched his guts up all over the hard wood floor.

Throughout the hall, the hushed sounds of weeping became evident in every corner. For most of those in attendance, the perverse acts they had taken part in would remain with them always, complete, and in vivid detail. Others would recall nothing. It didn't matter in either case. They were all tools of **Daagon** now, whether they knew it or not, whether they liked it or not.

They might as well be dead.

Thinking of death, Leo was surprised that no one had been killed during his brother's demonic-influenced orgy. Many were injured by their perverse couplings, and most would mend with time. Others, especially the babies, would suffer much in the months to come, and it would be a miracle if some escaped being crippled for life.

"The first lesson of the **Kaluti** is that **no one** shall place himself above the cause," Leon's father said wickedly. "This you have been taught from the cradle, but your lust for power has made you forget it."

"If necessary," Leon's mother interjected, "your father and I shall be delighted to teach you this lesson over and over."

"Will you now obey?" from the minister.

Leon acquiesced. Grateful to be alive, he watched his parents leave the stage and walk to the end of the auditorium. Still under their awesome power, only when they pushed through the heavy double doors did they release him. Landing on his back, the eldest twin turned over with pain in his eyes. To his surprise, his brother had reached under his shoulder, and helped him to stand.

"Thank you," he said in a throaty whisper.

"You're welcome," Leo replied, punching him as hard as he could in the stomach.

Before Leon could fall, Leo hit him once more on the temple, breaking his wrist in the process. Considering everything that had happened, it was worth it.

PART FOUR

RETRIBUTION

CHAPTER TWENTY THREE

Manhattan, New York--1997

Before Leo Braithwaite had been able to complete his unusual tale, a most unwelcome chill slithered its way into Utopia's anteroom. It was accompanied by a scent recognizable to everyone.

Fear.

Its effects different for each, Lt. Wesneski fumbled with his cigarettes as if he were unable to make up his mind whether to smoke or not. Lt. Conklin, on the other hand, had his coat collar pulled up high around his neck, and shivered as though he were freezing. Fear, however, was nothing new to Kevi Stone. He had experienced much in his youth, and he had learned to use it to his advantage. And though he never allowed himself to be consumed by its chilling, debilitating effects, in the past half hour, if asked, even he would have admitted to a shudder or two.

"That's quite a story," Conklin stated mildly.

"I take it you don't believe me," said Leo.

"I didn't say that."

"I wasn't finished."

"My apologies. Please continue."

Leo moved from the desktop and stretched his arms upward. "More than twenty years ago," he said, pacing back and forth, "when Leon and I joined the **Pains of Love**, we realized that Stone's group could very well be our vehicle to the television and radio mediums. Because of the enormous impact those mediums have always had on the American public, through it we hoped to proliferate our faith with even greater success. Everything within this room, everything that is happening now, and about to happen would have occurred decades ago if we hadn't made one tragic error." Leo caught Kevi's eye. "We underestimated our adversary. But as you can see, the **Kaluti** are a patient people. We knew we'd get another opportunity."

"My brother's moving to Long Island was only the beginning. Although my parents loathed the idea of his leaving Cameron, thinking he might lose sight of our cause, Leon proved them wrong by quickly establishing himself in business and politics, and becoming one of New York's most beloved figures. As much a surprise to us as it was to himself, with nothing more than raw human talent and intuitiveness, his influence surpassed our greatest expectations. Once he became one of the world's leading evangelists, a greater plan evolved. What the **Kaluti** intended to do by demonic force could still be accomplished through other means. All we would need is a powerful tool for leverage."

"Utopia," Kevi concluded.

"Yes," Leo said, "Utopia...and my brother's Christian Faith Ministry, which annually collects donations in the tens of billion dollars. Through Utopia, CFM, and my own considerable fortune from singing the gospel, our influence has spanned every international boundary, and because of the unimaginable wealth and power we controlled, we were determined to reshape the world. Even now you can see the benefits of Utopia's influence. In addition to its environmental contributions, a vast majority of foreign businesses and products have been expelled from this country while we, in turn, spread American goods and services throughout the world. Presently, the US exports approximately 80% of its goods to other countries, unemployment has decreased, the crime rate is down, as well as the national deficit, which has dropped by one-third, and the gross national product is up 72%. In the history of America, there has never been such prosperity." Purposely, Leo paused for dramatic effect. "In another ten years our influence would have encompassed the globe. Every nation on the face of the earth would have looked to us to solve their social and economic woes..."

"Excuse me," Harvey interrupted, "but if everything was going your way, why all this? What in hell happened?"

"Remember the Cuban/Haitian crisis in '94? Many of those that had died during that unfortunate debacle were **Kaluti**." Leo's voice turned bitter. "In their seek for asylum, in their quest for a better life in a better land, in their dreams of finding the simplest kind of prosperity, both Cuban and Haitian refugees died tragically, needlessly. Most of them drowned. And what of those lucky enough to reach this country alive? They were treated like chattel, penned up like animals...denied the privileges given others fleeing a land of oppression. That was a big mistake, gentlemen. A very big mistake. As a nation, the **Kaluti** were watching. And as you have yet to fully learn, we are a vengeful people."

"Wait a second," Wesneski said harshly. "Correct me if I'm wrong, but wasn't the American government instrumental in returning the Haitian leader, Aristides back to power? And in addition to the military aid, didn't we also offer financial assistance to rebuild Haiti's failing economy? What about all of those Cuban refugees that were inevitably granted citizenry here in the United States? Under the circumstances, I think our country was quite merciful, and exceedingly generous, considering the fact that we were being blackmailed."

"Think," Stone added, "of what would have happened if we had sent those refugees back. There would have been even more dead."

"That's not all," Conklin said harshly, "have you ever considered the price each American-born citizen must pay every time an immigrant takes his job, particularly in the southern states, where it is we that must be bilingual in order to apply for the lowliest positions? And what about the unemployment and welfare benefits that are diminished with each new uneducated, unemployed immigrant?"

Leo's moan was one of both emotional and physical exhaustion. "You've raised some good points," he said. "Unfortunately, the **Kaluti** would never see things the way you do. And don't forget we're talking about my brother. Since his youth, Leon has given substance and considerable credibility to an otherwise empty legend, and because he has always believed he was destined to rule mankind, our present dilemma was probably inevitable."

"Forgetting your brother's politics for a moment," Kevi Stone said softly, "I see now why you've hated him so."

Leo sighed heavily, a little surprised. "At least you understand."

Stone understood all right. He had seen Olivia Leander only once, but he remembered her quite well. She had that sort of something that a blind man wouldn't forget. Thinking back, he had heard the rumors that Olivia had been raped by one of Cameron's notorious street gangs, a practice pretty common in those days, but he had never considered that the twins might be responsible. He even recalled his mother whispering to his auntie that an orgy had taken place at Neptune's Union Hall. At the time, he didn't understand. Orgy was a word he was completely unfamiliar with, so like any youth, he shrugged it off as it something only grownups took part in, never realizing its true meaning.

"Pardon me," Conklin said suddenly, his eyes wide and curious, "but something just doesn't ring right. If you want **me** to believe this story of yours, you're gonna have to do me a favor."

"If I can."

"To begin with, I've interfaced with you and your family for almost fifteen years, and in spite of some of the things I've witnessed recently, I just can't accept the fact that a family as visible as yours can wield such extraordinary powers without ever having them discovered."

Leo said nothing at first. He just stared. "What is it you have a problem in accepting, Lieutenant? The fact that such power is real, or that it has existed under your nose for so long?"

"Maybe both," Conklin said indignantly. "I'm a cop. I deal in facts. Other than the trick that "Mourla" performed which could probably be explained rationally, I haven't seen one thing that suggests you, your brother, or your parent's are capable of things you claim."

Listening, Harvey asked, "What about his home?"

"Did you see where the fireballs came from?," Conklin asked, knowing that Harvey hadn't. Most of them were launched while they were inside Leo's tea room from a position impossible to view, the others while they were running.

"You don't know what you're asking, Lieutenant," the twin said grimly.

"I think I do," Conklin replied purposefully, shuddering a little.

It might have been a trick of the light, but the color of Leo's irises seemed to darken a shade or two before reverting back to normal. That wasn't all. The piercing, swirling intensity of the twin's occulars seemed to burn with uncanny, hypnotic power. "All right," he said in a tired voice, "if it's proof you want..." Standing quite rigid at first, he grabbed Conklin's arm and rolled his eyes back into his head. A series of twitches followed, for both. In a single instant, everything in Conklin's life was revealed to the twitching twin. Happiness, pain, frustration, death, even fear. "Two days ago, you were angry with your eldest daughter because she had struck her baby sister. As punishment, you've forbidden her to participate in her school's basketball game next Tuesday."

Astonished, Conklin snatched his arm away. "H-how could you know this?," he gasped, his eyes dazed, his face slack, sweat forming above his lips.

Leo grabbed Wesneski's hand unexpectedly and added, "You, Harvey, have been thinking your wife has been unfaithful, and you plan to have her shadowed once she returns home."

The Manhattan detective's beefy face flushed a bright crimson. "That's enough," he said sharply, lunging from his seat.

"What about you, Stone?," the twin asked. "Do you doubt my power?"

"I never have," Kevi answered, allowing Leo to take his hand.

Once more Leo's eyes rolled back into his head. His body shook several times before his breathing returned to normal. "N-nothing," he said, completely dumbfounded. "I couldn't see a thing. It's as though you have no soul...no mind. How?"

"Because I don't wish it," Kevi imparted. "The instant I'm aware of a psionic nexus being directed towards me, I instinctively shield myself against it. To date, my psychic barrier hasn't been breached...and won't be unless I wish it."

"Amazing," Leo said, shaking his head in genuine awe.

"What do you call it...this power of yours?," Harvey asked hesitantly.

"Psychometry," the twin replied.

"Psychometry," Harvey repeated softly.

"You have other abilities," said Kevi. A statement.

"Yes, but I'd rather not go into that right now."

"Why not?," Harvey inquired, his tone suddenly razor sharp.

"Well," Leo began evasively, "don't you think finding my brother's followers are more important than a bunch of parlor tricks?"

"I guess so." Harvey realized he was being put off. "What would you suggest?"

"Nothing," Leo said, detecting the investigator's taunt. "At this moment, I suspect my parents are making it obvious they are aiding the police...in fact, using themselves as bait to draw my brother's followers into the open."

"What happens when they find them?," Kevi inquired.

"I assure you, my parents can take care of themselves."

Beep! Beep!

When Conklin looked as his pager's tiny rectangular screen, a look of concern appeared on his face. "Do any of these phones work?"

"Not in here." Leo told him, "in the outer office there's a white wall phone to the right of the glass doors. You'll spot it easily. It's the only one not blackened by smoke. Dial nine to get an outside line."

"What's up?," Harvey asked.

"It's the Harper's. My men were told to contact me if anything unusual happened."

As the Lieutenant left the room, Kevi's thoughts drifted towards Nellie. He fervently hoped she wasn't in danger. When the detective returned, Kevi took note of the unmistakable look of gloom upon his face. "Is anything wrong?," he asked, his voice taut, his concern obvious.

"The Harpers are leaving town," Conklin said frustratingly, thinking ahead about what must be done. "Nellie doesn't want to be alone in that big house, so I suggested she stay with my wife and family."

Not particularly fond of policemen, Kevi felt a growing admiration for the Floral Park Lieutenant. Conklin certainly had nerve. In moving Nellie in with his family, he was deliberately endangering them.

"I've got to go," the Long Island detective said impatiently. "There're some very delicate logistics to be worked out if I'm going to get Nellie to the safe house unobserved."

"Before you leave, Lieutenant," Leo said quickly, "I have a request."

"What is it?," he asked, unable to look the twin directly in the eye.

"I'd like permission to visit my brother's home."

"What on earth for?"

"It's possible that just by touching some of the things at the murder scene, I might get a sense of who his followers are."

Thinking it over quickly Conklin said, "If you think it'll do any good, I'll arrange it." Then he said, "I'm going to need your car, Harvey. You can call for another to pick you up."

Wesneski tossed Conklin the keys and gave him his business card that contained his pager number. "Let me know how you make out," he said, "and beep me if you need a hand."

Twenty minutes later, two blue and whites pulled up in front of the UN building. During their wait inside the lobby, no one had said much of anything, nor did anyone speak once they were underway. It was just before they were about to leave the city that Kevi sensed something was wrong. It was the quiet. That's what bothered him. It bothered Harvey too. "Something bugging you?," he asked.

"Why's anything got to be bugging me," Harvey snapped.

"Don't bite my head off. I was just asking."

"Sorry. I-I guess I got a few things on my mind."

"It's okay. We're all a little on edge."

Through his rear view mirror the Manhattan detective glanced behind him. "Tell me something Leo," he said slowly, "just how does this psychometry of yours work?"

"I'm no parapsychologist," the twin answered, "but I guess you might say the resultant electromagnetic energy flows in two directions...sometimes giving insight to the future, which is often called "second sight," other times, it can tell you what has already occurred. Another way to look at it: Try to imagine that you are a movie camera filming a particular scene, only as each frame develops, you can see its past and/or future unfolding."

"You think you'll be able to discover anything at your brother's home?"

"There's always a chance, but I can offer no guarantees, especially with all the policemen that have been trampling about."

"They're professionals," Harvey said defensively. "They wouldn't have disturbed much."

"More than you know. As long as their presences remain, it may interfere with my perceptions."

*****

Two steps behind Leo and Harvey, Kevi trudged slowly up the winding staircase to Nellie's bedroom. Sickened by the pool of blood outside the bedroom door he felt a knot growing in his stomach. An even bigger knot formed once he discerned the burned silhouettes lying on the floor. Unaccustomed to such sights, he felt an irrepressible need to retch. And he would have, if Leo's throaty cry hadn't distracted him. One moment the twin was standing quietly just inside the bedroom door, the next instant he had fallen to the floor, his outstretched hands clutching at his chest. Pushing the bile back to the pit of his stomach, Kevi carried Leo from the murder scene and raced for the front door.

"Why'd you bring him outside?" Harvey asked.

"He was too connected inside," Kevi explained. "Whatever it was he sensed, he couldn't handle it."

Leo continued to convulse. Several times, in fact, his back had arched high off the ground even though he was out cold. As a Red Cross volunteer, Kevi had seen this kind of shock before. "It's his heart," he stated.

Harvey pulled Leo's clothes open, listened for a heartbeat, and took his pulse. "Nothing. Do you know CPR?" Kevi nodded. "You handle his heart, then. I'll handle his breathing."

Working together, Stone and Wesneski laid Leo flat on his back on the cold concrete front porch. Wesneski opened his airway and used the head-tilt, chin-lift maneuver to move his tongue out of the way. Next, he checked the twin's breathing by listening for the sound at his nose and mouth, but with the howling winds blowing as they were, it would have been impossible for him to hear a thing.

Stone checked Leo's pulse at the cartoid artery; the slight groove between the Adam's apple and neck muscle. When his sensitive fingers were unable to detect a pulse, he initiated the chest compressions. In tandem they worked; Wesneski with the mouth-to-mouth, Stone with the chest compressions. After several exhausting minutes Leo's sudden gasp was followed by a series of choking noises. Once more his back arched high. As soon as the spasm ended his breathing was restored. "W-What happened?" he asked, his voice a gritty whisper.

"You went into shock," Harvey told him.

"We had to give you mouth-to-mouth," Kevi added.

When Leo tried to get up Harvey held him down. "Don't try to move," he cautioned. "You've had a rough time."

Smiling wanly Leo said, "Thank you. Thank you both."

"Don't concern yourself," Kevi said sincerely. "There's nothing we can accomplish here, Harvey. Let's get Leo to the car and find out how Conklin's making out."

"You got it," the detective replied, already running down the driveway.

Kevi studied the twin's pained features for a moment. "You fool," he admonished, once he was certain Harvey was out of earshot. "What did you think you were doing back there?"

"I had to...," was all Leo could say.

"As soon as we can," Kevi said determinedly, carrying the twin to the car, "you and I are gonna have a serious one on one."

"Nellie should be moved by now," said Harvey, opening the car's rear door, noting the time. "I tried contacting Conklin by radio, but it doesn't work. Figures...it's a new car. The first phone we see, we'll call in." Harvey turned to look at the twin lying in the rear seat. "Were you able to see anything?"

"Not really," Leo replied in short agonizing breaths, "all of the images were jumbled up, and came so fast I couldn't get a clear picture."

"Don't worry about it," the detective said, hiding his disappointment, "maybe your parents will have better luck." A slight pause. "Speaking of your family, I think I might have done them **and** you a gross injustice."

"Don't concern yourself," the twin said dryly, "much of what has happened, or may still happen is our fault...ours alone. And even if my parents should lose their lives before this is all over, it would be a small atonement for the suffering they've caused."

CHAPTER TWENTY FOUR

On the corner of Linville and Eighth Avenue, outside an old fashioned bakery, nearly a mile an half from the Harper's home, Harvey Wesneski parked two car lengths from an open-air phone booth. Leaning his considerable bulk into the blustery winds, he sprinted across the slippery walkway, dodged a couple of kids who were sledding on the hilly street, and snatched the phone from its receiver. A brief conversation ensued.

"Something's wrong," Braithwaite related to Stone as both watched the detective gesticulating in a highly exaggerated manner.

After he had slammed the phone back on its receiver, Wesneski stormed back to the car. He had hardly gotten inside when he reached for his cigarette case lying on the dash board. Liberating a cigarette from one of its cells, he jammed it between his heavy, reddened jowls. "I'm afraid I've got some bad news for both of you," he said in a hollow voice, his cigarette hanging precariously from the corner of his mouth. "Nellie's been abducted."

"W-What...how?" Kevi stammered.

Harvey turned rearward to where the twin was sitting. "Your parents have also been taken."

"What in the hell happened?," Kevi asked, infuriated, concerned.

"A Quick and Ready laundry truck," Harvey began in way of explanation, "was the vehicle used to move Nellie to the safe house..."

"Wait a second," Kevi interrupted, "what do you mean a laundry truck?"

"The Harper's have used the Quick and Ready service for more than forty years, and routinely every week their laundry is picked up at their home." The detective took a long pull from his cigarette and exhaled slowly. "Instead of using a police vehicle, Conklin decided the laundry truck would be a better transport. That way, if anyone had been watching the house for any length of time, they would probably deem the pickup a normal occurrence. Since the Harper's laundry always takes several baskets, the plan was to hide Nellie in one of them, and spirit her away before anyone was the wiser. It was a good plan. In fact, everything went like clockwork until they reached the Long Island Expressway. That's where their truck was attacked."

"Didn't they have an escort?" asked Leo.

"Two. An unmarked vehicle a few cars in front, and one behind." The detective cleared his throat. "It didn't help much. The trace car was forced into a guard rail by a cement truck. The lead car was overturned when a garbage truck broadsided it, and both officers were trapped inside their automobiles before they could make a move."

"No one was killed?" from Kevi.

Harvey nodded.

"Well, that's a break."

"Several witnesses," the investigator resumed, "say two unarmed blackmen in Rastafarian getup were responsible for ramming the surveillance vehicles, and get this...one of them, with nothing more than his bare hands was able to tear the rear doors off the laundry truck, even after taking several hits in the chest from a .45 automatic. In spite of his injuries, this man was able to yank a officer from the van and toss him more than thirty feet into a lane of oncoming traffic. It was a miracle he wasn't killed. The other assailant snatched the driver from his seat and slammed him to the ground. As fast as things were happening, Conklin managed to get off a couple of rounds, shooting the "rasta" point blank in the neck and chest with his magnum. It didn't stop him. Before Conklin could fire another shot, the side doors were ripped off their hinges. He was taken from the vehicle and pummeled senseless."

"Is he all right?" prompted Kevi.

"Conklin sustained several contusions, a possible concussion, and some cracked ribs, but he'll be ok." Harvey lit another cigarette, took a couple of quick drags, before pressing it into the ashtray as if it was his worst enemy. "After Nellie was taken from the van, the injured "rastas" made their getaway in a stolen taxi."

Noting Harvey's expression Kevi asked, "What's the matter?"

"The cocky bastards pinned a note to Conklin's body with a warning. They promised to kill their hostages if the police continued to interfere."

"What else?" probed Kevi.

"They want Leo," Wesneski said, without turning. "If he doesn't surrender himself in a time and place of their choosing, they're gonna send his parents back to him...one piece at a time."

Saying nothing, Leo didn't seem at all surprised. Actually, it was what he had expected.

"I'm terribly sorry," Harvey said, "for both of you."

"No need to be," Kevi said grimly. "Our friends have won the first round. I assure you, round two will be different."

The detective gave the entertainer a curious gaze."You sound as if you've got a plan."

"I do."

"Well, don't keep it a secret, man. Tell us what you've got in mind."

*****

Haven Hills is reportedly one of the oldest villages contiguous to Long Island Sound, and though it possesses a somewhat rustic atmosphere, it isn't entirely without charm, especially for a fishing village. For several years, Leo's parents maintained a cottage near the High Point district overlooking Haven Hills's diminunitive seaport, just minutes away from an assortment of canneries and fishing boats scattered throughout the harbor.

Within a block or so of his parent's cottage, the twin became noticeably agitated. In fact, before the police car had stopped completely, he leaped into the snowy street and ran up the short walk way to his family's cottage, touching everything within reach--the mail box on the street side, the recently shoveled pavement, even the bushes that lined the pathway to the porch. "They have a tracker with them," he stated mechanically.

"A tracker?" Harvey began.

Kevi placed a forefinger to his lips.

This wasn't the time for asking questions. That time would come later. Realizing this, the Manhattan investigator forced himself to curb his natural inquisitiveness.

"He's a brute of a man," Leo muttered, ignoring the presence of his colleagues, his eyes wide, nose flaring, lips quivering. "His signature is quite strong. He's also a stealther."

When the twin touched the door he jumped as if he'd been shocked. The tingling sensation lingered for a moment, but vanished as soon as he grasped the knob firmly in his hands. Kneeling, he studied the lock mechanism. Quite literally, it had been crushed. In a falsetto enervated monotone he uttered, "My parents were having tea...here in this room when they were caught unaware. There was no struggle. In the presence of great physical power, resistance would have been futile. The two that abducted them were quite prepared for the type of psionic attack my parents could construct." In an emotionless voice he added, "They never had a chance to defend themselves."

As if she were still there, Leo touched the chair his mother had been sitting in at the time of her abduction. "I can see them," he said, ignoring the anticipated jolt of pain. "Both are from Jamaica, speak English, but addressed my parents in **Kaluti**."

Expanding his awareness, Leo moved around the room slowly, using his psychometric abilities to trace his father's aura. For long minutes he was frozen like a statue, when suddenly he exited the cottage hastily and headed for the street. "They appropriated a car," he reported, "a fairly new Cadillac STS. No license plate. Just one of those thirty day stickers in the rear window." Turning slowly, he leaned his head back, clenched his fists, and spread his arms apart. "Got em!" he said finally, shaking himself free of his overpowering spell. "I know where they've taken my parents."

"Are you sure?" Harvey sputtered with surprise.

"Absolutely. The Bronx. Give me a map, and I'll point right to them."

"Good job," Harvey said approvingly, surprising Leo when he slapped him on the back. "I can say it now, but when Kevi suggested this plan, I thought he was completely nuts...you too, for going along with it." Thinking of all the crimes he could solve the detective mused aloud, "Man, I'd give anything to have that kind of power."

"No, Harvey," Leo said, shaking his head," I don't think you would. More times than I care to mention, my peculiar gifts have been nothing but a curse. You can't imagine how often I wished I was like everyone else."

"Maybe you're right," the detective said thoughtfully. "Maybe it does have its draw backs. Right now, though, if you were a girl, I'd kiss you."

"Sorry, Harvey," Leo said, smiling demurely, "you're not my type."

Harvey laughed a gravelly laugh, and delivered another thunderous blow to the twin's shoulder. "Now we check on Conklin."

"That's the plan," Kevi chimed. "Now that we know where Nellie and Leo's parents are, once we figure a way to rescue them we shall deal with their abductors in a manner appropriate to their deeds."

"In a manner appropriate to their deeds," Harvey repeated. "Stone, you have no idea how good that sounds."

*****

Nellie's first thoughts when she had awakened was that she had been placed in a coffin alongside her husband and son. It was that cold. So cold, in fact, she felt as she were suffocating. But if she wasn't dead, what then?

Then she remembered. She had been taken by force from the laundry truck. Shuddering, she found herself thinking of Lt. Conklin and the other officers that were with her. The sound of the driver's bones shattering when he was slammed into the pavement echoed loudly in her ears. Only one thing could have been more horrible. That was the gigantic black brute that had treated metal doors as though they were paper. To call him hideous would have been an enormous compliment. An icy grin, indicating his evil, sadistic tendencies was permanently fixed in the middle of his distorted features, while a half dozen teeth filled his chasmal mouth, each one a dull yellow and smelling of decay. His right eye was completely covered over with dead hairy skin, while the other wandered in perpetual motion.

Several times since regaining consciousness Nellie had asked to have her hood removed from her head, or to at least have her bonds loosened. Silence was her only response. While It was certainly in the realm of possibilities that her captors hadn't understood her, she doubted it seriously. Calming herself, she allowed her other senses to compensate for her blindness and visualized her surroundings. Because of the echoing acoustics and the way sound carried, she was certain she was being held in an ancient, abandoned building, and by timbre alone, she numbered her captors as four, all of which were sitting in rickety wooden chairs, quite possibly around an equally rickety table.

A tiny bell echoed throughout the room.

Chilled more than she thought possible, Nellie reeled. To her horror, the ominous chime struck a familiar chord in her memory. As her heart fluttered uncontrollably, she was certain of two things: First, a meeting was about to begin. Second, she was going to die.

"Are we covered?" a croaking voice asked. "This is not the time for making mistakes."

"Someone watches even as we speak," came a reply.

"Good. What of the two that were injured? Are they both well?"

"Fayaan is one of those on lookout. Kotuu died an hour ago. We disposed of his body as soon as our escape was successful." A moment of silence followed. "Kotuu's spirit is now one with our dark lord."

"**Daagon** be praised," someone said softly.

"**Daagon** be praised," the gathering responded.

Nellie wasn't at all surprised that her abductors were speaking in her husband's ancient, native tongue, and it was most unfortunate that she had been able to understand very little. Only a few words here and there. Versed in many island languages, Leon had tried to teach her **Kaluti** several times in the past, but it always eluded her.

The cold, night air swept suddenly around her feet. While she was unconscious, her captors had taken her boots and her gloves. Luckily, the mink coat she was wearing kept the rest of her body from freezing, and though she loathed it, the hood at least kept out most of the wind. Her hands and feet, however, had grown numb from the cold. "Damn you!", she shouted exasperatedly. "You've bound me to this infernal chair and placed me in what must be the coldest part of this room. If it's your intent to kill me, get it over with."

A scraping sound echoed quietly, almost as if someone had moved a chair away from a table.

Nellie didn't have to see to who it was to know the heavy footfalls were being made by an extremely large individual. Trembling, she wondered if it was the ugly brute that had abducted her. Her musings ended the moment a heavy hand struck her face. The agony that followed was too intense for description. Lying helplessly on her side, the widow gasped weakly, grateful the heavy footsteps were moving away.

"Dear God in Heaven," she prayed in a small voice. "Please take me now..."

Her prayers unanswered, Nellie took a moment to catalogue her injuries. A tooth felt loose, her nose felt broken, and a trickle of blood rolled down her back. When she was knocked to the floor, one of the slats in the chair had broken and dug into her lower spine. "Maybe I'll bleed to death," she mumbled, spitting blood inside her hood. But there was little chance of that. The cut was a minor one. Still, she could hope.

Suddenly, in English, a voice said, "Don't antagonize them, dear..."

"B-Brother Cal? I-Is that you?" Nellie asked, surprised to hear her father-in-law's somber, gritty baritone.

"Yes, daughter," the minister whispered coarsely.

Nellie cringed suddenly. She had always hated being called "daughter." It had always made her feel as if she were some sort of...non-person. In almost thirty years, her in-laws had never called her by her given name. It was only fair. She hadn't called her father-in-law, "father," as he often asked her to, or her mother-in-law, "mother." The bridge of hatred that stood between them was too great for either side to cross.

"Quiet, traitor," another voice spoke. The sharp sound of a powerful blow followed. It was accompanied by an agonizing cry from Nellie's father-in-law.

"Cal," Nora Braithwaite screamed, "are you all right?" When there was no reply, the aged minister's wife began to beg. "Please, don't hurt him, he hasn't been well. This insufferable cold has already taken its toll. Cal," she said, "can you hear me?" When her husband didn't answer, Nora Braithwaite became incensed. "Remove this hood and untie me you cowardly bastard, and I'll gut you like the slimy pig you are."

"Really now," the evil voice spoke again.

Another blow.

It was followed by Nora's scream. Then, laughter. Evil, maniacal, unbelievably cruel.

"The next one who speaks dies an instant later," the first voice promised. "There will be no second warning."

Nellie's mind whirled in confusion. Convinced that her in-laws were responsible for the deaths of her husband and son, and her abduction, to discover them prisoners like herself, left her completely dumbfounded. "Why them?," she asked herself. The answer came an instant later. Bait. Her abductors wanted Leo. Once he was captured, the **Kaluti** could make a clean sweep of the entire family. Again, why? What could have turned the tribal elders against their most ardent supporters? If anyone knew, Brother Cal and Sister Nora would. Unfortunately, they weren't in a position to reveal their knowledge to anyone.

As the meeting resumed, Nellie listened intently to the mostly unintelligible conversation still hoping she might learn something that would provide some of the answers to her questions. In spite of their frequent whimpering, she knew that Brother Cal and Sister Nora were listening too.

"I ask a favor," said one of the voices at the table.

"What is it you wish?"

"After those who are marked for death have gone to meet our dark lord, some of us will return to our homeland. I wish to stay, at least for a time."

"For what reason?"

"To dispose of the dog, Conklin, and his family, as retribution for our fallen brother. It was the cop's man that killed Kotuu, who is also my blood kin. I believe I have the right."

"We are all blood kin in one manner or another," a harsh voice spoke, "but as you say, you have the right. So be it then. You may avenge your fallen brother."

"**Daagon** be praised."

"**Daagon** be praised," came a reply. "Will you require assistance?"

"No. If I cannot avenge my brother on my own, then by **Daagon's** eyes, I deserve to meet the dark lord before my time."

*****

The traffic on the Long Island Expressway wasn't as heavy as expected, but on the Van Wyck, it was bumper to bumper, moving a few inches every couple of minutes.

"Back in your folk's house," said Harvey Wesneski, "you called one of the guys a "stalker." What's that mean exactly?"

Leo Braithwaite leaned slightly forward. "A stalker is a **Kaluti** that can track someone without being detected, that's unless the person he's tracking can recognize his signature."

Wesneski inched his vehicle ahead. "That's another thing. I'm not certain I understand what you mean by "signature.""

Stone said to Leo, "Explain it in layman's terms, if you don't mind."

Braithwaite paused thoughtfully. "Many cultures believe every living thing has an aura of energy emanating from it. If someone like myself, is sensitive to that energy, through psychometric means, and others, they can track a person or an object almost anywhere. Even across great distances."

"Sounds incredible," Harvey said.

"But true," the twin stated. "Through psychometry, I can locate any member of my family anywhere in this country, as long as they are living."

"Unbelievable..."

"Not really," Stone jumped in. "Some psychics have been able to locate missing persons and precious objects just by placing a pinpoint on a map...sometimes even if the object is halfway around the world."

"Ok then," Harvey asked, "what's a "stealther"?"

"Like a "stalker," Leo said in reply, "with one exception. A "stealther" has the ability to subvert the psionic nexus emanating from one with psi talent."

The detective turned to give the twin a puzzled look.

Leo snickered. "Think of it this way, Harvey. A psionic nexus is the link that connects my family's telepathic abilities together. Their psionic core, or rapport make their thoughts one whenever their powers are joined. A field of energy comparable to that of radar is created, giving them an extended awareness in all directions. Often, an electromagnetic flux is generated, in which incredible energies can be discharged from their bodies much in the manner of an electric eel, only infinitely more dangerous. This incredible energy can often create a nearly impenetrable barrier."

"A force field," opined Kevi.

"Exactly."

"So what this "stealther" did was jam your parent's radar-like signals," Harvey speculated.

"Yes. But even more accurately, he disrupted the link between my parents without them knowing it, creating the illusion that their power was functioning properly when in reality it wasn't. The feedback energy they received wasn't of their own making. It came from the "stealther." My parents weren't able to tell the difference."

"Whew," the investigator exclaimed. "There's so much I don't understand."

"Join the club," echoed Kevi.

*****

From the Van Wyck, Harvey Wesneski turned onto the Interborough Parkway an hour later, and headed towards Floral Park. According to the map, the Darian Medical Center was no more than ten minutes on the southeastern side of Floral Park. They were exiting onto Rte. 24, heading eastbound when his pager went off. Reaching inside his suit jacket, he pulled the pager out, looked at its blank screen, and set it down. Harvey then reached for his belt and extracted another pager. Its screen was also blank. Puzzled, the detective raised an eyebrow.

They all had heard the ringing, but no one had any idea where the sound had come from.

"The glove compartment," Leo suggested.

Kevi looked inside the small compartment, pulled out a pager hidden beneath the owner's manual, and handed it to Harvey.

"Must be one of the other cop's," the detective said, turning it off, placing it on top of the dash board.

"Why so many beepers?" Kevi inquired.

"I only have two," Harvey replied defensively.

"Wouldn't one serve as well?"

"I guess so," the detective replied, holding up the one he had taken from his belt, "but this one is for the old ball and chain. The other's for work."

Kevi shook his head.

Frowning, Harvey said, "Look, you don't know my wife. Long ago, I learned not to give her a means of contacting me whenever she wanted. The truth of the matter is, she can be a royal nuisance at times. For example, with all that's going on, if she was here right now, she'd be calling me every half hour for one thing or another. So this beeper," he indicated the one clipped to his coat pocket, "is for work. While this one", he indicated the one clipped to his belt, " is for her. It has a very special function. As soon as my wife buzzes me, my service will ring her back, wherever she is, and tell her that I'll return her call at my earliest convenience." Wesneski's smile darkened. "It's sad, but I never do..."

Kevi's deep brown eyes widened. "Why not?"

Harvey scowled. "Because she has no respect for me, or my job," he said, his anger unexpected. A pause. "You know, to this day, I can't figure out why I married her. She's everything I despise. New England blue blood. Old money. You know the type? Can't do nothing for themselves. Completely helpless without their servants." A snort. "Wanna here something funny? One time she beeped me just to tell me she was lost...in our own house, for pete's sake."

"You're kidding?"

The detective gave Kevi a quick look. "I admit our home is rather large," he continued. "In fact, it's more than 30,000 square feet."

"That's quite a house."

"Yeah, it is," the police officer agreed, "but the servants manage to find their way around okay. How come she can't? I've asked myself a thousand times, why would I marry someone like that?"

"Love. Isn't that usually the reason?"

"You'd think so. Me, I'm not so sure anymore. We've been together for more than twenty years, but in the past fifteen I can't remember us ever expressing our affections to one another. Whatever the attraction was doesn't exist anymore."

"How did you meet?" Kevi asked, "that is, if you don't think I'm prying."

"No," Harvey said softly. "It's no big secret or anything. We met in college. Both of us attended Harvard. Can you believe it? Me, a Harvard grad?"

Kevi was indeed surprised. Although Harvey often pretended to be a big dumb cop, Kevi hadn't been fooled an instant. From their very first meeting, he sensed a superior intellect behind the police officer's puppy dog eyes and lumbering, Colombo-like manner. Still, he would have never guessed the detective had attended one of the most prestigious schools in the country.

"I completed my undergraduate," Harvey resumed, "and graduate studies in law, at the very top of my class. Summa Cum Laude and was class valedictorian both times," he added without boasting.

"How did you end up being a cop?"

"I wanted to be a defense attorney, but when a close friend of the family was murdered and later acquitted by some clever shyster, I realized practicing law was not for me. Not unless I was a prosecutor. I never got the opportunity. In the interim, I entered the police academy, not realizing it at the time, it was what I really wanted. Later, I discovered I could make and even greater contribution to society by putting the scum bags who prey on the weak either behind bars or in their graves."

During their brief association Stone had known there was something about the portly investigator that disturbed him, but he was unable to put a finger on it until now. In all the papers, months ago, Harvey had been decorated for bravery and "performance above and beyond the call of duty" for risking his life to save a score of children held hostage by some whackos in one of the parochial schools in east-side Manhattan. Only the three assailants had gotten hurt. Afterwards, he was the recipient of numerous citations from the Mayor, the Governor, and the President of the United States. He had even refused a captaincy just so he could remain a street cop. "You should be very proud," Kevi said sincerely.

"Yeah, I guess so," Harvey said quietly. "Did you ever hear of the Carltons?" Kevi indicated that he hadn't. "Well, they practically own the state of Massachusetts. They make the Rockerfellers, the Duponts, and the Gettys look like a bunch of potato farmers. That's the family I married into. Me, the only child of immigrant stock, whose family had to borrow against everything they owned just so I could get an education, married a girl who by inheritance alone possesses unimaginable wealth. And though we're as far removed as the earth is to the sun, and have as much in common as oil and water, by some miracle we fell in love."

Kevi noticed the iciness in the detective's tone. "You make it sound like you did something dirty."

"I don't mean to," Wesneski replied, his face reddening suddenly. "It's just that sometimes the things she does really gets under my skin."

"Look, Harvey," Stone said, sensing the detective's obvious torment. "I can see this is a painful subject. Believe me, I wasn't trying to pry."

"I know you weren't, but I've told you this much, you might as well hear the rest." Adjusting his rear view mirror Wesneski said, "You were right Leo...about me thinking my wife being unfaithful and all. It's true I've given it some thought to having her followed. But not to catch her in any wrong doing. I'm not looking for either explanations or recriminations. I just want to know where I stand, that's all. That's not too much to ask, is it?"

"What did your wife study?" inquired Leo.

"Art," Harvey Wesneski said with contempt. "The thing of it is, she hasn't got a single iota of talent. She can't paint, sketch, sculpt, or anything. All she knows how to do after seven years is appreciate it, and to advise all her rich bitch friends of which objects d'art to buy. You should see our estate. I live in the Briarwood section of Staten Island...I'm sure you both know what that means." Presently, Briarwood contains the most expensive real estate in the state of New York. "The house itself costs in the ten of millions," he said, "but the art inside is worth more than a hundred mil'. And guess what? I can't tell one painting from another. Ain't that a hoot?"

Leo admitted it was. "So what's she doing out of the country?"

"Don't know for sure," Wesneski said bitterly. "We've grown so far apart lately, my singular focus has become my job. My wife, on the other hand, manages to keep herself busy with a plethora of debutante balls, charities, trips abroad, and Heaven knows what else. Actually, the only time we see each other is when she wants an occasional dance between the sheets. I know I should mind, but quite honestly, I don't. Hell, any sex is better than none. Then, there's the fact that she's so wanton, so damned uninhibited." Without realizing it, the detective was licking his lips. "I've got to admit, she may not be much of a wife, but she's always been one helluva lay...uh, that is, until about three years ago when she decided to get interested in body building."

Assuming the police officer and his wife were in the same age group Stone said, "Don't you mean body shaping?".

"Nope," Wesneski said, reaching for his wallet, handing it to Stone with the photo section already open. "Check out the first three pictures."

Stone raised up the detective's wallet so the twin could see. Wesneski's wife was indeed a breathtaking beauty. She had sunny blond hair, a smile that could light up the world, and a body like Lenda Murray. The bathing suit she was wearing was thinner than dental floss, but it successfully displayed her firmly sculptured body. And though he preferred his women soft and shapely, Stone had to admit the detective's wife was one sweet honey. In the most recent picture, she wore her hair like Sean Young in the film called the "Boost," which is who she looked a lot alike; a blond Sean Young, only with muscles.

"She's very beautiful," Kevi commented, and handed the wallet to Leo Braithwaite who had been devouring the picture with his pale, blue-grey eyes. "Niiiice," the twin said unabashedly.

"Yeah, well, I'm willing to bet neither of you have ever made love to a body builder before."

"Can't say that I have," Stone replied.

"Me neither," Braithwaite admitted.

"That's what I thought," Wesneski concluded. "Tell me Kevi, when you make love, how do you like it to feel? What I mean is, you wouldn't enjoy it very much if it was all dry inside, would you?"

"No way. It should feel warm, soft, and moist."

"What about you Leo?"

"I like mine nice and wet."

"And you Harvey?" Kevi asked curiously.

"I want to hear a splash when I get in there."

CHAPTER TWENTY FIVE

Since Kevi was unfamiliar with the new Algonquin Expressway on which they were travelling, he studied the map he had taken from the console.

"Once we get over this rise," Harvey said putting on his shades, "the Medical Center should be on our right."

"Look at that sun," Leo said, his voice filled with awe.

"Ain't you the romantic," Harvey said innocuously.

Not in the least offended, the twin continued to gaze out of the window, appreciating the way the sun's rays shone through the trees growing profusely on both sides of the busy highway. Because winter was his favorite season, he took particular enjoyment in how the warm sunlight reflected its rays off the newly fallen snow. Although it was only an illusion, it was as if there were countless, gleaming, shimmering diamonds lying about the land.

Nearing the crest of the hill, a car that had just gone over the top veered suddenly to its right. The vehicle directly behind it skidded in the other direction into a thick growth of trees, its occupants avoiding a crash by the barest of inches. Approximately six car lengths behind them, Harvey touched his brakes. If there was a slippery surface or an obstruction on the other side of the rise he wanted to be sure he could avoid it. Suddenly, there was light. Intense, blinding light.

On instinct, Kevi yanked the steering wheel to his right and stepped on Harvey's foot. Jamming the accelerator to the floor, he guided the police car off the highway and into a field of deep snow. While they hurtled downhill at breakneck speed, two enormous fireballs fell upon the two vehicles that had been behind them, destroying them instantly. "Head towards that dirt road," he barked, "into the woods."

Another fireball was heading their way. The snow-filled trees provided some cover but not nearly enough. Like a madman, Harvey drove down the slippery, bumpy field. Rough going all the way, it was virtually impossible to avoid the many ruts and dips hidden beneath the eight inch deep snow but the detective did as best he could. Reaching the dirt road finally, the heavy Chevy skidded sideways onto its snowy surface, making it into the wooded area scant seconds before a fireball destroyed the old wooden bridge they had just crossed.

"Where in hell are they coming from?" Leo screamed in stone terror, his eyes looking outward in every direction.

"Chopper," Harvey shouted knowingly, recognizing the muffled whup, whup, whup sounds of its blades whipping the air. "I've got some bad news guys. Unless we can jump a lake, we're about to run into a serious dead end."

"How big is it?" Kevi asked, weighing their options.

"Hell, I don't know. Forty or fifty yards across, I guess. Why?"

Noting the speedometer--it read fifty--Kevi did some quick calculations. "At this speed there's no way to jump that distance."

Harvey gave the entertainer a crazy look. "I was joking!"

"I wasn't. But that doesn't mean we haven't a way out of this mess."

Harvey's eyebrows arched upward. "I-I'm listening..."

"Then do as I say, when I say it. Don't think about it, or try to rationalize it...if you do, we're all gonna end up dead."

"W-Whatever i-it is you're gonna d-d-d-do," Leo stuttered, "it'd better be fast. Another fireball is heading right for us."

139

"Lake coming up," Harvey screamed fearfully.

The instant the blazing meteor struck the trees, it knocked them apart like ten pins, sending much of its burning debris flying ahead into the path of the speeding automobile. Displaying uncanny skill, Harvey swerved this way and that and somehow avoided the blazing limbs. Fifty feet from the lake, another fireball was launched. This is the one they feared most. There were no more trees for cover.

The detective was just about to put on the brakes when Kevi yelled, "Floor it! And when you get to the lake don't stop."

"Are you crazy? We'll drown in those icy waters."

"Do as I say, damn you, or would you prefer burning to death?"

"W-W-We're not g-gonna m-make it," Leo shrieked hoarsely, feeling the intense heat from inside the police vehicle.

Blazing intensely, the fireball grazed the car's bumper the same moment it was propelled through space into the murky depths of the frigid waters. Only a miracle kept the gas tank from exploding. It would take another miracle to save the vehicle's occupants.

As soon as the automobile broke through the thick ice, its front window was blown inward. Water rushed in from everywhere. Gritting their teeth, Leo and Harvey were unable to control their shaking. Much more fortunate than the others, the sub-zero temperatures hadn't affected Kevi at all.

"B-Been n-n-n-nice kno-knowing y-you," Harvey said through chattering teeth, his lungs feeling blistered by the cold.

"Shut up," Kevi snapped, calculating that they had only dropped about fifteen feet. "Everybody take a deep breath. We're gettin' the hell outta here." And with a single blow, he knocked his door completely off its hinges.

Unable to believe his eyes, Harvey sat stunned for a moment.

Reaching across the detective's chest, Kevi hit the door with everything he had. As it swung open, the car began to tilt sideways. In desperation, Wesneski tried to open his seat belt, but the mechanism was jammed. Ripping him free easily, Kevi yanked the detective from the automobile, and pushed him towards the surface. Turning quickly, he noticed that while Leo was struggling with his door, his bright, blue-grey eyes flashed panic and fear. In a single move, Kevi was outside the sinking police vehicle. A sharp blow from his elbow smashed Leo's window inward. Placing his feet against both sides of the door, he tugged prodigiously. After he had snatched the door completely open, he took Leo by the waist and both swam towards the surface.

Just above them, not more than a dozen feet away, Kevi could see Harvey thrashing wildly in the murky waters. Somehow the detective's bulky overcoat had gotten wrapped around his feet. Sinking fast, Harvey clawed the frigid waters in frantic desperation. Reaching him in seconds, Kevi grabbed the portly police officer by his ample waist and kicked for the surface. For the twin and Harvey's sake, he hoped he could make it in time. He also hoped whoever was in the helicopter wasn't waiting overhead.

Three heads broke the surface. Luck was with them. The copter was nowhere in sight. But they weren't out of the woods yet. Leo gasped painfully and Harvey sputtered repeatedly. Looking them over quickly, Kevi knew that if Harvey and Leo didn't receive proper medical attention, both men would perish from exposure. Placing them back to back, he gripped their belts in his hand, and swam the thirty-odd yards to the other side of the lake, avoiding the thick ice when he was able, breaking it apart with his powerful hands when he couldn't.

Once on shore, Kevi draped Harvey and Leo across his broad shoulders and raced down the snowy road in the direction of the hospital. Less than twenty yards away, a seven foot wire fence with a sign that said, "PRIVATE PROPERTY! NO HUNTING! NO FISHING! BY ORDER OF THE DARIAN

POLICE," stood directly in front of him. Ordinarily, a fence this height wouldn't have concerned him, even with the burden he carried, and under normal conditions he could have jumped it easily. Unfortunately, the frigid waters had sapped much of his strength. But not enough to prevent him from ripping the chain link fence apart in his bare hands. Like a handful of stale pretzels, the links crumbled between his powerful fingers, littering the clean white snow at his feet. With no other obstructions before him, Kevi raced across the snowy lawn into the antiseptic lobby of the Darian Medical Center.

The instant the electric doors closed behind him, a quiet pandemonium erupted. Nearly everyone in the lobby began to cower with fear. Covered with mud as he was, much of it frozen to his clothing, any resemblance to a human being was quite indistinguishable. One lady, Kevi hoped wasn't a patient, fainted dead away. After a few seconds, once the hospital staff's initial fears were overcome, the mud-covered entertainer was besieged. While a trio of doctors stood at his side offering their assistance, Leo and Harvey were whisked away in separate directions. Refusing their aid, Kevi headed for the cafe next to the gift shop. Curiously, an entourage of assorted onlookers followed in his muddy wake.

While she regarded the mud-covered man with fearful interest, an elderly blue-haired lady nearly dropped the pot of coffee she had just lifted from its electric hot plate. Smiling politely, Kevi Stone took the steaming pot of coffee from her shaking hands, extracted a muddy twenty dollar bill from his pant pocket, and laid it on the counter. After he had selected a suitable cup and saucer, he sat at a window where the warm morning light poured in. Gulping down his first two cups, he poured himself another. By the time he finished his third, he had fallen into a deep, welcome sleep.

*****

Awakened by the chatter that surrounded him, Kevi discovered a young candy striper was taking his pulse. "He's conscious," she announced to the resident standing at her side.

A youngish doctor with bifocals perched precariously at the end of his nose took a clipboard from the trainee and began to write. "You're a very remarkable person, Mr. Stone."

"You know me?"

The bespectacled doctor pointed to the dresser on Kevi's left. His wallet, money, credit cards, etc. had been cleaned and laid neatly on the table. "Oh you were quite unrecognizable when you came in here, but by now, I imagine everyone on the grounds knows who you are."

"The two I brought in. Are they okay?"

"By all rights, them and you should be dead. But you don't have to worry, your friends are fine. As a matter of fact, Lt. Wesneski has been a considerable pain since regaining consciousness." The doctor smiled. "I for one won't be sorry to see him go."

"That's Harvey for you," Kevi said, realizing the doctor was only kidding. "Where is he now?"

"Both of your friends are visiting another police officer that was brought in earlier. If you like, I'll ring them for you."

"Conklin?" The doctor nodded. "That won't be necessary," Kevi said searching for his clothes. "I'll see them soon enough...as soon as I get something to wear."

"Not a problem. Hope you don't mind wearing hospital blues. Your clothing was so badly damaged, we thought it best to throw them out."

After he had dismissed his young nurse, the doctor removed a uniform from the closet, complete with shoes, socks, pants, and shirt. Shedding his hospital gown, Kevi started to get dressed.

"You interest me, Mr. Stone," said the doctor, eyeing him curiously. "Would you mind telling me how someone as slenderly built as yourself can carry five hundred pounds of dead weight so easily?"

"Well doc," Kevi replied as he put on his modesty garments, "for more than thirty-five years I've lifted weights religiously, almost fanatically you might say, and in all those years I've never taken a week off. So, even at forty-seven, I guess I'm probably more fit than most people half my age."

"I think there's a little more to it than that," the doctor said suspiciously. "I've heard your friends' tale of how you rescued them from what could have been their watery graves."

"You know what they say about adrenalin."

"Yeah, well, neither adrenalin, or your weight lifting regimen explains why you look like a man in his late twenties."

"Soul food?" Kevi suggested with a smile.

"I think not," the doctor replied, fairly amused.

Kevi decided to change the subject. "Hey doc," he said, "at one point, I'm a little blank. The last thing I remember is walking through the lobby. After that, things get a little hazy."

"Understandably so, I'd say. Well, after you had frightened our staff and our patrons half out of their wits with your imitation of the Swamp Thing, we took charge of your friends, seeing to their needs immediately. You, on the other hand, refused our help, brushed us aside rather brusquely, I might add, entered our once immaculate cafe, bought a pot of steaming black coffee, and in less than a minute, you consumed the whole thing. I know, because I watched you the entire time. After your last cup, you leaned against the window and was asleep in seconds."

"Don't remember any of it," the entertainer said, combing the tangles from his hair. After he had pocketed his personal effects he studied himself in the mirror. "Well doc, how do I look?"

The young doctor smiled approvingly. "Better than when you came in here."

There were two armed hospital security guards standing outside Kevi's door. Both were assigned as his escort. Noting his surprise, the doctor explained that until he and his friends were discharged, no one would enter or exit the grounds, and all emergencies would be diverted to the nearest medical facility. Lastly, no one was allowed to communicate with anyone outside the hospital. These measures were considered necessary and were implemented by Conklin at the moment of his admittance.

Harvey's rotund figure sitting astride a soft-cushioned folding chair with an unlit cigarette between his lips was the first thing Kevi saw when he entered the tenth floor hospital room. Lt. Conklin was lying in the bed closest to the bathroom. Leo Braithwaite, however, was resting his feet on a stool and was sitting next to a sunlit window.

"The doc taking good care of you?" Harvey asked, shifting his cigarette from one corner of his mouth to the other.

"Sure," Kevi said, "Feel like a million bucks...thanks to the good doctor here."

"I don't think I had very much to do with it," the resident replied honestly. "Uh, Lieutenant, I must ask you not to violate hospital regulations and smoke in this room."

"Doc, with the way my lungs feel," Harvey admitted, "the last thing I want is a cigarette. But sometimes I kinda feel funny if one isn't handy."

A former smoker, the doctor nodded. "Before I sign your releases, I want to check everyone over once more. Who's first?"

"Me," volunteered Harvey, moving to the doctor's table.

After he had taken the detective's pulse and blood pressure, the resident removed his stethoscope from his lab coat pocket. "I would prefer that each of you stay at least twenty four hours," he said instructing Harvey to breathe deeply, "but I can't force you. I also realize the sooner you leave this hospital, the sooner we can get back to its normal operations. I believe the necessary arrangements have been made for your departure."

Within the hour, an ambulance pulled up to the side entrance of the medical center with two policemen inside, both dressed as medics. A few minutes later, six men total, departed the restful community of Darian and headed north to a place in which they could plan their next move.

CHAPTER TWENTY SIX

Leo Braithwaite had made himself as comfortable as possible on the ambulance floor the instant it had gotten underway. His eyes closed, legs folded, and chin on his chest, he stretched out his hand.

Kevi Stone, sitting on the floor directly across from him, his knees up, took the twin's hand instinctively. A moment after their fingers were interlaced, both felt a tingling sensation in their limbs followed by a light buzzing in their heads. The psionic nexus between them had been established.

With extraordinary clarity a profusion of images rushed into their minds. It was almost like having x-ray eyes. Only more so. The human eye can perceive only so much raw data, mostly because of its limitations; nearsightedness, farsightedness, color blindness, etc. etc. Stone and the twin's perceptions, however, were from a different source entirely. The mind's eye. It missed nothing. Every blade of grass, every flake of snow, and every heartbeat of every individual in every vehicle within a hundred square yards could be discerned easily, as if under a microscope.

Exiting the Major Deegan thoroughfare finally, the bright crimson and white ambulance rolled leisurely onto the Saw Mill Parkway. A short time later, the vehicle slowed before stopping on a lonely country road. Not at all surprised, before the two police officers dressed as medics jumped from the medi-van, both Stone and the twin had known the cottages was their destination.

As soon as Conklin was lifted inside, he used a pocket-sized portable telephone to place a call to the adjacent cottage. Seconds later, his wife and three children burst into the living room door with two armed police officers following close behind. To allow the Long Island detective and his family the privacy they deserved, Leo, Harvey, and Kevi remained on the front porch.

His restlessness growing, Harvey reached for a smoke and lit it. After the first puff, he coughed coarsely several times before extinguishing it in the blanket of snow covering the cottage's front yard. "These things are gonna kill me yet," he choked.

"Give them up," Kevi suggested.

"Don't tell me, you're one of those people that have no vices."

"I never said that. I just don't have any that are hazardous to my health...except for hanging around you."

"Verrrry funny."

While Leo rested on the knee-high wooden bannister he motioned to Kevi before pointing into the woods. "See it?"

"See what?" Harvey wanted to know.

"Both of these cottages," Kevi replied, "have an escape tunnel that lead into the woods, and two vehicles hidden at the tunnel's end." Turning, he faced the front door. "The fireplace is its access, and there's a cache of arms hidden behind it."

"How do you know all this?"

"We scanned it," Leo said evenly.

Harvey shrugged a little, letting out an uneasy sigh. "I'm almost afraid to ask what that is."

"Don't you ever watch the Sci-Fi Channel?" Kevi asked.

"Nope. Never have the time."

"Extra-sensory perception," Leo disclosed, "or what is sometimes referred to as **sight beyond sight**. From the moment Stone and I entered the ambulance, we scanned every living thing, a hundred yards or so, in all directions for the entire trip."

"You gotta to be kidding me," the detective said, scratching his head, believing he was being put on.

"It's true," Kevi said with a laugh. "If I hadn't experienced it myself, I wouldn't have believed it either."

The cottage door opened suddenly and everyone turned simultaneously. Clinging tightly to each other, Conklin's wife and three children stepped quietly onto the front porch. Although tears were still in their eyes, their sad expressions were no longer present. "Take care of our man," the detective's wife said softly, her eyes filled with warmth.

"We'll do that, ma'am," Harvey replied enviously, watching the lovely young woman and her three blond hair, grey-eyed siblings being escorted back to the cottage next door.

"We don't have many options," Conklin said gloomily, spreading a large map across his knees. "If Leo's right, and the Furrier's building is where his parents and Nellie have been taken, getting them out won't be easy. The condemned building sits alone on a tiny, city block surrounded by a half dozen other condemned buildings." A pause. "Whether its day or night, an assault of either kind is gonna be difficult." Conklin took a moment to draw several circles on the map with a red felt marker. "Each of these six buildings can be used as lookout points, which means we must locate their spotters somehow, and eliminate them before they can communicate with their confederates, otherwise the lives of our assault team, Nellie, and Leo's parents will be jeopardized immediately."

"They certainly picked the perfect spot," Wesneski said, quirking and eyebrow.

"So where does that leave us?" Stone asked.

"Dunno," Conklin said uncomfortably. "As far as I can see the only advantages we have is they believe you, Harvey, and Leo are dead."

"I hate to shoot holes in that theory," the twin inserted, "but it's possible they know we're still alive."

"How?" Conklin asked. "How could they know?"

Leo tapped his forefinger against his temple. "The same way I know where **they** are," he pointed out. "The same way I know Nellie and my parents are still alive. Another thing, if the **Kaluti** have someone with abilities greater than mine, before we come within a mile of that building they're gonna know it."

This was news Conklin didn't need. Purpling in anger, he slammed his fist against the metal railing of the gurney. He regretted it an instant later and clutched his ribs tenderly.

"Take it easy, Bob," Harvey advised. "There's no point in getting upset."

"There must be another way in," Kevi said earnestly. "One they don't know about."

"There is," Conklin said jauntily. He shuffled through the few prints that laid cluttered on his bed until he found the one he was searching for. "Assuming our friends are infallible as the rest of us, I'm hoping they selected this building because of its seclusion and nothing more. If I'm right, we have a chance." Conklin held up an aged coffee-stained print. "This is a complete layout of the entire building, and the only one in existence. As you can see, there's an old sewage canal that leads into the basement of the building. Actually it's a corrugated metal culvert large enough for several people to move through with relative ease. I'm betting only a handful of people know it exists."

Leo and Kevi's eyes met furtively. Each knew what the other was thinking. Just as they were able to discover the escape route from the cottages, the enemy might have someone capable of detecting the sewage canal. For the moment, though, they decided to keep this knowledge to themselves.

"You're thinking of sending a team through the sewer," Harvey concluded.

"Yep. At the other end, there's a floor grating made of heavy steel that will have to be penetrated, as well as a four foot by four foot sump with a grating that can be breached rather easily. After that, it's a piece of cake." Conklin laid the drawings on his lap. "Leo, you know more about the **Kaluti** than the rest of us. When would you expect them to make contact?"

"Midnight...Sunday."

"Why Sunday?" queried Stone. "I can understand the longer they wait is to their advantage. It's a battle of nerves they'd surely win. But they've got to realize given enough time, retaliatory forces will eventually be mounted against them."

"I was thinking of something else. This Sunday is very important to the **Kaluti**. It's what they call the Night of the Blood Moon, our most holy day."

"Which means," Harvey prompted, his guts telling him he wasn't going to like the answer no matter what it was.

"Minutes before the hour of midnight, when the moon is in its last quarter, Nellie and my parents will become a blood sacrifice." Leo tried to contain a shudder but failed. "Only when they are dead will we be contacted."

Harvey looked at his watch. "That gives us a little less than thirty six hours. More than enough time to mobilize."

"I beg to differ, sir," said one of the police officers dressed as a medic.

"What is it?" Conklin asked, noting Sgt. Wilson's sour expression.

"Sir, you've met my father..."

"Yes. What's your point?"

"Well, sir, one of the first things a farmer like my father learns is when to plant and harvest his crops, and to old timers like my old man, the Farmer's Almanac is his bible."

"What're you driving at?," Conklin asked, his impatience mounting.

"Well sir, I hate to be the one to tell you, but the moon will be in last quarter tomorrow night...not Sunday night."

Conklin's face paled. "What? Are you sure?"

Sgt. Wilson picked up the morning edition of the New York Times. "It's easy enough to check, sir," he said hurriedly flipping through its pages, folding the paper to the weather section, before handing it to his superior.

There it was, in black and white, for all to see. 11:02 PM, Saturday night, was the moment the **Kaluti** would strike out at a sleeping America. But first, their helpless captives would die.

"That doesn't give us much time at all," Conklin said distressingly.

"No, sir," Wilson replied somberly. "It doesn't."

*****

Nellie was freezing so badly she wanted to die. At least it would end her misery. Lying on her side as she was, her muscles ached even worse than before. Her teeth chattered loudly and her body quivered uncontrollably. Much to her surprise, though, she had fallen asleep. The funny thing was, the instant she was awake, her thoughts were of sleep again.

Her final sleep. The sleep of death.

And then, she noticed something that had given her hope. The voices in the room no longer spoke in hushed whispers. The tones were much more boisterous, which meant something had gone wrong, or at the very least, the situation had changed somehow. If she only knew what they were saying.

"We do not tolerate failure," a raspy voice hissed nastily.

"It couldn't be helped," another intoned.

"Explain yourself," raspy voice commanded.

"We appropriated a helicopter as instructed and would have eliminated our enemy as they approached the top of the hill, but at the last second they avoided our attack. We then chased them through the woods and forced them into the lake. The car sank quickly, but we couldn't wait to be assured of their deaths."

"Why not?"

"Three police copters prevented us by giving chase. Fortunately, we were able to elude them, but only after putting down in a heavily wooded area, where we were fortunate enough to steal a car and make our escape."

"Why didn't you blast the interlopers out of the sky?" raspy voice asked harshly.

"Our koth fura was spent," the other explained. "Even his abilities has limits."

"Will he be rested enough by our holy night?"

"He feels confident," the other intoned.

"Good. Your explanation is satisfactory, however, we will not tolerate another failure. From anyone. Is that understood?"

"It is understood."

"**Daagon** be praised," raspy voice chanted.

"**Daagon** be praised," the other repeated.

CHAPTER TWENTY SEVEN

"Are you certain you can find your parents once you get inside?" Conklin had asked Leo.

"That's the least of our problems," the twin said in reply. "Finding the lookouts are."

"Then here's what I suggest," the Floral Park detective said, jotting down his thoughts as he spoke. "Two teams equipped with infra-red head gear will search the six buildings as soon as its dark enough. Their job: seek out and sanction the lookouts." He pointed to a print. "Once they're eliminated, you, Stone, and our Swat teams will cross this open field under the cover of darkness to this docking door which is on the darkest side of the building."

"A diversion," Wesneski concluded.

"Exactly. With Stone and Leo's...er uh, peculiar abilities linked together they'll be more cognizant of the dangers, so it'll be up to them to create the diversion, and either engage or retreat the enemy as the situation dictates. With any luck, they'll gain access to the building without being discovered. Since they'll be the most vulnerable, they should have the best retreat."

"Before they move, though, I'll lead another team through the sewer," posed Harvey Wesneski.

"Correct," Conklin said, offering a smile to Stone and the twin. "Once you've received a communique from our "dynamic duo" telling you where the hostages are, you will all meet on the main floor before proceeding to effect their release." The detective's voice turned cold. "Any resistance you meet along the way will be dealt with expediently."

"Oh, you can count on that," Wesneski promised.

"Pardon me, but I don't think Leo and I should go in together," Stone said abruptly.

Conklin's eyes flared. "Why not?"

Taking the blue print lying on the detective's lap, Stone drew two oblong circles upon it. "Two reasons", he said. "First, by separating, Leo and I can use our powers more efficiently. Second, and more importantly, I know exactly where the hostages will be."

Conklin's forehead wrinkled into many lines. "Where?"

Stone showed him the print indicating the circles. "Here," he said. "On the fourth floor. All the electrical power within the building was de-energized long ago, so how do they plan on running their transmitter?"

"By tapping into a transformer adjacent to the building," Leo Braithwaite realized.

"That's right," Conklin choroused, digging through the mess of papers on his bed. "There's at least six operating transformers all tied together. They'd only have to tap into one to draw from the others."

"The closest one is to the west side of the building," Stone added.

"Then we can stop them easy," Sgt. Wilson said with a sudden burst of enthusiasm, "at least from using that neurotransmitter thingamajig. All we have to do is get Con Ed to shut down the grid for the whole area."

"True," Lt. Wesneski said, "but if they have a generator of their own, one in which they don't need outside power, already in operation, and acting as a backup, we'd be no better off than before. Even if we got Con Ed to lose the grid, it would only alert them, and possibly accelerate their plan."

Wilson yielded. "Sorry sir, didn't think of that."

"There are two stairways inside the building," Kevi Stone resumed. "One on the north side, one south. If Harvey and his men proceed up the south side which is closest to the basement entrance, and Leo and his team proceed up the north, should resistance occur, our adversary's forces will be split in two, giving me a chance to reach the fourth floor unobserved. It's quite possible I may be able to rescue the hostages while Harvey and Leo's teams draw fire."

"How do you intend to get to the fourth floor?" Wesneski asked.

Stone showed the detective the first circle he had drawn.

"From outside," Harvey Wesneski muttered, surprise in his eyes.

Stone pointed again.

Wesneski blinked. "The wall?" he said with even more surprise.

A nod from Stone.

"But that's impossible. You'd have to climb out of one of the second or third story windows to reach the fourth, and our surveillance of the building shows its completely covered with ice. Besides that, you'd be out in the open, with no cover at all."

"I'm willing to risk it," the entertainer told him. "It's a difficult climb, but not an impossible one."

"You think you can do it?" Conklin asked, his eyes wide with disbelief.

"Certainly."

"You're right," Conklin admitted approvingly, "about splitting up, I mean. I can see that now. Since we don't know what we'll be up against, we're gonna need every advantage we can get. I just wish we could be certain the hostages are really in the building. I hate risking lives for nothing."

Leo reached for the portable telephone next to Conklin's table, and extended the antenna fully. Punching the number keys rapidly he said, "If its visual confirmation you want, I believe I can provide it."

Conklin arched both brows high. "How do you plan on doing that?"

"Every move Nellie has made since my brother's death has been scrutinized by some friends of mine. Including when she was abducted from the laundry truck." Moving to the far end of the living room, Leo whispered softly into the telephone. His conversation was brief. "It's as I've told you before, my parents and Nellie are in the Furriers building...along with eight of their abductors. That's not all," he said, snatching a map from the wall, laying it across Conklin's legs. "There are only two look outs." The twin indicated the two buildings. "One here...the other there. Exactly which level or room they're in is not known, but neither of them are armed. I guess you know what that means."

They most certainly did. The **Kaluti** were supremely confident that their hell-spawned abilities alone were enough to deal with any opposition raised by an armed police force.

"Why haven't you mentioned any of this before?" Conklin asked, eyeing the twin thinly.

"I would have eventually," Leo said apologetically, "but my friends had to be sure."

Now that they had some kind of game plan to work from, Stone was certain Wesneski and Conklin could solve the necessary logistics required to implement the assault. While the two police officers hashed out the particulars, he grabbed the phone and placed a call. He had hardly spoken a few words when everyone's eyes swung in his direction. "My Vietnamese housekeeper," he explained. "I'm giving her instructions to contact my family, my band in Australia, and my lawyers should she not hear from me within the next twenty four hours." A minute later, he hung up.

"Where did you learn to speak Vietnamese," Harvey inquired. "In the military?"

"No. I've always had an affinity with languages. Including Vietnamese, all the Spanish languages, Portugese, Chinese, Japanese, Haitian, Jamaican, Bahamian, and **Kaluti**, I speak a total of fifteen languages...fluently."

"Impressive," Harvey said admiringly, taking his turn on the phone. When he was finished he said, "You know there's one thing that's been bothering me about this whole thing."

"What's that?" Kevi wondered.

"Well, assuming the bastards are unable to neutralize our attempts to stop them, I fail to see how they plan to escape. With the exception of a couple of apartment buildings, an occasional gas station, and a convenience store, that area in the Bronx is one of the most unpopulated and isolated in the entire borough. They're boxed in. Don't they realize we can have every cop in the city move in on them at any moment, cutting off every avenue of flight?"

"And so we shall," Conklin inserted.

"They must have a contingency plan we're not aware of," Harvey said, thinking aloud. "Whatever it is, it must be a doozy."

"They need no such plan," Leo Braithwaite said sardonically. "The **Kaluti** prefer death to failure. If you think this is just another kidnapping or terrorist act, you're all in for a rude awakening. This is a holy crusade by an amoral people whose patience is unswerving, whose brutality is without equal, and whose powers may exceed your best technology in armed warfare. The word defeat doesn't exist in their vocabulary." Sighing heavily, Leo looked into the faces of the two detectives. "I had hoped by now you'd understand, but it's obvious you've been unable to appreciate the real horror that will follow should our mission fail. Don't you see," he said, stressing his point, "the first to fall will be those in closest proximity to their transmitter's powerful waves. Every man, woman, and child within a mile of here, which includes your precious policemen will be brought under their control instantly. Think of it this way, the bigger your police force, the bigger the **Kaluti's** army becomes."

"I thought the purpose of their infernal machines was to control by subliminal means," Harvey asked, his voice growing tight.

"It is," Leo said patiently, "but the instant their equipment is energized there's going to be an incredible surge of alpha energy, and those closest to it will immediately fall under its influence."

"We simply can not allow that to happen," Conklin spouted histrionically, thinking of the innocent civilians that could be possibly involved in their little play. "I no longer care how this mess started, and though I hate to say it, I can't concern myself with the lives of our assault teams or the hostages. Their lives are forfeit. Yours also. If a few must be sacrificed to preserve the lives of millions, then so be it."

"You sound as if you know how to stop them," Kevi Stone stated.

"I do." Conklin's blue eyes blazed intensely. "We simply cannot allow this malignancy to spread. If you fail, gentlemen, I will have no choice but to have that building destroyed. Do you understand what I'm saying? I'm going to give you the greatest degree of latitude I possibly can, especially since I can't be with you, but at such time when I determine our mission has no chance of succeeding, the latest being exactly one minute before they start their infernal machines, I promise you that building will be reduced to rubble."

"How?" the twin asked skeptically.

"Does it matter?"

"No. I guess not."

"Take my word for it then," Conklin said icily, "if you fail, every living thing in that city block will die."

CHAPTER TWENTY EIGHT

Bbbbrrriiiiinnnggg!!!
Each time the phone had rung it was Harvey that had answered it. Although Wilson was closer, the Manhattan detective would cover the length of the room in one elongated step and snatch the phone from the coffee table before anyone could move. "Speak to me," he said gruffly.

A soft buoyant voice spoke into the receiver. Harvey recognized it immediately. He had heard it several times within the last few hours. As he listened to the news he and his colleagues desperately awaited, his intense brown eyes turned soft and forlorn. But only for a moment. Clearly, his disappointment and frustration was indicated even before he slammed the phone back onto the cluttered coffee table.

"Settle down," Kevi cautioned. "You're burnin' up energy you're gonna need later." In the beginning he had managed to ignore Harvey's incessant pacing and constant swearing, but as the day wore on the detective's pointless exhibitions began to wear on his nerves, and everyone else's.

Harvey spun on his heels, his eyes full of fire. "How you can sit there so calmly?"

"Discipline," Kevi imparted. "The years I've spent waiting to fight has taught me how to control my emotions."

"Well, I can't do that," Harvey muttered moodily, reaching for a chair, trying to decide whether he should sit or remain standing. He chose the former. The next instant, though, he leaped to his feet as if he had been given a hot seat.

"I can teach you," Kevi offered. "When this is over, you can work out with me and my band. You'll not only learn how to become more focussed, but more relaxed as well."

His eyes twinkling at the corners, Harvey regarded Kevi's youthful features carefully. "You actually believe we're going to win this thing, don't you?"

"Certainly."

Harvey smacked himself on the knee. "Dammit if I don't believe you."

Twice, the interior lights of the cottage blinked on and off.

"Tate, check out back!" Conklin barked to the patrolman at his side. "Wilson...the front."

"What's going on?" Leo asked, puzzled.

While Conklin contacted the men protecting his family Harvey explained. "You know the intrusion device you showed me? It's been engaged." Harvey checked the clip in his Smith and Wesson .45 automatic and removed a spare from his coat pocket. "Which means we have a visitor."

Realizing the device of which the detective referred to worked on a laser eye beam principle Leo asked, "Couldn't a squirrel, deer, or some other animal trip it?"

Brakes screeched.

"Not unless they've learned how to drive."

"No one out back," Tate called out.

Wilson separated the curtains with his revolver. "It's a ranger," he announced, his surprise genuine.

Conklin swore. "Dammit! I gave strict orders...doesn't he know this property is restricted?"

"He's checking out our tire tracks," Tate echoed, positioned at the window opposite Wilson.

"He's sure to find the ambulance," Harvey muttered to no one in particular.

Tate turned. "Sir, he's coming up the walkway."

"That does it," Conklin barked. "Wilson, go out and explain to him that if he's not gone in exactly two seconds flat, he's gonna be arrested for endangering innocent lives, and for obstructing justice."

"Yes sir," the sergeant replied, reaching for the door handle.

Leo tensed suddenly. "No," he rasped, snatching Kevi's hand, their minds melding into one.

An instant later, a tall fair complexioned black man with blazing red eyes and dreadlocks tucked beneath a ranger's cap stepped boldly into the living room. A chilling maniacal laugh accompanied him. It was a laugh that promised death.

Instinctively, Tate fired his weapon into the intruder's chest. The bullets never reached him. In a moment too incredible to measure, a wind of hurricane force appeared--seemingly from nowhere, yet everywhere at once--blew the officer's half dozen spent pellets across the cottage's hard wood floor.

Amazingly, everyone but Stone had been propelled backwards into the room and were pressed tightly against the wall. But even his great strength barely withstood the mighty wind. Nearly blinded by its force, tears seeped from the corners of his eyes only to be whisked away by the increasing gale. His ears popped and his lungs felt as though they were filled with water. In seconds, the hurricane-like bluster ripped his clothes from his body a piece at a time, until all that remained were shredded briefs, socks, and shoes.

Above the howling gale, the imposter roared an obscene chant over and over again, his body shaking violently. And then, the impossible happened. Stone had taken a step forward. And another. As the imposter's crimson eyes glared with surprise, he raised his arms high.

Fighting back the fear, Stone crushed the cry forming in his throat.

Suddenly the ranger's pale anemic features began to change. Then he spoke. "Hello, Butch."

Kevi Stone's heart stopped in mid-beat as his father's handsome face appeared in front of him. Even more surprising, he had been called by a nickname given him ages ago. A name only his father had used.

"How are you, son?" Poppa asked, offering a familiar embrace.

Dead and buried for more than thirty years, as much as Kevi wanted to believe his father alive, needed him alive, dreamed of having him alive, his mind was unable to accept the incredible. His movements a blur, with fingers extended, he struck the imposter squarely in the chest, his blow so forceful it penetrated clothing, muscle, and cartilage. As shock appeared on the ranger's face, Kevi's powerful fingers clutched his evil heart and snatched it from his chest.

His eyes glazed over, his jowls hanging loosely, blood draining from his face, the imposter stared in horror at the gaping hole. By all counts, he should have been dead, but powerful supernatural forces were hard at work in keeping him alive.

Grimly, Kevi Stone smiled. Holding the still-beating heart gently in his hands, he shoved the pulsating organ into the imposter's open mouth. "Time to die," he said, harnessing the rage within him, using it to augment his great strength. Summoning all the energy within his sinewy limbs, Kevi struck the ranger an awesome blow to the forehead. The results were horrifying. Blood, bone, and brains splattered all over the room as the imposter's head was ripped from his neck and shoulders. The remainder of his body went flying from the living room, over the front porch banister where it landed some twenty feet into the snowy front yard.

The instant the imposter's body touched the snow-covered ground, a tremor of great force created a fissure in the earth more than a yard wide, and six feet deep. Much like an earthquake, everything within the cottage that wasn't nailed down was shaken from its perch. With the exception of Conklin, who was still strapped to a gurney, everyone had been knocked to their feet.

Nearly a minute passed before the tremor finally subsided.

The first to rise, when Kevi stepped onto the front porch, the ranger's body exploded into a million pieces. All that remained of him was the stain of blood, gore, and fragments of bone lying atop the clean white snow. And with his death, the powerful winds that had wailed so fiercely dissipated into nothingness.

Throughout the cottage, the smell of fear hung thickly in the air. Leo, Harvey, Conklin, and the two Floral Park police officers were each drenched in its gamy scent.

As Kevi studied the faces of the five frightened, he realized their fears were not of the imposter, but of him and the violence he exhibited. "It was the only way," he said grimly, not realizing that covered in blood as he was, he looked more animal than human. "It was either him or us."

"Geez, Stone," Harvey said, trying to calm his rapidly beating heart. "I'm sure glad you're on our side."

"It's not over yet," the entertainer said, heading for the bathroom.

"Whadaya mean?"

"There's another," Leo explained, wiping the blood from his face with a shirt sleeve, "the brother of the one now dead. The one we should fear most."

"Where is he?" Harvey asked, peering through blood-stained curtains.

Leo pressed his hands at both temples. "Heading this way. He knows his brother is dead and he awaits us in the woods. He's blocked the access road but doesn't know of our escape tunnel." A pause to control his frantic breathing. "Like his brother, he's an elemental...one without telepathic abilities, but a formidable adversary just the same."

"Then he won't know about my family," Conklin hoped, adding hastily, "we've got to get everyone out of here and next door."

After they had activated the escape hatch behind the fireplace, Wilson and Tate armed themselves with automatic weapons, fragmentation grenades, and other explosive devices. Once Conklin was certain the occupants of the cottage next door had made their escape he gave the order to retreat into the tunnel.

"He's here," Leo Braithwaite announced, his fear suddenly overtaking him.

"Get to safety," Kevi Stone ordered, his body dripping wet as he emerged from the shower. "I'll deal with him."

"No. You don't know what you're up against."

"For Pete's sake," Wesneski growled. "This is no time to be stingy with information. Tell us what we need to know."

"There's no time," the twin shrieked. "We've got to get out of here."

Suddenly, a boulder the size of a small sofa came hurtling through the roof. The results were instantaneous. Sergeants Wilson and Tate dove into the tunnel as if they had seen a ghost, and were quickly followed by Harvey and Leo, both who acted as if they had witnessed the same spook. His fears not as great as the others, as quickly and as gently as he was able, Kevi Stone lifted Conklin from the gurney and followed the others through the dimly lit lanterned tunnel.

Running neck-and-neck with Harvey, Leo shouted between heavy, staccato-like breaths, "That's what I've been trying to tell you. An elemental is the most formidable of all **Kaluti** abilities. So far we've encountered the pyrokinetic, and the one that can control wind and water, but the one after us is infinitely more dangerous. He can control the earth itself, and being a true telekinetic, he has an affinity with almost everything organic and inorganic in

153

nature. If he senses us, every blade of grass, every tiny pebble, the very ground itself will do his bidding."

Out of breath Harvey asked, "If elementals aren't telepathic, how did they find us?"

"They were being directed by others."

"What in hell are we up against?" the detective asked with a gasp.

"Possibly more than we can handle," Leo said, wheezing harshly. In that moment, the narrow tunnel in which they were in started collapsing behind them. "He's found us. For he who is one with the earth, a man made tunnel is an anomaly that can easily be detected."

Racing overhead, unencumbered by winding turns and half lit corridors, the elemental was more than able to match his quarry's steps. As he closed in, he commanded the concrete tunnel walls to push inward, and to bury his enemy beneath sixteen feet of earth.

Suddenly, his angry cry filled the chilling afternoon air. His prey was getting away. Altering his course around the small half frozen pond he had come upon him unexpectedly, he increased his pace, hoping to regain the precious seconds he had lost.

Wilson and Tate were the first to break through the thicket of snow-covered bushes disguising the escape tunnel, and to run into the warm, afternoon sun. The others emerged seconds later. Ten feet away, an armored van, cleverly concealed, awaited them.

They would not reach it.

Crack...crack...crack!

By themselves, trees had uprooted. As a result, everyone stopped dead in their tracks. Suddenly, an oak, the closest to the van, teeter tottered for a moment, before falling between them and their vehicle. To astonished to flee, the sextet watched the scene with incredulity as a trio of oaks fell upon their transport, literally crushing their only hope of escape.

Braithwaite screamed. With the exception of Stone everyone responded by jumping with fright. Taking only an instant to break the powerful spell fear had placed upon them, like a herd of frightened sheep the police officers trailed the twin into the woods.

With every step they took, branches from trees and snow pummeled their bodies. Even the weeds and bushes seemed to have living strength within them and attempted to drag them down. Huge oaks moved about as if they had a will of their own, falling left and right, seeking to crush their human quarry beneath their massive weight. Rocks of every size flew at them with frightening speed, bludgeoning them unmercifully.

Not exactly built for foot races, particularly through a dense snow-covered forest, Wesneski took a moment to get a second wind. When he looked up, he noticed that everyone else had stopped too. A huge lake stood in the foreground. There was no place else to run. But as he looked into the sun, a familiar sound reached his ears. Breathlessly, he pointed skyward.

Gruffly, Conklin shouted into his field telephone. "Able Baker Charlie! Grid delta twenty...code red."

In response, a large camouflaged Army chopper turned tightly in their direction and landed less than thirty feet from the lake shore. Four men leapt to the ground in cover formation, automatic weapons at the ready. A few precious heartbeats later, the sextet bordered the copter and were fifty feet into the air before the **Kaluti** pursuing them could be seen running into the clearing. As he shook his fists defiantly, boulders, rocks, trees, and snow obeyed his every command. Impossibly, the sky became filled with objects that hurtled towards the copter with missile-like speed.

"Get us outta here," Harvey screamed, his words swallowed by the copter's groaning engines.

Jerking suddenly into a tight left turn, the noisy aircraft spilled each of its occupants on their backsides, but somehow it managed to evade the missiles that were being projected from the ground. Wesneski and Tate were the first to regain their feet, and to fire on the **Kaluti**. Both missed.

The moment Stone reached the copter's cockpit, he instructed the pilot to swing back around. Grabbing the Law's rocket Wilson had carried, he placed it upon his shoulder. Once the police officer had delineated its operation, Stone outlined his plan.

"It can't be done," Wilson stated skeptically.

"There's only one way to find out," Kevi said, climbing out onto the heavy metal skids of the noisy copter. While the aircraft circled wide towards the clearing, Kevi pinpointed the **Kaluti's** last location.

"He's there," Leo affirmed, pointing.

Harvey ordered the pilot to move in closer. Bad idea. A rock the size of a football came from out of nowhere, striking Kevi in his side, nearly dislodging him from the copter's landing gear.

Standing in the clearing, the **Kaluti** raised his arms high and bellowed a challenge to those above him. Harvey, Tate, and two of the Manhattan Swat team replied in kind by sending a hail of bullets in his direction. None scored a hit. The copter jostled suddenly and Harvey and Tate were nearly catapulted from its open doorway.

"An enormous surge of electromagnetic energy," Leo shouted in explanation.

The copter banked again. Harvey Wesneski continued to fire in short bursts, but the way the craft was being buffeted by the electromagnetic field generated from below he was unable to get a clear shot. By the time he was close enough to get the elemental into his cross hairs, it was too late. Boulders, doing a cartoonish rock dance, gathered, and covered the elemental completely, creating an impenetrable barrier. Swearing, Harvey continued to fire anyway, his bullets ricocheting like rice off glass.

The copter dipped suddenly. "We're all going into the drink," the pilot yelled, "if we don't get the hell outta here."

Kevi moved to the middle of the copter's landing gear and leaned backwards until he hung upside down. He would only get one shot. Even if the copter hadn't been skipping about the way it was, he had a one in million chance of success. A huge tree uprooted and flew towards him. Ignoring it, Kevi aimed and fired.

The same instant the missile blew up the barrier the elemental had erected, a huge elm tore off the copter's landing gear, and sent the aircraft spinning out of control. Listing at a thirty degree angle, its blades chopped at the water like a giant egg beater, throwing a misty spray high into the air. The pilot screamed in fear and gritted his teeth, unaware that he had bitten through his tongue. While he and his co-pilot gripped the controls tightly, by sheer willpower alone they tried to regain control of their floundering aircraft. Nothing happened at first, and for a moment or two it seemed as if a crash was inevitable. Then, just Inches above the swirling waters, the pilot and co-pilot leveled the aircraft finally and guided it into the afternoon sun.

Death would have surely claimed him if Kevi remained on the copter's landing gear. Given a choice of falling sixty or seventy feet into a half frozen lake, or to be crushed by a flying tree, he chose the latter. Gratefully, he heaved in a healthy portion of frigid air which nearly froze his lungs. His deep brown eyes alert, he noticed a distorted shadow fall upon the waters. Halting his swim to shore, he warned the copter away.

"Where's he going?" Wilson wanted to know.

"To make sure the **Kaluti's** dead," Leo shouted back.

"Is he?"

Leo pressed his fingers to his temples. "Not by a long shot. He buried himself below ground before the rocket struck."

"Let's land this thing," Harvey growled, "and finish it while we can."

"No," Leo barked. "Stone wants to do it alone."

*****

An explosion erupted just as Kevi emerged from the lake's icy waters. A chasm six feet wide and nearly twenty feet deep appeared suddenly in front of him. Only his lightning quick reflexes kept him from falling into it. As his hyper senses homed in on his quarry, a sudden pounding filled his ears. Cupping them with both hands he followed the cannon-like beacon inland.

Like a jungle predator, Kevi waited, thinking it appropriate that in just a few moments the hunter would become the game. Half-naked and buried beneath the freezing snow, he held his breath, becoming one with the terrain. It was the only way to fool the fiend that was stalking him.

Pausing a moment, the elemental opened his mind. His eyes closed tight, he expanded his awareness in all directions. Danger. But from where? Steeling himself, he opened his mind even more. Nothing. One thing was certain. A careless error and he'd be as dead as his baby brother. Still thinking of his fallen sibling, the **Kaluti** stopped to study his surroundings. He couldn't have made a bigger mistake.

Like lightning, Kevi sprung upon him like a wild animal and thrust his arm elbow-deep through his body. His chest cleaved in two, a mixture of hate and rage emanated from the **Kaluti's** blood-filled mouth. As Kevi pulled his arm free, he knew that he had severed his enemy's spine and that his heart had been pushed through the back of his rib cage.

Turning slowly, the **Kaluti** noticed a single strand of gory sinewy flesh was the only thing that kept his pulsating organ from falling to the ground, and he watched with horror as it bobbed up and down like a yo-yo. Still, even as his life fled from his body, his knotted hands managed to find his enemy's throat. But there was no longer any strength in his bony fingers.

Effortlessly, Kevi removed the **Kaluti's** gnarled digits from his neck and watched the light of life fade from his enemy's eyes. Even while dying, the elemental smiled. Suddenly, Kevi knew why. The instant the elemental had fallen to the ground, the electromagnetic flux that was every part of his life force created a shockwave of such proportion, trees, rocks, snow, everything within a hundred square yards was blown sixty feet into the air.

Baarrrrooooommmm!!!

"What was that?" Harvey asked anxiously, surprised.

"The elemental...dying."

"And Kevi?"

"Quiet," Leo snapped. "I'm scanning now." Five minutes passed. "Our rapport has been destroyed. I can't sense him anymore."

Harvey choked. "You mean he's dead?"

"Look down there," the twin shouted angrily, pointing. "Do you think anyone could have lived through that?"

Offering no reply, the detective glared at the huge crater in the earth below. "The bastards'll pay for this," he said savagely, "oooh are they gonna pay."

For the better part of an hour, Harvey, Leo, and four of the Swat team did a foot search of the immense, burned out crater and its immediate surroundings. Because there wasn't a single trace of Kevi or the elemental, both were presumed dead.

"Stone knew the risks," Conklin offered morosely as the copter made one final pass over the huge, smoking crevasse. "With, or without him, we still have a job to do. I'm certain he'd agree that effecting the release of the hostages, and stopping these bastards are of greater importance."

Agreeing, Harvey said determinedly, "As soon as its dark, we strike and may God have mercy on their souls, because I sure as hell won't."

CHAPTER TWENTY NINE

A group of kids, six or so, most of them in their early teens, were playing in the snow-covered field just outside the Furrier's building. Engaged as they were in snowball fights, sledding, and playing tackle football, they never once realized the dangers lurking nearby. It was a good thing too.

"Shall I get rid of them?," a gruff voice asked, as he peered evilly through a boarded up window.

"They are no threat," a raspy voice returned. "Let them enjoy their time. They have so little left. However, since losing three of our number, we mustn't relax our vigilance."

"When will we make our demands?," another asked.

"Dusk," answered raspy voice, the leader. "It will give little time for our enemy to mount an assault. Now that Stone is dead, whatever pitiless attempts the police make will be squashed immediately."

"Yes, but because of Stone," another spat, "we've lost two of our most powerful elementals. Their talents will be sorely missed."

"That is true," the leader replied, "but we have no need to concern ourselves. Our power shall prevail."

"**Daagon** be praised," the other agreed.

"**Daagon** be praised," the leader intoned.

"More children coming," rumbled a deep, gravelly voice.

Through broken and partially boarded windows the worshipers of **Daagon** watched the scene below with interest. It appeared at first, the youths were of rival gangs, indicated by their heckling and whizzing of snow balls at one another. But after a time, the dozen or so teens gathered together with a common purpose. In the hours that followed they labored without ceasing, sculpting with the newly fallen snow.

"What're they doing?" someone asked.

"Making a fortress," came a reply. "An impressive one, I might add."

Almost ten feet high, the half-moon shaped fortress was built directly against the Furrier's building faded red brick wall. A steep slide for their sleds, windows, cannons, and cannonballs, all sculptured from snow, the gleaming structure was a source of pride for the young teens. Once completed, they separated equally and took turns at storming its slippery walls.

"Police," a quiet voice spoke suddenly. "Shall I...?"

"Be still," came an equally quiet command. "If they're here to rout the children, we shall do nothing. If not..."

Two policemen emerged from their snow-covered blue and white. With clubs in hand, they ordered the young teens forward. Gathering up the snowballs they had just made, the kids ambled cautiously towards the men in blue. They wanted no trouble. They were only playing and were bothering no one. Nevertheless, the police officers scolded them, pointing out in graphic detail the hidden dangers playing near condemned buildings before informing them of their trespass. But when a billy club was raised, not to attack, only to emphasize a point, the kids reacted defensively and buffeted the two men with a barrage of snow balls. Surprised and outnumbered, the patrolmen raced for their car with the young teens in hot pursuit.

For twenty minutes or more, the fearless youths assaulted the blue and white, yelling and gesturing obscenely, celebrating their rowdy, noisy victory over the invaders of their turf. Each time an officer would open their door or roll down a window they were greeted with a snow ball in the face.

Things changed quickly when another blue and white rolled onto the scene. In unison, the four police officers leaped from their vehicles and rushed the angry teens. Though the teens still outnumbered the authorities, they were scattered in all directions. The four policemen pursued them, but with youth and knowledge of the terrain giving the teen's the advantage, they failed to take a single prisoner. Finally, after profusely shouting their frustrations and their hatred of teenagers in general, they gave up, leaving the area a few minutes later.

"It is time," the leader said to one of his subordinates. "You know what to do?"

The subordinate nodded.

"Then go, and **Daagon** be praised."

"**Daagon** be praised," chanted the subordinate.

"Everything is going as planned," the leader announced to those assembled. "The trap is set. The final hour approaches."

*****

Wesneski's impatience had reached its limits. The proof of it was that his pacing had become even more frenetic, and his swearing had become even more graphic.

"You know," Conklin stated mildly, "you really should take Stone's advice and try to relax."

"I can't stand this waiting around," the detective grumbled, grimacing at the mention of the entertainer's name. "We should be doing **something**."

Conklin knew exactly what his colleague was feeling. He had also lost someone close to him. Unfortunately, he couldn't afford himself the luxury of mourning a few dead when millions of lives hung in the balance.

The moment the mysteriously delivered package arrived at the Floral Park precinct, Dr. Thomas was notified immediately. A single sheet of paper was taped to the outside of the shiny, stainless steel box. Scrawled in snake's blood, it was later determined as such, was an effigy of a two-headed snake and a large "K" from the **Kaluti** alphabet. Realizing its significance, Mike's team made every attempt to get the box open. Chiseling, drilling, torching, even subjecting its sharp corners with acids and other chemicals with corrosive properties failed to unlock its secrets. Since x-rays were unable to show what was inside, it was assumed the interior was lined with lead. With no other means of opening the box, short of blasting a hole in it, which would have surely destroyed its contents, Dr. Thomas was left with but one alternative--deliver the package to Conklin as it was delivered to her.

On the off chance the Long Island station was being watched by their adversaries, several decoys were used. Having found Wesneski and Conklin before, every precaution was taken to keep their whereabouts secret. To accomplish this, six decoys heading in six different directions, led false trails all over Long Island, while the real box was en route to a Harlem east-side flat.

"What took you so long?" chided Wesneski as he took the stainless steel box from the young patrolman's hands.

"Harvey, will you chill out," Conklin admonished, noticing the time. It was seven P.M. "Evans was following **my** orders. Thank you, Sergeant. You may return to your duties."

Ignoring the portly Manhattan Lieutenant, the patrolman saluted Conklin and left.

"Get a grip, Harvey," Leo Braithwaite said firmly. When their eyes met, the twin winked. "That's an order."

A brief smile touched the detective's face. It disappeared once he realized what he was holding.

Taking the box from Harvey's meaty hands, Leo set it gently upon the dining table. His nimble fingers caressed the cool metal tenderly.

"What do you make of it?" Harvey asked.

Leo appeared not to have heard him. Slowly, patiently, his long fingers covered the entire surface of the shiny cube probing for the mechanism that would make it open. Seconds passed. Finally, the top of the box opened slightly.

Harvey's eyes widened. "How'd you do that?"

"By pressing at the corners." Leo grunted as he pushed harder on the sides of the box. "A clever mind put this thing together."

As the lid began to open, a heavy, acidulous odor accompanied by a sickening scent of death and decay forced the two men back.

Placing his hand over his face, Conklin moved his wheelchair closer to the table to inspect the box's contents. Blood drained from his face, his eyes bulged in horror. The decapitated head of Nellie was inside, still moving, still full of life, hardly beautiful. A massive sense of fear overpowered the Floral Park detective, forcing a scream from his lips. So complete was his terror, he pushed himself backwards into a wall. His wheels spun relentlessly on the aged carpeting, and ceased only when his stomach had discharged its contents.

"What is it?" Harvey asked, jittery.

"Nellie," Leo said coldly.

Harvey peered into the box, fear, rage, and sickness burned its way into his stomach. Hundreds of writhing, hissing, hideous snakes in a variety of colors squirmed in an out of Nellie's eye sockets, as well as the openings of her nose, ears, mouth, and neck. His body twitching in fear, the tiny hairs on the back of his shoulders stood straight up the instant she spoke.

"Traitorous one," she said darkly, her head turning slowly towards her brother-in-law. "The hour draws near when you shall surrender yourself to us. We shall tell you when...and where. Refuse, and your family will die."

As Nellie's maniacal laugh echoed loudly within the small room, Harvey was unable to squash the desire to puke.

Calmly, emotionlessly, Leo removed a butane lighter from his pocket, ignited it, and tossed it into the box. The flames thrust towards the ceiling, burning intensely.

Jumping back not a moment too soon, Harvey narrowly escaped being singed by the sudden torrent of flames. The stench that followed was so powerful it tortured his sensitive lungs. A few seconds later, the blaze flickered out, leaving hundreds of bony skeletons covering the bottom of the stainless steel, lead-lined container.

"The snakes and the message were real," the twin explained, a mixture of rage and hate in his voice. "The face of Nellie was just an illusion."

"But that was her voice I heard." Tasting the bitter bile in his mouth, Harvey noted with disgust that his egests had covered his expensive footwear. "And her laugh..." He shook his feet repeatedly, his left first, and then his right.

"No. You heard what your mind told you to hear."

"Close it," Conklin ordered, visibly shaken by what he had seen, his face the complexion of chalk. "We have less than two hours to rescue the hostages and destroy these bastards."

"Or die in the attempt," Harvey added.

"Or die in the attempt," Conklin repeated.

*****

An hour after dark, a worn, battered vehicle moved through the empty city streets of the Bronx and took a position just two blocks from the Furrier's building. Under the cover of night and the swirling snow--it had blown steadily since late in the afternoon, more than four inches had fallen--the mobile command center, which at first glance was nothing more than an aged cargo van parked between two derelict vehicles in the abandoned neighborhood. It would not be noticed. A dozen or more similar vehicles already dotted the avenue, all looking as though they had been entries in a winter demolition derby.

Conklin and two of his men were the van's only occupants. All were sitting before an astonishing array of electronic devices, waiting, watching, and listening for signs of activity within the building they were staking out.

So far there was none.

To all appearances the vehicle looked at least fifteen years old. It was rusted from its roof to its rims. Its tires were completely flat and dry-rotted, but surprisingly enough, they could be inflated and fully functional in a matter of seconds. In addition to being one of Floral Park's best kept secrets, the unusual vehicle contained an assortment of highly sensitive sophisticated surveillance devices within its heavily armored sound proof walls, and carried armaments that would make 007's gadgets look foolish in comparison.

"How's it going, Harvey?" Conklin asked, adjusting his headset, awaiting a reply.

"No problems so far. It's a good thing you thought of using insulated wet suits. It's cold as hell in here, and the muck is waist high and thank God for the SCBA's (Self Contained Breathing Apparatus)...it certainly keeps the stench out."

"I tried to think of everything," Conklin replied pleasantly. "Let me know when you reach the canal door."

"Roger that."

Conklin indeed hoped he had thought of everything, otherwise precious lives would be wasted. In his entire career he couldn't ever recall feeling so helpless, and he particularly hated the idea of sitting in relative safety while others might be going to their deaths. But someone had to monitor the assault teams' movements and send in the backups should something go awry.

"What the...?"

Startled, Conklin jerked forward. His hastiness was rewarded by one rib grating against the other. Gritting his teeth, he boosted the power on his transmitter so Leo's team and the Able-Baker units could hear what was happening. If any one team was taken out, an alternate plan would be implemented. "What is it?" he grunted, swallowing back the pain.

"Dammit, Bob! You didn't tell me there'd be rats down here, and it looks like they're really pissed off."

"Sorry, Harvey," Conklin said, amused and relieved at the same time. "I didn't think anything could live in that filth. What's happening down there?"

"A sewer rat decided to attack Slattery, that's what's happening. That was a **biiig** mistake. Your boy impaled it on his Crocodile Dundee knife." Harvey's heavy breathing seemed loud within the cramped vehicle. "Geez Bob, where did you get these guys...the Rambo Military Academy?"

"You wanted the best," Conklin said proudly. "You got 'em. Slattery was in the Seals, and Cartwright was in the Delta Forces."

"I can believe it," said Harvey. "A rat about the size of a cocker spaniel I had as a kid leaped at Cartwright, and he rung the filthy s.o.b's neck like a chicken. You hear that awful squealing? Rambo and his brother here are using their flame throwers on the vicious bastards." The squealing continued for several minutes. Finally, there was silence. "Stupid rats", Harvey breathed loudly. "Decided to fight instead of run. I'll give a hoot once we reach our objective."

"I copy...keep me apprised," Conklin said. Recalling what the character on Hill Street Blues used to say to his men at the end of each briefing he added, "And be careful out there."

"You got it," Harvey said, missing Conklin's wit entirely.

"Still no word on the Able-Baker teams?" came Leo's voice over Conklin's headphones.

"Nothing yet," the detective answered. "You know the drill. They won't transmit until they're ready to engage the enemy."

"You're coming in a little garbled, Lieutenant. Can you adjust."

"Certainly." Conklin tweaked a dial on his console. "You sure your information was correct?"

"I'd stake my life on it," the twin replied. "My friends have assured me the lookouts haven't moved since early this morning. Don't worry, I'm sure we'll be hearing something soon."

"That's what I'm afraid of..."

"You have every reason to be," an evil voice said abruptly.

"Wh-Who is this?" Conklin asked, his voice hoarse and throaty with fear.

"Death," roared the voice. "The two officers you sent will bring only a moment of amusement. The others, however, have already been dispatched by my brother-in-arms in the building nearby."

Conklin's face reddened suddenly as hate and rage swelled inside him.

"You were warned not to interfere," the evil voice related. "Listen, and listen well. This is the price you pay for disobedience."

The screams that followed only intensified Conklin's ire. Two men from his Able-Baker team were dead, and two more were dying in a manner he could only imagine, and there was nothing he could do about it. "You black-hearted bastard! I'm gonna kill you for that. I'm gonna rip out your heart and feed it to the rats, you filthy son of a bitch. You hear me?"

The men flanking Conklin were hand-picked because of their competence, their intelligence, and because they each had nerves of steel. But after listening to the horrible screams of their colleagues, both became as shaken as their superior.

"For your sake," the voice continued, "let us hope further lessons will not be necessary...Aaaaahhhh!!!!!!"

Chuka, chuka, chuka!!!!

Conklin's pulse exploded. Accompanying the horrifying scream he had just heard he was fairly certain he recognized that muffled sound. "That's an automatic weapon being discharged," he hazarded, "with a silencer. But who...?"

Silence. Conklin hated it. With noise, an experienced ear could often determine what was happening.

"The two lookouts in both buildings have been eliminated," a cold mechanical voice spoke evenly. "My deepest sympathies for your men." A pause. "Twin, if you're listening, you now have a clear path to the Furrier's building. Under the cover of darkness, you will be able to escape detection from everyone but myself. If I'm wrong, any opposition you encounter, I will deal with immediately. Once you get inside the building, proceed to phase two of your plan. Good luck."

"W-Who is this?" Conklin asked, dumbfounded. "Identify yourself at once." More silence.

Conklin ground his teeth until his jaw had begun to ache. "Leo, do you copy?"

"I heard him, Lieutenant," the twin answered, his voice tinged with fear, sweat oozing through his clothing. "I'm afraid I'm as much in the dark as you. I couldn't place the voice. Whoever he is though ... sounds like he's on our side."

Conklin swore. "But can we trust him?"

"Since he obviously knows who we are, and what we're up to ... have we a choice?"

"I guess not," Conklin answered in a defeated tone.

"Time is growing short, Lieutenant," Leo said uncomfortably. "Proceeding as planned."

Conklin wasn't a happy camper. Not at all. Four more of his men were dead. And that hurt. That hurt bad. Good men who were only doing their jobs had died horribly. Not only that. An unknown player had taken an interest in the game, and he knew things only a handful of people were supposed to know. Conklin glanced at his clock. The twin was right. Time was running out. For everyone. Less tha eighty minutes to "zero hour."

*****

For twenty minutes Harvey's team used their mini-lasers against the thick iron grating to the sump. Once it was breached, he signaled Conklin the moment he was in the basement of the Furrier building.

As promised by their unknown ally, Leo's team crossed the open field safely, and assembled outside the docking area almost the same moment Harvey's team entered the basement.Using their Mini-lasers and the howling winds as cover, the twin's team of four men cut through the security locks and entered the building quickly and silently. Once inside, they engaged their infrared head gear which enabled them to see in the pitch blackness. The motion detectors they carried would instantly identify any movement other than their own.

Leo was the only one unarmed. As his team stepped into the cold silent building, the four policemen took up position, two to his front and two to his rear. their job: to protect him at all costs. It had been his and Kevi's task to find his parents and Nellie, and to warn both teams of the dangers. Now he must do it alone. "Harvey, do you read me?" he whispered through the tiny but extremely sensitive transmitter-receiver in his helmet.

"Affirmative."

"We're inside the building approaching the north stairway. Stone was right," he said, pressing his fingers to his temples, his senses reaching out. "The hostages are on the fourth floor." a short pause."Nellie's ok," he added, "but my parents aren't doing so well. I count six, maybe seven others.Can't be sure until I get closer. signal me when you're at the south stairway."

"Hold up," Harvey said quickly. "Are you sure there's no one else in this building other than us and those on the fourth floor?"

"Positively," Leo replied. "Why?"

"Because somebody's moving towards us as we speak. No tellin' how many. Our motion detector's are going crazy. Doesn't matter though ...cause they're gonna get some lead in their butts when they open that door."

"Should we assist?" Leo asked anxiously."We're only one level up and can be there in seconds."

"No," Harvey insisted, ridding himself of the cumbersome SCBA.

"We'll call you if we need you, otherwise stick to the plan."

While Harvey waited for the intruders to enter the huge sliding door, Leo and his team proceeded towards the closest stairway.

CHAPTER THIRTY

Twenty three seconds had passed since the twin's last transmission. For Conklin it seemed like twenty three hours. And though the mobile command center's engine had been silent for more than an hour, he felt incredibly cold, in spite of fact that the vehicle's interior temperature was a crisp, comfortable seventy-two degrees. Loathe to admit it, he knew that it was his fears that chilled him so completely.

Thinking then of his Manhattan counterpart, the Floral Park detective noticed Harvey's gold cigarette case lying atop the communication console. He just couldn't understand it. How could anyone become addicted to such a disgusting habit, particularly when there were so many others to succumb to? Suddenly, he felt an overpowering craving for a cup of strong black coffee. This was his preferred addiction. Unfortunately, the contents of the two thermoses he had brought along had been consumed in the first hour of the stake out. Curious, he reached for Harvey's cigarettes and inspected them. Even as a kid, often pressured by his peers, he had refused to pollute his lungs with what his father often called the "black death." Now, a grownup, who sometimes detested his own addiction to caffeine, Conklin discovered he was actually considering lighting up one of Harvey's cigarettes and taking himself a much needed drag. One cigarette, that's all he would need. A little something to take the edge off, something to calm his tautly stretched nerves.

Bbbbrrrrrrppppp!!!

Startled, Conklin dropped Harvey's expensive cigarette case to the floor, inevitably jarring a half dozen of the disgusting little killers from their cells, spilling them around his feet.

Bbbbrrrrrrppppp!!!

There it was again. The sound of an automatic weapon being discharged. It could mean only one thing. One or both of his assault teams were in trouble, each possibly battling for their lives. Taking a chapter from his colleague's book, he began to swear. Repeatedly and proficiently. Except for waiting, and maybe praying, there was little else he could do.

*****

Disturbed by the fearful screams and rapid gunfire blasting into his headset, Leo anxiously awaited word from Harvey. None came. Every instinct told him to say "to hell with the plan," and rush to the aid of the three men that were only a level below, and he would have, if his men hadn't alerted him to the shape that moved across the warehouse floor. Barely catching a glimpse of it, the twin's fears were amplified. Neither the motion sensors he and his men carried, or his psionic abilities had been able to detect the swift-moving, ghost-like figure.

"Aaarrrrgggghhhh!!!" he screamed suddenly, the pain unreal.

Useless for the past few minutes, the motion detectors indicated movement and beeped loudly into Leo's headset, its warbling pitch assaulting his sensitive ear drums. But that was nothing compared to the internal klaxon that rang so voluminously throughout his skull. Once engaged, there was no way to tune out or turn down its powerful reverberations. Ignoring the relentless tintinnabulation as best he could, he checked the four by four screen on his detector. At least three men moved towards them. Closing his eyes, his hyper senses confirmed those readings. Before he could discuss his findings with his four associates, the signals vanished from his screen and his mind. As he expanded his consciousness even more than before, he probed the energy field shifting around him. His mind locking onto an anomaly, he and his men started in the direction where the ghost-like figures were last detected.

*****

Harvey screamed like a madman. Or at least like a man that had surely believed he had gone mad. What he saw couldn't be real. But there it was. A snake of monstrous proportions had splintered the three-inch thick wooden sliding door into kindling with a single blow from its mighty head. And with a swiftness inconsistent with its size, it had both of his men within its powerful coils. Back-pedaling faster than he thought possible, Harvey escaped being the reptile's first meal of the day. His heart filled with fear, he watched his men struggle in the clutches of the hissing beast. Slattery used his knife, to no avail, to stab the monstrous scaly reptile in its side, Cartwright was unable to move. His arms were pinned to his side.

Surprisingly nimble for one his size, Harvey dodged the snake's long, powerful tongue, escaping capture by inches. Suddenly, he realized he had an insufficient knowledge of reptiles and was quite unable to determine in which species the snake belonged. Whatever it was, he knew it wasn't indigenous to the United States, or anywhere else on the planet. From end to end, the reptile measured more than sixty feet in length. Nearly five feet in diameter at its thickest point, it was greater than a foot thick at the tip of its tail. A monster if there ever was one, its huge, gaping mouth was capable of swallowing a man his size effortlessly.

Seconds flew by. The battle was not going well. Harvey and his men were beginning to tire, the snake was not. It's thick elongated tongue continued to dart out in whip-like fashion keeping the portly detective at bay. His weapon useless, every time Harvey would steady himself to fire into the creature's face, Cartwright and Slattery would be shifted in front of him.

There was no doubt about it. An evil intelligence was at work behind those blazing reptilian eyes.

Brainstorming, Harvey broke two flares in his hands and threw them at the beast with the hopes he might blind its lidless eyes. No such luck. Enraged by the sudden brightness, the reptile whipped his tail and slammed the detective into the wall. Listing a moment before falling to his knees, Harvey imagined himself being hit by a runaway freight train. He had barely enough wind to release a single, agonizing gasp.

Sensing his prey's helplessness, the huge snake raised its head high to strike. Desperately, Harvey shook the cobwebs from his brain as he looked for his rifle. Knocked several feet away, he knew there was no way he could get to it before the snake got to him. Swearing, he pulled a pair of .45's from his garments. The reptile closed quickly. Unfortunately, Harvey had no time to aim. As the monster's cavernous mouth loomed above him, his last thought was that "this is a helluva way to die."

Then, from out of nowhere, a swift moving figure dressed in a skin tight, spandex body suit leaped through the air and landed upon the beast's enormous head. Wrapping his legs around the reptile's huge neck, he bludgeoned the leviathan unmercifully with a huge fire axe.

Despite his surprise, Wesneski reacted immediately. His adrenalin pumping the necessary strength into his bone-tired limbs, he leaped to the aid of the stranger who had just saved him. His hopes died. As before, each time he aimed his pistols, the snake reacted instantly and moved his men in the line of fire. Reluctantly, the detective dropped his weapons to the floor. While the monstrous reptile tried to dislodge the dark clad stranger fiercely banging upon its head, Wesneski raced some twenty feet to the far wall, extracted a fire axe from its broken glass cage and attacked the ophidian's hard scaly belly with the ferocity of a madman. A half dozen strikes later, Cartwright was free.

The stranger's attack was relentless. Still, with each blow he delivered, the reptile banged him unmercifully into the ceiling above, and to the walls to the left and right of him. A normal man would have been crushed to a pulp.

Wesneski cried out a warning. Too late. The reptile's tongue had already snatched the stranger from its head and was forcing him into its foul, cavernous mouth. Helplessly, the detective watched in horrified fascination. In another moment, the stranger would be crushed between powerful reptilian jaws. At least that's what Harvey first thought. He was wrong. As if it were the most natural thing to do, moving with the swiftness of a gazelle, the man in black leaped from the beast's mouth and wrapped his arms around its mighty jaws. It was amazing. He was actually holding them closed.

Harvey's heart beat excitedly. There was only one man with that kind of strength. But he was dead. Or was he? Whether he was or wasn't didn't matter for the moment, because even though the viper's tongue was only partially trapped between its jaws, the beast was still capable of killing the stranger by slamming him against the wall.

When Cartwright got to his feet, he discovered his weapon lying beneath the enormous bulk of the slithering leviathan. Each time he came within inches of reaching it, the snake's immense tail would whip forward and send him flying. Wesneski had much better luck, and he continued to hack away at the monstrous reptile's raised underbelly. Slattery, who was still in the clutches of the beast managed to get one arm free, and was using his knife to dig into its steel plated hide.

The monster bucked suddenly. As it showed signs of weakening, Wesneski and Cartwright attacked with renewed vigor. The beast, however, was far from dead. With a swish of its mighty tail it scattered the officers across the floor as if they were little toy soldiers.

Craning its huge head upward the beast prepared to dash the stranger against the floor. Waiting for just such a move, at the very last moment, the man in black leaped from the reptile's neck, rolled across the floor, and righted himself with the agility of a gymnast. The angered ophidian hissed loudly, flashing towards him, jaws agape.

Wesneski screamed another warning, but neither he nor Cartwright had reached their feet to be of any assistance to the stranger.

Moving like a mongoose, the man in black bobbed, weaved, and dodged with surprising nimbleness. As each of the reptile's strikes missed their mark, the stranger's axe delivered a heavy blow. But the moment he leaped over the beast's whipping tail, he slipped and fell in a thick, viscous pool of snake blood. Lying on his back momentarily stunned, when he looked upward he was thinking that his luck had run out.

The huge reptile must have thought so too.

Still, the stranger managed to evade the monster even though it matched his every move. Hissing loudly, the beast forced its foe into a corner of which there was no escape.

His elbows bloody from his fearful, backwards crawl, the stranger ignored his pain and searched for an avenue of escape. There was only one chance. If it came, he would have to be ready for it. His heart thudding like a big bass drum, he waited. And then, it happened. As the beast prepared to strike, the very moment it opened its yawning, slime-filled mouth, the stranger leaped inside.

Harvey's mouth dropped to his knees. His heart pounded in his throat. He couldn't believe his eyes. Shocked, he could do nothing except watch the powerful jaws of the reptile close slowly around his rescuer.

"Aaaahhhhhh!!!"

Although the stranger's agonizing cry had sent chills running across Harvey's spine, instead of freezing him into immobility, it spurred him to hack away at the monstrous reptile's bloody innards with maddened motivation.

"Aaaaarrrgggghhh!!!!"

Like organic steel the stranger's powerful resilient body straightened within the snake's gaping jaws, even while standing shin deep in its hot, sticky gruel. Barely able to keep his footing, he continued to press upward, ever so slowly, until the beast's jaw stretched completely open. Powerful muscles tightened and pushed even harder.

"Sssssssssss!!!!"

Hissing in agony, the reptile tried to force its prey him from its mouth with its tongue. It would have succeeded if the stranger hadn't forced its jaws completely apart. Shaking its head violently, the hideous, venomous viper released Slattery and had thrown the stranger against a wall nearly thirty feet away.

His rifle in hand, Harvey retreated to a place of safety and emptied clip after clip into the brain of the horrid beast. The instant Cartwright and Slattery reached their weapons, they did the same. For the next ten minutes the stranger and the three police officers watched in silence as the reptile jerked its smelly entrails onto the concrete floor.

*****

"Anyone hurt?"

"I knew it was you," Harvey said, adjusting his visor.

Removing the black scarf covering his head, Kevi wiped the snake's foul gruel from his face and neck. "Really? How?"

"You're the only one I know foolish enough to jump into that beast's mouth. What on earth were you thinking?"

"Dunno," Kevi said, smiling openly. "I admit it's not exactly the smartest thing I've ever done."

"Then why'd you do it?"

"It seemed like a pretty good idea at the time."

Shaking his head in disbelief, Harvey found himself laughing heartily. Suddenly he felt better than he had thought possible. Stone was alive. That was the reason for his euphoria. Just how he was alive didn't matter. There he was, though, fashioning his shoulder length hair into a pony tail, beaming his infectious smile. Harvey shook his head once more. Never one to make friends easily, he was delightfully surprised how much he actually admired and respected the entertainer. Not because he had just saved his life, or the lives of his men. It was more than that. In the short time he knew him, Harvey considered Stone one of the most honorable men he'd had ever met. He actually thought of him as a friend.

It had taken almost a half hour, but as soon as their communications were restored, Conklin related three important details to the bone-weary quartet waiting in the basement.

First, they had little time remaining before he ordered the building's imminent destruction.

Second, an extremely powerful surge of electromagnetic energy was emanating from the top levels of the building.

Finally, he had lost contact with Leo and his team.

CHAPTER THIRTY ONE

Strongly electromagnetic, the forces swirling around Leo and his men continued to wreak havoc on their sensitive instruments. They could neither send or receive to Harvey's team a level below, or to Conklin who was monitoring them from just a few blocks away, and each time Leo mentally probed his surroundings, a superior psionic power blocked his efforts. Yielding finally, he moved his team stealthily up the north stairway. With each step he took, his fears intensified. Not for himself, or even for his family. But for the men that followed him blindly. Too many deaths had already occurred because of him, and he wanted no more blood on his hands. Reaching the second floor, he and his men fanned out and covered every possible means of attack. Like the floor below, there was no sign of the enemy.

Two floors to go. That's where the hostages were being held and where their enemies awaited them. But it was between the third and fourth floors, they were attacked. Like wraiths they came, silent and invisible. Neither Leo's finely tuned senses or the sophisticated devices he and his men carried were capable of detecting the beings that assaulted them.

They were not from this world.

They were from Hell.

It was probably instinct more than anything else that made Leo turn, but as soon his hand reached for his mouth, the scream that began in his throat died before ever reaching his lips. In horror, he watched helplessly as a pair of sinewy hands reached up through the concrete floor, snatching one of the men covering his rear. While the officer's agonizing screams saturated the still, malodorous air, his body was pulled through solid concrete as though it was without substance. His clothing, however, remained tangible and reacted to the natural law of physics, and wouldn't yield as flesh and blood had. In what seemed like endless seconds, the policeman's body seeped through the cold concrete floor like water through a sieve, leaving nothing except a milky white substance floating atop a thickening pool of blood.

His fears tight in his throat, Leo screamed for the other officers to flee. Under normal conditions they would have needed no warning, but fear and shock had frozen their minds as well as their limbs. The youngest officer vomited all over his compatriot's garments before leaning over the concrete bannister. Another was rigid with fright. The eldest, although fearful, also seemed dumbstruck. All would die if they didn't retreat quickly.

In unison, the duo closest to Leo stepped backwards up the stairs, discovering, much to their chagrin, their feet were also cemented to the floor. Barely visible in the blackness, a pair of hands reached up through the steps and held them both prisoner. Then, like their unfortunate colleague, all too slowly, they were pulled through the concrete floor an inch at a time.

Leo shrieked in horror. He could do nothing except watch the policemen die. In fearful desperation he tried freeing both of the officer's legs, but the forces that held him would not be denied. After he had yelled a warning, the youngest officer, a rookie, aimed his small but formidable automatic weapon at the hands that seized him and squeezed off several, short, sporadic bursts. Incredibly, the hail of bullets passed through the ebony, vascular appendages, sending concrete chips flying in every direction. Still, each time Leo had kicked them, he felt as if he had struck steel. Knowing that he was going to die, the elder officer, a seasoned veteran of many battles, with just a year left on his retirement, pulled his gun from his holster, made the sign of the cross, and began to pray. Helplessly, the twin watched in horror as the officer pointed his pistol just below his right temple. When he pulled the trigger, the silent spit echoed loudly in Leo's ears, leaving him repulsed and filled with shame.

Three men dead in seconds and one to die just as horribly if he didn't find the courage to kill him. Falling to his knees, the twin begged the remaining officer for forgiveness. To his surprise, an understanding passed between them, at which point the officer yanked two fragmentation grenades from his chest and pulled the pins with his teeth. Fearfully, shamefully, cowardly, Leo raced up the stairs, reaching the fourth floor a moment before the explosion occurred, narrowly escaping with his life. When the dust finally settled, he turned to look down the stairs, shrinking in horror. Virtually unscathed, the hands from Hell continued with their grisly task, dragging the remainder of the mangled corpses through the crumbling concrete steps. His eyes swelling with tears, Leo felt sickened for not having the courage to die with those delegated to protect him.

"Welcome to your death," a cold empty voice echoed suddenly from down the narrow hall.

A tall, slender figure with billowing robes approached. With hate in his heart, Leo started towards the thin man with the bulbous head. Even through his diaphanous robes, he could tell the ancient figure was the boniest person he had ever seen. His face was like an angel's, soft, pure, innocent. His eyes, however, were a startling contrast to his angelic, majestic appearance. Blazing with unbelievable fury, they seemed as old as time itself.

"Everyone dies," Leo heard himself say, surprisingly without fear, and removed his head gear. He would no longer need it. The creature's eyes alone were capable of illuminating the darkness. "The trick is to be prepared for when it comes. I am. The question is...are you?"

The bony figure's laugh was cold, brittle, almost musical, much like the sound of precious crystal breaking. As he removed his arms from his enormous sleeves, he raised his hands slowly to his acrocephalic head. Leo knew then that a psionic battle was about to begin. Crushing his fears, he vowed to destroy the man responsible for the deaths of the four policemen.

It started as a tiny glow in the middle of the ancient's forehead, and then it grew. A bolt of pure electrical force struck Leo squarely in the chest. If it hadn't been for the padded Kevlar body armor Conklin had insisted he wear, he would have been killed instantly. He wasn't far from it. He nearly broke his neck rolling down the hallway and tumbling down the concrete steps into the wall below. His mind a haze, his heart pounding like a trip hammer, he tried to rise, discovering as he did, he was lying in a pool of blood. His skin crawling, Leo's soul grew as cold as the bony creature at the top of the stairs. Getting to his feet as quickly as he was able, the twin searched his mind for a defense against the fiend sauntering towards him. He had only one chance, one fraught with peril, and certain death if it failed.

Zzzzzzssstt!!!

Striking his unprotected neck, a second bolt of electricity knocked Leo backwards, forcing the wind from his lungs. Through burned and bleeding lips he gasped in pain with barely enough strength to move. "In the name of honor," he said weakly, begging, "grant me a quick death."

"What do you know of honor?" the **Kaluti** asked hatefully, their eyes meeting for the first time. "You've turned your back on your family, and your people. You deserve to die the most horrible death imaginable."

"Is there no room in your heart for mercy," Leo pleaded, "for a brother?"

"Mercy is for the weak," the **Kaluti** hissed, "and as far as being a brother..."

Unable to evade the blow, Leo was kicked brutally in the face. A bright light exploded behind his eyes. His jaw slightly dislocated, his nose almost certainly broken, pain filled his brain before spreading throughout his body. "A favor then," he begged, spitting out a tooth. "Grant me one favor. Let me choose my own way of dying."

"That is not our way," the **Kaluti** said, "and yet I'm interested to know what death one such as you would select."

"Search my mind, if you will. I know not what you call it."

The **Kaluti's** eyes brightened for a moment. Aware of Leo's psionic skills, he could in fact sense a challenge from his fallen foe, but because he was so sure of his own power he could only feel contempt for the cowering figure at his feet.

Leo gasped as his mind opened against his will. Barrier after barrier was penetrated, pushed aside with ease.

"You have chosen the most feared death of all," the **Kaluti** said with surprise. "You have greater courage than I anticipated."

"What is it called?"

"In our language..."Koli noratana fetu." It is also my title. It means..."

"Soul stealer," Leo completed. "That makes you a witch doctor."

"I prefer high priest."

"Whatever..."

"Your soul shall be my greatest tribute to our god," said the priest, licking his lips. "But why die in such a manner?"

Leo looked at the blood stained floor. "If those not of our faith can go to their deaths so bravely, can I do no less."

"Compassion," the priest said reproachfully, "is an emotion for the weak."

"And sometimes for the strong," Leo taunted.

The **Kaluti's** eyes glowed suddenly. Because of his foe's remark, he wondered if something had been hidden from him. The ancient sage flash probed his enemy's mind once more to be certain. "Your bravado is wasted. What can you do? I know your every thought. Your psionic arsenal is nothing."

Leo muttered quietly.

"Incantations will not serve you here," the high priest assured him. "I can summon the appropriate counter spell in an instant."

"There's one spell even you have no defense against," Leo said pulling himself to his feet. "Do your worst evil one. Do your worst and die."

The high priest's head began to glow like a beacon. An instant later, a beam of pure energy shot towards the twin with devastating results. The wall around him was completely disintegrated. But Leo was left unharmed. Sneering he said, "If that's the best you can do...you're in big trouble."

The priest's eyes blazed in awe. He couldn't have missed, and yet the bolt seemed to go right through the twin's body. Disconcerted, he launched another attack. The results were the same. Reeling, for the very first time in his life the priest began to doubt his ability. As he caressed his brow with an ancient bony hand, he redoubled his efforts by launching his most powerful beam of all. Once more, it passed through the twin, its force creating a huge crevasse where the stairs had been. Rocking on his feet, the priest backed up a step and actually contemplated flight. Before he could move, a strong, slender arm reached from behind him and cut off his wind.

"Wha-Who?" he asked, struggling with his unknown assailant.

"You were defeated from the beginning," Leo whispered in his ear. "I wanted you to read my mind...so that I could plant the idea that my power was of no consequence, knowing all the time your arrogance would make you believe it. When you raised your shields expecting a psionic assault, you never realized the moment you looked me in the eyes, I had already slipped past your defenses."

"H-how?" the priest asked, still struggling.

"Hypnosis. While you were wasting precious energy on a nonexistent target, I walked right past you."

The twin turned the ancient bony figure around to face him. A glimmer of understanding showed in the priest's eyes. "Truly, you have no honor," he choked.

"You're right," Leo replied, snapping the bony priest's neck as easily as a dry twig, "I don't."

Because his hatred had fueled his adrenal glands to capacity, giving him a source of energy never before tapped, Leo picked up the elderly priest easily over his head and tossed him into the gorge. Without remorse, or giving his enemy another thought he climbed the remaining steps and headed for the room where his parents and Nellie were being held, completely oblivious to the four phantom-like figures floating towards the floors below.

CHAPTER THIRTY TWO

Four men moved silently through the darkness. Stone, who was weaponless, acted as point. Wesneski, Slattery, and Cartwright, their weapons at the ready brought up the rear. Since leaving the basement and heading for the main floor of the Furrier's building, a once busy dock alive with activity for a once thriving business, none had spoken. But not for long.

"What was that?"

"Shhhhh," said Stone. Adding in whispers, "a rat".

"What the hell are you whispering for?" Wesneski inquired. "After all the racket we made in that basement killing that snake, and the way sound echoes through this building, you think for one second our friends don't know we're here?"

"I'm sure they do," posed Stone, his eyes wary. "But do you think it wise to broadcast our position? Or maybe you prefer being ambushed."

"Don't think I'd like it much," Wesneski said quickly, adjusting his infra-red visor. "You mind telling me something else," he said, this time in whispers.

"Not at all."

"How can you see so well in this blackness?"

"I've always had exceptional vision. As a matter of fact, until I was six, I didn't know there was a difference between day and night."

Harvey shook his head in amazement. "You know, there are times when you really give me the creeps."

Kevi snickered. "I like you too, Harvey."

"One more question. How'd you managed to survive that explosion?"

"Luck mostly. I assumed the elemental was like his brother, so I expected the electromagnetic flux he used to amplify his powers to increase exponentially at the moment of his death. I was right. You've experienced the tremor associated with the ranger's demise. The same thing happened with his brother, only with more destructive results. Before I could move, a huge fissure opened beneath my feet and sucked me straight to the bottom, closing over me as I fell." A pause. "I had a helluva time getting out," he said uneasily. "Took me almost two hours digging my way upwards. I nearly suffocated on the way." Another pause. "Man, I wouldn't wish that on anyone."

"Me neither," Harvey intoned, visualizing the experience in his own mind, admiring the entertainer's tenacity to survive, believing that no matter what the odds, or how formidable the obstacles he would continue to cheat death.

Luck had nothing to do with it. Nothing at all.

Halfway up the stairwell, Wesneski and Slattery discarded their motion sensors and communication devices. The electromagnetic field had grown much too strong. It changed nothing. He and Slattery would take the south stairs. Stone and Cartwright, the north. Along the way, they hoped to meet with Leo and his team, or at least discover some clue to what might have happened to them.

Drip...drip...drip...

The intermittent, almost melodic sounds echoed loudly in the tomb-like silence. Because they were expected in an old building, Stone and Cartwright ignored them. Before long, they discovered a vast hole in the stairwell. Cartwright grunted his disappointment. They would need repelling equipment if they were going to cross the gaping chasm. "How do we get past this?" he asked, inspecting the hole more closely.

In addition to being fifteen or twenty feet across, to get to the next level they would have to negotiate a vertical climb of at least sixteen or seventeen feet, with no visible protuberances at hand.

"Easy," Stone said, hefting the policeman by the waist.

Before the officer could utter a word, the entertainer had taken two steps back, leaped across the fifteen foot chasm, and lighted on the other side with the grace of a ballet dancer. The instant Cartwright was released, he dropped to his knees, heaved in several gulps of air, and clutched his chest as if he had suffered a coronary. "Man, you are a machine," he said admiringly, leaning over to study the abyss he had just navigated. Flashing a smile hidden by his visor he added, "You ever think about a career in law enforcement?"

"Nah! You guys don't pay enough."

"You got that right."

Halfway up the stairs, Stone and Cartwright came upon the uniforms, weapons, and equipment of Leo's team. They also discovered the source of the dripping.

Blood. Gallons of it.

"What the hell?" Cartwright exclaimed, feeling a sudden queasiness coming over him.

Stone's sharp eyes studied the grisly scene. He had never seen so much blood.

Drip...drip...drip...

Stone covered his ears with both hands. It was only his imagination, of course, but each drop of blood striking the cold hard concrete echoed in his head like a sledgehammer striking an anvil. Steeling his nerves, he led the way to the next level.

"I don't like this," Cartwright said, as if aware of a presentiment. "I don't like this..."

A fiery ball illuminated the darkness suddenly, striking the police officer squarely in the chest, killing him before he could complete his sentence. It happened so fast, so unexpectedly, the blazing orb, which was about the size of a softball, burned through his body like a hot knife through butter before continuing on its destructive path.

A series of flaming balls, each growing in size, hurtled suddenly towards Stone. But he was not easy prey. With gazelle-like speed and agility, he raced up the steps towards the man launching the still growing meteors. Empowered by bloodlust alone, every pore, every molecule, every vessel of his blood cried out in rage. One more step and death would follow death. Twisting his body left, then right, he somersaulted over the **Kaluti's** head. Then, swooping like a hawk, he loomed in for the kill. Fear stood prominently on his enemy's face. But Stone was beyond compassion. It had been burned out of him with the horrible demise of his companion. Inches away from delivering a killing strike, his keen senses caught something lurking in the shadows, and it moved quickly. Twisting in mid-air, Stone rolled with the bucket-sized fist that would have struck him high on the temple, absorbing the heavy blow with his right shoulder. Even so, the concussive force was so powerful, his flight was redirected. Completely helpless, like a rag doll he was flung into an open elevator shaft where certain death awaited him some fifty-five feet below.

*****

A frightful howl echoed throughout the increasingly cold building. It wasn't the first. There had been three. Each with a frequency that could be measured with some degree of accuracy. Who or what it belonged to was anyone's guess. Even the direction from which it had come was impossible to determine.

Slattery gave Wesneski a nudge.

The detective nodded.

An eery glow moved towards them. Both agreeing that a hasty retreat would be wise, the two men returned to the main floor, and took up a defensive posture behind one of the foot-thick stainless steel freezer doors, where in years past valuable furs were stored.

Quickly, the two officers checked their weapons. Their arsenal consisted of several clips of ammo for their submachine guns, a half dozen concussion and fragmentation grenades, a double-barreled sawed-off shot gun apiece, a flame thrower, and for close work, knives that could disembowel with a scratch.

An icy chill tugged at Harvey's spine.

In pairs, each dressed in long, diaphanous robes, four men floated down the stairs. Carrying no lighting of any kind, the deep, pitch blackness was illuminated by their eyes. Almost angelically they descended, landing as if they had invisible wings of gossamer. Once they had formed a line from shoulder to shoulder, a ponderous, oafish figure was the first to move. Quite deliberately, he pointed to where Harvey and Slattery were hiding.

Grinding his teeth together, Wesneski fired a quick burst from his automatic weapon. In that same moment, the oafish man's head leaped from his shoulders and rolled across the concrete floor. Stopping only when it had reached the northeast wall, in horror, Harvey watched the undead body stagger about like a monster in an old Frankenstein thriller, still pointing in his direction, before it finally crumpled into a heap a few seconds later.

Instinctively, Wesneski and Slattery opened fire on the three men approaching.

"Why don't they fall?" Harvey howled, discharging an expended clip, jamming another in its place. This time, though, when he pulled the trigger, his gun jammed. Discarding it immediately, he yanked the sawed off shot gun that was strapped to his back, aimed it, and squeezed both triggers.

The detective's heart went cold. The shot gun wouldn't fire either.

Slattery screamed.

And then, Harvey.

Suddenly, both men were whisked into the air and slammed into the ceiling by some unseen force. Their weapons, which had already ceased to function were then torn from their fingers and had fallen to the floor. Around and around the two men whirled, faster and faster, both becoming dizzier than they ever thought possible. When the whirling finally ceased, they fell to the floor, landing hard amidst their useless weaponry.

"You have killed a brother," the leader of the trio snarled, "and you have committed the greatest blasphemy of all by destroying a symbol of our deity. For these crimes you shall die...slowly, painfully, horribly. You will beg for mercy. And then death. But it will not come. As we delight in your screams, we shall rend your limbs from you as easily as one would rend wings from a fly, and just as a fly lives for a time, so shall you, until we rip your heart from your steaming, hot flesh.... before sending you to meet our lord and master."

"You sound pissed," Harvey remarked, his head still spinning. "Let's say we forget our differences and go have a brewskie?"

The leader advanced a step, his eyes blazing more intensely than his compatriots. "We shall see if you are as flippant once we've commanded your colleague to rip your loins from your body...with his teeth."

Outwardly, Harvey shrugged with indifference. Inwardly, he reeled, and was grateful his visor hid his face. "

"Oh yes," the **Kaluti** said smiling, piercing Harvey's veneer of bravado. "I've just sensed a delicious taste of fear from you." A brief pause. "An even greater punishment comes to mind," he announced to his cohorts flanking him. "Brothers, we shall delight in watching these swine tear each apart, but only after they indulge in some perversities I'm sure they will find...stimulating."

For the first time in Harvey's life, he found himself cowering. He had no fear of death. He had been a cop too long, and he had faced the grim reaper many times. But to be used as a sexual puppet for the perverted pleasure of others was something that deeply terrified him. His captors knew it. Unfortunately, there was little he or Slattery could do to prevent it.

"Let us begin," the leader exclaimed. "Up!"

One word, and both police officers were lifted into the air. As if by unseen hands, their clothing was ripped from their bodies, piece by piece. Within seconds both were naked. Struggling was futile. The two police offices were in the grips of a power neither could understand.

Wheeeeeet!!!!

The unexpected, shrill whistle had made all heads turn.

Without their infra-red headgear, Wesneski and Slattery were almost totally blind in the darkness. Even so, both recognized the twin shells hurtling towards them.

LAWS rockets.

Instinctively, they closed their eyes, not so much from the intensity of light illuminating the almost total blackness, but from the explosion that would erupt within the space of the next heartbeat.

Baaaarrrrrrooooommmmm!!!!

Suspended in mid-air as they were, Wesneski and Slattery were caught in the sudden concussive backlash, and like weeds in a hurricane, they were slammed into the wall above the huge freezer door. Unconscious before falling to the floor, blood flowed heavily from their ears, nose, and mouth.

Within the flickering, burning brightness, a figure in black strolled towards the three fallen **Kaluti**, two of which still hovered near consciousness. The leader, obviously the strongest of the trio tried sitting up. Kneeling next to him, the man in black placed an automatic pistol equipped with a silencer at his temple.

The **Kaluti** shuddered as he stared into the deadest eyes he would ever see. "Force field?" the man speculated.

The **Kaluti** said nothing. His mouth was so filled with blood the best he could manage was a painfully wet gurgle.

The figure in black offered a becoming smile. "Thought so," he said before pulling the trigger. He shot the other men as well. Twice. Two bullets apiece in the head. He then reholstered his weapon and kneeled next to the two policemen. Both were still alive but wouldn't be for long if they didn't get proper medical attention. After he had given them several exhausting minutes of first aid, he grasped each of the officers by a leg and dragged them to a place of safety outside the Furrier's building.

CHAPTER THIRTY THREE

"It's time, sir," the young police officer said exasperatedly as he attempted to adjust his instruments to the changing electromagnetic field.

Conklin gave the sergeant sitting next to him an empty glare.

The officer didn't notice. While he alertly awaited his superior's instructions, his eyes remained fixed upon the instruments in front of him.

Seconds passed. The silence within the command center had become increasingly uncomfortable. For nearly an hour, there was no word from either team, and the only indication of any activity in the abandoned building was the energy flux the three men had been monitoring.

The young sergeant glanced at his senior officer for a moment. The way Conklin was staring at the clock was as if he were trying to mentally cause time to stand still. Beads of sweat dotted his wrinkled brow, and his lower lip was chewed until it had begun to redden.

There were two reasons why Conklin had contacted his former Naval Captain. First, the elderly officer was probably one of the greatest authorities on the subject of high energy electromagnetic fields. Second, as Admiral of the nation's newest aircraft carrier, "Thor," he was responsible for some of the finest aerial assault aircraft in the world, two of which were the latest versions of the Navajo SK-401 Kill Strike armored helicopters, unquestionably the ultimate in attack aircraft. Completely armored, anything less than a direct hit from an eight inch gun would fail to knock it from the sky. Nearly four times bigger than its predecessors, the flying battleship possessed unprecedented maneuverability, speed, and range, along with the latest technology in radar, communications, and armaments.

Conklin remembered the first time he had seen the fantastic battleship in the papers. There had been a leak at the copter's manufacturers; some disgruntled worker, it was believed. But once the media got wind of it, there was a nationwide outcry from the American public condemning the first nuclear powered, nuclear armored copter, which in fact cost more than ten billion dollars of the taxpayers money, and because of the furor created by certain defence and antinuclear lobbyists in Washington, only two copters were completed. Both were assigned to the aircraft carrier, "Thor." Each of the two multi-billion dollar aircraft were capable of navigating and operating in strong magnetic fields, or any high energy field that would prove disastrous with standard aircraft. It was this technology Conklin desperately needed. In addition to the Admiral's seemingly inexhaustible knowledge, and because the craft could be remotely controlled from a distance of more than twenty miles, these were crucial ingredients to his scheme.

The moment Conklin realized that the world he knew would be irrevocably changed if the **Kaluti** weren't stopped, he laid his cards on the table, hoping that he could persuade his old friend to aid him. In the end, it didn't take much persuasion at all. The Admiral had known Conklin for more than eighteen years, and never in that time had he considered his young friend an alarmist. If Conklin said there was a conspiracy, there was a conspiracy. Nothing more needed to be said.

"It's time, sir," the sergeant repeated, disturbing his superior's reverie.

Conklin took another look at the clock above him. "You know what to do, Sergeant."

The young police officer nodded. After he adjusted the dials on his console, he spoke softly into the tiny mike at his lips. "The watch word is

imminent...I repeat, the watch word is **imminent**..."

A moment later, a voice Conklin immediately recognized as his dear, old friend could be heard over his headset. "Message understood. The watch word is **imminent**."

Conklin removed his headset, leaned back in his chair and closed his eyes. Within minutes, the two remote controlled copters would reach their designated points. Each twenty miles easterly and westerly of their target, both would launch four of the deadliest, most destructive non-nuclear missiles devised by man. The code word had been given. The watch word was **imminent**. Nothing could stop the force he had set in motion. In a matter of minutes, everyone and everything within in the Furrier's building would be destroyed.

*****

As soon as Leo walked into the room he knew that if he wasn't extremely careful, Nellie Braithwaite was going to die in a manner he preferred not to watch. Hooded and tied to an old, wooden chair, she squirmed helplessly as a huge, ponderous brute stood next to her, his lone wandering eye daring him to advance. Readying himself, the twin's eyes drifted towards his parents. Much to his surprise, in the next instant he was hoisted into the air by their considerable telekinetic power. Recalling the first time he had witnessed his parents' incredible abilities, his fears began to grow.

"The prodigal son returns," a voice vacant of all emotion announced. "Your death, and the deaths of those who follow you shall serve us well today."

With untold black hate in her eyes, Leo's mother stood next to her husband. "It saddens me, son," she said in a contained voice, "to think that we would be betrayed by one of our own. Your brother was right about you all along, and we were blind. We believed in only his hatred of you, and thus were unable to penetrate the web of lies you have woven so cleverly. But even you are capable of making a mistake. A mistake you shall surely rue."

"We wanted to destroy you the moment we discovered your treachery," the minister chimed, "but Stone and too many outsiders were present to take the chance."

"The funeral..."

"Yes, the funeral," the minister said perniciously, echoing his son's thoughts.

Fear swallowed Leo's brain as his parents effortlessly slipped passed his mental defenses. Desperately, he tried to force their psychic presence from his mind, but their combined energies would not be denied.

"Because of you," the minister continued, "we were forced to make some adjustments in our plans. I can assure you, however, your brother's dreams... and ours will soon be realized." After a pause he added, "But now comes the time for penance. One must pay for one's transgressions. For you, son, the price of betrayal is death." Pointing to Nellie, the minister said in a voice from the grave, "And death for this tainted bitch and her offspring...once we find him. Both shall die at a time of our choosing. But you shall be the first to experience the justice of the new order."

Leo stiffened with fear. In spite of the freezing temperatures within the dilapidated dwelling, his body felt unusually warm. A few seconds later, he was burning up all over. Almost at the same moment the invisible flames had touched his skin, the thick, smoky scent of his smoldering clothes reached his nostrils. His nose afire, before Leo could take another breath, he was naked as his brother those many years ago, and just as helpless. Then, slowly, his weightless body started to spin.

"Pain," his mother shrieked.

Leo shrieked in reply. His skin bubbled from the invisible flames as his body continued to whirl ever faster. As the centrifugal force increased with each revolution, blood oozed through the pores of his burning skin, but more profusely from his nose and mouth. Like water tossed into a whirling fan, Leo's precious body fluids whipped around the room, covering his parents in its warm, coppery essence. Sick to his stomach, Leo was sickened even more by their joyous, incessant cackling. Like two naughty children, the two octogenarians danced about, reveling in his gory rain of blood.

Leo's last thoughts were of how he had failed. Not just himself, but everyone that believed in him. In a way, his entire life had been a failure. He could never be the dutiful son he had portrayed for so many years, nor could he give allegiance to the race that bore him. It was because of this he would die and countless others after him. Because of him, many would suffer horribly, needlessly, endlessly. None would find peace or glory in the world beyond. Torment their only reward, every sentient being on the planet would find themselves dancing to the strings that **Daagon** pulled.

*****

An anguished cry of agony awakened Nellie with a sudden jolt. As its shockingly lugrubious wail sent chills bolting through her cold, stiffened body, her fear within was released. Above her and to her right echoed the horrible screams that had awakened her. They were accompanied by a swishing sound she was unable to conceptualize in her mind. Something splattered against her hood. Biting back a scream, her naked feet felt a searing heat, as though she had been sprinkled with molten steel. No. Not steel. Blood. Realizing the truth, she clenched her teeth and squashed her fears. Her mind whirled with activity. Could it be that it was her rescuer being tormented so? Always believing someone would eventually come for her, she hoped their attempt wasn't in vain.

Another scream caused Nellie to shudder quite uncontrollably, possibly, because it seemed so familiar. As the anguished cry resounded in her ears, she suddenly realized that it was within the realm of possibilities, even if they were remote, one of her abductor's was being tormented. She fervently hoped so. If that were true, then something definitely had gone wrong.

While her senses reached out into her prison, hope sparked within her breast. Since the beginning of her captivity, other than Brother Cal and Sister Nora, she had counted at least eight individuals within the cold, musty room. Sometime during what she had hoped would be her final slumber, those numbers were reduced by half. "If only I could see," she muttered through chattering teeth. But she couldn't. Regardless of what might have happened, or what was happening now, she was as helpless as ever.

*****

Within the pitch black darkness of the elevator shaft, Stone hung precariously by his fingertips. Seconds ago, as he was falling, he thought his death was certain. Fortunately, though, his great strength and instinct for survival hadn't failed him. Peering below at the grave that could have been his, he began to appreciate the small miracle it had taken for him to snag the only protuberance within reach. Death could still claim him if he wasn't extremely careful. The ledge he had been fortunate enough to grasp was slowly crumbling between his fingers and would give way at any moment. Pressing his legs against the elevator shaft wall, he leaped backwards, snatched the greasy elevator cable between his arms, and slid almost a dozen feet before his powerful legs halted his descent.

Slow going at first, as Kevi started his climb, every foot he gained he lost almost half as much. It didn't matter. In addition to his great strength, an even greater resolve gave him the necessary fuel to continue. Between floors, a plan formed in his mind. Instead of exiting at the next level and following the trek he had taken previously, he decided to climb to the top floor, leave the elevator shaft, deal with the opposition, if any, then hasten to the floor below where the hostages were being held, and if at all possible, effect their release. Considering all he had been through, even though it was sort of spur of the moment, his plan was as good as any.

Forcing the fifth floor elevator doors partly open, Kevi's uncanny hypersenses--specifically his incredible sense of smell--detected a recent spoor of two people. Although several hours old, their scents were as readable as foot prints made in snow. Should they ever meet, he would know their owners instantly. Slowly, cautiously, like a ghost with a grim purpose, he exited the shaft, surveying his surroundings with each step before heading for the stairs.

Fourth floor.

Kevi's ears began to prickle. That meant danger.

And something else. Fear.

Moving with cat-like stealth, he hugged the walls as he moved down the narrow hallway.

A door opened unexpectedly, spilling light into the darkness.

Kevi waited, ready. But no one came out.

A trap? Almost certainly.

Without making a sound, he stepped closer to the door which was slightly ajar. When he was just about to push it open a gritty voice speaking in his native tongue said, "Please come in, Mr. Stone. We've been expecting you."

CHAPTER THIRTY FOUR

The wooden door creaked on rusted hinges, echoing loudly, as Kevi pushed it open. Without fear he stepped boldly into the room, his keen, dark eyes observing everything at once. The door slammed behind him, suddenly, and on its own accord. Unfazed, his gaze became riveted on the scene in front of him. Suspended in mid-air, naked, and upside down, Leon's body was completely covered with blood. To the right of him were his parents, also covered in blood, their arms interlaced. Both wore triumphant expressions on their faces. Kevi reflected no surprise. From the beginning he had believed the minister and his wife led the **Kaluti**. Regarding his former sweetheart, his heart pounded inside his chest. Tied to a chair, squealing as she struggled, a monster of a man standing next to her held a fragile shoulder in one gigantic paw. "I'll give you exactly one second to remove your hand," Kevi snarled, his blood on fire.

Grunting in reply, the monster offered a twisted gash for a smile.

"You are in no position to give orders," the retired evangelist said vehemently.

Like an uncoiled spring, Kevi leaped for the gigantic brute, striking him a prodigious blow, sending him flying into the minister and his wife. "That's where you're wrong."

A painful yelp was followed by Leon's abrupt impact with the floor. He slipped into unconsciousness a moment later. Ignoring the twin for the moment, Kevi ripped Nellie's ropes apart like threads and removed the hood from her head. A seething rage swelled within him as he carefully studied her injuries. To weak to stand on her own, he helped her to her feet.

"Oh honey," she sobbed in surprise, her arms around his neck, "I knew you would come."

"Shhhh," he said comforting her. "Everything's going to be all right." Even without turning, Kevi knew the brute was getting to his feet. The minister and his wife, however, were still lying on the floor, their legs entangled, both momentarily stunned. "See to your husband," he instructed Nellie. "We will have need of his power before this is over."

Nellie reeled in shock. "H-Husband? My husband...is dead."

"No, honey," Kevi said gently, putting his arm around her shoulder, "your husband lies there. And if you expect to see your son again, you must do as I say."

"L-Lex? Alive?"

Nellie fainted dead away.

Catching her as she fell, Kevi shook her roughly. When she didn't respond he slapped her across the face. "This is no time for hysterics," he admonished, pushing her towards Leon lying face down on the floor. "Your husband needs you. We both need you."

Kevi's ears prickled again. With uncanny speed the brute rushed at him with outstretched arms. With even greater speed Kevi spun, ducked beneath the brute's gorilla-like attack, and delivered a crushing blow to his rib cage.

More than seven feet in height, weighing in excess of five hundred pounds, swift, and possessing strength possibly exceeding his own, Kevi had no doubt the monstrous fiend was responsible for knocking him down the elevator shaft. Ordinarily, he would have enjoyed pitting his great strength against that mountain of muscle. Unfortunately, there was little time for such a contest. If Conklin kept to his timetable, in less than four minutes the entire building would be destroyed. Confident he could handle the minister and his wife, in spite of their arcane powers, Kevi allowed himself sixty seconds to defeat the hulking beast. Not much time. It would have to be enough.

The brute's lone wandering eye studied his adversary carefully. His monstrous snarl, which for him was a mischievous grin, stood prominently on his face. Tenderly, he rubbed his ribs.

"That was just a love tap," Kevi said cockily, his hands upon his hips.

Scowling, the monster struck with cobra-like speed and delivered a wicked kick to Kevi's shin, taking him completely by surprise. Although a glancing blow, it sent a bolt of pain straight to the entertainer's brain, and just as quickly, even more viciously, the brute launched a powerful right hook towards his opponent's head.

Reading the blow easily, Kevi avoided it. His right leg, smarting as it was, would hardly incapacitate him, but caused him enough discomfort for his movements to become stiff an awkward. Once again, the brute attacked, this time, with an uppercut that missed Kevi's chin by inches. Kneeling quickly, Kevi took the offensive. In the blink of an eye, he rained a dozen blows upon the brute's unprotected groin. Howling in agony, the monster raised his log-like arms above Kevi's defenseless back. Instinctively righting himself, Kevi struck the behemoth beneath the chin with the top of his head. Howling again, the brute held one hand on his groin while the other rubbed his jaw. Kevi howled also. His head buzzed as if filled with bees. Taking the advantage, he kicked his evil opponent in each shin, his feet aching from the effort. It was like kicking concrete. Roaring, the brute dove for him with deceptive agility. Like liquid lightning, Kevi melted beneath the hurtling mass, positioning himself at the proper moment, and with the impetus the brute had already obtained, he sent him flying into a wall with astonishing force.

"Kill him, you lumbering idiot," the minister's wife shrieked as she moved towards her errant daughter-in-law, "or by **Daagon's** eyes, you'll pay with your life."

Even during his battle with the brute, Kevi had observed things had taken a foul turn for Nellie and her husband. Because of her recent hardships, Nellie was no match at all for the evil crone who gripped her by the hair. Leon hadn't fared well either. Each time he tried to rise, his father would kick him brutally about the head and face.

Thirty seconds left.

While the brute was still on his knees, Kevi Stone leaped through the air and aimed his feet for the behemoth's gigantic solar plexus. The instant his powerful legs connected with that rock hard body, all the air contained within the monster's massive frame was released in an instant.

"EEEEeeeeeeee!!!!"

Quickly, Stone covered his ears. He had never heard had anything so loud. The brute's squeal was in fact so voluminous, it reminded him of the foundry's steam whistle that announced each eight hour shift in the town of his birth. Just as atonal, and just as cacophonous.

The beast's one eye rolled a blood red. Slowly, with great effort, he somehow regained his feet. Rocking from left to right, he trudged forward with renewed determination. Standing his ground, Stone waited. The moment the beast was within reach, he flurried into his unprotected face, turning it into a bloody, pulpy mess. Blinded, the brute swung his great arms wildly, desperately hoping for a lucky blow. But Stone was as elusive as the winter air, and just as cold. Because the monster had hurt Nellie, he felt no sympathy.

"This ends now," he growled, ducking beneath a pair of thick, flailing arms.

From the floor, Kevi swung a double uppercut from knee level, upward to the brute's unguarded chin, lifting the 500 plus pound monster clearly from the floor, snapping his brutish neck in two. Landing thunderously, the brute jerked spasmodically for several seconds before finally expiring.

"You filthy blackguard, you'll pay for this," the minister's wife shrieked, staring with disbelief at her dead grotesque servant.

Turning quickly, Kevi caught Nellie just as she collapsed. Adding to her other injuries, she acquired numerous scratches upon her face and neck from her struggle with her mother-in-law. The battle between father and son continued, but had taken a different turn altogether. Leon had somehow summoned the strength to rise, and was effectively contending with his father. With Nellie in one arm, Kevi separated father and son, purposely slamming the elderly minister to the floor.

"You're just like your old man," the former evangelist said acidly, his breath escaping in short, husky gasps, "sticking your nose into things that don't concern you. That was his mistake too."

Kevi's eyes burned with hate. "W-What do you mean?" he demanded, his throat feeling constricted, his chest on fire.

Puzzled, the minister asked, "You never knew?" A pause. "I would have thought your mother would have told you by now."

Before the reverend could blink an eye, Kevi had lifted him into the air by the throat. "My mother only **suspected** you were responsible for my father's death. Now that I know you were, you're gonna tell me why. Refuse...and your life ends this very second."

"He was going to the authorities about us," the minister's wife said answering for her husband. "Somehow he had gathered evidence of us sacrificing a teenage girl and her family within our church walls." Recalling the incident, the old witch cackled with amusement. "The virgin and her family actually thought they were attending a baptismal." Another cackle. "You should have seen their faces when they learned they were taking part in one of our blood sacrifices."

Disgustedly, Kevi cast the old man aside.

"Fearing his strength," the minister gurgled from the floor, "we asked him to join us in our cause, but he rebuked our proposals."

"Fool that he was," the minister's wife snorted. "Just think of it...Haitian, Jamaican, Bahamian, Cuban, all the **Kaluti** believers forgetting their differences and assembled under one banner. With our combined demonic might we could rule the world." Spitting at Kevi's feet she added, "And your stupid, visionless father wanted nothing of it."

"His Christian upbringing was too firmly implanted," the reverend said disparagingly. "We had no choice but to remove him from the play."

Kevi's rage augmented, and his hate. Even if he hadn't made a promise to his mother more than two decades ago, he fully intended to avenge the death of his father. But in his own way. One in which he wouldn't have to dirty himself by putting his hands on their filthy, putrid flesh. "It's over," he said helping Nellie to her feet. "Your mad plan was futile from the beginning."

"It's **not** over," the minister hissed confidently, motioning to the stolen equipment humming quietly in the corner. "It's only just begun. **Nothing** can stop us now. In just a few minutes this entire city will be blanketed with powerful alpha waves, and more than ten million sentient beings will be subjected to its influence. On this very night, a new order shall begin."

"I've got some news for you, pal," Kevi spat, removing his shirt top, giving it to Leon to cover his naked, bleeding body, "unless we vacate these premises immediately, the only new order you're going to see is in Hell."

"What do you mean?"

"In less than two minutes," Kevi added coolly, "this building is gonna be blown sky high."

They wouldn't believe him, of course, which is exactly what he was counting on. Confident that he could get Nellie and Leon out of the building before it was destroyed, Kevi decided to leave his father's murderers to the tender mercies of the fates. If they survived somehow, the authorities would be waiting for them and if by some small miracle they managed to elude due process, they would never escape his vengeance.

"You lie."

"No," Leon retorted hatefully, pulling the shirt Kevi had given him over his head, tearing part of it to cover his naked loins. "After all the lives that have been destroyed in the name of your cause, do you honestly think we could allow you to continue. No, father. Even if our lives are forfeit, before your holy hour begins...you, your followers, everything in this building will be obliterated, and with them, your perverted dreams of a perfect world."

"Wrong, my worthless stripling offspring," the minister gloated. "Do you think we have planned for so long to allow you and a few bumbling policemen to upset our grand scheme? Even if this building is destroyed, there are four stations exactly like this throughout the city, all designed to target an orbiting satellite, precisely at the 23rd hour. And that's only the beginning. By midnight, the alpha energy our devices emit will blanket the entire country giving us several hundred million new slaves by dawn."

"For what purpose," Leon goaded. "You're gonna be dead. You'll never see your dreams fulfilled."

The minister's laugh indicated amusement. "Is it your desire to kill me, son? Fool. You haven't the power. And do you seriously believe that ending my life, or the life of your mother will destroy our great plan?" With unmasked hatred the minister said, "Watch and learn, son. Watch and learn."

Taking his wife by the hand, the minister raised their arms upwards, forming an apex. As their eyes rolled back into their skulls, the two necromancers fervently imprecated their hosts. "Kaliki notu Daagon, notu notu balaaka daki baruta kaliki."

Suddenly, from out of the ether, a swirling blackness appeared, causing the tiny hairs on Kevi's back and neck to leap about. Snatching Nellie and Leon by the arm, he raced for the open doorway and shoved Nellie into the narrow hallway. He was just about to throw Leon through when an unseen energy with sledgehammer force knocked them both backwards. Regaining their feet quickly, both instructed Nellie to get out of the building. Unfortunately, the ominous force that prevented their escape also prevented Nellie from hearing them.

"Kaliki notu **Daagon**, notu notu balaaka daki baruta kaliki!," the minister and his wife chanted repeatedly.

As if in reply to their invocation, a growing blackness spun around the room, snatching Kevi and Leon's breath away. Suddenly, the twin screamed. A great black scaly hand, seemingly part of the floor had reached out and grabbed him. Hastening to his side, Kevi kicked the monstrous extremity. Kicking a steel girder would have been more productive.

"**Daagon!!!**," Leon howled, realizing why his parent's were so unconcerned with the building's destruction. "They're using the neurotransmitter to amplify their abilities...to call the dreaded one into our world."

From nothingness another black hand appeared, perpendicular from the other. It reached for Stone. Dodging left, then right, he tried to evade its Atlantean clutches, but while the monstrous appendage moved effortlessly through the roaring wind, Stone's movements were comically slow, lethargic, as if he were wading through a pool of molasses. Trapped in a corner, he was snatched by the waist and lifted from the floor.

As the room grew blacker by the second, a halo of energy forming around the heads of the minister and his wife became the only light.

Suddenly, at ceiling level, a holographic likeness of a two-headed snake appeared.

"**Daagon!!!**," Leon croaked, his fears even greater than before. "He hasn't crossed over yet, but if he solidifies, it'll be the end of mankind."

Recalling the stories his mother had told him as a teen, Kevi knew that if **Daagon** entered the world as a living, breathing entity, every weak-willed, desperate, hopeless, faithless individual would become prey to its evil influence. No matter how hideous he was to gaze upon, each of those men, women, and children would believe the dark god their **Messiah**. And in exchange for answering their prayers, they would find their bartered souls had become fuel for the demon's unholy appetites. Literally, it would become the end of the world. Evil would reign over good, until all good in mankind perished from the face of the earth, and all would become one with the body of **Daagon**.

"Kevi...!"

In comparison to the howling winds, it was a subjugated whisper at best, and yet Kevi had heard someone call his name. But that was impossible. The black tornado whirled so fiercely he was almost totally deaf. The instant he felt a sudden tugging in his mind he instinctively erected his mental defenses.

"*Don't shut me out,*" a voice pleaded. "*It's me.*"

"Leon?"

"*Yes. Listen closely. My folks are too engrossed to realize we share a mind-link. We must use these few brief moments to our advantage. Nod if you understand.*" Kevi complied. "*Good. Conklin's force will never make it in time. The **Dark One** will be firmly rooted in our world unless we act now. There's only one way to defeat him.*"

"H-How?"

"*Our faith?*"

"O-Our faith?" Kevi's mind sputtered incredulously, thinking that Leon certainly picked a peculiar time to have suddenly gone mad.

"*I'm not mad,*" chided the twin, reading Kevi's thoughts. "*It is our faith that is being tested tonight, and nothing else. Since the dawn of man, this battle has been waged in the souls of men. And since that time the noble of heart have succeeded in preventing mankind's destruction. The **Dark One** is a force of spiritual evil. Only a force of spiritual good can defeat him. And Kevi, if we fail, this will be the final battle. There'll be no others. That's what's happening tonight. It is our Christian faith against one as old as time itself.*"

"But what can we do?"

"*Not only are we of one mind, and of one heart, we are also of one spirit. In spite of our differences, our weaknesses, or our shortcomings, we remain a force for good. Our cause is not only righteous, it is just.*"

"This is hardly a time for a sermon," Kevi opined.

"*Be that as it may, the only thing that can save us now, and the world as we know it...is prayer. That, and an undying, unyielding faith. As my parents pray to their evil god, we must also pray to ours, and believe ours the stronger. But if we harbor the tiniest of doubts in our hearts...our world is doomed.*" A pause. "*Do you still know the scriptures on faith you were taught as a child?*" Kevi nodded. "*Everything that we pray for, we must believe we have received it.*" Another pause, this one briefer than the last. "*Whatever you do, answer me truthfully...have you accepted Jesus Christ as your personal Savior?*"

"I have," Kevi Stone replied without hesitation, "long ago."

"*Do you also believe that Christ is truly the Son of God, and that He died for our sins, rose from the grave to walk amongst men before His inevitable ascension to the Throne?*"

"I do..."

"*Then in our Christian tongue, join me in the Lord's prayer.*"

And with all the hope, all the faith their hearts could muster, they prayed aloud:

"Our Father, which art in Heaven
"Hallowed be thy name
"Thy kingdom come, thy will be done
"On earth as it is in Heaven..."

Although their utterances were little more than a whisper in the swirling madness, from their very first syllable **Daagon's** emergence into the present plane was instantly denied. Throughout the room the darkness was being consumed by a soft, gentle light.

Music was in the air. Heavenly music that defied description. It wasn't just melodic. Incredibly tangible, it affected their senses, touched their bodies, as well as their souls.

"Give us this day our daily bread
"And forgive us our trespasses
"As we forgive those who trespass against us
"Lead us not into temptation,
"But deliver us from evil,
"For thine is the kingdom,
"The power, the glory, forever...
"In Jesus's name we pray...Amen."

"The light," Kevi said reverently, *"look into the light. Do you see?"*

"Yes," Leon replied excitedly. *"Angels! Angels from heaven...thousands of them."*

"A-Angels?"

Kevi was stunned. He saw no angels. He saw an army. The **Army of God**. Literally thousands of soldiers attired in uniforms of gold, riding thunderously upon mighty white stallions that blasted fire from their nostrils. Seven abreast they came, in an endless column, pouring from Heaven's shining gates, their armor and weaponry glistening brightly, almost as brightly as the crosses which stood prominently upon their breast plates and shields.

Their enemies were demons of every sort. And somehow Kevi knew these were the possessed souls of **Daagon**. Those that were too weak to resist his evil influence were liberated instantly by a gentle touch of the soldiers' golden swords, while those that came to the demon willingly were hacked down without mercy and burned with an incredible fire. And though they were outnumbered ten to one, the **Army of God** remained unscathed. The demonic hosts, however, were trampled beneath the horses' hooves, until none were left to challenge the power of the **Father. His** power remained absolute. **His** justice was swift and true.

A feeling of warmth began to penetrate Kevi's body. A sense of joy he had never known filled his soul as the victorious army began to fade, and though his eyes remained closed, he observed and understood the peace and contentment etched on the twin's face, realizing that even though they were of one mind, one heart, one spirit, their perceptions of the **Almighty** would always be different. Leon had seen angels because he was a man of peace. He, on the other hand, was a warrior, hence the wondrous army of the **Father.**

"Aaaaarrrrrgggggghhhh!!!! You have doomed us. You have doomed us all."

"You have doomed yourselves," Leon replied morosely, suddenly aware that the demon's evil grip no longer held him. With each passing moment, its monstrous form was beginning to disappear.

While most of **Daagon's** substance existed in the world beyond, the one great head that had reached into ours snatched Leon's parents from the floor. And with its tongue, the demon tossed their struggling forms into its hideously cavernous mouth, their screams becoming more tenuous as **Daagon's** dreaded image faded even more.

"You have won nothing Chrisssstianssss," the demon hissed. "As long as evil exists in the sssssouls of men, I remain victorioussss." The snake god's tongue tightened its grip around his captives. "One day thissss sssshall be your reward."

"Leon! Don't look!," Kevi screamed.

Shuddering in disgust, the twin's last image of his parents were of the demon god grinding their aged, broken bodies within his gigantic mouth. Blood from their mangled bodies splattered throughout the room, covering everything.

With even greater force, the powerful vortex continued to whirl, battering the Leon and Kevi unmercifully. Clinging to the floor in desperation, both realized they could still be sucked into that black hole from Hell. They could still die and for long seconds, the winds continued to howl, stealing the oxygen from both their lungs. Leon slipped into unconsciousness. If not for Kevi grabbing him when he did, he would have certainly followed his parents into the netherworld.

Finally, the winds abated almost as suddenly as they appeared, and when Kevi opened his eyes, it was to an empty room. With the exception of Leon and himself, there was nothing. Nothing at all. Everything was gone. The only evidence that anyone or anything had been within the room was the blood that covered the floors, the walls, and themselves.

Tearfully, Nellie burst into the room and ran into Kevi's arms. With little time left, he quickly draped Leon's inert form over his shoulder, took Nellie by the waist, and raced towards the top floor.

Scant seconds remained.

With one kick Kevi smashed a boarded up window and stood on a ledge directly above the snow fort the kids had made earlier. A signal light flashed in the distance. A heartbeat later, he leaped into the darkness.

They had fallen almost forty feet when the first missile destroyed the top floor of the building. The explosions that followed came too quick to count. As the crumbling debris hurtled towards the ground, the trio whizzed down the snow slide along the slippery hard-packed snow path towards the street.

Righting himself while sliding, Kevi raced through the darkness across the snow-covered field towards the blinking signal light he had seen, unable to protect Nellie, Leon, or himself from the exploding debris. A lithe figure in black met him an equidistant apart and took an unconscious Nellie into his arms. Together, they raced for the Medivan that had been appropriated just for this moment.

The noise was ear-splitting. The concussion from each explosion could be felt from more than a block away. Finally, there was silence. As Conklin had promised, the hundred year old building and everything else within that particular block had been reduced to a smoking pile of ashes.

"It was a good thing we were able to use the kids from our fan club to build that fort," Ricky Caldwell said, taking a swab from a jar and wiping the blood from Nellie's forehead.

While falling through space each of them were struck with pulverized stone, pieces of glass, and metal from the rapidly, crumbling building. Nellie and Leon were both unconscious and suffered many lacerations from the exploding debris, but for the most part their injuries were minor. The cuts and bruises Kevi received were already healing quite miraculously.

"Risky, I'd say," Stone said disapprovingly, "and don't be so smug."

"Who's being smug?" Caldwell asked. "We needed help. Only those kids could have gotten close enough to provide an avenue for your escape. Besides, every one of 'em volunteered." A brief pause. "How'd you like me and the fellas performance as the irate policemen?"

"Very convincing," Stone admitted, " but I thought I told you to keep the rest of group out of it."

Ricky Caldwell displayed his biggest grin. "After all these years," he said, removing a pen light from a first aid kit, inspecting Nellie's eyes for signs of shock, "you should know by now we never listen to anything you say."

"Harvey and Slattery?"

"Doing fine," said Ricky. "Both're strong men and'll pull through okay." He looked at his watch. "As a matter of fact, Timmy and the guys should have them at the hospital right about now." Noting his friend's dour expression he added, "Don't worry, nobody's gonna recognize them...not with Ronnie's gift for makeup."

"We haven't much time," Kevi said, looking back at the smoldering crater. "Conklin's men, the fire trucks, and everyone under the sun'll be moving in soon. Before they do, I want you gone from here."

"Stop gabbing then," said Ricky, handing his associate some bandages for Leon's wounds, "and give me a hand."

Kevi smiled. "And thanks. I know what this must have cost you," he said, realizing how much his friend hated the idea of having to kill again.

During the Viet Nam conflict, Ricky was a Special Forces mercenary working behind enemy lines. He had seen and done more than his share of sanctions during his tenure. And though decades had passed since his time in the war, he hadn't balked about having to kill. Surprisingly, he was coolly efficient, empty of emotion, and completely without mercy. From the very moment he pulled the trigger, he resigned himself to the fact that he would always remain a soldier. "I was just thinking," he said amusingly, "in addition to my being your engineer for your solo projects, our group's engineer, senior vice president of our production company, not to mention the fact that I'm always bailing you out of one thing or another, don't you think I deserve a raise?"

"Not!"

An impish smile appeared on Caldwell's face. "That's all right old buddy," he said with a hint of sarcasm. "That's alllll riiiiight. See if I save your butt again."

"Oh, shut up," Kevi said with a smile. "Get in the van before I shoot you with your own gun."

"Yes suh, massa boss man!"

CHAPTER THIRTY FIVE

"Son," Leon said, "I'd like you to meet a very good friend of mine."
"It's a pleasure, sir," Lex said, pumping Kevi's hand enthusiastically. "Between mother and I, we have all of your recordings."
"Really?"
"Yes, sir."
"I see you have my latest CD. Would you like me to autograph it for you?" Lex's blue-grey eyes danced with excitement. "Gee, would you?"
"It'd be my pleasure."
After Kevi had signed the inside cover, he reached inside his jacket pocket for a small white envelope and handed it to his godson. Lex. His godson. He still couldn't believe it. For more than twenty years he had been wrong. Wrong about Nellie. Wrong about Leon. Wrong about everything. All those years of hating. And for what? "Inside," he said with a smile, "are four front row seat tickets and a couple backstage passes to my band's concert next week at Radio City."
"Get out of town!" Lex exclaimed excitedly.
"See for yourself."
Lex tore open the envelope and held the tickets and passes as if they were made of pure gold. "Gee, thanks."
Bing! Bong!
"I'll get it, Pop," Lex said, moving to answer the door. Stopping in mid-step he asked, "Mr. Stone, will I see you before you go? My girlfriend's coming over, and I'd really like you to meet her."
"Is she a fan too?"
"Is she ever..."
"Then I'll be glad to stick around."
"Gee, Mr. Stone, you're the greatest," Lex said, and disappeared from the den.
"I must apologize for my son," Leon said, a little embarrassed, "but he's always wanted to meet you."
"No need to apologize. He's a fine boy. You and Nellie should be very proud."
"Coming from you, that means a lot." Leon then offered Kevi a chair in front of the fire place. Once they were seated, he poured two glasses of mint tea, both with a shot of Remy Martin.
"I thought you only drank gin," a gritty baritone boomed unexpectedly.
Kevi turned and smiled. "Hello Harvey, you're looking well."
"I'm still a little sore in places, but I guess I feel pretty good." The detective's sharp brown eyes drifted towards the twin.
Because of the cool look he had been given Leon said, "I guess you've come to arrest me."
"That will depend on the answers I get," Harvey said dryly.
"I see," Leon said in a small voice, offering the detective a seat next to Kevi. "What is it you'd like to know?"
"Your brother's murder..."
"It wasn't murder," the twin said haggardly. Lowering his voice a notch he added, "It was self defense."
"Proof?"

"Only my word. And the truth."

"I'd like to hear it," Harvey said with icy aloofness.

"What's the point?" Leon flared suddenly. "You've already made up your mind about me. From our first meeting you've had me tried, convicted, and sentenced."

"With good reason, I'd say," the Manhattan detective said condescendingly, "but for the record, I'd like to hear your story anyway."

"I would too," Kevi said in earnest, his eyes full of warmth.

Leon regarded his boyhood enemy and friend for a moment. "All right," he relented, addressing Kevi only. "Maybe **you'll** know the truth when you hear it."

Of all the rooms in the Braithwaite's lavish home the den was the family's favorite place. Often, Leon and Nellie would relax in front of the fire, sipping fine brandies, and dining on expensive cheeses wrapped in Lebanon Sweet Bologna. As for their son, the den was perfect for conducting his Boy Scout meetings--he was an Eagle Scout--and entertaining his friends, specifically his lady friend, Annie. Very often the spacious, quiet room served as a haven where every member of the household ventured to relax, or to escape from their everyday problems, or just to reflect. Reflection, however, was the last thing Leon wanted at the moment. Particularly, when it concerned his much too recent past.

*****

With the telethon over, he and his son had headed for home. Though tired from the day, before they were within a block of their property both became acutely aware of the latent psionic energies emanating from inside.

"Uncle Leo," Lex acknowledged.

"And another," Leon assented, "I don't recognize him. Do you?"

Lex shook his head.

Sensing danger, and desiring his son to be as far from it as possible Leon said, "Lex, you go and visit with your friends. I'll see what your uncle wants."

"Pop..."

"It's okay," Leon said quickly. "I'm sure there's no danger."

"All right, Pop," his son capitulated, "but be careful."

Leon smiled. "Ain't I always?"

As Leon climbed the spiral staircase, he was glad he had sent his son along. There was no doubt that danger awaited him. The evil that had invaded his home was so thick it nearly choked him. And because his brother had never visited him without the accompaniment of one of his parents, his fears were increased. This was a bold move on Leo's part. A bold move indeed. And who was the stranger? That was the other thing. Assuming the servants had let them into the house, they most certainly would not have conducted them to his bedroom.

"Hello, brother," Leo said, his eyes cold as death. "You look tired."

"What're you doing in my bedroom?" Leon demanded, his pulse racing, his heart fluttering out of control.

"Calm yourself bro'. I've got someone I'd like you to meet."

Leon moved towards the bathroom door.

"Lex?"

No. That was impossible. Lex had just left him. Then who?

"This is **my** son," gloated Leo, as if reading his brother's mind. "Lindsay Lee Crawford Braithwaite."

Leon felt himself stagger. He could scarcely believe his eyes. The young teen's looks, mein, and mannerisms were exactly like Lex's.

Quite casually, Lindsay pointed. An instant later, a tiny fireball exploded from his fingertip.

Luckily, Leon's sixth sense had told him to duck. Missing him by inches, although the marble-sized ball of fire wasn't meant to kill, it would have caused him considerable injury.

Leo erupted with maniacal glee. "Tonight you die, brother," he promised. "You've poked your nose into my affairs for the last time. And what did you accomplish, I ask you? Nothing. Absolutely nothing."

Leo nodded to his son, and Lindsay pointed again.

This time Leon was ready.

At his fingertips, a solid shield, a foot in diameter, constructed from the free floating molecules in the air deflected the fireball into the bathroom and set it ablaze.

Leo howled in amazement. "Well, well, well...it seems I'm not the only one that has been reading mother's sacred book. I'm impressed. My goodie two shoes brother has been a bad boy." Leo's look became mischievously confident. "Let's see what you've learned, shall we? It'll be like old times."

As his son stepped left, Leo stepped to the right. The next attack would be simultaneous and would come from both sides. Raising his hands, Leo moved his fingers as if they had been frozen. At his fingertips a blue glow glistened. Lindsay's fingers also glowed, only his was a bright crimson.

While Leon's buttocks were pressed tightly against the padding of his waterbed, he received a blast of blue fire from his twin, red from his nephew. Together, they completely shattered his molecular shield and knocked him to the opposite side of the room. Looking up from the floor through a thick cloud of steam, Leon could see his brother's cadaverous eyes glowing brightly, even more so when Lindsay embraced him. It was incredible. Their embrace doubled, quite possibly, tripled their power.

"Very good, brother," Leo said with a dead smile. "But not good enough." Pure electrical energy sprung from his eyes, scorching Leon's hair, destroying the vanity table behind him. "Hah!" he whooped. "You dare challenge me? Your powers are nothing."

Shakily, Leon rose from the floor, his pale, blue-grey eyes black with hate. "You think not," he said slowly. "I promise you, neither you or your hell-spawned child is going to leave this room alive."

"Oh? And how do you plan to stop us?"

Leon's face remained confident. "I'll give you a hint...Korati tonatu sokoffaii."

Leo's tight features went slack with fear.

"What is it?" Lindsay asked, unable to remember a day when his father had been afraid.

"It seems," Leo replied, his voice quavering just a little, "my dear brother has invoked the one power he knew I had never mastered. The joining of souls."

Lindsay was confused, and reasonably frightened by the incredible energies his uncle was generating.

"It seems I've underestimated him," Leo went on to say, his fears rising. "Just as our two souls are now as one, my brother has taken the latent energies from his tainted wife and son, stored them within this house, and he is now harboring these energies within himself."

Understanding, Lindsay's eyes widened with fear.

"Don't make me kill you," Leon warned.

"Do you think this changes anything? Lindsay..."

The black forces that had been stored within Leo and his son's souls surged together suddenly an erupted with incredible force.

"Noooo," screamed Leon, covering his eyes, his molecular shield forming all around him.

The resultant explosion was incredible. The fiery energy that had burst forth was instantly absorbed by Leon's formidable defenses and discharged back towards its source, consuming both boy and father in their own conflagration. As their screams filled the room, Leon could feel his brother and nephew's thoughts reach out and touch his mind. His body rocked as if a million volts of electricity surged through his body. Every hair on his body felt singed, and prickled with energy. An even worse experience, Leon could feel every moment of his brother and nephew's dying, as if a part of him was dying too.

Finally, when he uncovered his eyes and ears, the first thing he noticed was that the entire room was completely covered in blood, and that the burned husks of Leo and Lindsay lay at his feet. "Your madness has been your own undoing," he whispered to his brother's still smoking corpse. "Burn in Hell, you fool...burn in Hell."

*****

"So it was **Lindsay** that was found beside your brother's remains," Harvey said. A reasonable deduction since it was Lex that had let him in only moments ago.

Leon nodded.

"Your brother intended to replace you." A statement.

"Yes. As children, Leo and I learned to mimic each other perfectly, so perfect in fact, that even our parents couldn't tell us apart. It was a game we played often...with everyone. That alone was a crucial element to my brothers plan. With the aid of his illegitimate son who could pass himself off as my own, he needed only to remove Lex and myself from the scenario to conduct his perfidious affairs in the open and none would be the wiser."

Harvey shook his head. "Sooner or later someone would have discovered..."

"Nothing," Leon finished. "Absolutely nothing. My brother and I, my son and Lindsay are identical twins in every sense of the word. Except for some well-hidden scars, there are no physical differences between us."

"There has to be," Harvey interjected. "Fingerprints for instance..."

"Our fingerprints," Leon said patiently, "our teeth, our physical confirmation, including musculature, and vascularity are completely identical. A retina scan, even a DNA charting would fail to discern a single dissimilarity."

"Your voices," Harvey hedged, forgetting momentarily that he had already been fooled more than once by Leon's incredible vocal abilities.

"Can be mimicked easily," Leon said in his brother's thunderous bass.

A touch of fear reached Harvey's spine. "It was your voice on the 911 operator tape," he realized.

In Wesneski's voice Leon said, *"I doubt there's a human voice in existence we can't duplicate perfectly."*

"H-How is this possible?"

"It just is," the twin said pensively, in his own pure, countertenor voice. "My brother and I, Lindsay and my son are more than doppelgangers, Harvey. In our bloodline, at least one male sibling conceived by us would be born an exact twin, complete with their father's abilities."

Harvey gave the twin a blank stare.

Misreading it as a look of disbelief Leon suggested, "Test us if you wish. Me against my son. What you'll discover, with the exception of age and size my son and I are completely identical...down to our individual alpha rhythms."

Harvey's heavy, beefy hands started to shake. He wanted a cigarette so badly he could almost taste it. But because his lungs still ached from nearly drowning in the lake less than a week ago, he decided against it. He settled for a drink instead. "How come you didn't use this power at your brother's home?," he asked, his voice quavering even after sipping his gin. "You could have saved the lives..."

"I would have if I could," Leon replied morosely. "Unfortunately, my power is strongest in my own home. In my brother's, I was impotent."

A brief silence.

"It was you who wrote **kotaii** on the family portrait," the detective surmised, his voice suddenly loud in the quiet room.

"Yes. I wanted to be sure the police would utilize every resource to protect my wife. I figured once she was safe, I had only two problems remaining: One, to convince my parents my brother and son were killed by our elders, which wouldn't have been hard at all. The elders were already displeased with him. And two, maintain my charade and protect my real identity. I failed in both." Leon turned slightly to his right. "Stone's unexpected appearance at the funeral was one of the reasons. He unnerved me so much, I ended up giving myself away."

"By kissing Nellie," Kevi posed.

"Yes. That was the worst thing I could have ever done."

"Why?," from Harvey.

"My brother hated Nellie intensely. Except sexually, he would have rather died than touch her. It was in that singular moment, my parents discovered I was not who I claimed to be, and so, they naturally concluded I had murdered my brother."

"When did you discover your parents were involved in your brother's nefarious machinations?"

"Not until I stepped into that room in the Furrier's building. Knowing them as I do, I had my suspicions several times, but I had no real proof." Leon poured himself another glass of mint tea, this time, with a double shot of Remy Martin. "Prior to my brother's demise, my parents and I had many talks, in which they assured me they wanted nothing to do with his mad schemes. Like a fool, I believed them, possibly, because I wanted to. While I was their captive, though," he continued, the hard lines of his face growing cold with hate, "they delighted in telling me how they had always shared my brother's dreams of glory and power. As **Defti Garugatu**, my twin would be their conduit to undeniable, irrefutable, god-like power." A thoughtful pause. "Only now that it's all over, do I realize how foolish I was to even think that I could trust them...or continue to deceive them." Thinking of the men who had lost their lives in defense of his own he added, "Ever since we left the hospital in Darian, they were one step ahead of us. They knew every move we made. Dear God, the lives that have been lost..." As his voice trailed off, Leon hung his head low, as if he were quietly weeping.

Harvey, too, was thinking of the policemen that had lost their lives, some of which hadn't had a chance to fully appreciate the dangers they faced. "The day before your brother's death," he said changing the subject, "Dr. Pothiz and "Mourla" flew into Miami from Capi, changing flights upon arrival, and flying to Atlanta. A few days later, they flew into Chicago where a cabby took them to the Sears Tower." The detective's eyes narrowed thinly. "For what purpose?"

"If you know they've been in those cities," Leon said with real surprise, "you must know they've visited others as well."

Harvey nodded.

On a foot stool contiguous to his chair, there was a folder. Flipping it open to a page that was purposely folded back, Leon handed it to the detective.

"These are the exact addresses Dr. Pothiz and 'Mourla' visited."

Harvey studied the single sheet of paper briefly. His beefy red face indicated understanding. "In each of these cities," he began to read in a dry monotone, his brows arched into a V, "atop these structures, a receiver-transmitter was placed, creating a network of...why didn't you show us this before?"

"To tell the truth, I never had the chance."

"These devices...were to neutralize your brother's alpha neurotransmitter?"

"It's what we had hoped. Theoretically, they would draw the alpha energy from each satellite, much like a lightning rod attracts lightning. Once the energy field came in contact with the building's antenna, our device would subvert my brother's neurotransmitter by discharging its energy into a concrete structure, rendering it harmless. In a nutshell, it was designed to make each of Leo's transmitters impotent...no matter where they had been placed. And though ours were fabricated in haste, my colleagues believed they would still work. After all, it was their technology that was stolen in the first place."

"Their technology?," Harvey inquired interestedly.

"Yes. In the mid-sixties, Dr. Pothiz and "Mourla" were considered the **Kaluti's** most faithful followers. They were quite obsessed, as my family was, in making our nation the greatest in the world, which was the reason they developed the alpha-adrenergic neurotransmitter in the first place. Years later, after meeting my wife and son, something happened. Having seen through our facade, and because we freely admitted our Christian beliefs, we naturally expected the direst of consequences, but instead of denouncing us, or exposing us as we had anticipated, they painstakingly scrutinized our lives and our theology. Then, very much to our surprise, in years to come, and in confidence, mind you, the two scientists became the greatest supporters of the Christian faith my family has ever known. Unfortunately, my brother discovered their secret. And if he knew..."

"Your parents knew," the detective finished. "Which is why they wanted them brought to this country."

"Exactly. Considering the incredible influence Dr. Pothiz and 'Mourla' held as elders within the **Kaluti** community still living in the Caribbean, my family's minions had no choice but to eliminate them...here, where they were most vulnerable."

"It was Dr. Pothiz and 'Mourla' that helped you destroy the equipment in the Utopia offices then." A statement.

"Yes. You've seen 'Mourla's' abilities. They would have certainly paled in comparison with the "koth fura" we encountered, but they were considerable enough for our purposes."

The detective offered a brief smile. "How'd you manage to lock the dead bolt once you left the room?"

Seemingly on its own accord, Harvey's gold ball point pen jumped from his fingers, danced in the air, and floated towards Leon's outstretched hand.

"Telekinesis," the police officer stated, shaking noticeably. After all he'd experienced in the past week and a half, it was still an unsettling experience to see an object at the mental caprices of another.

"Like 'Mourla,' I can only do little things," Leon apologized, noting the detective's discomfort. "My brother and parents were much more proficient. But you're right. When I exited my bedroom, I turned the key telekinetically, locked the door behind me, then waited for my wife to arrive. But I missed her somehow." Leon winced. "I almost died when I saw her going up the stairs." Wincing again he said, "With Nellie's untimely arrival, I realized that all the plans I had made had gone awry."

"Plans?" Harvey asked. "What plans were those?"

"I wanted to have just discovered the bodies..."

"Before your wife came in the house, you mean."

"Yes. I would've gotten her away in a hurry, and would've explained later. Once I knew she and my son were safe, I would've notified the police. But Nellie arrived too soon." Leon swallowed hard. "I nearly went crazy when I saw her tumbling down our stairs. Then, when I heard Lex's scream behind me, I was even more frightened. I thought he had gone, but because he feared for my safety, he doubled back to check on me. He was in complete hysterics when he saw me kneeling over his mother. After I assured him she was all right, I told him what had happened and what must be done. That's when I placed the calls from my car phone, mimicking my wife's voice both times..."

"Wait a second," Harvey interrupted. "We checked the service of your cellular in your car. No calls were made from that number."

"In my son's car, there's another cellular, one you didn't check. How could you? His car wasn't around and that particular phone is registered to Utopia."

Harvey nodded. "Continue."

"The moment Lillian and the police arrived, my son and I sneaked away from the scene before being discovered. Incidentally," Leon pointed out, "it was my son and his Boy Scout friends that managed a watchful eye on Nellie during her abduction."

Harvey's eyes glowed intensely. "You know, I've really underestimated you." In a disdainful tone he added, "You've got to be one of the most cold-hearted bastards I've ever met."

"I did what was necessary," Leon pointed out. "I'd do it again if it meant preserving the lives of my family." His eyes narrowed. "And so would you if the circumstances were similar."

"Maybe. Maybe not," Harvey grunted. "You know, you could have saved yourself a lot of trouble if you would've told me the truth from the beginning."

"I was fighting for time," Leon said earnestly. "Besides, would you have believed me?"

Harvey said nothing. His eyes told Leon everything he wanted to know. "I thought so. Even now you're having trouble."

"You're wrong," the detective said, getting up from his chair, putting on his overcoat. "At least about now. I believe you. And so will our superiors, once Conklin and I get together and concoct something we think the brass'll buy."

Leon's hopes lodged in his throat. "I'm not under arrest?"

"You know what the Miranda Act is?"

"Of course," the twin answered, understanding. "Thank you," he said warmly. "Thank you very much."

"How's Conklin doing?" inquired Kevi.

"Fine." Harvey paused slightly. "Now that I think about it, there are a couple things he wanted me to ask."

"Anything," Leon responded eagerly.

"For the past two days, an investigative team has been sifting through the rubble of the Furrier's building, hoping to discover those responsible for razing it. So far, they've found nothing. Considering how it was blown up, that's quite understandable. The funny thing is...there isn't a single trace of blood, bodies, clothing, weapons, or even that humongous reptile we battled in the basement. Can either of you explain that?"

"Those things no longer exist in our plane of reality," Leon imparted. "With the demon defeated, everything that was connected to him has gone back to his world."

"Hmmm," Harvey said, thinking it over, "maybe that's why we can't find any of the equipment your folks boasted about. It might also explain why Conklin's old Navy buddies weren't able to find any residual energies in the alpha and electromagnetic spectrum. Guess it means everything's back to normal."

"What was the other thing?" Leon asked.

"The person or persons responsible for eliminating the two assailants who took out Conklin's Able-Baker teams," Harvey said. "Bob would like to thank him...them. As a matter of fact, so would I. Whoever it was saved me and Slattery's hide."

"Now there you got me," Leon said honestly.

"I wish I could help," Kevi admitted, shrugging his shoulders.

The detective gave both men a cool look. "Thought I'd ask anyway," he said, donning a striking fedora, his instincts telling him one, maybe even both were lying. "Stone, can I drop you?"

"Yeah, Harvey, I'll be a few minutes though. I have an appointment with some young fans of mine."

"Take your time. I'll wait for you in the car."

"Thanks again," Leon said, shaking the investigator's hand. "My family and I can never repay you."

"Yes," Harvey replied grimly, "you can."

Leons brows arched high. "How?"

"By not letting it happen again..."

*****

"Don't you think you should have told him everything?," Kevi asked.

Leon turned slowly, his eyes wary. "Whadaya mean?"

"Like who you really are."

Leon flinched. "Y-You know?"

"I've always known. But only recently, have I understood the reason for your deception. You were born Leo Antoine Braithwaite, but for most of your life you've used your brother's name, Leon Aloysius Braithwaite."

"H-How...how could you know that?" the twin asked, astonished.

"When I look into someone's eyes, Leon, I see their soul. Having seen yours more than thirty years ago, I'd know you anywhere. Nellie could too. You couldn't deceive her as a kid, and you wouldn't have been able to deceive her at the funeral if she hadn't been so distraught over believing her son and husband were already dead. But that's not all. The moment you exited your Jeep Cherokee, I recognized you instantly, and not by your eyes."

"How then?"

"Remember that rumble we were in. Your right knee was damaged, and for awhile your limp was quite pronounced."

"I haven't limped in years," the twin argued..

"To one who recognizes body language as easily as I, your limp is as plain as the nose on your face."

Just then, Lex poked his head into the den's doorway and asked, "You about through in here, Pop? I've got some of Mr. Stone's fans here to meet him."

"Yes, son," Leon replied. "He'll be along in a minute."

Lex beamed brightly before closing the door.

"You've asked me why I didn't tell Harvey everything," Leon said. "What good would it have done? And what's in a name anyway? Whether the world knows me as Leon or Leo, it's my deeds that make the difference."

"Maybe you're right," Kevi said thoughtfully, reaching into his pant pocket. "What are you gonna do about Utopia? Rebuild it?"

"Yes," the twin said determinedly, "and this time it won't be perverted by greed, avarice, or power."

"I sincerely hope so," Kevi intoned. "If you need any help, give me a call."

"I'll do that, and I appreciate your kindness," Leon said, shaking Kevi's hand. "Now, you'd better go before my son and his young friends come in here and hog-tie you."

Kevi's infectious smile beamed brightly as he turned to leave the room. At the door, his smile grew even wider once he realized the note he had taken from his pant pocket, the twin now held in his hands.

Leon couldn't have been more surprised. The note he had been given was done completely without his knowledge. Less than a square inch in size, Kevi had somehow placed it in his hand when they had shaken. Stuck between his thumb and index finger, it was held securely in place by a tiny piece of transparent tape. His curiosity aroused, Leon took a moment to unfold the tiny note, which in actuality was a recent newspaper clipping. Taken from the morning edition of the New York Times, the article simply read:

"Evangelists, Christian Scientists, and ministers from almost every corner of the globe have announced an unprecedented televised alter prayer. For the first time in history, every Christian with a radio or television can become an active participant in a very special ceremony. A tremendous undertaking for any one organization, The Christian Faith Ministry, formerly under the auspices of Reverend Dr. Leon Braithwaite, will be responsible for establishing the satellite link up that will connect the entire planet. Planned for Easter Sunday, the 24 hour long alter prayer will be communicated in every country, every province and city, in every civilized tongue, and shall be presided over by the Pope.

Having been born a cynic, even this reporter is aware that this unparalleled event is resultant to the inexplicable, inestimable increase and interest in the Christian faith. A miracle? I would say so. Throughout America, churches have become packed day and night with old, new, and current members reaffirming their beliefs. Even those hopeless miscreants thought lost in our country's cults have turned away from their former tenet and have found peace and contentment in Jesus Christ, our Lord and Savior. Never before has this country exhibited such a feeling of warmth from its teeming populace. And never before has this feeling of love manifested itself in almost every beating heart.

America is not alone in this respect. The entire world is agog over this miracle.

This reporter can only think that maybe there's a chance for the human race after all. And though we might not ever understand the blessing that has been bestowed upon us, particularly at this time when there's been so much human suffering, I can only state that this incredible gift is not for understanding. No, my Christian friends. If anything, it is for receiving."

"Things aren't normal at all," Leon said to himself, proud that he was partly responsible for absolving so many lost souls. "Things, in fact, are better than they've ever been."

EPILOGUE

While Kevi performed on the Braithwaite's brand new Chopin piano, he delighted in the fact that each of his fans were young, wide-eyed, and bubbling with excitement. It was exactly the diversion he needed. For a few brief moments, the captivated teens were able to take his mind far from the events of the past week and a half.

A lot of living had gone in the last ten days. A lot of dying too. Thinking of those that had perished by his hand, he discovered that though there was some remorse, he had no regrets. A heavy burden had been lifted from him, almost as if his soul had been purged. And for the first time since his father had passed away those many years ago, he finally felt at peace within himself.

Sitting alone by the fire, Leon poured himself a large Drambuie from a black and gold decanter into a fine silver goblet. Somewhere between being mildly intoxicated and hopelessly drunk, he nearly missed the knock on the door. "Come in," he slurred, unaware that Kevi was already standing at his side.

"What's wrong, Leon? What's bothering you?"

"I'm supposed to give this to you," the twin moaned, handing Kevi a note neatly folded and smelling of his wife's perfume. "It's from Nellie. She hates me, you know. I-I'm almost certain she's still in love with you."

"Did she tell you that?" Kevi asked, reading the sheet of paper in a single glance.

"N-No, but..."

"But nothing. You know Nellie. She's honest to a fault, and always speaks her mind...that's unless she's changed in the past thirty years." Taking the twin's drink from his trembling hand Kevi said, "This isn't like you, Leon. You're the last person in the world I thought'd be feeling sorry for himself. And as for Nellie hating you, get a grip. She's angry with you, yes, and probably has every right to be. But you know as well as I, once she looks the whole thing over, she'll realize the choices you made were the right ones."

"H-How can you be so sure?"

Kevi sighed heavily. "Ever since our minds first linked, I've been bombarded by jumbled up memories that weren't my own. That's not all. After I had gotten you out of the Furrier's building, while you were unconscious, I pushed past your barriers and read your thoughts. In that single probe, I've discerned all of your hurts, joys, hopes, dreams, successes, failures, even your fears. And because you've mind-melded with Nellie several times throughout the years, her memories, which had become part of yours, were also disclosed to me." A brief pause. "As much as I hate admitting it, I envy you."

Leon's eyes widened with surprised. "Envy me? Why?"

"Because I have never known two people more in love with each other. And because you have something I've always dreamed of having, something I never had...even with Nellie those many years ago."

Even intoxicated, Leon noted Kevi's wince. "What's the matter?"

"My son," he said solemnly. "Through that part of Nellie which is also part of yourself, I saw his conception...and his death. And through Lex, I know what he meant to you." A brief pause. "You see, Leon, I know everything about you...every thought and emotion you've experienced in your entire lifetime. I also know how much Nellie loves you, and of all the happiness you brought her. But most of all, I know better than you how much you worship the girl we both love." Turning, Leon's eyes indicated no surprise. "I admit it. I still love her. I've always loved her. Maybe I always will. But she'll never hear those words from me. What Nellie and I shared ended years ago. What has happened, happened, and was meant to be. I know that now."

Leon's eyes began to swell. "Me...my family, we don't deserve such a friend."

"You're wrong, Leon. It was you that reawakened my faith in my fellow man, in addition to strengthening my faith in the **Father**. And that's something I can't ever repay." A slight pause. And then, a smile. "You know, I don't mind telling you, I was kinda scared when you told me that only our faith would save us. For a moment or two, I thought you had gone nuts. But once I had taken a moment to peer into your open heart, once I saw how deeply you believed, how deeply you truly love your fellow man, I was provided with the necessary spark to rekindle my own faith. Because of you, Leon, I've seen what few will ever see in this life...the true wonders of Heaven. And because of you, I know with all my mind, with all my heart, and with all my soul...**there is a God.** That's what you given me, Leon. And that's a gift few can give." Kevi paused once more to look at his watch. "I've gotta get going. Nellie's waiting." He touched the twin gently upon his shoulder. "And don't worry," he said with a smile, "she'll be home soon."

Leon choked. "How can I ever thank you?"

"Continue to take care of my godson...and his mother."

*****

"So Leon's going to step down as leader of his ministry," Harvey said, driving eastbound towards the city park where Nellie was waiting.

"Uh huh," Kevi replied solemnly. "He feels unfit. In the defense of others, he has taken lives. He can never don his robes with that on his conscious. It's kinda sad when you think about it. Of all people, Leon knows that our Lord forgives, if you are truly repentant, and yet he hasn't found a way to forgive himself."

"What about Utopia?"

"Oh, he'll devote the rest of his life to it. Fortunately, the only damage that's been done has been by his family."

"And besides us, only a few will ever know what happened," opined Harvey.

"Yep. With Leon at its helm, Utopia will continue with its fine and noble works."

"What about you and Nellie?"

"I love her, if that's what you mean. But she's still married. Even if she weren't, I'm not the kind that goes sneaking around."

"I wasn't trying to eavesdrop, but while you were entertaining the kids, I heard Leon and Nellie quarreling before leaving the house. I think she intends on divorcing him."

"For what reason?" Kevi asked. "I'm certain she cares for me, but I'm also certain she's still in love with her husband. It wouldn't make any difference anyway. There's a bond between Leon and I that goes beyond friendship. One forged by love, hate, death, and a lifetime of experience."

"Then whatever you do, you lose," Harvey concluded.

"That's right, whatever I do, I lose."

"That's a shame," Harvey said sadly. "That's a damned dirty shame." Their car slowed to a stop. "Here we are," the detective announced. "You sure you don't want me to wait for you?"

"No thanks. My limo will be arriving shortly."

"Well, take it easy then. And when you get a chance, give me a call."

"I will, Harvey," Kevi said softly. "I will."

*****

Lost, forlorn, and looking quite out of sorts, Nellie stood alone in the center of the city park next to a huge fountain that had frozen over more than a month ago. With her back to him, Kevi watched the winds catch her hair and whip it lightly in front of her face. Because she had expected him to enter the park from another direction, when she turned she was startled for a moment. An instant later, she was in his arms, kissing him gently on the lips. Her tears poured from her eyes as she pressed herself against him. "You're going away, aren't you?"

Kevi removed a hanky from his pocket and wiped Nellie's tears, but was very careful in not touching her nose. The brute had broken it, but not so badly that it would mar her natural beauty. Even with her bandages, she was still the most beautiful woman he had ever seen. "Next week's concert at Radio City is the beginning of our world tour," he explained.

"That's not what I meant," Nellie said, sensing his evasiveness. "Will I see you again?"

"Of course you will," he lied, "but don't you think you and Leon are going to be awfully busy? It's going to take both of your concerted efforts to make Utopia the organization it once was."

"I don't care about Utopia or my husband anymore," Nellie said bitterly.

"You're being unfair, don't you think? And just a little bit cruel?"

"Unfair?," she asked. "Cruel? After what he's put me through?"

Kevi nodded. "If you think you're the only one that has suffered, then yes, you are being cruel. And selfish. And that's not like you. That's not the Nellie I used to know. Listen honey, your husband has risked his life several times to save you and your son, and I've never met a person more devoted. You should be proud to have him."

"My pride and my love died when I believed my family dead. You have no idea how that feels. For the past week and a half I've had nothing to live for, and more times than you can imagine I've prayed for death."

"It was the only way."

"No! I don't believe that. There had to be another. If it were me, I would have found it."

Kevi swallowed hard for what he was about to do. "If that's true, Nellie, you wouldn't have married him in the first place."

As Nellie pulled away in shock, Kevi realized these were the harshest words he had ever spoken to her, and that they had cut into her heart like an old, rusted rapier.

"Oh honey," she cried, trembling, her hand shaking as she reached for her mouth. "How I must've hurt you. After all these years, you've never forgiven me."

"You're wrong, Nellie," Kevi said gently. "I've forgiven you years ago, although until lately, I hadn't realized it. But that's not important. What is important is that Leon needs you. Now more than ever before. And deep inside you know you need him too." Taking her head in his hands, Kevi turned Nellie's face upward and kissed her lightly on the forehead. "Go home," he said softly, "please. Go and be happy as you have been all these years, as you should be, as you will be, for as long as you're with him." Hugging her tightly, he pressed his lips against her cheek one last time. As much as he wanted to, he couldn't tell her how he truly felt. And as much as he needed her in his life, he knew it could never be.

While they walked towards the street together, Kevi realized that Nellie would never call him. Not as long as Leon was there. Nor would he call her. Too much time, and too much hurt was between them. What could he give her anyway? She already had everything she needed. She had her life back. She had her family. And most of all, she had love.

Walking the rest of the way alone, when Nellie reached the end of the path, she turned and waved, tentatively. There was a sadness in her face that Kevi knew he'd never forget. If he called out to her, she would return to him. That, he also knew, and it took all of his inner strength to resist the temptation. Losing sight of her finally, as she turned the corner, a tear rolled slowly down his face. In that moment he began to weep.

Nellie had walked out of his life forever.